Dark Dahlias Rite

A Dark Reverse Harem

Mimi Baptist

Cassandra Doon

Editing provided by T.J. Walter

Cover photography by Michelle Lancaster

@lanefotograf / www.michellelancaster.com

Cover Model: Brodie

First Edition 2025

"When you lie down with dogs, you get up with fleas."
– JEAN HARLOW

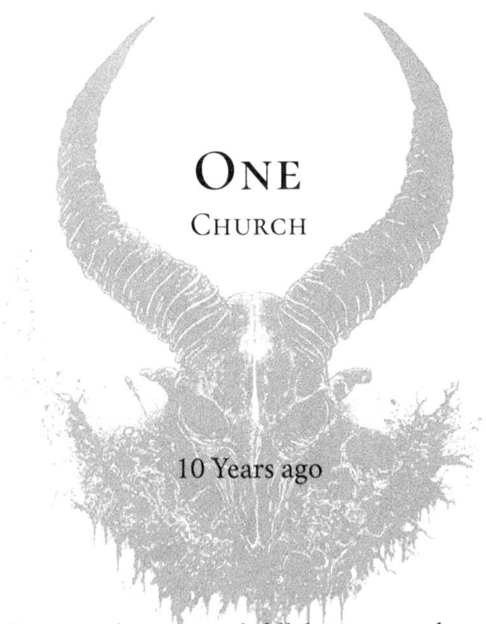

ONE
CHURCH

10 Years ago

I went to the crossroad, fell down on my knees
(Robert Johnson)

ROBERT JOHNSON WAS a nobody just like us, from a small neck of the woods in Mississippi. I am lying on my back like a corpse on the cold, grimy, carpeted bedroom floor in the trailer, gazing up at the blackened mold that is slowly consuming the corner of the wall just above my window, whilst I listen to Robert Johnsons alluring voice, killer guitar skills and spellbinding lyrics.

As legend goes, the aspiring bluesman went to this spot between Highway 61 and 49 in Clarksdale, Mississippi – a place we now call the Devil's Crossroad, - he fell down on his knees, like he says he did in his lyrics and waited by the side of the deserted crossroad in the dark of the moonless night, and the Devil himself came to him. By tuning his guitar, the deal was sealed for the bluesman's soul he was guaranteed a lifetime of easy money, women and fame. Only that lifetime was merely a year for poor Mister Johnson, that's when it clicks, and I know what we must do to get out of this fucking hellhole that our premature coffins have begun to be lowered down into.

I get up and run like a madman to my older brother's bedroom, barging in without bothering to knock.

"Church." He utters, not pleased with my careless entrance.

"At least you are not wanking one out like last time." I smile smugly at him, as I slam the door closed behind me.

"Fuck you. What do you want? I need to finish off crunching the numbers to see if we have enough cash to pay rent this month."

Bishop sits crossed legged in the middle of his bed bent over a mess of papers that surround him. It must be bad if shit is scattered all over his bed as he tends to be a neat freak, always striving for complete control.

Our father left a few years after I came along, I was probably 3 and Bishop was about 7 at the time. From stories I heard from my brother he wasn't a good father, or husband. He was always drunk; he beat Momma constantly and Bishop had coped a few lashes on his back from his belt to. Maybe it was a saving grace that he had abandoned us, but that also meant Momma had to work harder to keep a roof over our heads and food on the table. She had two full time jobs which meant she wasn't home a lot, so Bishop pretty much raised me.

When I was 16, she got pretty sick, it was, cancer but the doctors caught it too late. Perhaps if Momma had stopped pretending she was ok when she obviously wasn't and actually had gone to the doctors sooner, she could still be here. But when you are short on cash every month and don't have health insurance, stuff like that takes a back burner. In the end she wasted away to nothing but skin and bones, a living skeleton. And then she was gone.

Wasting away like a consumption patient
Soon to be but stardust dispersing in the erasing wind
Bugs and critters will feed on your decaying flesh that is now
vacant
How can life be this unkind?
It takes, and it takes
Dirt, mud and bloody roses filled with thorns
Covering the rotting casket you lie in, and breaking our feeble faiths
Long forgotten memories of tear stricken mourns

I wrote those lyrics on the day of her funeral, back then our band Hell's Angels was just me and my best friend Parrish, which was mainly goofing around with some of his foster dad's musical instruments, but after that day Paragon of Virtue's Inferno was born.

Parrish's tale is way darker than mine; his daddy killed his mummy in cold blood with a knife as he hid under the kitchen table below them. Her blood dripped down from the table above him, creating a spill. which little by little coursed through to his 8-year-old rocking body. The poor fucker has a thing for knifes now, go figure. while his daddy is used as a bitch in prison, by somewhat worse monsters than him. Serves him right, death would have been too good for someone like him.

He ripped her apart, staining her skin with something as delicious
as wine
Now he gets broken in by prickling joysticks in a vicious line

Bishop took over managing our small garage band and even learned how to play the bass. To this day I don't know how he copes with my sorry ass, the band and his job at the Rosson's garage. He had finished school 2 years before Momma got sick, and has been delaying college since then, he had even been offered a full ride scholarship that meant He could've been out of this God forsaken place yet, he decided to stay. I fucking hope he knows how much I appreciate everything he's done for me so far, if it wasn't for him I probably would've ended up dead in the gutter by now.

He got us gigs at the only bar in Friars Point and some other places around the Mississippi river. The pay was shit and yes, they were stinky, sticky and filled with the worst drunks, that couldn't care less about the music that echoed around the four walls that they would find themselves in, but at the end of the day Beggars couldn't be choosers.

We needed a drummer desperately, couldn't be a band without one really. That's how we fucking ended up with Abel Rosson. Bishop had gone to the Rosson's house to go over the books for the garage with Mr. Rosson and heard Abel playing from his bedroom. Desperate times called for desperate measures and yet I still can't stand the guy.

Silas Rosson, Bishop boss isn't Abel's dad, he's his uncle. Abel's parents used to live in a trailer next to ours, more often than not, they were high as a kite neglecting little Abel on a frequent basis. The 10-year-old Bishop couldn't stand his harrowing crying, so he used to sneak him over to ours all the time. Four years later, one horrid night, shit hit the fan. Abel was 6 at the time, and how this came to be still can't be fathomed by any of us as a raging party seemed to be taking place at their trailer. His parents couldn't pay some sort of debt to a drug dealer from Friars that happened to have a eye for little boys; but you can piece together the rest of the details. The police came and so did family services. his parents lost custody of him, and he ended up with a strict for punishment disciple of God that is his uncle. The guy was never caught and is still roaming lose to this day.

He says I am dirty thanks to sins I didn't choose to commit
That my soul is damned to burn if to God's words I don't submit

"Why follow someone like sheep, that gives you nothing but misery and agony? Our souls are condemned no matter what, may as well get something in return." I tell Bishop.

"What the hell are you talking about, Church?"

"Call the others, on this moonless night we are going on a field trip."

We are all here, me, Bishop, Parrish – who's now rocking blush pink hair, - and even 16-year-old Abel snuck out of the house. I tried to explain as much as I could on our drive here in Bishop's beaten down 1967 Chevy Impala, and everyone seems to be on board with what we are doing tonight.

When we arrive each of us takes a junction on the Devil's Crossroads.

Remembering the lyrics, I walk into the heart of the crossroad and bury the box containing a picture of us 4, some graveyard dirt that I took from Momma's grave and a bone from a black cat. That last item was not as hard to come by as I thought it would have been, all I had to do was drive to Lulla, go to crazy Miss Wynae's witch shop; the woman has all types of wacky juju stuff. The way she eyed me had been Creepy, it was like she knew exactly what I needed the bone for.

The moment I return to my original spot on the crossroads, I dusted off my hands on my skinny black jeans, Parrish says "May the fallen angel that rejected God, listen to our prayers and answer our calling."

"We want what you gave Robert Johnson all those years ago." Bishop states in a forbidding tone.

" We are ready to pay the fee you redeem, unprejudiced for our request." Abel remarked.

"Is that so boys?" An eerie deep voice sounded from behind me.

This dark skin man, wearing an immaculately tailored black three-piece suit with matching black button-down, and shiny, black Oxford shoes, gives me a sinful smirk the instant my gray eyes land on him.

I swallow dry, as he begins to circle me like a shark in the wake of smelling blood.

"Ok. I will give you what you want, and as payment for my gracious handout, I will collect your souls in a year."

"No." I protest.

"No? "

"Church." I hear Bishop call out anxiously.

"Give us another price."

"Church, what the fuck are you doing?" Abel says disgruntled.

Parrish chuckles and utters "It looks like he is negotiating with the Devil."

The man before me looks me up and down,

"I like your style, boy. Ok. Sacrifice a pretty, pure girl as an offering and I will grant you a quick buck, all the pussy you desire and your names in light's for the world to see."

I peer at the rest of my band members, before replying to his words.

"How does that guarantee you won't come back to us in a year to drag our souls to hell with you?"

"On the strike of the year, give me the blood of a virtuous girl to reset the deal, and your souls will be spared."

Well, it sounds easy enough, right…

"I believe it's time to go"
(Robert Johnson)

Once more the bluesman Johnson ghostly voice penetrates my ears, as we drive away from the Devil's Crossroads, and

Satan himself. Sometimes a deal with the Devil is better than no deal at all. At least it gives us a chance to do something, be something, get out of the shadows of our rough upbringing and past.

We intend to go through with our side of the bargain.

But how long will we be able to keep dancing with the Devil?

Two

Abel

The woods of Friars Point feel alive, pulsing with an energy that doesn't belong to the living. Whispers coil through the trees, faint and insidious, like the voices of the damned threading their way into the marrow of the night. Each step I take lands with ritualistic precision, the cadence of our movements syncing with the relentless pounding of my heart. It hammers against my ribcage, a drumbeat that seems to echo through the dark, keeping time with the sins we're about to commit.

We move like shadows, cloaked in black hoods drawn low to conceal our faces. Our anonymity is a shield—not from judgment but from the weight of what we are. Sinners, murderers, bound by a deal we dared to make.

The clearing comes into view, bathed in pale moonlight that spills over the crude stone altar at its center.

She lies there, his offering as promised. Her form is slight, fragile, hands and feet bound with ropes that dig into her skin. Her breath comes in quick, visible puffs of air that vanish almost as soon as they form, with each exhale a silent plea for a mercy she'll never find. Her eyes, wide and shimmering with tears, dart frantically, taking in the twisted tableau around her. They're full of terror— a terror no one should ever know, let alone endure.

"Ready?" Church's voice cuts through the stillness, a whisper so sharp it feels like a blade against the quiet. I nod; my throat tight.

Words fail me, not from fear, but from the grotesque thrill that courses through my veins. It's a sickness I can't explain, an anticipation that turns my stomach even as it consumes me.

Church steps forward, his silhouette merging with the night, his presence commanding as he takes his place at the altar. The rest of us form a circle around him, a congregation of the damned witnessing a perverse ritual that mocks anything sacred.

"Pro Satana ipso," Church intones, his voice steady, revenant. "Virginem in lecto tuo collocamus, donum tibi offerimus, pactum nostrum honoremus."

The blade gleams in the moonlight, a crescent of silver poised above her trembling form. Then it descends. The sickening sound of steel meeting flesh cuts through the night, followed by the wet spray of blood that paints the air and surrounds. Her gasp is fleeting, drowned by the guttural chant that rises from our throats, a hymn to the abyss.

I watch, transfixed, as the life drains from her body, her essence pooling on the stone and soaking into the earth. It's an offering, a gift to the dark deity who holds our souls in his grasp. The air hums with a power that is both intoxicating and hollow, a rush that promises everything but delivers nothing. In this moment, we're gods—creators and destroyers of worlds that exist only in shadows.

The ritual ends, the sacrifice is complete. Her last breath lingers in the air before vanishing into the night, and as silence reclaims the clearing, one thought grips me: Will the Devil truly keep his promises?

The hum of the tour bus engine is a low, steady dirge beneath the cacophony inside. Laughter bounces off the walls, sharp and reckless, mingling with the clink of glass bottles and the stale musk of sweat and beer. We sprawl on the leather seats, kings of this rolling dominion, heading toward another city for us to conquer with our music and presence.

I lean back, my gaze flicking lazily to the muted television, that shows the news scrolling by in fragmented headlines, completely ignored by everyone around it, until one headline grabs me like a hand around the throat. "Turn that up," I say, my voice sharp, cutting through the din. Church, lounging nearest the remote, obeys my command without hesitation.

"...breaking news out of Friars Point. Authorities have discovered the body of a young woman, her throat brutally slit in what appears to be a ritualistic style killing. The victim has yet to be identified, there are no witnesses to the crime and an investigation by local authorities is underway..."

The bus falls silent, the air growing heavy and charged as the words sink in. The image on the screen shifts, showing a blurred image of the woods that we know all too well—the altar hidden among the trees where we spill blood for power. My chest tightens under the weight of our shared guilt, the unspoken bond we have that both binds us together and sets us apart from the world.

"Shit," Church mutters, his voice barely audible, cuts through the silence like the edge of his knife. The sound ripples through the group, a grim acknowledgment of what we have done.

"Keep cool," I remind them, my voice measured and steady, even though my pulse quickens. "It's just another mystery for them to chase. They've got nothing!"

As if to punctuate my words, the news anchor's tone shifts to a lighter note and her face brightens as she moves on. "In other news, the new rising star rock band, Paragon of Virtue's Inferno continues to skyrocket. The controversial group who are known for their dark lyrics and enigmatic stage presence, will be performing in Charlotte tonight, where fans are already lining up outside the venue for the sold-out show."

A collective exhale passes through the bus, the tension easing just enough to make way for the smug satisfaction that comes with hearing our names being celebrated.

"Looks like we're still the darlings of the damned" I quip, a smirk tugging at the corner of my mouth. The others chuckle, their laughter tinged with the mixture of relief and subversiveness we all feel.

"Let's give 'em one hell of a show," Church says, his gaze meeting mine. Theres a fire in his eyes, something feral and unrestrained, like a reflection of the blood that ties us together.

"Always do," I reply, leaning back into the worn leather seat.

The images on the screen blur into insignificance as I close my eyes, letting the rhythm of the road carry me into thought. Tonight, we'll ascend the stage, the heat of a thousand bodies fueling our fire. They will cheer, scream, and worship us for what they can see, while oblivious to the darkness we wear like a second skin, the shadows of our sins trailing us wherever we go.

Present Day

Sunlight pierces through the half-drawn curtains causing me to stir, the blade of gold light severing the darkness of last night's indulgences. slowly consciousness claws its way back as the warm and heavy scent of sex clings in the air. The motion of sheets rustling beside me draws my attention.

She—a tangled mass of chestnut hair spilling across the pillow—shifts, her body a silhouette against the morning light. With an unabashed stretch, she rolls onto her back exposing her bare skin that gleams while her breasts and nipples become exposed, and they pucker in unintended defiance with the warmth from the bed and the room's chill. A smirk twitches across my lips; such a shameless vulnerability, it's almost poetic.

The other, a raven-haired siren stirs from her slumber. Her lids flutter open, revealing eyes like midnight storms, that cut through the haze of my waking mind. Her voice is like silk wrapped around gravel, rich and suggestive. "Do you need me to help with that?" My gaze drops to waist level, noting the stirring beast below the sheets. Her hand reaches out, fingers ghosting over my semi-hard dick with the promise of pleasure. It's an offering, a submission to the power I wield, even in the aftermath of decadence.

"Yesss please," I drawl, stretching the words out like a caress, "that would be lovely."

The world narrows at the sensation of her touch and the fabric shifting as she sits up. My hands find their natural place behind my head, creating a casual throne for a king among sinners. The pillows cradle me as I lean back against the headboard, every muscle in my body singing a hymn to the carnal worship that is about to unfold.

Her mouth descends, the wet heat enveloping me, drawing a hiss between my teeth as i close my eyes and surrender to the rhythm of her devotion, the suck and pull, each movement a testament to the control I command with my mere presence. The band, the fame and the whispered rumors—they are but distant echoes against the immediacy of her lips on me.

In this room, in this moment, I am the master of my fate, the architect of pleasure and pain. Outside these walls the world awaits, ready to be bent beneath the will of Paragon of Virtue's Inferno. But for now, I can bask in the decadence of flesh on flesh and the sweet slide into oblivion.

THREE

HARLOW

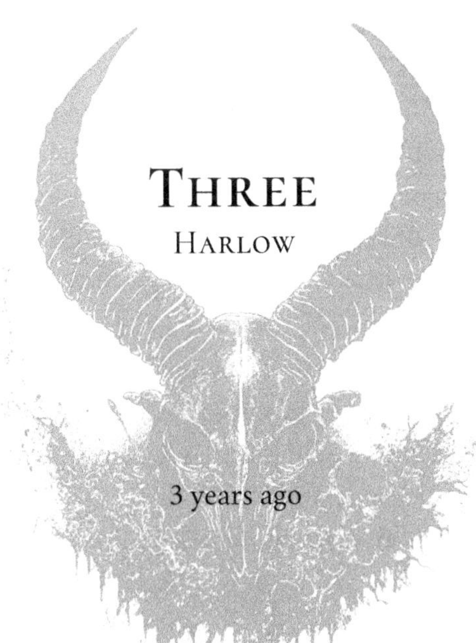

3 years ago

I AM WEARING A GORGEOUS, white pleated swing style halter dress that reaches just above my knees. Mother dearest picked it for today's sermon. Once more I have my hair down, making my natural dark blonde curly hair frame my heart shaped face.

According to mother dearest, I was blessed with perfect porcelain skin, luscious eyelashes and plump lips, and it is repeatedly told to me that I don't need any of that fakeness, so it is little to no make-up for anything. As I stand rooted to my spot at the altar of my father's house of prayer, before his herd-as he calls them- a disturbing image flashes before my eyes. Instead of the beautiful white chapel that is painted in a rainbow of colors from the light shining through the stained-glass windows, a shadowy darkness fills the space, tainting it in a hue of grays, almost as if I had entered a film noir.

The nicely dressed brethren are blackened shadows sitting in the pews of the chapel, and when I look down at myself, my snowy white dress is no longer pristine, as rivulets of crimson red bespattered it. I look down hanging low at my front by a strap going over my neck and across my shoulder, is my most prized possession, my old spruce acoustic guitar, that over the years has been covered in stickers, doodles and some of my favorite lyrics.

While leaving one of my hands behind the neck of my guitar and lifting the one from the strings above the rosette up to my neck, it swiftly becomes clear what the red liquid is, it's my blood. I am bleeding from a slash on my throat. I start to panic, what is happening?

"Harlow?" I hear a faint male voice call from behind me.

As I turn around to look at who has called me, I see is four husky men, in all but black, with horror movie masks covering their faces. Who are you? I open my mouth to ask but my voice fails me.

"Harlow." The stern tone of my father snaps me back to reality and out of the nightmare I found myself in. Standing behind me, vision slowly changes from the masked men to my father dressed in his preferred 80's prom style of powdered blue tuxedo pants with the matching jacket worn over an open-collared shirt with the ruffles and blue trim. Somedays I pray that someone tells my father that this isn't in fashion anymore. I mean, you would think as a preacher he would adorn himself better, a bit more... plain and modest, like a normal preacher, but not him, he has all the hallmarks of a pompous and boastful sinner.

I clear my throat, whilst orbiting back around to face his

herd. Stringing the first note on my guitar, I open my mouth, the words just spilling out like sweet nothings.

Sweet as sugarcane
Pretty as a peach
But You don't allow me to be vain
As that is not in the written words You preach
Sour as vinegar
Ugly as sin
All of the profane and corrupt that rather suffer
Than let the Holy ghost within
I have been blessed with the beauty of heavenly innocence
But why give me wings if You were going to break them?
I have been cursed with a silken voice of a lovely Lorelei
Then why bound me to earth amongst unfaithful men
Making me the Pied Piper of Your sanctified genesis
To turn the ones that have forsaken You Lord, Your fallen and
condemned
To guide the sinners and the saints towards the hands of the divine
Amen

"Amen." The whole congregation repeats after me.

"My daughter, Harlow Abaddon, everyone." My father says as he comes to stand by me. "We were truly blessed by the Lord, to have been given an angel of our own." He states as his cold hand lands on my lower back, triggering me to shudder.

Broken wings heal. Broken wings heal. Broken wings heal.

I keep repeating those words to myself over and over, like a mantra because as long as they don't clip them, I can still fly.

"Bow child." He says in a hushed tone so only I can hear him. I do as father commands; after all I will be damned if I don't.

I walk over to place my guitar in its case and descend the few steps from the altar to sit next to mother dearest in the front row, making sure to set the case under the pew we are sitting on before the reprimanding begins and as if right on cue;

"Your voice was hoarse quite a few times during the song, Harlow. That won't do." she whispers harshly.

I reply with the only acceptable response for her,"I'm sorry, mother."

"Don't be sorry. Be better." she demands quietly.

I want to tell her that if she hadn't made me practice all day yesterday, before this morning's performance, then perhaps my vocal cords wouldn't be raw and gruff sounding, but I know better than to do that.

As if perfectly timed Father begins his sermon, and everyone falls silent to his forbidding blarney.

I always wonder what people see when they look at me.

Do they see the Cherished and doted upon preacher's daughter, with the picture-perfect life, I assume that's what they see, right? Wrong.

You want to know what I fear more than not being able to fly away and leave this place, the dark, damp, putrid closet below the stairs in our kitchen. where being slapped in the face constantly, grabbed, dragged and violently shoved was not punishment enough. No, my mother went and took a page from Stephen King's book 'Carrie' and created her own 'prayer closet', Not that I think she has ever come across the actual story, in any shape or format, and I know if she finds out I have a weird obsession with anything horrorish then mother dearest will probably lock me in the closet and throw away the key for my punishment.

This chapel-fashioned, tiny room under the stairs is packed with religious paraphernalia of everything imaginable. From portraits and small statues of every saintly figure to a life-sized crucified Jesus in the center with an altar below it that holds a frayed-old-Holy Bible that looks like it came from the lord himself and has candles everywhere. Excerpts from the Holy book are written all over the walls with my shaky handwriting from years of punishments and being told. "Maybe this way His words will sink in that stupid head of yours." My mother used to balefully utter from the other side of the door.

If you are questioning where father was during all of this, that would be anywhere else but home. His herd is more important than his family, always has been, and if by some miracle he is in the house then he does nothing and says nothing to stop the abuse, which makes him just as bad as the abuser.

After a while I learnt not to speak my thoughts out loud, not to disobey, not to resist and rebel against their teachings. I learnt that if I followed my parents every wish and command, like a loyal faithful daughter then I wouldn't get beaten and wouldn't end up in the closet.

I'm 16 years old and I have no friends, not true ones I have made myself anyway, mostly because the ones that mother dearest and father approve off are kids from families that are part of the congregation, and… well… I don't know if they are actually my friends or if they are my parents´ eyes and ears, that rat on me once we are done playing.

I have never been kissed, or touched lovingly my whole life, much less sexually. And in all likelihood, I am defiantly going to die a virgin.

Mother dearest says I am too graceful and beautiful for my own good, and that I will tempt only lust, gluttony and greed from men. Like the sins of others can be blamed on my hands somehow. All I have is my guitar and my voice. Yes, my verses and ballads are tainted by the Lord, but at least I can say something using these then when I usually cannot. Perhaps, someday, someone will hear me sing and they will want to rescue me from the unfortunate prison I find myself in. Maybe that person will see beyond the mask I wear, to see the hurt, woe and torment behind my smile and electric blue eyes and save me.

"May the Lord bless you and keep you." My father finishes his sermon. like I always do, I tuned out during the whole sermon, it's not as if I don't know every word in that book. If there was a test at the end of his Holy teachings, without paying an ounce of attention I would still pass it with flying colors.

As the sermon concludes, the three of us gather outside by the door of the only chapel in the outskirts of the quaint little town- where we live- of Chapel Hill, Tennessee, in the guise of the close-knit family that we are meant to be, everyone comes to pay their high praises to my father. Things go by the quotidian that is this sham of a life, that is until a very well-dressed gentleman-with deep brown hair, hazel eyes and olive skin, in a mocha-brown Chino pants, with a perfectly tucked in off-white knitted polo shirt and perfectly polished penny loafers- approaches my father.

"Your daughter has the voice of an angel, Pastor Abaddon." The man comments as he removes the sunglasses from the half-buttoned polo collar and sets them on his face. Shaking this stranger's hand my father replies "Thank you. The Lord has definitely been kind to us when he gifted us with such a talented daughter."

"I don't believe I have seen you around these parts before, Mister." My mother cuts in.

"First time in Chapel Hill for me, ma'am."

"Where are you from?" My father asks.

"Nashville, born and raised."

"And you came all this way to hear my sermon?" My father utters beaming proudly.

"Actually, I travelled here for her, Sir." The man states while bestowing me with the most genuine smile anyone has ever given me that it brings a blush to my cheeks, and I can't help but smile back at him.

"I don't think we caught your name yet, Mister." My mother says crudely. She does not sound pleased with the direction this conversation has taken.

"Where are my manners, I'm sorry." The man begins to speak as he digs for something in his front pocket, pulling out a card that he then hands off to my father. "My name is Gabriel Mourreau. I work for Columbia Records; I am a music producer for Provident Label which mostly focuses on Christian music, we think Harlow Abaddon could be our next rising star."

And just like that I can feel these fictional wings tear through the skin on my back, rip perfect holes in the back of my dress as they stretch out wide, free from the heavy chains that have been keeping them barred and broken inside of me for so long.

FOUR
BISHOP

Present day

THE LEATHER of my chair creaks underneath me as I lean back, the dim light from the desk lamp casting long shadows across the room. This office is my sanctuary made up of dark wood and secrets, it suits me perfectly. it's where control pulses like a living thing. Although It's quiet now, save for the distant echoes of laughter and the strum of an unplugged guitar from somewhere down the hall. They all have their own places to call home, but this house, it's our true north. Here, in this den of musical prodigies and midnight whispers, we are more than just a band; we are brothers bound by rhythm and rebellion.

My phone vibrates against the mahogany desk with a breaking news alert, tearing through the silence. The screen lights up with the face of an angel—or so they say. Harlow. The name is like a sweet toxin on everyone's lips. Her eyes, as bright as spotlights, seem to stare right through the headlines that scream about her meteoric rise. I scroll, moving my thumb over the glass as if it could smudge away her innocence as I read the headline that proclaims in bold letters "Local Singer Harlow Strikes a Chord with Heaven,". A snort escapes me. Heaven doesn't know the tune we play, the dark symphonies that have been composed in the dead of night. I can almost hear Church's voice, that note of fascination he has whenever he utters her name, but I push the thought aside. She's just a girl, caught up in the chaos of newfound fame, singing praises to a deity that has no sway over the likes of us.

Leaning back in my leather chair, I drum my fingers on my dark mahogany desk that's seen more secrets than the stars have seen nights. Church's obsession with this Harlow chick has been gnawing at my curiosity for weeks. Every time I catch a glimpse of his screen, there it is—her name, glowing like some digital mantra. I think it's time I see what the fuss is about.

In a few taps, her world spills onto my screen – a live performance captured for the masses to replay endlessly. The stage is awash with pale white light, making her white dress gleam like she's some kind of modern-day seraphim. Harlow stands there, a slender figure amidst a flood of applause, her hands clasping the microphone like it's her lifeline to the divine.

"Show me why you're worthy of my brother's time," I mutter to myself, pressing play on the video.

The opening chords strum through the speakers of my phone as Harlow lifts her head to face the crowd. She's enchanting, I'll give her that, with those wide eyes full of longing and lips parting to start spilling her soul into the mic.

Her voice, it's like honey laced with silver, and she belts out her love for the lord or whatever deity has her so wrapped up in rapture.

"Sing it, saint," I sneer, watching as she sways with the rhythm, her arms raised high, embracing the adoration showered upon her by the sea of faces lost in worship.

"Believe it, the Lord is fantastic," she croons, her voice soaring over the notes effortlessly, and for a split second, I understand the allure. There's something so pure and untainted about her, a disparity to the murky depths we dwell in.

I lean forward, with my elbows on the desk completely drawn in to the aura she creates despite who I am. Her conviction is almost tangible, her belief a shining armor that she wears proudly under the spotlights. But it's that same light which makes her shine is the one that casts the longest shadows, and we, we are the kings of shadows.

"Harlow," I breathe out, the name comes out like a whisper of wind stirring the dying embers of a once roaring fire. "You don't know it yet, but you're dancing on the edge of a blade." My gaze doesn't waver from the screen, from the spectacle of purity that's about to be stained. She is the last piece, the final note in our grand performance.

I flick off the video, the screen going black like a mirror reflecting a distorted image of my smirking face. A game is afoot, and I'm never one to fold when the stakes are this high.

The video is like a ghost in my mind now, the image of Harlow burned into the back of my eyelids, haunting me. I can't shake it—the vision of her, all dressed in white, pure as the sinless sky. It irks me, gnawing at the edges of my thoughts like a persistent rat.

I lean back in my chair, hands behind my head staring up at the stucco ceiling of my office. Church's fascination with the girl has my stomach in knots, a tangled mess I can't unravel. Sure, she's hot—no denying that. The kind of hot that makes men walk into walls and women whisper behind their backs, but that heat is backed by a faith so fierce it makes my teeth ache.

A god chaser. That's what she is—a beacon for the devout and desperate- And Church well, he's tracking her every move like a hound on the scent. But we are not those who kneel; we bend the knee to no one but ourselves—and the dark secrets that bind us.

My lips quirk up at the thought, a devilish grin spreading across my face. The idea comes slowly at first, then all at once like sunrise over a blood-soaked horizon. She would be perfect—the final offering. Ten years we've danced with the devil; ten years we've fed him sacrifices to keep our souls from damnation and our names in lights. Each year, the price gets steeper, the demands more challenging.

"Harlow, darling," I say to no-one, my voice laced with a darkness that matches the ink etched all over my skin, "you might just be the masterpiece we need to complete the gallery."

A god lover offered to the devil—that's poetry, that's art, The beauty in the irony, a delicious twist of fate that I relish with every fiber of my being. We promised him ten sacrifices —a decade of devotion to our own survival. And now, as the clock ticks down, I can think of no better climax to our unholy symphony, to present the devil with an angel.

"Sorry, sweetheart," I chuckle, the sound hollow. "But the

stage is set, you're the star of our show, you just don't know it yet."

I flick my thumb against the screen, a series of quick texts dispatched like harbingers of the coming storm. My fingers dance across the keyboard with practiced ease, each tap an echo of the drumbeats that pulse through our music. It's time to bring the band together, time to reveal the final act in our dark concerto.

"Get to the office. Now." The words stare back at me, stark and unyielding as I hit send, the message wings its way to Church, Abel, and Parrish. Each one of them bound to my will, to the fate we've all chosen.

Minutes drip by like wax from a candle, I fix my eyes on the door, the anticipation building within the walls of this opulent sanctuary we call a home. There's a thrill in the wait, knowing they're coming, knowing what I'm about to propose.

The heavy door swings open, and Church strides in, his presence filling the room with a silent expectation. He's dressed in all black, as always.

"What's up?" His loud voice reverberates against the bookshelves.

"Wait," is all I say, my gaze locked onto his with a smirk I continue "We're not all here yet."

Church nods, a slight tilt of his head, and saunters over to the couch. He sinks into it, the cushions swallowing his frame as his eyes hold mine, questioning but patient. The others will be here soon, then I'll unveil the plan — Harlow's fate entwined with ours, by the very hands that seek to save her soul.

"Patience," I murmur, more to myself than to him. "The final scene is about to begin."

The office door opens a few minutes later as Abel and Parrish stride through, one by one with sweat glistening on their brows like a sheen of determination. They've been pumping iron downstairs, sculpting their bodies into temples that mock the sanctity they're about to defile.

"About time," I grunt, watching them slump into the chairs with the haughty grace of bears settling into their cave.

Abel, the ever defiant one, leans back, stretching out his legs as if he owns every inch of the space between us. He produces a cigarette from nowhere, the smoke dangling lazily between his fingers before he lights it, the flame briefly illuminating the dark hunger in his eyes.

"What's up?" he drawls, smoke curling around his words, an insouciant challenge.

I can't help but smile—a crooked, knowing smirk. They have no idea the kind of storm I'm about to unleash. I watch as smoke from Abel's cigarette snaking towards the ceiling, a hazy omen in the stillness of my office.

"Church," I nod at him, the name more a title than a brotherhood now. He's leaning back against the couch, his posture relaxed but eyes sharp, always waiting for the next play in our infernal game.

"Abel. Parrish." My voice is the crack of a whip, snapping their attention to me fully. "I trust you've been... productive?"

"Always," Parrish replies, his tone cool and collected.

I lean forward, elbows resting on the desk, my hands clasped together as if in prayer. But we haven't prayed to anything holy in an exceptionally long time.

"Good," I say, the word tinged with the hint of dark satisfaction. "Because I've found her."

"Found who?" Abel's smoke falters, a cloud dispersing in confusion.

"The last sacrifice." The words roll off my tongue, heavy with significance. A grin unfurls across my face, wicked and triumphant. "The one who will seal our pact with the devil himself."

"Who is she?" Church asks, leaning forward now, beneath his cool exterior his interest has been piqued.

FIVE

HARLOW

GABRIEL MOURREAU certainly opened more than a window for me, but overall, he also opened a door for father and his holy preaching to reach thousands more people helping to persuade them into giving him most of their life savings, even convincing some to seclude themselves in this small community he has established in the outskirts of Chapel Hill.

The first year was a bit shaky, a struggle to come up with an image that would please both the record label and my parents, lyrics that were predominantly God related yet girly enough so people around my age could identify with them and finally, finding a tune that would tie with what I was trying to say. Somehow, we ended up with a mashup of pop-country with a bluegrass folk vibe.

When it comes to my appearance, my hair became a light old money blonde instead of my natural dark blonde-which apparently makes my electric blue eyes pop, especially with a black liner around the perimeter of them-. Accentuating my face is the near perfect curls that waterfall down over my shoulders and back unless it is up in braids, these are my go-to hairstyles for the image created with colorful clothes, especially swing dresses, oh, and let's not forget the good old cowboy boots that are meant to be made for walking.

But even with all of that, according to Gabriel, the most important thing about me is my voice.

"Your voice is what enchanted me. Your voice is what's going to… 'bring all the boys to the yard'." I remember giving him a half-suppressed laugh at his words.

"No boys." My mother dearest had said.

Gabriel just ignored her as he continued, "Everything else is simply background noise, as long as we put emphasis on your beautiful vocals, whatever is echoing behind it doesn't matter."

The moment my first single came out 'By the grace of You' I went from a nobody who grew up in the middle of nowhere Tennessee, to the sweet daughter of a preacher, the small-town girl next door everybody loved. When my debut album 'Deception of an Angel' was released, it reached number one that day, by the next week it had gone platinum.

I spent the rest of the year touring. Either doing small shows by myself or being the opening act for people like Gabby Barrett, Anne Wilson and Riley Clemmons.

Now, with a new album looming on the horizon, the route to take doesn't seem so clear to me, although I think everyone would be happy if I just carry on doing what I did previously, but all that does is pluck my dainty white feathers, one by one, if it continues there will be none left, and without those feathers, I won't fly no more.

Once more I am held captive and made into a liar

By You, your words and what everyone else wants me to be
Just a Pretty white dove caged in rusty barbed wire
Forever the virgin daughter of a preacher from Chapel Hill,
Tennessee

As I halt my manipulation of the strings on my guitar, A single tear breaks free Because once more these words won't see the light of day, so what's the point in what I am doing right now? mother dearest calls them Too whiny, but I continue Writing them down, erecting a melody for it and singing them out loud.

After overhearing one of my 'complaints' as she puts it, she spit her venomous words at me yet again "You ungrateful brat, questioning His chosen righteous path for you." At least, long gone are the days where something like this would land me in the 'prayer closet', but it doesn't stop the slaps that come my way, every now and again.

I put my guitar back in its case and make my way out of the house, treading carefully over the graves and headstones that make up our front yard, to head into father's church. Our house is on the same grounds as the chapel and the old cemetery. Funny enough, graveyards are my safe haven. I love to sit against an old, sunken headstone, in poor condition and write. The dead below my feet are my confidants, my only friends in this place I can tell all my secrets to After all, no ghost has told on me yet.

Growing up, we were the only family living on the outside of Chapel Hill, but since I became someone, and with all the money flowing in--not just from my career but from father's 'herd' sending him money from all over the US--father began to build a community sheltered by the woods around us. Right now, there are a good 100 families living in newly built houses that surround the church's grounds, perhaps 333 people in all, including me and my parents, while Chapel Hill's sign claims only 931 souls.

As I enter the chapel through the ornate, arched double doors that lead into the narthex, I stop before crossing the threshold into the nave and aisles as I can hear mother dearest and father arguing.

"I don't know what that boy is thinking, but I don't not like it." My mother says, pacing along the altar.

"It doesn't sound like a bad idea." Father remarks as he shrugs.

"Have you fallen and hit your head, Claude?" She stops in her stride to scold my father, placing her hands on her hips to emphasize how displeased she is. "Bishop McGrew wants to convert his band's tour with Harlow's."

Wait, what? Bishop McGrew from Paragon of Virtue's Inferno? He wants me? I mean, he wants us to tour together? Why?

I have listened to some of their songs, they are dark and disturbing. But ohhhh, the lead singer Church's voice, we'll let's just say that my legs feel like jelly every time his sexy mouth utters anything with that gravelly voice.

And they are all hot as hell. Forgive me father for I have sinned, many times, by looking at images of those gorgeous specimen online. Look, I may be a virgin, but I am not a prude, I have eyes that allow me to see the sacrilegious beauty of all four of them.

Church with his ashy blonde hair always in a James Dean

style, pale gray eyes and piercing on his lower lip. Rolling Stones magazine had an unholy and ungodly picture of him without a shirt on, and you could see his tattoo of Devil wings that covers his back completely, I drool just thinking of it.

His older brother Bishop, same ashy blonde hair as Church but shoulder length, with similar pale gray eyes but with a hue of green around the iris. And then there's Parrish with rich hazel eyes, now he's a bit more out there with his style, spiked short pink hair, with an array tattoos with things like rainbows, unicorns and other fantastical cute creature you can think of as well as a plethora of piercings; from his tongue, one in each cheek dimple, one in his left nostril, left eyebrow, his right ear is covered with them, while the other is completely bare, nipples (yes, both) and while I don't listen to gossip, according to some statements in that same magazine, from girls he has been with, his dick is also pierced. Just the thought of that makes it harder to swallow.

Finally, there's Abel with medium length dark brown hair that constantly falls over his dark brown -almost black- eyes, his skin has more of a light olive tone, unlike the other guy's paler complexions. Abel's sinful body is a mix of black and grey wash tattoos, mainly consisting of Paragon of Virtue's Inferno lyrics. I saw an image of him wearing reading glasses whilst holding what appeared to be 'Twilight' by Stephanie Meyer, what a wet girl's dreams.

"I thought you said she hasn't finished recording her new album yet."

"She hasn't. But Gabriel implicated that we could do a bigger tour focusing on her debut album that did so well. given her first solo tour was so small, that way we can promote and introduce songs from her follow up album to build up the anticipation or whatever."

"Ok. And why don't we want Harlow to do it with… what's the band called again?"

"Paragon of Virtue's Inferno." Mother dearest says with nothing but venom in her words.

"Interesting name." Father comments.

"Hell's Angels, dear, that's what it means. Devil worshippers, all four of them. And their fans are a bunch of sinners ready to burn in hell."

Father hums as he starts to listen to the voices in his head – I know that's exactly what's happening because he gets this distant look in his eyes when they begin to speak - and nods in agreement to whatever was just said. "Didn't the boy mention something about wanting to bring different people with different tastes together? Try something that hasn't been done before. How is that not similar to what we are trying to achieve here?"

"You're kidding me, right? Do you want these boys to taint Harlow's image? Because that's what they will do with their dirty money, drugs and sex." You forgot the Devil, mother dearest, I think to myself. "I did not sacrifice 19 years of my life to watch my own flesh and blood become a Devil's whore." And there it is.

Mother dearest speaks of me like I am a chore that must be done right or else. How dare she talk of sacrifices? I have been slaughtering my soul away to please her from the moment I left her womb.

"Contemplate with me, my dear." Father says as he wraps an arm around my mother's shoulders. "What better way to bring the Lord's word and will to fruition then by converting every soul that this band has, by your claim, condemned to eternal damnation?"

"You think those people will follow where she leads blindly?"

"Have you heard our child? We will have them on their knees and praying to me in no time." Don't you mean God, father?

"Well, I suppose we can at least go to their show in New Orleans and see what we might be working with. Mister McGrew said he would have a contract ready to sign by then."

"There you have it." Father concludes.

Six

Parrish

THE STAGE QUAKES under the weight of our music, the pulse of Paragon of Virtue's Inferno rips through the sultry New Orleans night. I'm in my element, letting the electric currents from my guitar surge into the sea of bodies, that crash like tidal waves against the barriers.

"Listen to them," I mutter to myself, a wicked grin splitting my face as I soak in their frenzied cheers. The venue is swarming with fans, each one thirsty for the dark symphony we conduct. The Shadows play along the walls, twisting with glee as they feast on the heightened emotions of the crowd that is trickling over the edge of insanity. Tonight, the darkness is alive, as it feeds, it grows!

As the chords shred the atmosphere, I can't help but think about Harlow and her mother. They're supposed to be here somewhere, amidst this congregation of chaos, ready to bind herself to us – to me – with a simple signature, written in ink. Bishop's been tightening the noose on that contract, and I wonder... how will Harlow stomach this congregation of lost souls?

"Will she find beauty in the madness? Or will she run, scared from the monster we've become? " I muse aloud, the thought lingering like smoke on my tongue. My voice barely rising above the cacophony, but it's not meant for anyone else's ears. It's an echo of the challenge that lies ahead; a game of power and seduction, where the stakes are as high as the heavens we seek to burn.

"Harlow," I whisper her name like a prayer—or is it a curse? —while scanning the crowd for a glimpse of her purity amongst the damned. I can almost picture her, wide-eyed, heart racing with the kind of adrenaline that only fear, and desire can brew together.

"Let's give 'em hell," I announce to the band, they respond with a collective nod you can see the hungry look on their faces.

We're ready to pull Harlow into our orbit, to show her a world where virtue is set aflame, and from its ashes, a new order rises—one where we reign supreme in the darkness, unchallenged and unrepentant.

"Welcome to the Inferno," Church growls into the mic, my gaze is locked on an invisible point in the pit, "where angels fall, and demons rise."

The crowd roars its approval, a beast with a thousand mouths, and I can't shake the feeling that tonight—the strings of fate are about to be pulled taut, ready to snap.

The final, reverberating note of my solo screams through the charged air, clawing its way to the rafters. Sweat beads on my brow as I throw my head back, letting the roar of the crowd wash over me like a tidal wave of raw energy. My fingers ache, but it's the sweet pain of victory, of domination over the senses of every soul in this pit of hedonism.

And there she is, almost ethereal.

She stands at the perimeter of chaos, an untouched lily amidst a swamp of sin. The stark white of her ankle-length dress cuts through the dimness— like a beacon calling out to those who still harbor some semblance of innocence. My heart hammers, not from the exertion of the performance, but from the sight of her—Harlow.

"Damn," the word slips from my lips, barely audible over the din of our fervent congregation. She's fucking beautiful, a masterpiece that would make saints weep and devils repent. She's been sculpted from alabaster dreams and given breath, standing amidst this sea of depravity like she's wandered out of some celestial garden by mistake.

An angel among demons? No, more than that—she's the definition of what defines us, the untouched purity that makes our darkness all the more delicious. She's the promise of redemption, that we can never seek because our paths are paved with the thrill of damnation, rather than the climb toward salvation.

I feel it—the pull of her presence—as if she wields a gravity all her own, ensnaring the attention of every lost soul here tonight, including mine. It's a power, quiet yet potent, and it stirs something primitive within me, a desire to possess, to claim, and to corrupt.

"Let's show them what it means to burn," I murmur under my breath, guitar strapped against me like a weapon of war, ready to lead the charge into the darkness where only the bold dare tread.

I lean into the back up mic, my voice a purr of dark velvet. "How we doing tonight, New Orleans?" The crowd roars back, fierce and hungry, but I barely hear them. My eyes locked on Harlow's silhouette, a beacon of purity.

Her mother's face is a canvas of outrage, pale and tight with disapproval. I smirk, wondering how she'd react if she knew the plans Bishop had laid out for her precious daughter's future. A twinge of something uncomfortable knots in my stomach, a jabbing reminder that maybe I shouldn't have indulged in that last-minute line before the lights went up. But the show must go on and I'm a master at playing through pain—or pleasure, for that matter.

Harlow's mother leans down, lips moving rapidly as she speaks words lost in the cacophony. They're turning to leave, retreating from our infernal embrace, but then it happens— Harlow pauses, casting a glance over her shoulder, her eyes finding mine through the shifting bodies and strobe lights.

It's a look that sears straight into my core; I swear for a moment the world tilts on its axis. There's recognition there, a flicker of curiosity that dances in her gaze, and suddenly I'm not so sure who's corrupting whom. She sees the danger, that much is clear, but what sends a jolt of adrenaline coursing through my veins is the dawning realization that she might just be intrigued by it.

For a heartbeat our connection is electric, a spark that threatens to ignite and consume us both.

With One final glance, she's gone, swallowed up by the night and the mass of people seeking their own salvation or damnation. But it doesn't matter. Harlow has left her mark on me, a promise of a game more dangerous than any I've played before—a game of power, control, and irresistible temptation.

"Let's crank it up," I say, my guitar once again alive in my hands. We're going to give them a night they'll never forget. Because in this world of shadows, where we walk the line between reverence and rebellion, I am a prince—and I will not be denied!

43

SEVEN

Harlow

"Laissez les bon temps rouler." (Let the good times roll.)

That's New Orleans for you. A place where sinners come to play, amongst the ill-omened energy buried deep inside every brick, nail, piece of wood and steel that make up these streets of sin.

We landed in the Big Easy with just enough time to get to the venue and take our place in the thick of the crowd. Once more I don't get to see anything, apart from what rushes past the window of whatever transport gets me to and from these places. It unsettles me, especially driving to the concert location itself, passing by all the haunted history that stains the French Quarter and not being able to take the time to tour any of it. It all looks so eerily beautiful.

I have been to quite a few places in America and Canada, with either my small tour or the ones I did with other artists, but I never see anything beyond my trailer, tour bus or the venue. Always imprisoned in some sort of confinement

I am taken by surprise as we arrive at an old warehouse in the heart of the shipping district. Inconspicuous from the outside, yet as you go in, vintage murals, brick walls, exposed wooden beams that hold the mezzanine and roof that houses a massive crystal chandelier that adorns the almost 8,000-square-foot space., a cute speakeasy bar is hidden off to the side. Paragon of Virtue's Inferno are top cats in what they do, so I am wondering why they are doing smaller venues like this instead of big arenas? I mean, I can see the appeal i suppose, it has an almost ghostly appeal with how dark and spine-chilling it is inside, it ties with their vibe perfectly, it also makes it more personal for the fans.

Mother dearest hasn't uttered a word to me since we left Chapel Hill. But I am used to her silence. I prefer it to her telling me everything I am doing wrong, knocking me down with her sharp, jagged, saw like words.

We are standing in the far corner of the mezzanine on the outskirts of a mass made up of interesting looking people who have, tattoos, piercings, and different hued hairs. black clothes seem to be the predominant color of choice, even mother dearest is wearing a black swing maxi skirt with a dark gray, drop shoulder knitted sweater. which makes my maxi-tiered white lace dress stand out. Every girl in here is either flaunting their legs or graced with a flimsy top that covers barely anything.

"Whores." I hear my mother say under her breath. As the lights somehow get even dimmer, plunging the space into utter darkness, this low hum starts to fill the air around us as the band come out on stage. I am gripped by them the second the spotlights shine down solely on each one. The pictures I have seen of all of them, do not hold a candle to what is before me now. The moment Church opens that sinful mouth of his, I am done for. I thank God for the loud music that consumes the locus that I find myself in because I am certain a moan breezed past my lips, and I certainly wouldn't want mother dearest to have heard that.

the concert progresses with more harrowing and appalling words, telling haunting and dark tales, I feel myself get sucked in by it all, like something about it just captures my attention. It's alluring, yet scary.

I can feel the hairs in the back of my neck stand up as if something is lurking in the shadows, it's like it's watching and keeping a very close eye on me, or perhaps it's the boys, the fact it seems like they are all looking right at me. The urge to run away, with a tail between my legs, is strong but despite that, I am rooted in place like it's the Elysian Fields in the Underworld, like I am one of the joyless souls haunted by regret for the choices made or not made in this mediocre life, slowly becoming an asphodel flower.

"How we doing tonight, New Orleans?" Parrish utters in a boyish husky voice, and the crowd goes wild. I don't think my fans have ever screamed for me like that, It's almost savage in nature.

He then smirks, making his dimple piercings glint as the lights above him hit them at just the right angle. I feel a little flutter in my stomach at the sight, which quickly turns sour by mother dearest leaning down to speak in my ear.

"I have had enough of this unnatural show of vice, debauchery and depravity. These people will never repent, look at them, they are clinging to every filthy thing that leaves their lips. "Let's go Harlow." She turns away to leave after she's done uttering her thoughts.

Sadly, Like the obedient good girl I am, I follow in her footsteps, but I suddenly pause, realizing What mother dearest had just said; All I do is be penitent for sins she laments on my behalf, yet the only thing I mourn is not being able to do anything worth regretting. In that split second I decide that I want to be in bed with the Paragon of Virtue's Inferno boys, go for a swim and even drown in treacherous shark infested waters as I bleed because at this moment it feels as if she has embedded the tip of a knife into my heart.

I cast one last glance over my shoulder, at the beautiful boys I never will be given permission to see in person ever again, my eyes latching on to these arresting hazel eyes of Parrish, that are staring straight at me. For a moment it feels as if There is this charged up instant, where energy just seems to slash right through me, Zapping me from my mournful thoughts.

What in the heavens was that?

Candidly, I see the danger these boys are selling, and I want it; at least then I would have something of my own to repent for.

"Harlow." Mother dearest calls out sounding irritated.

Just like that, my hope to have something more for me than this life I am riding out is shattered. I will be Forever trapped, forever caged.

As I come close to her, mother says "What was that McGrew boy thinking, dragging us here to this satanic gathering? I am not burning in hell as a consequence of this imprudence. I would rather break a leg than sign a deal with those Devils."

We begin making our way to the stairs that lead to the ground floor, if I thought it was dark before, even with the few lights from the stage, this hallway is even darker. It doesn't help that there are doors at both ends separating the stairway from the rest of the space out there, and the only lightbulb above us is flickering on and off. Ok, now that's some horror movie-bad juju- I'll tell you. I stop at the top of the stairs, but mother dearest just continues to go right on down. She is really that keen to leave this whole satanic gathering-as she called it- behind.

"Mother." I try to warn her; at the exact moment, the light goes completely off.

Among the darkness, I could swear I see the shadows move down in the direction of mother dearest, but that could have been the sudden blackness playing tricks on me, making me see things that aren't really there. plus, I am a bit spooked with all of this devilish talk, so I might be conjuring ghosts up in my mind too.

In the wake of that, I just about see mother lose her balance, her blackened figure falling forward and tumbling down the stairs. Thud after thud is all you can hear, with low muffled noises of the concert behind the doors that separate us from everyone else.

"Mother." I repeat again, this time with a shaky, fearful voice.

The bulb lights back up like nothing was ever wrong with it, at full force, blinding me in the process. Moaning of pain echos in the enclosed space, coming from the bottom of the stairs, making me take tentative steps in that direction.

I rush the last few steps, falling on all fours next to a pretty bruised up Mother that is lying on her back, her leg bones protrude through the skin and muscle they are meant to be buried under. It looks to be broken not only at the shin but at the ankle too. "Mother." I say in shock at what's before me.

. . .

It's been a few hours since we arrived at the hospital. Mother's bones have been put back in place, casted and she is now resting comfortably on pain medication, in a private patient room. Me? I am wandering through the wards, still trying to gather myself since the accident.

Back at the venue, I hadn't known what to do. Mother's dearest had to yell at me to go and get help, only then did I move. I found a nice security guard that radioed over to a first aider on site, who after seeing to my mother called an ambulance for us straight away.

As mother was being cared for by a doctor at the Ochsner Baptist Medical Center, I called my father to tell him the news of what happened. "Why are you calling me, Harlow? I can't do much from Chapel Hill, now can I? Call Gabriel." He comments over the phone, not a shred of concern over his wife's wellbeing.

Gabriel was a lot more helpful, he said he would call the hospital and deal with everything over the phone, Bless his heart. He instructed me to go back to the hotel room Bishop had arranged for us to stay in after the show. Since our original flight back to Nashville wasn't until the morning but I couldn't muster the courage to go there by myself. It's funny you spend most of your life asking for a bit of breathing room, to have some separation and freedom from the people that control every little thing about you, but the moment you get a taste of it, even if it's bitter, you don't know what to do with it. So that's why I have been walking around aimlessly through the hospital while mother is asleep.

Just when I approach her room, I hear a honeyed male

voice speak from within. "You did the right thing, Mrs. Abaddon. Your daughter will be in good hands. We will take care of her." Is that Bishop McGrew? Gabriel did say he was going to try and contact the boys to let them know what had occurred, I just didn't expect one of them to come around.

I linger just outside the half open door, my back to the wall, doing the most I can to be able to hear what's being spoken inside without being noticed.

"You better not spoil what took me 19 years to make perfect, Mister McGrew." Mother dearest warns.

"Oh, trust me, we have no intention of morphing Harlow into anything, she's ideal for what we have planned just the way she is." Bishop expresses in a solemn manner.

Mother simply hums in reply.

"Since we are all done here, I will let you be." The manager of Paragon of Virtue's Inferno announces, sounds not far from the door, so I try to move out of the way, unfortunately I am not fast enough. Bishop opens the patient room door fully, bumping right into me. The only reason I don't fall to the floor on my ass is because his rough hands hold me at the waist.

"Well, well, well… what do we have here?" Gradually I lift my eyes over to the face that just uttered those words and what I see takes my breath away. An impure, yet gorgeous, Cheshire cat like grin consumes his features. "Eavesdropping, Harlow. Such a Bad girl." A blush must paint my cheeks, not only from embarrassment from being caught snooping, but from the way he just said "Bad Girl.".

I open my mouth to say something in return, but all I manage to do is a little squeak.

His gray eyes dilate at the sound that just left my throat,

and as if waking himself from a dream, or perhaps nightmare, he steps away from me. His shirt is now wrinkled from where my hands fisted themselves while he held me.

"Your mother will no doubt tell you this once more when you go in there, but I may as well give you the good news. You will be joining me and the rest of Paragon of Virtue's Inferno on tour." I'm what? There is no way mother dearest signed the contract after the stuff she mouthed off at the concert. "In addition to that I will be taking the reins as your manager during her recovery." He what? "We will see you in a week, little mouse." And with that he's gone.

EIGHT

ABEL

I AM PERCHED on the cold metal step of our tour bus, a lit cigarette dangling between my index and middle finger. The sun is relentless, scorching the earth beneath me, but I don't mind the heat. It's a small penance for the sins that cling to me like a second skin. The Smoke curls up into the clear blue sky as I draw back another lungful of nicotine-laced relief.

A rumble of conversation pulls my attention to the dust cloud billowing down the road. As Harlow's entourage arrives. They are an overdone parade of followers and flunkies, instantly I can feel My lips twist into something that could be a smirk or a snarl; it's hard to tell these days.

She steps out of the sleek black car like she's descending from a higher plane, and hell, maybe she is. Nine suitcases follow her, each carried by someone who looks more put out than the last. Amidst the chaos of her arrival, she stands there, untouched and radiant. "Damn," I mutter under my breath, not caring who hears, it's not just the sunlight that makes her hair glow like molten gold; it's something about her—a light from within that makes the hollows of my chest ache with a strange hunger.

. It's not often something so pure comes into our world, I can't help but watch, transfixed, as she surveys her new domain. The defiant tilt of her chin tells me she's no damsel, and I can certainly appreciate that because Damsels break too easily, and I have a feeling Harlow's made of tougher stuff.

The smoke from my cigarette blurs my vision for a moment, and I rub my eyes with the heel of my free hand. When the haze clears, she's still there, shining amidst the grime and the shadows of our existence.

"Should be interesting," I say to no one in particular, already weaving stories in my head where she's both the villain and the savior, but then again, aren't we all a bit of both?

Harlow strides into my line of sight with her arms crossed. Gone is the ethereal white that draped her during that night at the concert, replaced with leggings that cling to her like a second skin and a T-shirt that exposes every curve beneath. The sun catches in her hair, setting it ablaze with light, but there's an edge to her now, a sharpness that wasn't there before.

"Trying to blend in?" I quip to myself, smirking at the thought. Angels don't walk among mortals without conse-quences, and she's no exception, not anymore.

My gaze flickers over to the small trailer our crew has parked just a stone's throw from our bus. It's a sad little thing, trying to be a sanctuary in this wasteland of sin and metal. They're showing her the ropes, pointing out the flimsy locks, and windows that might as well be made of tissue paper for the protection they offer.

"Safe," I snort quietly, knowing full well the illusion of security we've spun around her. She steps inside the trailer, and I can't help but admire her bravado or whatever it is that lets her walk into the lion's den with her head held high.

"Always the angel, thinking she's above it all," I mumble, though part of me wonders if she sees the bars on her cage or if she's truly that blind. Harlow's presence here is like a spark near a powder keg, and I'm too intrigued by the promise of flames to look away.

"Welcome to the fold, Harlow," I whisper to the empty air, a smirk curling my lips. "Let's see just how long your wings last."

I inhale a deep drag from my cigarette and let it linger in my lungs. My gaze doesn't stray from the small trailer and as if on cue, the thought that she's about to trade the makeshift sanctuary for the chaotic confines of our tour bus, sends a jolt of anticipation through me, the kind that's half dread, half delight. With the image of her sitting there among us flashing in my mind, being pressed against all of her soft curves that freely on display, in those skin-tight leggings and well fitted tee. It's the simplicity of her that gets me—she could be anyone's girl next door, except for the fire I swear I've seen flickering behind those wide eyes. Then there's that mouth, lush and probably untouched, which sparks a hunger I haven't felt in a long time.

"Bet she's never tasted a real man," I muse, the thought unbidden and raw. A part of me wants to be the first to have her lips wrapped around me, to see if an angel chokes, or swallows down sin like its salvation.

"Fuck," I curse under my breath, shaking the image from

my head. It's like I'm some horny teenager again, not the seasoned son of hell I've become.

I shouldn't even be thinking about her like this. Harlow's here for a purpose—a dark one at that. I've chewed up and spat out women far more experienced than her without a second thought. Yet here I am, caught up in fantasies about a virgin sacrifice meant to keep us all breathing. Stupid doesn't even begin to cover it.

"Get it together, Abel," I chastise myself, the name feeling like another layer of armor I've strapped on. "She's just another mark."

But even as I say it, I know marks don't usually come looking like damnation dressed in innocence, nor do they make the beast inside me sit up and take notice. I pull my shirt away from my skin, suddenly feeling too hot, too tight and too much.

"Control," I hiss, the word for me is a command, a mantra. Control is what keeps us alive in this world, where power is both currency and a cult. I can't afford to lose mine—not over Harlow, not over anyone.

A smirk twitched across my lips as I watched Bishop make his play. The bastard's got a way with words, and it looks like he's pouring pure honey into Harlow's ear, trying to sweeten her up. His body language screams interest—leaning in, nodding, flashing that damn charming smile of his. He's too close, too damn attentive and for a moment, I wonder if he's forgotten the plan.

"Typical," I mutter under my breath, the smoke curling from my lips like a sly serpent tasting the air.

But he's not the only one ensnared, it seems. I catch the subtle shift in Harlow's stance, that unspoken dance of intrigue between predator and prey. A low chuckle escapes me, ain't this a sight? An angel drawing sinners ever closer, weaving a spell without even realizing her power. It's a dangerous game she's stumbled into, and I can't help but want to be a player if only to see the flush in her cheeks when she learns the rules.

Drawing in the final drag, I roll the taste of tobacco and temptation over my tongue before flicking the spent cigarette away. It tumbles through the air, a small spark against the gravel, its glow dying as swiftly as my restraint.

"Time to introduce myself," I mutter, pushing off from the trailer with purpose, boots crunching on the ground beneath me.

"Harlow," I call out as I approach, my voice a dark melody that cuts through the space between us. Her head turns, those wide eyes locking onto mine, and I feel that jolt—the one that comes when you know you've caught someone's full attention.

"Abel," I offer my hand, not a question but an assertion. "Looks like you'll be riding with us for a while." My gaze is steady, daring her to look away first.

placing her warm hand in mine, she responds, "Nice to meet you, Abel. "Her voice soft yet steady, a hint of steel beneath the velvet.

"Welcome to the circus, Harlow," I say, my thumb brushing against her skin—a fleeting touch, but enough to see the reaction I was hoping for. A shiver, a glance away, then back again. She's strong, but even angels have their breaking points.

"Thanks," she replies, pulling her hand back with a grace that tells me she's no stranger to handling the unexpected.

"Should be quite the show," I quip, stepping back to give her room, but not peace. Never peace. Because in our world, peace is just another word for submission, and neither of us is submitting—not yet anyway, and certainly, not without a fight!

NINE
HARLOW

WHY DOES it feel like I am walking into a trap? You know, like one of those live bear traps, hidden amongst the dead and decaying leaves, broken branches and dirt that snap their jaws on you, digging their sharp teeth in your flesh so deep that the more you try to free yourself the worse you make it.

The car I am in rolls to a sudden stop. I guess we have arrived. I am scared, yet excited. This is the first time I am not under mother dearest shadow, and it's a weird feeling of separation and emancipation that buries itself in my heart. Not that she didn't do her best to add her input on everything, which is how I end up with 9 suitcases packed full of hand-picked items by her. But as I got off the flight, I couldn't stand the idea of strolling in here, wearing another pretty dress, so I bought myself a pair of leggings and a cropped tee at the airport. For once I wanted to feel normal, not like this circus freak that she parades everywhere.

I open the door and step out of the car, as I take in my surroundings, I snap it shut behind me. My entourage deals with the suitcases and music gear, scattering themselves to wherever they need to be.

My band isn't big, normally it is just me and my guitar, but I still have Ada who is my backup singer, but she also plays guitar, bass and piano, and her brother Abraham on the drums. They are twins from father's congregation and live in the compound he has created. For this tour they decided it was better to drive themselves in their own car to the places we will be performing and stay in hotel rooms. As they put it, ever so kindly, they didn't want to be in the presence of evil for too long.

I see Abel sitting on the metal step of a tour bus, puffs of cigarette smoke leaving his lips. They are very pretty lips. God, is it me or did the Miami heat just get even more scorching?

Bishop's sweet like honey voice fills the humid Florida air, "Welcome to the madhouse, Harlow."

"Mister McGrew." I note, softly tipping my chin up.

He chuckles, getting remarkably close to me. "Yeah, no. That won't do, little mouse." The older McGrew comments in a hushed tone. "Call me Bishop." A pause as he gazes into my eyes. "Or Sir." I swallow dryly at his last words.

"Fine. Bishop. Are you giving me the grand tour?" I ask him whilst doing a little spin, clasping my hands behind my back and walking backwards in the direction of a small trailer.

His thumb brushes over his lips and in its wake, a crooked grin is left on his face. "Wow those were a lot of words. What happened to my tongue-tied girl?" He questions, as he gets right up next to me again in just a few big steps.

I honestly don't know how to respond to that, so I stay

silent. I turn back around so I am walking side by side with him now. Our arms keep brushing and goosebumps break out on my skin.

"This will be your trailer." Bishop states opening the door for me like a gentleman.

"Miss Abaddon." One of the Paragon of Virtue's Inferno crew members races towards us with some keys in hand. "These are for the locks on your trailer, miss. There's three on the front door, and one on each of the windows on either side. as he is leaving, he hands the keys to me and says "This should keep you safe."

Safe? From who? Or what? Stepping inside what, up close, seems to be a traveler's wagon or circus trailer, without all the flamboyance on the outside. "It's cozy." I mutter while taking it in. At the far end there is a massive bed which takes up the width of the trailer, you probably can fit 5 people in that thing. To one side there's a little kitchenette and on the other a dinette, composed of one chair and a little round table. "No bathroom?" I ask.

"You will only be sleeping here, but you will travel with us on the tour bus. You can shower there." The older McGrew makes it known.

"I guess I will be peeing outside then." I remark as I step down to stand next to him.

"You can pee on the tour bus too, little mouse." Bishop says leaning in to loom over me. "Wouldn't want you to flag out those fetching ass cheeks to the world."

"How do you know they are fetching?" I utter with a boldness which is very unlike me. Also, far apart from normal behaviors, is the smile that Bishop is giving me now, it is charming, sweet, and genuine and not at all like the scowls and crooked grins he usually has on display.

"There's more to you that meets the eyes, isn't there?" He nods his head as if he is observing me for the first time.

I don't get to say anything back as someone calls out in a solemn, dark melodious voice "Harlow." I turn my head, my eyes locking with these almost back pits. A jolt travels through my spine, at the intensity of his gaze. "Abel." He introduces himself as he offers me his hand. Wow, how formal. "Looks like you'll be riding with us for a while."

We get held captive in each other's eyes, neither of us daring to look away.

"Nice to meet you, Abel." I respond to him in my most mellowed voice as I give him my hand to shake.

"Welcome to the circus, Harlow." He says.

Abel's thumb brushes against the back of my hand, and my body shivers at the sensation, which makes me glance away to gather myself.

What is wrong with me? First the goosebumps as Bishop's skin touched mine, and now a shiver that just seized my whole body with Abel. I refuse to look weak in front of these guys, so I lift my eyes back to the sinful man that is still holding my hand.

"Thanks." I reply with a bit of a husky voice, pulling my hand back with as much grace as I can muster.

"Should be quite the show." He informs me while throwing an up to no good smirk my way and a quick wink in Bishops' direction.

All the older McGrew brother does is shake his head like he's had enough of Abel antics. His arms are crossed over his chest with his slim fitted shirt sleeves rolled up to his elbows, making his forearm muscles pop up. Now either I am aroused by this or I kind of just peed myself.

"And that's the rest of the Scooby gang coming our way." Bishop announces.

I barely have the time to react properly as Parrish just steps right into my personal space, making me take a few steps backward until I am up against the trailer's wall. But he just keeps coming forward and I end up pinned to the wall completely with him hovering above me.

I squeak.

"There is my little mouse." I hear Bishop note.

"Big boo-boo, pretty doe, you should've stuck with the dresses. I just love a nice pair of skin-tight leggings. Makes me want to cut them legs out with my knife." Parrish states as cool as I cucumber, making me lost for words.

Huh, What?

"You shouldn't play with knives they are dangerous." I tell the alluring boy with the pink hair after a few heartbeats.

Parrish is not wearing a shirt; his skin glistening with sweat giving his tattoos a nice shine. It's a crazy array of color and fantasy creatures, from a stunning mermaid circling his left arm appearing as if it is diving into his hand, to a unicorn jumping away from his heart that leaves a rainbow in its wake, a reverse cross on his sternum holding a pink bunny styled as if it was Jesus, amongst many, many, others. But the ones that capture my full attention are the three fairies below his belly button casting their eyes below the waistband of his Calvin Klein boxers, sticking out from the exceptionally low-slung denim shorts.

I snap my eyes back to Parrish's hazel ones. God, I am

trying my hardest not to fall into temptation here, but these guys are not making it easy.

"Nah. The danger lies mostly in the person that wields the sharp object." He informs me as a very much morally wrong Joker smile paints his face, foregrounding his dimple piercings.

"So, you aren't dangerous?" I question.

"Mary, we are the perfect characterization of perilous." Dear God, that voice. My knees go weak, the only reason I don't fall to the ground is because Parrish is keeping me upright with his own body still pinning mine, but he definitely picks up on my slight knee jerk when his eyebrow arches in question.

I peer behind Parrish to catch a glimpse at the possessor of the ungodly and unholy voice. Church.

"My name is Harlow." I tell him.

"Sure thing, Mary." Church replies.

What?

I was just about say that aloud but got distracted by feeling of someone playing with one of my curls, twirling it around his finger and pulling it to his noise to take a big inhale I look over to find that it is Parrish, sniffing my hair. "Hmmm wild raspberries, rose and pink pepper. Aren't you appetizing, pretty doe?"

I don't know what to make of this guy, he keeps saying weird and disturbing things that kind of chill my blood but give me an eerie tingle on my lower back. My brain is trying to catch up with everything that is happening, when someone says "Ok. I think that's enough, we need to get this show on the road.

· · ·

Chop-chop, everyone on the tour bus." Bishop with his controlling and overbearing personality, should put me off and yet it doesn't.

"Wait. About the riding situation." I say just as Parrish steps away from my personal space, pouting. Why does that sight make my heart melt for him?

"What about it?" Bishop asks me.

"I ummm, don't know how comfortable I am about being in the same confined space as you lot for that long. I don't even know you." I admit.

"Well then it's a great opportunity to do so, don't you think, angel?" Abel states, as he looks me up and down like he's sizing me up. "I definitely wouldn't mind getting to know all of you." Is he flirting with me? Oh, of course he is.

Great, so Abel wants to get in my pants, and I am to be in the same coffin as them. There's so much a girl can take before her will bends and breaks. And I so don't want to be another one of the silly naïve girls that fall for his, or any of the other Paragon of Virtue's Inferno members, charms."

"I'm your manager now, and I am telling you to get on that tour bus, Harlow."

"How about the trailer?" I mean, not that the trailer is any better, is small and cramped and there's no bathroom.

"No." He utters forbiddingly.

"How about I jump in one of the entourage cars?"

"No." Bishop shouts. "Tour bus. Now." That domineering tone was probably meant to frighten me and make me apprehensive, therefore compliant, which it does, but it also makes me want to be defiant and stand my ground, all to see if I can drive Bishop to lose control. That isn't me though, so, I do as I am told.

I stomp past them all, just in ear shot as Church tell the others. "Great, we have an entitled princess with a stick up her ass for a roommate, how fun."

The audacity of that guy. He barely uttered anything to me, and when he did, it was to call me someone else's name. And I'm the spoiled brat? Church is the one with a stick up his ass and probably a chip on his shoulder, the jerk.

Him, I don't like. At all.

I climb into the tour bus and sit by myself on the bench seat near the front of the bus. The boys come inside soon after and settle down by the dinette. The tour bus motor roars to life and that kind of quietens the voices at my rear as the boys talk amongst themselves whilst they begin to play cards.

I am officially in hell.

TEN
CHURCH

I AM FUCKED. Downright fucked. Unconditionally, totally and devilishly fucked.

Harlow has not even been here for more than a few minutes and I am already addicted. From her old money blonde curls that frame her beautifully angelic face, to her unblemished vampiric looking skin, covering her entire willowy figure and don't get me started about those perky tits paired with that perfect apple-bottom ass, and her fucking scent is an aphrodisiac made up of Madonna lily, peach and lychee that is beyond intoxicating. her sweet and innocent goodie two-shoes façade with that killer curiosity might just work with our devious plans.

Ive been in the habit of using and abusing anything to do with Harlow since I accidently heard one of her songs. One of the many groupies I fucked had one of Her songs she had set as a ringtone for a friend that was... how did she put it? A prude with no taste, but One word out of that holy mouth of Harlow's and I have been Fucking obsessed ever since.

I don't fuck the same girl ever. I just toss them out after I am done, but as this girl was leaving, Harlow's voice echoed in the hotel room, and I couldn't just let the slut go in the wake of that. Instead, I made her play Harlow's song on repeat as I took her from behind brutally. I might've taken it a bit too far, forcing her face down on the mattress with my hand on the back of her head, first it was her screams of pleasure, then her wails of desperation as air became hard to come by. She thrashed and jerked to no avail, while I thrusted violently in and out of her. I came just as Harlow hit a heavenly high note and by then the bitch stopped moving.

Oh well, just another damned soul no one cared that much about, missing right after one of our shows. Normally the shadows take them. Haunting them, taunting them, playing with their food before dragging them down to the burning depths of hell. This one was on me though, whoops, Harlow made me do it. I blame her, and her bewitching voice.

Bishop was not pleased with me that night. Him and the other two idiots had to help me dispose of the body in the Chicago River. I don't know what my brother was stressing out about, there are that many bloating corpses in there, even if the pigs do come across her, they will probably think she was a mob hit or something. After all it is their dumping ground and has been since Al Capone's time. So, we are in the clear.

Harlow Abaddon is my drug of choice. Don't get me wrong, I still do Line after line of any powder and pill that gets thrown my way, the delicious Devil's drink, but it's Harlow that gives me the highest high, and the worst withdrawals when I don't get my fix of her.

When my dear brother told us he had the perfect girl for our last sacrifice, the one that would seal our pact with the devil forever, I thought great, after 10 years of killing random bitches, we will finally get to just enjoy the party. while I do find pleasure in slashing someone's throat and watching them choke on their own blood, struggling to breathe, as life leaves their dull, vacant eyes, -Just the thought of that evil act sends a thrilling and satisfying shiver up my spine- But then he uttered her name, and I felt like I'd just been stabbed in the heart. I wanted to punch Bishop's pretty face until it was a mangled, broken mess of exposed bone and blood everywhere; but when the other two idiots agreed, I had to go along with the madness.

The fucker, it's not like I can't see the bigger picture, I'm not blind. Harlow is the perfect offering and yet, it feels like I would be giving away half of my soul to the bastard? Which is stupid because Satan already owns our sorry asses. That's why we need this final girl, the ultimate slaughter of an earthbound angel that will unbind us from the pact we made 10 years ago. So, it is her or us and sadly, I am too selfish to burn in hell for a girl.

New Orleans, now that was a show, because she was there. The moment I set foot on stage; I was like a dog on a leash as I got pulled right to Harlow. She was the only thing I saw, a vision in all white that I wouldn't mind painting in blood and cum.

I haven't touched another pussy since the one I killed. Not out of fear I would do it again because I couldn't care less if I did, it's just that no-one rivals my personal paragon of virtue, my princess, my Harlow. The most fucked-up thing is Blue fucking balls. I can't fuck her, she must be pure for the sacrifice. I wonder if my brother will let me fuck her dead pussy though, just so I get to feel heaven at least once.

"How we doing tonight, New Orleans?" Parrish's unchaste voice howled in the packed venue, followed by the screams of our devoted fans, and my princess's pretty, blue eyes locked with those of my best friend.

I didn't get time to be jealous, as Harlow's mother said something to her straight after and they began to walk away. For a split second, I prayed that she would leave and never come back, that would be it, the end of that, we wouldn't have to slaughter her for our own greedy needs. But my princess paused and looked back at us. All of us. The message was there, behind the words she didn't speak, but cried out with her eyes was that of someone begging to be saved. She saw us as a way out, from what I don't know yet. As I looked at the other idiots, they all seemed tortured, by the goddess before them just like I was. Fuck, I should've known then that we had bitten off more than we could chew with Harlow.

"Church." I heard Parrish call out my name. "Don't let her go." He mouthed to me. I bobbed my head, and chanted some Latin words that I knew would make the shadows do our bidding. "Egredere, egredere, ubicunque es coepiscopi mei, et fac jussa mea. Expurgate quid obstat quin nostrum virginem capiamus."

I swear on everything unholy those shady fuckers have a twisted sense of humor. I asked them to get rid of her mother, yet they simply decided to make her trip and fall down the stairs breaking her leg, but I guess it still got the job done.

Bishop never told me how he manipulated Harlow's mother to not only sign the contract merging our tours but to, also hand over managing my princess's music career to him. Ive got to give it to my brother, when he wants something, he gets it. Which terrifies me, especially when I see him look at my girl like she's his.

Harlow just graced us at last with her presence on this sweltering Miami morning, joining us for the tour. Bishop has been all over her, like a dog with a fucking bone. This trying to sweeten her up is beyond him, making her trust him, and therefore us. He's my brother, I would know that the fucker is as enamored by her as I am. It's the same way he knows the extent of my obsession with her. And then there is Abel, who saunters to her like she's his new plaything. I want to hate them for wanting what is mine but only a fool wouldn't fall at Harlow's feet, so I can't fault them. Parrish being his devious self, gets right in Harlow's personal space and ends up pinning her to the trailer. The green-eyed monster doesn't come out; instead, I get turned on by seeing my girl in the arms of my best friend. ------That's new.

She is obviously attracted to all of us, you can see it in the way her body responds to our touch or simply our proximity. The little shudders, the blushing cheeks and trying to avert her eyes. Harlow seems to know she should run and hide, yet she keeps drawing closer. She is just as affected by our presence. That realization throws me off guard, which pisses me off, making me go full asshole on Harlow. I can't have her like me, if she does, I will fall harder and make corrupt her and I can't be the one that damns us all, Not Again.

I call her Mary, after Jesus's mother. The eternal virgin. Someone ought to explain to me how a so called 'virgin' ends up pregnant, and how she is still considered one even after giving birth. Don't Christians know the concept of a hymen rupture? Even if she wasn't penetrated beforehand by her darling husband José, or whoever she was rolling around the sheets with, behind his back, that shit certainly got destroyed when Jesus came out. Therefore, no longer a virgin. But I digress.

As a very bratty but cute Harlow stomps into the tour bus, I can't help myself but poke the bear one final time before we set off. "Great, we have an entitled princess with a stick up her ass as a roommate, how fun."

"Smooth, you fucker." Abel says as he digs his hands in the front pockets of his black, ripped skinny jeans. "Way to leave a great first impression."

"Fuck off." I utter.

"That attitude definitely won't win you any brownie points with my little mouse." Bishop tells me in his sweet as honey tone. What is it with this 'MY little mouse' bullshit?

"At least one of us hasn't forgotten why the daughter of the preacher is here." I grumble as I start moving towards the tour bus.

"Sounds to me like you are the one with a stick up your ass there, bestie." Parrish notes, draping an arm over my shoulders. "But it's ok, I know how to relieve some of the pressure and make it pleasurable." The pink haired idiot says, giving me a cheeky wink.

Fucked. Unholy fucked, The bunch of us, and yes, I am including my princess in that.

Eleven

Parrish

I LEAN BACK into the leather embrace of the tour bus seat, a smirk playing at the corner of my lips. This is fun. Who would have thought that hurtling down the highway in a cramped tour bus with a little brat would be so damn entertaining? The road hums beneath us, a steady vibration flowing with the adrenaline coursing through my veins.

Up ahead, Harlow's figure is rigid, she's clutching the sides of the front seat -her knuckles white- perched more towards the edge, as if she's ready to sprint off this metal beast the second it grinds to a halt with her eyes fixed on the endless stretch of road as it unfolds like a dark ribbon before us.

"Trying to put as much distance between us as possible, Pretty doe?" I call out, my voice laced with amusement. It's just funny; she can't escape us now. Not with the miles of open land flanking either side of the bus or with the next stop hours away, and certainly not with the way we've all but woven her into the very fabric of our twisted future.

She doesn't turn, doesn't acknowledge my words, but I see the slight stiffening of her shoulders, the way her grip tightens even more—if that's even possible. The defiance radiates off her in waves, and I can't help but be drawn to it, like a moth to the flame.

The corners of my mouth twitch upwards as I watch her resolve waver, then steel once again. She's a puzzle and I've always loved a challenge.

I've let Harlow stew in her own simmering pot of defiance up the front of our tour bus while the rest of the band and I sprawl across the cramped quarters, instruments and egos both vying for space.

I can't resist the pull of her resistance any longer. It's like an itch under my skin, a siren calling to the darker parts of me that love the chase, the game. Rising from my seat, I saunter down the narrow aisle, each step predatory. I drop into the empty seat beside her, close enough to feel the tension rolling off her in waves.

"Enjoying the view?" I ask, leaning back and stretching my arm across the top of her seat—a casual gesture that's clearly anything but.

Harlow shoots me a glare sharp enough to slice through steel. I grin, loving the fire in her eyes. "What do you want, Parrish?"

"Ah, straight to business." I chuckle, amused by her curt tone. "Let's play twenty questions, shall we?"

Her brow arches with disdain. "No, thank you."

"Really? Not even a little curious about me?" My smile fades just a fraction as she turns to look out the window, brushing me off again. She's not playing the game like they usually do, and it irks me more than I care to admit.

"You sure about that?" I press on, reaching out, my finger tracing the line of her jaw. Her skin is soft, warm, and I slowly trail downwards, grazing the column of her neck, flirting with the edge of danger as I brush over the swell of her breast.

"Please don't touch me," she murmurs, voice low but laced with steel, making me pause. Yet, her body betrays her words, a subtle shiver running through her at my touch.

"Ah, pretty doe," I say, voice dropping to a husky whisper, "you like it, don't you? Maybe you're not as innocent as I thought." The smirk returns full force as I stand, leaving her with the ghost of my touch and the promise of more.

My laughter echoes in the confined space as I retreat to my original seat, leaving her flushed and breathing hard. The game has only just begun, and I'm relishing every moment of it. The power, the control—it thrums through me, electric and alive, the same way the beat of the music we live for does.

The moment the bus grinds to a halt, Harlow is on her feet, darting toward the exit with a desperation that's almost comical. She's like a caged animal finally spotting an escape, and I can't help but chuckle from my perch at the back of the bus.

"Running won't help, Pretty doe," I mutter under my breath, though she's too far ahead to hear.

I rise, stretching out the kinks in my muscles, anticipation coiling in my gut. Tonight. The word thrums through me, a promise whispered by the shadows that cling to the corners of the tour bus. We're not set to play until tomorrow, which means tonight is ours—free, wild and ripe for the taking.

"Time to set up camp, boys!" I call out, clapping my hands together. The rest of the band stirs, sluggish from the road but quickening at the sight of our temporary home—a sprawling venue surrounded by a sea of tents and makeshift shelters.

"Let's get this over with," I say, grabbing gear from the

storage bay. My mind isn't on work though, it's on the thrill of the night ahead. It's on Harlow—her defiance, her fire, the way she squirmed beneath my touch and lied with her protests.

"Easy there, Parrish. Save some of that energy for the stage," Bishop teases, slinging an amp over his shoulder and falling into step beside me.

"Stage has nothing on what I'm planning," I shoot back with a grin, my voice low enough that only he can catch the edge in it.

"Careful now," Abel chimes in, while winking towards me. "We wouldn't want our little one to get spooked."

"Spooked?" I scoff, dropping the gear beside the designated tent area. "Nah. She's curious—can't help it. You saw her eyes. They're hungry for something new... something dark."

"Something like us," Church concludes, smirking as he joins our huddle, our collective excitement palpable in the cooling air.

"Exactly." I glance at her trailer, catching a glimpse of Harlow's retreating form. She's a splash of color against the drab backdrop of roadies and metal, a beacon that draws me in despite myself.

"Tonight, we'll give her a taste of who we really are," I declare, my words slicing through the twilight.

It's a vow, a dark promise, I intend to keep.

As the sky deepens to indigo, I feel it—the pull of the night, the call of the wild within our music-tainted souls. It's going to be one hell of an evening, and I can't wait to see how our pretty doe fares on the hunt.

"Let's make this a night she'll never forget," I say, a feral grin splitting my face. And with that, the last slivers of daylight fade away, leaving us cloaked in the embrace of dusk and the thrilling unknown.

The night wraps around us, a perfect cloak for our dark intent. We've donned our costumes, black as the secrets we keep, masks alight with an eerie glow—a band of spectral predators on the prowl. I can feel my pulse thrumming in my veins, a rhythmic call to the primal game about to unfold.

"Ready?" I whisper, more to myself than to my brothers.

"Always," Bishop murmurs, his voice a ghostly echo. He fishes out the spare keys and with a soft click, the trailer door swings open.

Inside, the trailer is dark with only moonlight filtering through the curtains painting silver streaks across her sleeping form. She lies there, a vision of innocence, her chest rising and falling in the tranquil rhythm of slumber. My breath catches at the sight—our pretty doe so peaceful, so vulnerable, so utterly unaware of the shadows creeping into her sanctuary.

"Let's make it quick," I murmur, my gaze fixed on Harlow. "No noise."

Abel nods, silent as a wraith, as he slips inside. His hand, large and capable, gently presses over Harlow's mouth just as she stirs, her eyes fluttering open in confusion that rapidly spirals into terror. A muffled gasp slips from beneath Abel's palm, her body tensing as she awakens fully to her bound predicament.

Church moves with practiced ease, looping restraints around her wrists, securing them with a firmness that brokers no resistance. The fear in Harlow's wide eyes strikes a chord deep within me, igniting a fire that rages with wanting, with need.

"Shh," Abel coos, almost tenderly.

I edge closer, drawn by the mingling scents of fear and woman, breathing in the heady mix. Her gaze locks onto mine, a silent plea within the depths of those liquid orbs, but all I can think about is the taste of her skin, the secrets it might reveal under my tongue.

"Look at you," I tease, unable to keep the raw edge of desire from my voice. "All tied up with nowhere to run. But don't worry, we're not going to hurt you... much."

"Please," she mumbles, the word barely audible against Abel's hand.

Harlow's frantic movements are a wild dance of desperation under Abel's unyielding grip. Her muffled cries vibrate against his palm, the sound fueling the fire in my veins. I slip the blade from my pocket, its edge catching the dim light as I step forward, relishing in the terror widening her eyes.

"Shh, darling," I coo mockingly, "You wouldn't want to miss the show."

Bishop, ever the silent archivist, hoists his phone up, the lens capturing every tremble and shudder that courses through Harlow's bound body. The recording, a twisted piece of memorabilia for nights devoid of such delicious, fear filled activities.

"Easy, easy," I taunt, my fingers toying with the hem of her white nightdress—a symbol of her innocence—before gathering the fabric and drawing it up, slowly, torturously. She's a statue of pure dread, her limbs tensed and immobile as her sanctuary becomes an altar of darkness.

"Such a pretty little thing," I murmur, my voice laced with

venomous honey, "Do you know how much this white teases us, Harlow?"

With each inch of skin revealed, her breath hitches, and I can practically taste the sour tang of her panic in the air. The knife, now a wand of command, traces a path along her inner thigh, so close yet never piercing.

"Please," she chokes out, the word a ghost upon her lips.

"Please?" I echo, feigning consideration. "Oh, I intend to, sweet Harlow." My nose skims over the cotton that shields her most intimate parts—the barrier between her world and mine. The scent of her, a mix of fear and something more primal, fills my senses.

"Let's get rid of this nuisance, shall we?" I whisper, sliding the cold steel under the elastic of her panties. With a flick of my wrist, they fall apart, like useless scraps of fabric. Her body goes rigid, a doe caught in the snare, knowing that the hunt has only just begun.

"Better," I approve with a smirk. "Now, there's nothing between us but shadows and sin."

The tremors in her body have stilled, replaced by a quiet anticipation. Her eyes, wide and fixed on me, flicker with something new—a hint of intrigue beneath the fear. A defiance that makes my heartbeat faster. I lower my face to the delicate skin between her thighs, and though the hole in my mask my tongue traces the seam of her, tasting her sweetness. "Fuck," I murmur against her flesh, intoxicated by the flavor of candy and secrets. "Please," she whispers again, but it's not a plea for release this time. It's softer, breathier, like she's speaking directly to the dark desires coiling within me.

I can't help the smirk that curls my lips as I dive into her heat, pushing the mask up a little to free my mouth, feasting on her with a hunger that's been gnawing at me since the moment I laid eyes on her. My mouth envelops her clit, sucking with a fervor that draws a gasp from her lips. Her hips begin to move, no longer in an attempt to escape but to seek more of the pleasure that I'm offering. The pretty doe writhes beneath me, and I know—she likes this.

"Fuck me, little mouse, look at you," Bishop's voice slices through the thick air, his tone laced with wonder and wickedness. His words weave into the tapestry of our sin, binding her submission to our will.

Harlow's breathing quickens, her chest rising and falling in rapid succession. The power I hold over her is a heady feeling, one that fills me with a sense of dominion; as ancient and primal as the cult rites we perform under the moon's watchful eye. Tonight, under the cloak of darkness and inside her sacred space, I reaffirm my claim. We are the hunters, and she —the most exquisite prey we've ever cornered.

TWELVE

HARLOW

"PLEASE." I moan under Abel's palm. What in the heavens am I doing? I should be screaming bloody murder or something, not purring like a kitten to whatever Parrish is doing to me between my legs.

Yeah, I know it's them, the Paragon of Virtue's Inferno boys, all dressed in black like shadow demons in the night. Even behind the silly glow in the dark masks, I would sniff them out anywhere. Irrefutably, my men could be in a lineup of a thousand in disguise, I would still be able to tell who's who without trouble.

Wow, cripes, 'my men'? Where did that come from?

Their sensuous growly voices which echo, with my throaty whimpers, all over the otherwise silent trailer, are messing with my head. Or perhaps is the fact that they are ganging up on me together.

Why does that last thought excite me so?

"Fuck me, little mouse, look at you." Bishop's voice dances through the heavy air that surrounds all five of us, full of hope, and anticipation. I close my eyes at the sound, allowing myself to just feel.

Abel's punitive hand refuses to leave my lips, yet one of his fingers is now petting my cheek-invoking the same feeling as before when his hand was on mine. That feeling, mingled with Parrish's pierced tongue darting out to lick my clit, lapping at it in fast succession, before sucking on it once more; makes my whole body convulse in pleasure. I involuntarily pull on the restraints around my ankles and hands, straining against the bonds until they are so tight I am unable to pull further.

"Damn, Mary is coming already." Church says. The doofus is the one with a keen and strong grip on the restraints holding my hands above my head, his frame leaning over me.

As I open my eyes I gaze right at him. -Why are the prettier ones always the bigger and worst jerks? - But I can't hold his pale gray eyes for long, as mine roll back when Parrish's tongue suddenly penetrates my center, his piercing skimming along the inside of my pussy.

"Oh God." I whimper at the sensation.

"No God, here, angel. This is the Devil and his minions' playground." Abel utters, aiming a crooked smirk my way. His words awaken something in me and make me do something unexpected. I lick his hand. "Fuck." The drummer says as his hand finally leaves my lips and falls to my throat. He squeezes it with vehemence, forcing a squeak out of me.

"Rosson." Church and Bishop give a forbidding warning to the boy, very much in chorus.

"Marking your territory there, Harlow? Don't mind if I do the same." He roughly moves my face to the side and licks me from my jaw, passing the corner of my mouth, my cheek and he ends his journey on my ear, shoving his tongue deep inside. "Fucking delicious." He hisses.

"Not as tasty as her sweet pussy." Parrish remarks as he kisses my lips down there, proper French kiss, diving his tongue in and out of me. Mwah sounds marrying with licentious groans that drive me crazy.

"Are you planning on sharing at some point?" Abel asks the boy between my legs, as a purr flees my lips. If this is sin, then why does it feel so good? I am starting to question some of father's preaching here.

"Y'all can have your turn, as soon as my pretty doe comes for me one more time." Parrish licks the entirety of my slit after announcing that. Nibbles the delicate flaps of my labia and penetrates my soaking core with his tongue again.

"Greedy." Church says.

"Aren't we all?" Bishop tells his brother.

Tongue lapping, twirling and swirling around my inner walls, rubbing them in a nice riveting beat, "Please" I beg Parrish. I try to peer down at the boy giving me pleasure right now. A bit hard to do when there's a hand on my neck impeding some of my movement. Parrish is the only one adorned in a different color mask; his is Barbie pink, while the others are green. I can just about see Parrish's arm jerking at his side, his hand buried between his legs. Oh my God, is he touching himself, beating the meat, as he eats me out? That arouses me even more.

The other Paragon of Virtue's Inferno members seem to be supporting quite protruding tents under their slacks, obviously turned on by the sexual carnival taking place right now.

Bishop speaks again, "You two could perhaps show her girls some attention." A shiver moves up my spine at his words.

"Oh, someone likes that idea." Parrish notes, his breath brushing against my wet folds, intensifying the trembling that has shot over my body.

Abel and Church peer at one another. I don't think these two like each other that much. Luckily, that doesn't matter, since after Abel shrugs and Church swallows dry, making his Adams apple bob up and down within his throat, they both hike my nightgown further up my body to reveal my breasts. Their mouths descend upon them in no time.

Something is up with Church. It's like he's trying to push me away by being a jerk with his words, yet he can't help being drawn near, he confuses me, more than the others.

"Oh, yes." I moan. Parrish's tongue is now stiff as he thrusts it into me frantically, whilst the boys on either side of me are eddying their tongues around my nipples. Abel's hand is still on my neck, so he has taken on an interesting position on my body, this lower arm and elbow are right along my breastbone as he leans into it. Church, having let go of my bound hands, has one hand massaging the underside of my breast with a light as a feather touch, enticing goosebumps to pop out in his wake, while the other is getting itself tangled in my blonde strands on top of my head, by pulling and tugging.

How is this bad in the eyes of the church? I don't understand. Ok, maybe four guys is a bit wrong.

"Cripes." I scream, as Church bites my nipple and an orgasm rips through me once more.

Parrish drinks up my juices like he's a thirsty man,

humming in the process, sending sweet vibrations up my pussy, which prolongs my climax. He finally surfaces from between my legs as he straightens his back and sits his ass on his heels, cleaning his mouth with the back of his free hand while the other is under the waistband of his slacks still pumping his length.

"Ever seen a dick before, pretty doe?" I shake my head at his question. If I wasn't already blushing from all the filthy stuff being done to me, I would be at his words, at my admission and at the sight of what Parrish pulls out. It is pierced, and oh so long. I mean, I have nothing to compare it to, but that seems lengthy. "Better close that mouth, Harlow, or I will take it as an invitation to let myself in!" I shut my lips closed at Parrish's warning, reluctantly.

The two playing with boobs chuckle at the pink haired man's words.

The way Parrish looks down at me it's as if I am their salvation. "Damn, I'm sorry boys." He utters almost in pain as he begins to self-abuse himself like a man possessed, his hand moving up and down his penis at a relentless speed. A loud growl breaks loose from his parted lips as this white-hot sticky fluid shots out from his manhood and lands between my spread legs. His cum rivers down my sex making me shiver.

"Way to ruin it for the rest of us, idiot. Now how are we to taste her without getting a mouth full of you?" Church says irked.

What Parrish does next, just about makes me cum on the sight alone. He gets on all fours, leaning over me, reaches for Church with one hand, grabbing his face with a brutal grip, pulling it towards himself and away from my boob. In the aftermath of that, Parrish freaking kisses Church on the mouth in a Full on, tongue lapping kissing.

Once their lips fall apart, their eyes dilating with delirium, he asks Church, "Doesn't she taste fucking divine?"

Thirteen

Church

THE JERK that I call a best friend cums all over her pussy. Now how are we to indulge on her sweet nectar, without it being tainted by his sour and salty shit? And when I complain about it, the pink haired idiot pulls me in for a kiss. He shoves his tongue in so deep, down my throat, I almost choke on it. But then her taste permeates my mouth, and I end up devouring his mouth, extracting as much of her juices out of him as I can.

"Doesn't she taste fucking divine?" Parrish asks me when we split from our kiss.

She does. Like heaven. And here we are trying to corrupt her, making her into a sinner to rival our damned souls, when we, no doubt, should be putting a chastity belt on her pussy to protect her from our gluttonous, wolf like, sex drive. And probably on her rosebud and mouth too.

Bishop finally approaches the bed; he's been standing to the side, recording the whole thing on his phone. He kneels next to Abel, who's still feasting on her breast, and with the camera focused on her dripping core from above, Bishop skims his middle finger up and down her folds, marrying together her juices with that of Parrish. My brother then parts her pussy lips and sinks his finger inside.

"Oh." Harlow purrs, her body trembling at the intrusion.

She's such a good fucking girl. I let go of her hands a while back, yet Harlow is still keeping them firmly placed above her head, fisting the sheets below her hands with quite a bit of vigor. Bishop pumps in and out of her a few times, and I am spellbound by the vanishing and reappearing act of his finger.

"Rosson, tilt her head back and make my little mouse open her mouth wide." My brother instructs Abel. His fixation with controlling everything can be somewhat unnerving at times, but in the bedroom, it's fucking stimulating. Releasing her perky breast with a pop, and straightening his back to sit on his heels, Abel does as he is told. He moves his thumb, so it is right underneath Harlow's chin, and puts some pressure on it, causing her head to tilt. After he moves his index over her jaw and pulls down.

The moment Harlow's lips break apart; Bishop takes his middle finger out of her pussy and shoves it inside her mouth. "Now, lick it clean, baby girl." He tells her, his camera now aiming at her face. Harlow circles her tongue all around my brother's finger. "Fuck. That's it, all of it." Her mouth shuts, imprisoning the little fucker and she sucks like it's the most delicious lollipop.

I adjust myself in my slacks. I am painfully hard and in desperate need of release.

Bishop adds another digit, thrusting them in and out of her mouth as if fucking it. And Harlow, this girl we think is pure as a fresh snow, is slurping on them like she is starved. Shit, now all I can envision is my cock replacing them, boring myself deep in her throat. But we did say no jamming our dicks in any of her fuckable holes, as to not tempt the Devil or whatever, but I am already fucking seduced here.

Well, if Parrish can make a mess on her, then why can't I? I lower my waistband, making my hard on stand to attention and fist it. It appears I am not the only one having the same idea. Abel has pulled his fully tattooed, monstrous dick out and is jerking himself off already. The hand he had on Harlow's throat at long last removed, is now playing with her nipples and massaging her breasts. With Bishop entertaining her mouth, she definitely won't be shouting for help, not that I think she would. My brother deep throats Harlow with his fingers, keeping them there until she starts gagging on them and only then does he pull out.

Parrish's pierced length it's still on the loose. He has taken a curled-up position between Harlow's legs, his head on her upper right thigh while with the tip of his knife he draws invisible lines on her left thigh. He's so absorbed in what he is doing, like there is no one else in the dinky trailer but the two of them. A satisfied grin paints his face. That's disturbing. If I know my best friend as well as I think I do, the idiot is getting attached, and that's not good.

"Hmmm." I hear Harlow meow. When I look across at her she is ogling me, more specifically my cock. I shift my hand up and down a few times, her eyes following my movement with heated desire. I pause at the tip and with my thumb I spread around the few drops of pre cum that have made a break for it.

"Like what you see, princess?" Her eyes snap to mine at the sound of my voice. I give her a sinful smirk, before continuing the teasing, "Feast your eyes, Mary. I was blessed with a perfect arch that hits a nice pleasurable spot you bitches have inside your cunts. Would you like me to show you where it is?" I ask, whilst with my free hand I trail down her breastbone to her midriff, passing her belly button and over her mound, halting at her entrance for a split second before digging my middle finger in and curving it exactly right hitting her G spot.

Harlow jolts at the stealth onslaught, almost choking on what's filling her mouth.

"Dude." Parrish howls at me. As I peer at him to see what got his panties in a twist, I notice that Harlow is bleeding from a small cut on her leg. Shit, his knife must've pierced her skin when she jumped at my touch.

"Sorry." I say nonchalantly. Don't know why Parrish is so mad, maybe it's because he is seeing red, literally. It's not like he hasn't foreseen slashing her soft and delicate flesh, making her bleed for him. The idiot is a sucker for blood play as much as knife play. I am rather surprised he's hesitant to do any of it with Harlow, we are killing the girl so what does it matter.

Gazing back at my princess, she looks pissed. Luckily for me she can't snark back since my brother is still stuffing her mouth with his own fingers. Unluckily for her I can turn that frown upside down in the flick of a finger. Her eyes roll back just as she purrs yet again. A sacrilegious sound that I pray I can hear until my dying breath.

I zero in on her wet folds and synchronize the ramming in and out of her pussy with the wanking of my dick. Someone's fingers find Harlow's soft pink bud and rub furious circles over the desperate bundle of nerves.

"Please. I don't think... hmm" she moans, "I can take any

more of this." Those are a lot of words out of her mouth which means there's nothing occupying it anymore.

"Lying is a sin, angel." Abel says purposefully yanking on his dick and clutching to one of her boobs quite forcefully.

"You've been such a good girl so far." Bishop tells her and you can see Harlow melt at the smooth fucker's words. Or maybe, it's the way he is orbiting her clit. "Just cum for us one more time and we will leave you alone, my little mouse." You shouldn't make promises you can't keep dear brother. I know after tonight, I'm definitely not going to be able to back off and abstain from my princess ever again.

Between, Abel roughly gripping her breasts, Bishop cockily circling her little bud, me mercifully finger fucking her and Parrish lovingly licking and drinking up the blood from the knife wound, there is no way this girl isn't over stimulated. That's when Bishop smacks her clit violently and our girl squirts for us. Fuck. Watching my princess physically spasm beneath our touch as her juices pour out of her and dampen the sheets blow her, mumbling some incohesive words, drive me to spurt too.

I grunt. Shot after shot of white pearly cum lands on her beautiful pale skin around her belly. She looks stunning, all dirty with my hot seed.

"Fuck." Abel groans, as his own cum smears her pretty breasts.

Subdued by darkness
But her holy lustre still slashes through with a vengeance that can
harm us
Make us bleed and cum till kingdom come

Stained by immoral act
But her pure gentle sheen is unmoving before our stagnant murky
waters
Whilst we are hexed by her fucking witchcraft
Marked by masked men
But we are the ones blinded by her virtuous soft glow that we'll have
to kill in the end
Surrounded by sin and demons yet, it's an angel I still see before me
Or is she an Albatross?
Our carnal cross
Sent to destroy us

This was a mistake. We shouldn't have played with Harlow tonight. The idea was to have a bit of fun. Emancipate ourselves from this disturbing craving of hunger and thirst we seem to have for her body and soul. And give her a taste of who we really are. To shamelessly expose our perverted, depraved and unhinged darkness, before her pretty blue eyes. To see how far we could push her until she couldn't take anymore and tried to run from the predators that want to sink their knives, teeth and cocks into her.

The gospel is, Harlow is either a curious pussy, like Parrish said, purely looking for something new, something different from what she's used to, or she is already as broken as us. That last thought scares me, because if her soul is defaced and defiled like ours, then she was meant for us, and I can't sacrifice that.

FOURTEEN

BISHOP

WE STRIDE out of Harlow's trailer, the night air hanging heavy with the scent of spent desire and pine from the surrounding trees. The moon casts its voyeuristic gaze upon us as we leave her there, a goddess amongst tangled sheets, her skin glistening like an offering to some primal deity. I can't shake the image from my mind; it's seared into me like a brand.

"Damn, that was something," mutters Abel, his voice rough with satisfaction as we cut through the darkness towards our tour bus, a hulking beast that waits to swallow us whole.

"Shut it," I snap, the image of Harlow, so vulnerable yet powerful in her surrender, haunting me. My boots thud against the metal steps as I board the bus, each step echoing the turmoil inside me.

The others disperse without a word—one to purge the night's sins under scalding water, one to collapse onto their bunk, one seeking solace in sleep or the blue glow of the television. But not me. I need isolation. My sanctuary calls—a small room at the back of the bus, where I can wrestle with the hunger that claws at my insides.

I slam the door shut behind me and lock myself inside my room, the sound a declaration of war against my own desires. The walls of my room closed in, adorned with symbols and sigils that remind me of our purpose, of the power we wield and the control we must maintain.

The screen of my phone casting an unholy glow against the walls. My breaths come out in ragged pulls, my hand moving furiously over myself. There's no stopping, not when every swipe brings Harlow's image flashing across my screen, her body splayed out for us, a feast we devoured but couldn't satiate.

"Fuck," I curse through clenched teeth, feeling my muscles tense with every stroke. The video plays on loop—the raw sound of her pleasure, a siren song I can't resist. My grip tightens, and I'm lost to the carnal haze, chasing the high that only she seems to give. My dick is a relentless rod of need, each throbbing pulse a testament to the hunger she's awakened.

With a grunt, I spill over, warmth spreading across my skin. But it's no relief, just an echo of what was, because the memory intrudes—Harlow beneath us, her nipples pinched and tugged by eager fingers, her body shuddering under a torrent of release from all of us.

"Damn it!" I spit out, swiping at the stickiness on my belly. The image won't fade; it's etched behind my eyelids, a constant reminder of her taste, her sounds, her scent.

I crash back against the pillows, a harsh breath tearing through my lips. The ceiling spins above me, a mocking carousel of Images flash like lightning—the curve of her throat as she arches, the way she falls apart when I strike. Her shattered moans are a siren's call, and I'm the shipwreck waiting to happen. My fingers twitch, craving the wet heat of her mouth, the velvet vice of her sucking them deep.

"Never been this hooked," I confess to the shadows. "She's witchcraft."

Dragging myself up, I pace the confined space, a caged animal starved for one more taste. But a dark whisper snakes through my mind, a reminder of the pact sealed in blood and ambition. She's not ours to keep, not really. Harlow's our sacrifice, the key to keeping what we created for ourselves.

"Can't get lost in her," I growl. "Need to remember why she's here."

The ritual looms over us, a deadline as unforgiving as the grave. There's no time to find another, no escape from the fate we've chosen. We're bound to the darkness, and Harlow...she's the light we're all too eager to extinguish.

"We need to stay away," I command myself, knowing full well the others are lost to their lust, trapped in Harlow's web as much as I am. Parrish, with his dark desires barely leashed, his face when he saw her blood—it was a mix of horror and hunger that chilled me to the bone.

"Obsession's a bitch," I spit out. Church, though, he's the one that's really got me worried. He's always had a handle on things, but with her... damn. The way he looked at her, it wasn't just heat—it was like he'd found his religion. And that kiss with Parrish, shared in the heat of the moment, it's a ticking time bomb for our reputation.

"Publicity be damned," I growl under my breath. We've always played with fire, but this...this is playing with dynamite.

I stop my pacing, standing still as a statue as I take a deep breath. "We need her," I admit through gritted teeth. But it's more than that. She's ensnared us, and if we aren't careful, she will be the end of us before the ritual can even claim her.

"Control," I declare, the word slicing through the fog of desire. "Gotta stay in control." We have to come back to ourselves, remember the stakes. Our lives hang in the balance, and Harlow's the key.

"Stay away," I repeat, this time as a vow. If we can keep our distance, maybe we can salvage this, save ourselves and our reign. It's a slim chance, but it's all we've got.

"Stay the fuck away," I snarl, the words echoing off the walls, a desperate plea to the darkness that surrounds us.

FIFTEEN

HARLOW

THE SAME WAY they came into my, dare I say, safe and sound sanctuary, nothing impregnable about this trailer really, the Paragon of Virtue's Inferno members left, like things that go bump in the night, leaving a sweet and sour taste in my mouth, and a lot of salty, sticky stuff all over my flesh.

They just about ruptured my faith in His words. How can an act that feels this good, be bad? What's probably illicit is wanting all of them with the same fervor and appetite. This is not God's work, this connection was forged by fire, this is the Devils doing, I am sure. Ive never been this smitten with a male before, not enough to misbehave and disobey the rules set by my parents and by the church. No one ever drew me into their orbit by an unexplainable pull, not until Church, Bishop, Parrish and Abel. This isn't just attraction to four pretty guys, its passion, temptation, and a borderline obsession. I want to kneel at their feet and worship them like Gods for perpetuity.

Mine.

Abel was right, perhaps I was asserting ownership.

If I lick it, then it's mine, right?

And I long for them to establish dominance over me, make me theirs.

They have marked me just as thoroughly, with their dirty praises, their lecherous touches, their own pleasure, and I have never felt more alive. Even though tied up, I felt free, emancipated from the preaching that got shoved down my throat by my father and beaten into me by mother dearest. This moment with the boys was my awakening. I have been numb all my life, dying inside, for what? To end up at His gate when I am actually dead?

Before he followed the others in vacating the trailer, Church released the bindings around my wrists and ankles, caressing the bruised skin in an affectionate way. As I looked dead on at his pale gray eyes, I was stupid enough to think that he and I, and all the other Paragon of Virtue's Inferno guys, were preordained to be together, imminent to fall, the same as a bird with a broken wing. Destined or doomed from the start, simply meant to be; But then in a split second, something dark crossed over his face, tainting his demeanor.

"Rat on us, Mary, and Bishop will make you a porn star overnight. Got it, Princess?" When he said 'Princess' this time it sounded bitter and filled with venom. Definitely miles away from the teasing, jammed with desire, pet name that slipped from his lips while they were playing with me. Somehow that cut me deeper and drew more blood than the little accidental slash on my leg done by Parrish's knife.

Once alone it dawns on me, I'm a fool. They used me. They saw an easy prey and pounced without a second thought spared for the havoc they would leave in their wake. Those parting words from Church told me I was nothing but a bit of fun. They don't like me. Of course they don't. I am the preacher's daughter, the good girl, and they personify sinners, dirty money, drugs, alcohol and sex.

The angel and the four horsemen of the apocalypse.

No story ever ends well with those characters together.

"Stupid. Stupid. Stupid." I say over the silence that echoes in the trailer.

I get up from the bed, but as I try to stand on my wobbly legs, they don't support me and I fall to the ground, landing on my hands and knees with a big thud.

Stupid because I fell, For them.

This terrible ache settles in my chest as if I have been stabbed in the heart. I feel like I can't breathe, it's as though my lungs have forgotten how to suck in air. My whole body begins to violently shake, in such a way that it seems I was thrown into the frigid waters of the Antarctic. Instantly all it takes to trigger the floodgates to open and I begin to cry uncontrollably.

In the midst of my panic attack, I disconnect, not only from myself but my surroundings too. I get dunked in darkness as the room around me morphs and I am shoved back into the prayer closet.

"Oh God, no, please." The place that broke me so. Where I would be at the helm of fear, having lost control over all other emotions. The only place where tears would bust out and I would scream and beg. My own personal hell on earth.

Closing my eyes I sit back on my ass, my back to the edge of the bed, and bring my bent legs to my chest, hugging them tenaciously with both my arms, cocooning myself in a fetal position. With my head down, chin tucked to chest and my forehead resting on the knees, I howl the words that used to flee my lips in the past, "No. Let me out. Please. I'll be a good girl. I promise. Just please let me out."

Drained from the sleepless night, from the perverted act, and from the all-consuming panic over it, I barely left my stupid small trailer all day to avoid the band like the plague they are.

I had to wash my body from their seed in the kitchenette sink, because I refuse to crawl back in the tour bus like the wounded prey they made me. This was the only way I could lick my own wounds and keep some dignity.

Stupid silly girl, I thought the Paragon of Virtue's Inferno men were the answer to my prayers. Gabriel undid the chains around my wings and allowed them to heal, and I hoped that; these four would be the ones to burst open the shackles I wore around my wrists and ankles that were forever weighing me down and at long last allow me to break completely free from father, mother dearest and God's divine plan enabling me to fully spread my wings and fly. I did spread something alright, my legs.

At least we didn't actually have sex. None of them buried their manhood's inside of me, why is that? They could've. I was completely at their bidding and mercy, and I shamelessly wouldn't have opposed either. I wanted it badly. But in retrospective, knowing what I know now, it was a blessing in disguise they didn't even try. The McGrew brothers, Parrish and Abel might be sinners with no principles, but they cared somewhat not to cross that line. I wish I regretted what we did, but I don't. For a moment there, where we were all together, lost in one another's rapture, I felt absolute, like I finally belonged somewhere, with someone, or four someone's. But when they were gone, solitude crept up once more, and I was left with Church's parting words that hurt because I thought the boys felt at least a spark of what I had, but I was just the amusement for the night. How naïve?

I learned my lesson; if you play with fire, you get scorched.

What caused me to fall apart, was the thought of mother dearest finding out what happened and dragging me kicking and screaming, back to the compound to hold me captive there forever. Or worse. nailing shut the prayer closet with me inside until I become a rotting corpse. I swear that place was made to be my coffin. With someone by my side perhaps I would be strong enough to resist, but all alone I am an already cracked and fragile, porcelain doll that is on the verge of shattering completely. I'm weak. I don't want to be, but I don't know how to stop everyone around me pulling my invisible strings for their own sick pleasure, making me perform whatever twisted story they conjure up in their minds, like I am but a mere marionette in their hands.

"Miss Abaddon, you are on in 30 minutes." I hear one of the crew members say from the other side of my trailer door. "You really should be making your way backstage."

"Right." I clear my throat after that frail attempt to respond. "One second." I say with more creed this time.

I peer at myself in the full-length mirror. I am wearing a cute pink floral babydoll dress with a square neckline and 3/4 puffy sleeves. My worn-out white cowboy boots adorn my feet. And I did my hair in a side French braid to complete the look.

I lift my hand to my rose gold simple cross necklace and twirl it around my fingers. I only do this when I am on edge or feel uneasy about what's to come. The question is, what am I nervous about? The show, or seeing the Paragon of Virtue's Inferno men? How bad can this be?

I arrive backstage without bumping into any of the bands. Both crews, mine and theirs, are slaving away, moving around in the dark corner of the venue like shadows, to make sure this show goes on smoothly. I feel awful. I didn't even come out for a sound test this afternoon. How unprofessional of me.

As I am waiting by some road cases, -that seem to be scattered everywhere- for my moment to walk on stage, someone whispers in my ear, "I never got to play with your pretty pussy, angel." Abel's voice sends a shiver up my spine, or maybe it's just the feel of his fingers as they move up that middle line. Once he reaches the nape of my neck he grabs it forcefully. "I am saddened really. Be a doll and let me sink my face in between your legs before you have to on stage." I whimper as he darts his tongue inside my ear.

Cripes. What is wrong with me? I can feel my arousal soak my panties and creep down my leg. They don't like you. They are just using you for their sick pleasure. I remind myself.

"What did you say?" Abel asks. Oh, heavens, did I say that out loud?

"Miss Abaddon, your band is ready and waiting for you on stage." A crew member announces.

"Right." I free myself from Abel's hold. Grabbing my guitar

from its position leaning against the crates next to me, and I place the strap over my neck and across my shoulder.

"Harlow?" Abel grips my wrist with a punishing vigor, stopping me from getting on stage. I look back at the man with a full body of tattoos, thanks to his open sheer lace t-shirt, I can get a good peek of. Maybe the reason I came to a standstill was because of the way he uttered my name. Hurt and dejected, that's what he sounded like. My eyes lift to his. Oh, goddamn it… cripes I just swore, but forgive me father, Abel is wearing his reading glasses and somehow that is making my legs turn to jelly.

I am about to speak when, "Yo Mary, our fans are waiting for you to grace them with your presence. Move your ass." Church's deep voice is like a bucket of freezing cold water dumped over my head waking me up from the spell Abel had me in.

"Or don't. Gives me a reason to spank it." Bishop asserts right after his brother.

Parrish appears behind Church, draping his arm around the lead vocalist shoulders. "Oh, I like this dress, pretty doe. It's short enough that I can see the small cut from my knife on your breathtaking long legs." He says, palming his obvious hard on.

Do not cave in to their seduction and corruption again, Harlow. Fool me once, shame on them. Fool me twice, now that would be on me, and I am not falling this time.

Closing my eyes I harrowingly declare, "Y'all had your fun. Now leave me the hell alone." As I open them, my focus is solely on the man right in front of me. Staring deep into his dark brown eyes, I continue on, "You had your chance, and

you blew it, so go bury your face between someone else's legs."
Please don't, I am screaming deep inside my head.

I rip my wrist from his grasp and walk away.

"You think I won't? There's enough pussy being flung around my way for me to take a pick." Abel shouts at me.

I spin quickly around and yell back, "Suck a dick, Abel," before jumping on stage.

How bad can this be? Pretty bad.

Sixteen

Abel

THE JEERS erupt like a cacophony of crows, tearing through the charged air of the dimly lit underground club that we are playing at tonight. I watch from behind the curtain—Harlow's silhouette on stage, her electric blue eyes wide with shock as another full cup of beer is thrown on stage, narrowly missing her feet. The crowd is merciless tonight, their boos ricocheting off the grimy walls, and for a fleeting moment, my chest tightens.

"Get off the stage!" someone bellows, their voice slicing through the din like a knife.

In all my years drumming with the arrogance of a god among mortals, I've never flinched at the cruelty of our followers. I'm used to the darkness that clings to this place, to us, but the sight of her, defiant yet shaken, triggers an unfamiliar twinge of guilt within me—a sensation foreign and as unwelcome as sunlight in our shadow-drenched haven.

"Come on, Harlow," I mutter under my breath, willing her to summon that innate fire and spit back some smart retort that'll show them all. But she doesn't. Instead, she turns, chin held high, and strides off the stage with a grace that belies the chaos she leaves behind.

I shove the curtain aside and step into the path of her retreat, catching a glimpse of her pallor beneath the harsh stage lights. My fingers twitch, a stinging reminder of the beats I should be pounding out instead of standing here, snagged by a conscience I thought I'd long since buried under layers of ink and apathy.

"Guys, you're up," one of the techies' snaps, his impatience a sharp poke to my ego. He's right—I can't afford distractions. Not when there's so much at stake.

"Got it," I snap back, shoving past him with a scowl. I take my place behind the drums, the familiar gleam of the cymbals reflecting the twisted excitement in my eyes. As my sticks kiss the skin of the snare, igniting the crowd once more, I force down the guilt, bury it deep beneath the rhythm and roar.

But even as the shadows dance and swell around me, hungry for the frenzy we feed them, I can't entirely shake the image of Harlow being booed off that stage. And for the first time in a long time, I hate it.

The thrum of my heartbeat keeps time with the reverberating bass as I settle into the rhythm, sticks flying over the drum kit like they're an extension of my own limbs. The stage is an inferno of sound and movement, but my eyes can't help but drift to the wings where Harlow stands—her silhouette a stark contrast against the chaos.

She's motionless now, her electric blue eyes cast downward, the echo of the crowd's disdain still clawing at the air around her. But even in defeat, there's something unspoiled about her, something that flickers defiantly despite the darkness we're all drowning in. Her curls, golden and untamed, seem to hold whispers of songs yet unsung, and for a moment, I feel the pull—a strange urge to leap from my throne of beats and shield her from the contempt she doesn't deserve.

I grit my teeth, forcing my focus back to the skins and cymbals before me. My arms move with renewed fervor, driving the energy higher, feeding the frenzy. She has a voice that could soothe the savage shadows that lurk hungrily in every corner of this room, a voice that shouldn't be silenced by the ignorance of the masses. It's clear, pure, and it haunts me more than any demon ever could.

"Damn it," I mutter under my breath, the words lost in the cacophony. The feeling gnaws at me, insistent and unnerving. I want to help her—I want to tell her that she belongs on a stage far grander than this pit of vipers.

"Abel, hit it harder!" Church's voice cuts through the din, his command laced with that cheeky edge that usually draws a smirk from my lips. But not tonight.

"Watch me," I growl back, giving him a wicked grin. My sticks are a blur, each strike a challenge to the shadows that hunger for our souls. Beneath the surface, though, the pull remains a dangerous current that threatens to drag me under.

"Give them hell!" Bishop bellows from his station, fingers dancing deftly over the strings of his bass. His presence is commanding, the very essence of blunt force that anchors us to this realm.

"Always do," I shout back, half-laughing, half-snarling as I lose myself in the riotous symphony we create.

Parrish, lost in his own bloody love affair with his guitar, doesn't speak—his gaze fixed somewhere between madness and ecstasy. We are the lords of discord, each note a decree, each song a spellbinding tumult.

Yet, amidst the frenzy, I steal another glance at Harlow, our unwitting siren, and feel an ache in my chest—a yearning to reach out, to offer a hand that might guide her back to the light.

"Focus, Abel," I chastise myself, shaking off the treacherous sentiment. The show must go on, and so must the plan. But as I watch her retreat further into the shadow's embrace, I can't shake the feeling that something within me has irrevocably shifted.

Harlow's image burns behind my eyelids—innocent, radiant, her voice a melody that could soothe even the darkest of souls. But I can't afford such distractions; she is the linchpin in a plan far greater than any fleeting desire or misguided conscience. She is the key to our salvation, to our release from this hellish bargain we struck in desperation.

The thought clenches like a fist around my heart, squeezing until the guilt bleeds out. She needs to die, so we can live. It's a truth as cold and unyielding as the steel of Parrish's beloved knives.

I watch as the sea of bodies writhes and convulses, the mass of energy palpable, tangible. It's electric, this power we wield is an unspoken dominion over every soul in the room. They're ours, every last one of them, caught in the web of our making.

And then, from the corner of my eye, I catch it—the shift in the shadows. They peel away from the walls like ink bleeding into water, sinuous and silent. They creep, stretching and expanding—alive in a way that sets my pulse racing with a perverse thrill. Their otherworldly dance of darkness mirrors our own, a symphony of night to accompany the wildness we incite.

The shadows swell with each note we play, growing bolder, more defined. Amid the din and the feverish light, they coil around the throng, unseen but felt—a brush of cold against sweat-slick skin, a whisper in the ear of the entranced.

"Lost and found, we claim this ground!" Church howls, his pale hair a halo in the strobe lights, his tattoos a declaration of our covenant.

The music crescendos, a tempest wrought by four horsemen, each beat a nail in the coffin of our imprisonment. The shadows dance to our tune, and for a fleeting moment, we are the puppeteers of the night, commanding forces that should be beyond our ken.

"Give it up for your kings!" I shout; my voice swallowed by the roar of the crowd. Tonight, we reign supreme— masters of the stage and the creeping dark that yearns to break free.

A shiver races down my spine, but it's not the chill of the unseen—it's the thrill of knowing. I lock eyes with a girl in the front row, her gaze wide and unseeing as she sways to our rhythm. She doesn't know it yet, but she won't be tucking herself into bed tonight. The shadows have marked her; they've chosen their prey.

"Keep them on their feet!" I roar over the thundering drums, my voice a serrated edge cutting through the frenzy. The crowd surges like a beast with a single heartbeat, pulsating to our command.

My sticks are a blur, each strike fueling the fire that burns within this hallowed hall. The darkness feeds off their energy, growing thicker, hungrier. It wraps around the unsuspecting souls, whispering promises laced with malice. And as the girl with the wide eyes starts to stagger, I can almost taste the sweet scent of fear mingling with sweat in the air.

"Let the night consume you!" Church's voice rings out, a siren calling to the lost and damned. My lips curve upward. The demons feast tonight, and we are their harbingers, their dark maestros orchestrating a symphony of chaos.

I pound the drums harder, faster. This is our ritual, our legacy etched in shadows and song. The crowd is a writhing mass now, completely under our spell. They think it's just the music that ensnares them, but I see the truth. I see the tendrils of darkness licking at their heels, drawing sustenance from their delirium.

"More! Give them more!" Bishop bellows, his fingers dancing over the bass strings with practiced fervor. His command is unnecessary, I'm already three steps ahead, lost in the rhythm, a conduit for something ancient and powerful.

"Tonight, we're immortal!" Parrish screams, his guitar screeching an anthem for the end of days. In this moment, I believe him. We are untouchable, invincible as long as the music plays and the shadows feed. And feed they do, on every note, every beat of the drum. They swell with power, so thick now that the air feels electric, charged with the promise of oblivion. It's a dangerous game we play, but the stakes have never been higher. This is our path to freedom, our only chance to break the chains that bind us to this mortal coil.

"Rise and revel in the darkness!" I command, and they obey, a sea of bodies moving as one with the creatures that lurk just beyond sight. The room spins, the energy crescendos, and I know without a shadow of a doubt—we are the kings of the night, and someone won't be making it home.

Seventeen

Harlow

I HATED IT. As I stepped on stage and gazed at the crowd before me, I saw nothing but punk metal looking people -a sea of black- who were clearly only here for the guys. They booed as I sang my songs and threw trash at me. They hated me! I felt like I had died inside, a little bit more at the real-ization.

I don't know what was worse, my disaster of a set or, afterwards, hearing and seeing how much these people worship the Paragon of Virtue's Inferno. At that moment I knew I didn't belong here with them. This was a mistake. With that I ran back to my trailer and cried the night away.

In the morning, my tormented sleep was disturbed by one of the crew members, knocking on my door to tell me I needed to head to the tour bus as we were departing to the next town on the tour. I wanted to escape, perhaps I could disappear, start anew somewhere, anywhere. But something was telling me that they would find me, wherever I went. I just don't know if the 'they' would be, my so-called family or my guys, I mean the band. It's not like I belong anywhere else either, so may as well press on with this and suffer at the core like I have been doing all my life. At least I am not under mother dearest's thumb.

As I get inside the tour bus, it's eerily quiet. I guess the boys are still sleeping. Good. "I should take advantage of this and take a hot shower." I tell myself. So that's exactly what I do.

The water is scalding hot, and I scrub my skin so hard it turns a blush pink. What am I trying to cleanse away here, last night or the night before? I stay under the millions of droplets of water falling on my skin for a long time. I feel the tour bus come to life under my feet, the beast roaring as it sets on its way out of this town and onto the next.

It dawns on me, I am going to have to face the music, and by that, I mean the four guys, sooner or later, so I turn the shower off and as I move the curtain aside, I see that I am not alone in this tiny bathroom.

"Parrish." I squeal as I cover myself with the curtain.

"Oh, no need for that, pretty doe. Nothing we haven't seen before."

"Haven't you ever heard of privacy?" I ask him, clenching the curtain punishingly. The image in front of me is setting something in the depth of my belly aflame and I get this throbbing between my legs that I ease by trying to discreetly rub my thighs together. Parrish's torso is bare, with gray joggers hanging low on his hips, accentuating the nice v that points to a blasphemous part of his body, I'm drawn into the direct view of his beautifully camouflaged muscles that are accentuated with colorful tattoos. I have no idea if its the steam that fogs the room or my eyes once more playing tricks on me, but I swear I see the tattoos move on his skin.

He groans. "Don't do that."

"Do what?" I abandon my ogle of his sinful body and lift my eyes to his.

"Bite your lip like that Harlow, And I solemnly promise, if it draws blood, I will kiss you, and only the Devil knows what else because I won't be able to control myself."

"Are you ever?" I chuckle.

His pierced eyebrow arches, at the same time his dimpled ones lift. "Dear Harlow, the restraint I am showing you, I haven't ever shown with anyone else." This is him holding back? Cripes.

"Why? Why not just take all you want and be done with it?" Oh, my dear God what am I doing? What is wrong with me? This isn't me. First, I snap at Abel. I can't believe I told him to 'suck a dick', but his words hurt me, just as much as Church's did after what happened between us. The sucker punches keep telling me that I am just another notch on their bedposts. I hollered for them to leave me alone, yet I don't seem to be able to do the same. The second I approached their web, I was trapped, and now I wait impatiently for the deadly predators to devour me.

Was what happened during the show God's wrath? Was the Lord punishing me for my small fall from grace?

Parrish doesn't respond, instead he looks at me like I've burned him, causing him excruciating pain. His hands are fisted at his side. What... that's when I peer down at myself, and I notice that I have let go of the curtain and I am completely naked before him.

"Parrish" I don't have time to finish that thought as Church, wearing but his boxers, lets himself in with a blaring phone in his hand.

"Mary, your fucking phone hasn't stopped ringing. Here." And he just throws the phone my way. I manage to catch it just in time, but the instant I see who's calling, I wish it had dropped to the ground and shattered. Mother dearest is flashing across the screen. "Are you going to pick it up, or what?"

"Church. Chill dude." Parrish tells the lead singer. "Harlow." The way he says my name, so tenderly and sweet, screams 'you are not alone', it gives me strength and I pick up.

"Hello." I whisper with a cracked voice.

I shouldn't have answered, nothing good ever comes out of her mouth. She told me how Ada called to inform her how bad last night's show went. There was no concern for my well-being, no asking how I was, even though I asked how her leg was healing, forever being the doting daughter, yet she couldn't care less for me.

All I got was, "You're a disappointment, Harlow. You're supposed to be gathering a following for your father, Harlow."

The most dire of all, "There are other jobs you could be doing here in the compound, instead of whoring around with those ungodly and unholy men. If you don't do what you were sent to us by God to do, then what is the point of you?" And then she hung up on me.

We are still on the road, I have been sulking on the couch in the main area of the tour bus, looking out the window, watching the outside world dash past it in a blur. My back is against one of the arms of the couch as the rest of my body leaning towards the back of it. Knees bent up to my chest, with both arms hugging myself around my middle.

I know Church and Parrish heard all of the phone call.

They have all been looking at me funny, which means the other two know as well, which is just freaking peachy. Now they all know how dim and dull I am.

I'm dressed in an old baggy tee that says "What would Jesus do?" and a pair of jersey racer shorts in contrasting black and white. My hair is in a messy bun piled roughly at the top of my head; pretty sure I look like the mess I feel.

"I think it's been long enough. You can stop moping around now, little mouse. Why don't you come and join us?" Bishop utters.

"No, thank you." I say without glancing back at them.

"So, your mom is a bitch. She ain't here. Come and play with us, pretty doe." Parrish begs.

Play with them? I finally peer at the four of them, they brought out these weird looking cards. I remember seeing them the first time I stepped into the tour bus. Where I am seated, I am slightly closer to them therefore, I can pick out what they are now. Tarot cards, creepy ones. Most seem to depict demons or have some form of gore filled imagery. They send a blood chilling sensation up my spine.

On the dining table there's a pentagram reading mat, where they place the cards in a specific order to, well, I will be honest, I don't know the purpose of what they are doing, but I am not messing with that stuff. In the center of the pentagram a goat's head has been drawn out. The sigil of Baphomet. Mother dearest was right, they are satanic worshippers.

Once more, I say, "No, thank you." I make sure to frown as I do, making it clear of my disapproval and displeasure to what they are fooling around with.

"Don't be a judgmental prude, Mary. It doesn't suit you."

Church comments. Is that what it comes across as? The last thing I want to be is like my mother.

"I'm sorry." Why am I apologizing? "I just don't feel comfortable dancing alongside Satan like y'all do."

"He's not a bad guy once you get to know him." Abel states as he pulls a card from the deck and puts it to rest on one of the five points of the darkened star. He makes it sound as if they know the Devil, personally.

"I'll take your word for it." I say in response to his strange statement.

"Does your God answer you?" Church asks then. I cast a confused look his way. "When you kneel for Him and pray, does he give you what you want?"

"Well, no. That is not how praying works' stuff isn't meant to just fall on your lap." As I speak, I turn on my seat so that I am facing the boys fully; cross-legged with my hands limply together between my legs.

"You can fall on my lap any time, pretty doe."

"Why devote yourself to someone that gives you nothing?" Church continues, not fazed by the pink haired goof's cheeky remark.

"Why do you care?" I ask in return.

"I'm just trying to understand you." he notes.

"Why?" Church shrugs at my question, which makes me knit my brows at him. He's so ugh! I can't even with him sometimes.

Eventually, I tell him, "Hope."

"What about it?" Parrish asks.

"God gives me hope."

"That's stupid. Hope is not tangible, it's not really something you can possess, hold with your own hands. For that reason, it's not a thing someone can hand to you." Bishop observes.

Maybe not, but it's the only thing that keeps me going in this life that I am living. But it ain't mine, because the boys are right, He doesn't' grant you anything, no matter how many times you beg. I learned that the hard way, scratching the closet door until my fingers bleed from the wooden splinters, on my bruised knees, pleading to be free. He never answered, and neither did she. So, I hope that I am not just what He made me out to be, His angel, stuck on earth only to lead sinners to their savior, His prophet, my father. I hope that there is a family out there for me, where what binds us is stronger than blood. I hope that I belong somewhere, with someone that can see me for me, and love me even graced with the invisible cracks that are all over my body and soul.

"Hope is but a feeble dream." Abel announces. It might be a weak dream, and I might be a weak girl, but what else is there? Is not like there's a magic lamp out there I can rub for a genie to come out and grant my wishes. And wishing on shooting stars doesn't work either. Trust me, I tried.

"Ok. Maybe I don't want anything then." I am getting frustrated here. What do they want from me?

"Everyone wants something. You're no different princess. So, don't pretend that you are." Church says with a slight irk in his voice

"Ugh. Fine. Maybe what I want not even my God can give me." Because what I pray for is for Him to be gone from my life.

Eighteen
Church

I keep fucking things up. I can't help myself. I need Harlow at a distance. I need her to hate me, not look at me like I'm her savior. It's as if she could love me, love all four of us, even damaged with the cracks all over our bodies and souls. That's how she gazed at me as we were leaving her trailer the other night, like we were the answers to her prayers, so I had to break the spell, I had to hurt her. I hate myself for it.

"Y'all had your fun. Now leave me the hell alone." She told us before going on stage the next night, and I thought I'd accomplished what I had set out to do. She sees us for what we truly are, but shadows ourselves, demons who only do wrong, ruin everything. Then she turned to Abel and barked, "You had your chance, and you blew it. so go bury your face between someone else's legs." I got painfully hard at the spite and venom in her voice. Harlow is more than the angelic, sweet and innocent front that is portrayed, there's something else lurking underneath, the Damn princess has hellfire hidden in there too. When she told him to go "suck a dick," I just about came. Now that's a sinful image I can get behind, or in front of. Fuck.

Watching her get booed on stage with shit getting thrown her way, caused a weird heavy feeling on my chest. Why can't they see her beauty? She could be their salvation, instead they rather worship us, their damnation. That pissed me off. I wanted to kill the whole crowd. Make the shadows drag all their souls to suffer in hell for all eternity. How dare they dim and dull my girl's light?

And her mother. What the fuck?

I got woken up by this organ hymn, echoing through the tour bus nonstop. I'm a grumpy asshole when I get rudely awoken, or perhaps that's just my default mode, so I did shit without thinking, I barged in the tiny bathroom like a wrecking ball. Seeing Harlow naked and wet just about made me cave and fuck her against the wall, so instead I snapped, "Mary, your fucking phone hasn't stopped ringing. Here." I tossed the phone at her which she caught, but as Harlow looked at the screen a shadow crossed her face and her whole demeanor changed into that of a scared little girl. I saw the caller ID; it was her mother. Why was she staring at the phone like the person on the other end possesses the power to do her more harm than the two fallen angels before her? What dark tales is she hiding, my pretty girl? "Are you going to pick it up, or what?"

Parrish told me to chill. I will admit that last line was a bit unnecessary. When Harlow eventually picked up the call her voice was but a broken whisper.

This woman is not a mother. The things she yelled at Harlow are cruel, vile and evil. It's like she despises her own daughter, as if Harlow is nothing but a chewed-up piece of gum stuck on the bottom of her shoe that she desperately wants to get rid of. The bitch.

As I peer at the girl curled up on herself, staring blankly at the world rushing past her eyes, I realized we know nothing about her. We assumed she had the perfect life, a beautiful home with the white picket fence and loving family. How wrong are we? I'm afraid to know, because if it turns out she's just like us, a fractured soul with a fucked-up childhood that has seen how truly brutal the world can be, then she belongs with us. She was made for us. And here we are stringing her along, to sacrifice her to the Devil for the sake of our asses.

So, I poke around, hunting for answers to questions we are all dying to ask Harlow. I want to understand her, and that's exactly what I tell her. I mostly need to know why she would give herself to a God, that would allow bad shit to happen to such a good and gentle soul. He gives her nothing, and I ache to tell her, "We will give you everything, if you kneel before us. If you pick us over Him." But then I remember why she's here, and I swallow those words down.

Her gaze falls and she clutches the cross that hangs from her neck as she says, "Maybe what I want not even my God can give me." I am about to ask her what she can possibly mean by that, when she gets up suddenly and walks away from us, disappearing into the back of the tour bus. I guess that's us done talking.

Show after show she gets booed off the stage. Show after show we see her dwindle more and more, running away to her trailer to cry herself to sleep. However, there are these moments, where we push just the right button, pull just the right string, and she comes alive, giving us glimpses of that cute little inferno of hers. No one else can bring her back to life like we can, and that's a scary thought.

It's quicksand we find ourselves in, and we keep getting sucked down by it. Falling further and further for a girl we can't have. I want to make her ours. I want to fuck her and claim the drops of red she will bleed once penetrated for the first time. But Harlow is our offering to the Devil, without her we are fucked. I want to save my soul and those of my band just as badly, to live long enough to experience more than just music, sex and drugs. Want. Want. Want.

She walks around clutching that stupid cross every second of the day, obviously fighting her own demons. She wants us too; there's no doubt in my mind anymore. She has fallen for the big bad wolves that plan to slaughter her and hand her over to another guy, to Satan no less. We are giving the best thing that ever crossed our darkened paths, on a silver platter, to sin itself.

Unlike her God, he did answer our prayers, but nothing from the Devil comes for free, and now we are paying the price. Is it me or does it just seem too expensive this time around?

I see the look in Harlow's electric blue eyes every time we thank Satan or play with our cards. They are not as judgy as before, it's almost like a longing now, but she stands her ground for some unknown reason and refuses to join us. Stubborn girl. Harlow just sits there, hugging herself in a fetal position, on the couch, either reading or getting lost in the fleeting world rushing by outside the window.

She doesn't know this, but the cards define which demon gets to play what scenario in our upcoming show. It's a game of Russian roulette, but we aren't the ones at risk, the thousands of lives in the crowd at our shows, are the ones in danger of perishing.

"They are slandering her all over social media. Our following is wondering why she is even getting on stage to sing." Bishop notes, pacing the room as he looks at his phone with a grimace.

We are in a backstage room, coming off the high from being out there putting on a killer performance for our devotees.

"Because she's stronger than she looks." Abel comments from his stretched-out position on the only couch in the room, which is why the rest of us are standing. One of his arms is draped over his eyes, while his other dangles over the edge of the couch. His chest is on full display, and I cannot abstain from ogling him. He's not wrong though, our girl isn't weak.

"That or she has a thing for punishment." A slap sound follows Parrish words. "Ouch." My best friend rubs the back of his head, giving the stinky eye to Bishop, who has finally stopped his patrolling. "You should be pleased with that, you bastard. You do like to chastise your playthings, no?" My older brother lifts his hand about to smack Parrish again, but he runs away, while laughing maniacally to hide behind me. "Protect me from your idiot of a brother." He hugs me tightly around my middle, resting his chin on my shoulder.

"You're the idiot. Don't taunt him, you should know better Parrish." I reprimand him, as I place my arms on top of his and pivot my face slightly to peer at the pink haired dream.

"Maybe I'm a sucker for punishment." He tells me with

dilated eyes and a cocky smirk that foregrounds his appealing dimple piercings.

Maybe we all are.

NINETEEN

PARRISH

THE SWEAT on my body is still fresh from the blistering performance we just gave. I can feel the residual heat radiating off Church, Bishop, Abel, and myself as we step onto our tour bus. Everything's different since Harlow joined the tour. She's like a bolt of lightning that struck us all, changing the air around us.

Normally, this would be the part where we'd celebrate - party, get high, take groupies back to the bus... But not since Harlow came along. It's unspoken, but we've all changed our ways for her. And tonight, I'm itching for something more... something dangerously exciting.

I glance around the dimly lit bus, watching as everyone prepares to turn in for the night. Restlessness scratches at the edges of my mind. Fuck this, I think I need something more tonight. With determination fueling my every step, I stride into Church's small room. He's sitting on his bunk, strumming a few idle chords on his guitar.

"Hey," I say, grabbing him by the throat and slamming my

lips onto his. "I'm bored. Wanna go put on a show for our Virgin Mary?"

As I watch Church's wicked smile, I can feel the adrenaline already starting to course through me. "Yes," he breathes, anticipation heavy in his voice as he adjusts himself in his pants.

"Let's do this," I say, heart pounding in my chest like a war drum.

We tiptoe out of the bus, our footsteps light as a feather on the gravel. The night air is cool against my skin, and I shiver slightly, eager to get inside Harlow's trailer and see what kind of reaction we'll elicit from her.

The lock clicks open, and we slip inside, careful not to make a sound. Harlow's soft breathing fills the small space, and I find myself holding mine, captivated by the sight of her slumbering form.

The cold steel of the flick knife rests heavy in my pocket, a constant reminder of the thrill that's just a heartbeat away. As I climb onto the bed and straddle Harlow's sleeping form, I can't help but admire her peaceful beauty. The soft rise and fall of her chest beneath me is almost hypnotic, lulling me into a false sense of calm.

"Finally," I whisper, more to myself than anyone else. I draw out the knife and hold it to her throat, the cold edge of the blade presses against her delicate skin, as I lean in, my tongue tracing a path up the side of her face. The moment she wakes, her body goes stiff, eyes flying open wide with surprise and fear. She looks at me, sitting on top of her, and for a brief moment, I wonder if I've gone too far.

"What are you doing, Parrish?" she mumbles, barely

moving an inch. Smart girl; she must feel the blade's cold edge against her throat.

"Good girl," I say, my voice low and dangerous, a wicked smile playing on my lips. "You don't want to make any sudden moves now, do you?"

Her eyes dart between my hand and my face, searching for some sign of mercy or understanding. But all she'll find is the wild excitement of someone who loves pushing boundaries – hers and mine alike.

"Church!" I call out, never breaking eye contact with Harlow. "You're missing all the fun."

"Wouldn't dream of it," he replies, sauntering over to us with a predatory grin. He watches us closely, reveling in her vulnerability and my dominance.

As Church enters Harlow's line of sight, his grin stretches wide, grey eyes gleaming with mischief. "We were bored, Mary," he drawls, the nickname dripping with unspoken intentions. "So, we've come to play. Just lay still and thank us later, okay?"

A shadow flickers across Harlow's face, uncertainty warring with something else - curiosity perhaps? She stammers out a barely audible, "Okay." I can't help but let out a low chuckle; she's so damn innocent.

"Good girl," I murmur, licking her cheek once more before finally removing the knife from her neck. The tension in her body eases only slightly, as I gently guide her fully onto her back. My gaze remains locked on hers, asserting my dominance and making it clear who's in control. The sharp tip of the blade glides down her front, brushing against the fabric of her simple camisole top. With a quick, practiced flick, I pull the material down to expose her breasts, my eyes never leaving hers.

"Such a pretty little thing," I murmur, running the tip of the knife over her now-stiff nipples. She gasps, biting her lip as the cold steel teases her sensitive skin. It's thrilling, this dance between danger and desire.

"Please," she whispers again, but there's a newfound heat in her voice that betrays her true feelings.

"Please what, kitten?" I ask, smirking at her flushed cheeks and glassy eyes. I know exactly what she wants, but I want to hear her say it. After all, that's part of the fun – isn't it?

I watch Harlow's body quiver with anticipation, Church grinning wickedly steps up to the end of the bed. His grey eyes full of mischief as he reaches down, yanking her shorts off in one swift motion. Her exposed pussy glistens in the dim light, beckoning him closer.

"Hope you're ready, Mary," Church says with a devilish grin, "I'm tasting you this time. I need to drink up those juices." He spreads her legs wide, leaning between them, his messy hair brushing against her thighs as he starts to lick her wetness.

Harlow's moans fill the small room, and I can't help but revel in the sinful sounds escaping her lips. My cock twitches with jealousy at the thought of Church pleasuring her so thoroughly.

"Keep those pretty little eyes open for me, kitten," I warn Harlow as I climb off her and move behind Church, who's bent over in his eagerness to devour her. "Church loves being watched."

She looks up at me with a mix of fear and arousal in her electric blue eyes. I smirk, knowing that she's starting to give in to her desires, despite the twisted nature of our game.

Harlow's moans grow louder, the sound of a sweet symphony that sends shivers down my spine. I watch her closely, noticing how she no longer fights us. Her hands grip the sheets tightly, knuckles white from the intensity of her desire.

"Fuck," I mutter under my breath. She wants this — wants us. The realization ignites a fire within me, and I can't help but wonder why it feels so right.

"Ready for more?" I ask Church, smirking as I reach for his pants. He nods eagerly, biting his lip in anticipation. I pull his pants down, exposing his ass to me, and my cock twitches in response.

"God," he groans, arching his back as I place my fingers into my mouth, coating them with saliva. With a swift kick, I spread Church's legs apart, giving me better access to his ass cheeks. My wet fingers trace a path down his crack, finally reaching his tight hole.

"Here we go," I whisper, pushing my fingers inside him. Church moans at the intrusion, and I can't help but feel a sense of power coursing through me as I slowly fuck his ass with my fingers. My eyes lock onto Harlow as she watches us with unabashed interest.

"Enjoying the show, Harlow?" Church asks breathlessly. Harlow's eyes wide and full of lust, are locked on me like a predator stalking its prey. I can't help but grin at the sight of her so enthralled by our dark performance. "Oh kitten," I think to myself. "The fun we can have with you."

I pull my fingers from Church's ass, leaving him panting and wanting. I spit onto his hole before tugging my own pants down just enough to release my throbbing dick. Giving it a few long strokes, I feel my balls tighten as arousal courses through me. "Fuck, that feels good. ¨

"Like what you see, Harlow?" I taunt her, my voice dripping with desire and control. She doesn't answer, but the look in her eyes is enough.

"Are you ready, Church?" I ask, my voice thick with desire.

"Give it to me, Parrish," he growls, his body quivering with need.

"Watch closely, Harlow," I warn her as I line up with Church's hole, my eyes locked with hers. She's propped on her elbows, pupils blown and mouth agape as she takes in the scene before her. Slowly, I sink into Church, making sure he can feel every inch of me. The sensation is intoxicating, and Harlow's moans only serve to heighten it.

"Fuck, Parrish," Church groans, never breaking his attention from Harlow's pussy. He pushes two fingers into her opening, but only just. We can't risk breaking that precious virginity of hers. Harlow's moans grow louder, longer, and I can tell she's getting closer to the edge.

"Good girl," I encourage her, my voice low and dark. "Let go for us, Harlow."

I bottom out in Church's ass, giving him a few seconds to adjust before beginning to fuck him slowly. With every thrust, he moans and pushes back against me, meeting me halfway. The sounds of Harlow's pleasure are like music to my ears, spurring me on further.

My free hand reaches for the knife in my pocket. Drawing a small cut along Church's back, just deep enough for droplets of blood to appear, I can't help but revel in the gasp that escapes him. Running my fingers through the blood, I pump harder into his ass.

"Look at this, Harlow," I demand, holding my hand up, covered in Church's blood. Her eyes fixate on it, curiosity and lust swirling within them. With a wicked grin, I lick the blood off my fingers, savoring the metallic taste. It's the final push Harlow needs – she shatters beneath Church's touch, her orgasm washing over her as she cries out his name.

"Such a good girl," I praise, my voice dripping with satisfaction.

The walls of the trailer seem to close in on us as I fuck Church harder and faster, my grip tightening around his hips. He pushes back against me with equal fervor, his moans loud and unashamed. With one hand, I grab the back of his messy hair, yanking him up so Harlow can see every detail.

"Watch," I order her, my voice dripping with lust and control.

"Harlow," Church gasps between thrusts, "look at me."

His free hand reaches down to grasp his own dick, stroking it in time with my pounding. I can feel my balls drawing up tight, signaling my impending release. My eyes bore into Harlow's electric blue ones, daring her to look away.

"Church," I growl as I spill inside him, my body shuddering with pleasure. The feel of my orgasm is enough to push Church over the edge, too – he erupts all over Harlow's wet pussy, a low groan escaping his lips.

"Such beautiful chaos," I think to myself as I pull out of Church, the power of the moment intoxicating.

Church leans down and licks up his own cum from Harlow's pussy, holding it in his mouth. He stands and turns to me, a wicked gleam in his eye before spitting the mixture back into my open mouth. Without hesitation, I swallow it whole.

"Delicious," I murmur, smirking at Harlow who lies there, mouth agape and lust dripping from her eyes. She's completely at our mercy, and it feels like divine power coursing through my veins.

"Hope you enjoyed the show, Mary," Church says, pulling his pants back up.

TWENTY

HARLOW

REFLECTED at me through the desilvering mirror, which taints my image with black spots, is a girl wearing a pale gray- like the McGrew brother's eyes- two-piece set with white lace detailing on the ruffle sleeve crop top and edges the layers of the ruffle mini skirt. An elastic panel around the waist of both top and skirt accentuates my curves. I paired the look with white trainers, and my hair is up in a crown braid, adding cute little butterfly clips to give my rather dull look a bit more color and that whimsical feel.

We've toured most of the east coast USA and are now moving inland on our tour. We arrived in Cincinnati, Ohio, last night, after traveling most of the day from Augusta, Maine. This show is different, instead of indoors, we are doing it in the open air, in the famous Spring Grove Cemetery. Our stage is the Dexter Mausoleum. A gothic revival building, with sandstone walls adorned with vines, give the structure a ghoulish feel, a chapel sits behind the mausoleum with. The crypts below, and the stairs on either side that lead to the chapel's entrance from where we will be performing are blocked off with rusty black iron gates, and our audience will watch us from amongst the graves.

I love cemeteries, I weirdly feel at home in them. I spent most of the morning wandering the grounds, while the crews got everything ready for the evening. I found this beautiful grave in all white marble, an imposing angel with spread out wings almost looked to be eclipsing the headstone, reaching down as if awaiting to take the soul buried under its feet and fly it away to the skies above. Maybe if I lay beneath it, it will take me as well.

I must've sat there for hours, my back to the gravestone with my legs flat on the dirty ground, talking to the ghosts that rest in this place. I kept getting lost in my mind, going back to two nights ago, when Church and Parrish paid me another sexy visit. I was taught that people loving the same sex was an abomination and sin. How can someone judge such a beautiful thing as appallingly? I could watch them come undone in each other's arms any day. The deep affection, passion and devotion shared during the intimacy between the two best friends, in that moment was given my way too. Having them make me a part of this carnal dance filled my empty heart with this sense of belonging. Damn, I am falling hard but I don't think I am the only one.

This time there were no brutal words in the end that cut deep and made me bleed, just a little taunt with a wicked smirk on both of their faces as they left me, a silent promise that they are not done with me and that they never will be.

Has Satan at last sunk his claws in my skin? Am I a sinner now? Why don't I care if he has and if I am?

Maybe I am weak because I must keep pretending that I am. That's the role I was given by other people. But with them, I don't have to pretend, these men keep peeling off the facade of layers created to enclose me; The preacher's daughter, the sweet, innocent good-girl next door, and the earth-bound angel chosen to shepherd lost corrupted souls. I worry if they continue, all that will be left is me, the real me. In fact, this last time, with Church and Parrish was the second time Ive ever felt like the Harlow I was always meant to be. The first time being when all four of Paragon of Virtue's Inferno snuck into my trailer.

The shadows that follow my guys, I mean the guys, around have been somewhat more restless than usual, or perhaps because I don't ignore their presence anymore, I see them more often. They just seem to be lurking everywhere. I still don't understand this dark game they play with them, and I continue to refuse to join them. I keep clutching the cross around my neck, waiting for the instant it will burn the skin of my palm, branding me as unholy.

"Why am I resisting the inevitable? I should just give in, right? I prayed for regret. They can be mine. I want them to be mine." I whispered to the messenger of God standing tall over my head. I have fallen. I am no longer an angel, like the one I am staring at, being held captive by Him, forced to be at His side, no longer imprisoned by His word. So why do I keep suffering for Him, singing high praises about something I don't believe in anymore? Did I ever accept Him as true? Or was that another thing I put on a false front for? "I think I am done pretending. Please, forgive me. Or don't." I closed my eyes then. "I don't care Because you certainly never did, and I am done giving you all of me." When I reopen my blue eyes, I swear I see the angel cry red tears. That makes me jump to my feet, but as I look back at its face the phantasm blood is gone.

"Little mouse, you look," someone starts but never finishes their sentence. I look past my image in the mirror, seeing Bishop standing behind me by the now wide-open door for the little office inside the chapel that I have been using to get ready for tonight's show in. He is wearing his usual show attire, of black button-down shirt, with the top five undone, long sleeves rolled up, tucked in a nice pair of black distressed, skinny jeans. His shoulder length ashy blonde hair escapes from behind his ears, veiling some of his facial expression, as his eyes drop to my feet and ever so slowly lift back up, skimming every inch of me, until they meet my own eyes in the reflection. The warmth and longing written in them is unmistakable.

I chuckle, "Never pegged you for the speechless type, Bishop."

He finally moves the strands away from his face, swallowing dry before saying, "That's a bit too much leg, don't you think, Harlow?"

I turn around so I can glare at him, crossing my arms over my chest. "Are you my stylist now too?"

"All I am saying is your other outfits were less, aaahhh... revealing." Bishop seems tense as he speaks, his hands clenching and unclenching. What demons is he trying to keep at bay there?

I want to say something along the lines of them being bad influences, walking around with no shirts on, with their mouthwateringly lickable flesh and biteable muscles on full display. Abel and Parrish's low hanging shorts or joggers or Church in his boxers, doesn't help the devilish heat that comes to life in the depths of my belly. Bishop is a bit more put together, but I have caught sight of him wet and wearing only a towel quite a few times. There's only so much a girl can endure, you know? Maybe I wanted to give them a taste of their own medicine. If I have to ache for them, then they should too.

Instead, I let my arms fall at my sides and utter in defeat, "I guess, I can change if you want." And just like that, I am back to being weak and letting other people dictate my life.

"No." Bishop forbiddingly howls, grinding his teeth.

"No?" I ask, confused.

"Just," Bishop takes a deep breath, closing his eyes for a second. When his pale gray orbs find my electric blue ones, he growls, spins around and leaves. What in the heavens was that?

I am still staring at the doorway dumbfounded when a crew member comes to let me know it's time to go on stage. I have been mentally preparing myself all day to get booed off stage once more, and I am sick and tired of crying over it. I think what hurts me the most, is not their fans' wrath and hate towards me, it is waiting for the guys to suddenly realize they made a mistake by bringing into their world and send me packing. I don't want to leave. How stupid is that? That must make me a masochist.

As I am making my way to the stage, I see Church and Parrish hiding in the shadows, their heads close together in a hushed conversation, and for some reason that image makes me smile. They are adorned in ripped light wash super skinny jeans, but while Parrish is wearing a white, low-neck and oversized armhole singlet, Church is freaking topless, his demon wings out for everyone to see.

"What are you smiling about, angel?" Abel asks me, spinning his drumsticks around with his fingers. He's sitting on a road case right by the chapel's only available opening, which happens to be the entrance to the stage. He is only in a pair of vintage-looking loose denim shorts, that reach just past his knees.

"How beautiful your kind of havoc looks." I tell him and then walk out.

The night is painted black, the stars covered up by dark gray clouds, and so is the horde of people before me. I begin singing my first song and the crowd wastes no time throwing empty bottles and cups at me. The difference, from all the other shows before, is that someone actually manages to hit me in the face with a full cup of beer, which makes me stop singing mid-song. Silence follows, from me, from my band, from them. Not even the critters of night dare utter a sound. Silence so loud I wonder if I went deaf.

I take a deep breath, peering at my band behind me, the looks of pity in Ada and Abraham's eyes fractures something within me.

Gazing down at my feet I whisper, "I am ready to dance with the Devil." I chuckle at my own words and lick my lips tasting the beer they have smeared me with. I turn my electric blue eyes to the crowd and walk right to the end of the stage.

I pray

I scream those words out, just like Church does when he sings this song of theirs. These folks want Paragon of Virtue's Inferno, then I will give them what they want.

Please keep the nightmares at bay

The ones where he cuts her and bleeds her dry
The ones where he abandons her to slowly die
A seemingly innocent child I as, but you stained me in red
Now I am messed up in the head
Cause I can only love with my knife
And be the bad dream to my future dear, dead wife

I pray

My voice takes a haunting melody as I sing the song with no background music. The crowd just stands there quiet and still as if in an enchanted daze.

Please make their echoes decay
I don't want to remember anymore
How they loved the high more than me
I don't want to remember anymore
How he loved me, so I became the fee
I don't want to remember anymore
The way he reminded me of the sins I didn't wish to commit
No, I won't submit
But I pray

I pray

I know what these lyrics are about. It's their stories. It's their darken beginnings, the ones that turned them into the snarly, bloodthirsty wolves they are today. Why I picked to sing this song? Maybe I want them to know I see them, the real them,

and I ain't running away. Because I ain't afraid of the four big
bad wolves.

'Cause I gave credence to You when he walked away
No more drunken beatings 'cause you thought momma had slept
with Jack
Or Zak
No more lashes to slice through my brothers back
'Cause you were just a fucking slack
I pray
'Cause I lost my faith the day You didn't allow her to stay

Church's voice breaks right here every single time he chants
this part, and mine does too.

I pray to the one that will actually hear our craves
We rather pay his price than be Your blind obedient slaves
You should've thought of the consequences before You took all the
good out of us
You just to unjust

I pray
Yeah, I pray
Just not to the one that leads me astray

When I am done, a few heart beats go by before the crowd goes crazy, cheers and howls echoing in the darkness. I smile at their response to what I've just done. My whole body is vibrating with some sort of euphoria.

Is this what being seen feels like? Is this what being alive feels like?

I sense a presence at my rear, but I don't need to turn around to know who it is. Church's arm snakes around my middle as a hard, sweaty chest gets glued to my back. He lowers his face to my ear and tells me, "Sing 'Home' with me, baby."

TWENTY-ONE
CHURCH

"SING 'HOME' with me, baby." I hoarsely whisper into Harlow's ear. She must sense my fast-beating heart from my harsh breaths against her back, combined with the tremble in my hand holding her to me. She must know the chaos she just unleashed on all of our hearts.

Harlow tilts her head back and pivots it slightly, it coming to rest on my bare chest as her electric blue eyes find my pale gray ones. They do this triangle dance around my face, from one eye to the other down to my mouth and up to my ashen pools again, then she gives me a gracious smile and says, "Ok."

My princess lifts the microphone to her lips, without breaking our gaze, and sings the first line of the song.

Run baby run

You should've run, baby. Thats the naked truth.

Bishop and Abel were both perturbed by something, as Harlow took to the stage for her set. This aura of an impending fall and our demise written all over their faces, as they both watch her like vultures awaiting the right time to devour her.

Through the last home of the ones that came before you
Buried six feet under like you will be too

Harlow continues, spinning around in my embrace so she's facing me.

Hide baby hide

When she screams those words directly at me, I dig my nails in the flesh of her lower back, certainly leaving half-moon indentations in her delicate porcelain skin.

From the wayward pretty nightmares that desire to wolf you down

"We don't fade into obscurity in her eyes. She sees us and she isn't looking away." Bishop had said just as Harlow began to sing one of her Godly songs. Heckling from the crowd soon treading on the heels of her angelic voice, and so did the sound of crap being thrown at her.

All so our souls in sea of fire don't drown

"Only a paragon of virtue would see the lure in our neglected, cracked into a million splinters and consumed by darkness souls, but still want them. Even love them for their faults and flaws." Abel had uttered in a hushed tone. That's when it happened, the moment where everything went eerily quiet and still, just after a cup smacked Harlow in the face, dousing her in whatever drink was in there. Whatever worthless piece of shit managed to do that; they are dead. I am sending the shadows straight to them tonight.

You could've run, baby. Yet, you didn't.

Run baby run
If we catch you then you will be our final girl, baby please
'Cause we are bored of begging on our bruised knees
Too broken to love and be loved
So may as well ritually slaughter you and bathe you in blood

I howl after Harlow is done with the first verse. We are so lost in each other it's as if we are the last two people in the world.

For a little while, it's just me and her, and I am going to drink up this pretty poison like nothing else matters.

Hide baby hide

We both beg one another.

My screwed-up mind seems to be trapped between the echo of what arose before and what is taking place right now. How a somewhat numb Harlow, peered behind her at the twins that make up her band. She didn't seek comfort or mercy in these people, but whatever she saw in their expressions made her crack. From where us four were standing, buried inside the darkness of the chapel, hiding from her view, we could see my princess's alluring features perfectly. Submission and acceptance oozed out of her. She laughed quietly and mumbled something to the blue corn moon, that I don't even think the ghosts in this place could hear, before turning back around; full of confidence and with a haunting new faith in herself. Harlow spread her angel wings and showed the insignificantly weak, mortal critters that stood before her the

power she really, fucking holds.

Our sweet sacrifice

I sing.

Your untouched body is the only one that can satisfy our dark
appetite

Of all our tracks Harlow could've chosen to cover and she picked 'I pray'. Did she do it on purpose? What is she trying to tell us? She can't see us. If she did, she would've run.

Harlow, I beg of you, fucking run.

Too late to run home, baby, run home
The need to rip you open until you are choking, gasping, dying
for us
It's a hauntingly, obsessive lust

Too late to hide away, baby, hide far away
Your gore in the tip of our knife and in our hands embedded, always
and forever
As you lay spread out on the altar of our sick pleasure

My princess takes over the song we are performing, looking at me like I hung the moon and starts.

Fuck.

When Harlow finished chanting 'I pray', before the crowd raptured in hail and praise from my girl, and I walked on stage, telling her sidekicks to beat it, I knew, in that fucking instant, I couldn't kill her.

We got cursed, baby, as Eve got bitten
The price for our souls' fuck ups once written, can't be unwritten

This is the punishment, yours and ours
Nowhere to run and hide, baby, 'cause we would find you in a crowd
of thousands

Our sweet sacrifice

Harlow and I hit that last note, and in a muted tone I say to only her, "More like our sour sacrifice." She frowns, not understanding the meaning behind my words. How could she comprehend how perilous the situation we find ourselves in is? 'Home' is about her, and she doesn't even know it.

The last girl. The last sacrifice. The last hope.

How silly, the things we prayed for prior to her. Fame, money and pussy, are all but fool' trash now, dim in comparison to what Harlow fucking Abaddon is. I pray to thee dark Lord for all of our souls to be free, and that includes Harlow's. But how can that happen if she's the key?

We are a bad disease that eats away at you. We are complete and utter destruction. We are death. She can't want that. She can't want us.

Twenty-Two

Bishop

THE STAGE TREMORS beneath the cheers and screams of the crowd, quaking with the raw energy of a hundred writhing bodies lost in euphoria. My gaze, though, it never wavers from Church and Harlow — my brother and our siren vocalist — as their voices twist and meld into an enchanting symphony that ensnares the crowd's collective heartbeat.

"Listen to them," I murmur under my breath, the words drowned out by the cacophony of the crowd's rapture.

Church is different tonight. Every note he belts out, it's like he's reaching out, trying to touch something only he can see. His grey eyes, nearly mirror images of my own, are alight with a fire I've never seen before. They catch Harlow's electric blues and it's like watching a storm brew over the ocean — unpredictable and mesmerizing.

It's damn dangerous, this game they're playing with fate. With every harmonious crescendo, I can feel the pull, the tether that binds him to her growing stronger. An obsession, igniting like dry wood caught in hellfire.

He's always been the cheeky one, the heartbreaker with a

devil-may-care smirk. But now, there's no trace of that boy. In his place stands a man bewitched, hanging on every word that spills from Harlow's lips. It's a sight to behold, and a curse to comprehend.

"Damn it all," I mutter, feeling the weight of the revelation crushing against my chest. Our lives, built on chords and chaos, now hinge on the whims of a woman whose voice could command armies or crumble empires.

"Captivating, isn't she?" The words are not my own, but they echo inside my skull, taunting me with truth I cannot deny.

"More than captivating," I concede, my voice heavy with a realization that tastes like ash on my tongue. "She's got him. She's really got him."

Not once has any girl come close to lacing her fingers around Church's wild heart. Yet, here she stands, Harlow Abaddon, doing just that without even trying — or maybe she's trying harder than any of us know.

I watch Church lean closer to her, his body language screaming words he hasn't yet found the courage to say. And right then, I understand the depth of the inferno we're all standing in. This isn't just about a song or a performance. It's a dance with destiny, and the stakes are our very souls.

"Be careful, brother," I whisper, knowing full well he can't hear me. My fists clench at my sides, knuckles whitening with the effort to stay rooted to the spot while every instinct screams to drag him back from the edge.

It's an obsession, a wildfire, a love that could spell our undoing. I steel myself against it, against the temptation to intervene. For now, I'm forced to watch — watch as Church falls headfirst into the abyss that is Harlow Abaddon.

The crescendo hits, a thunderous wave of sound that threatens to sweep us all into the void. Church's voice melds with Harlow's in a harmony so flawless, it feels like the world pauses; holding its breath for them. I stand there, rooted in the shadows cast by flickering stage lights, feeling the raw energy pulsing between the pair as they pour their souls into the final notes.

"Fuck yes!" someone shouts, and then the whole place erupts, applause cascading like a waterfall as the audience screams for more. The noise is deafening, but it's nothing compared to the silent storm brewing within me.

Church throws his head back, his laughter mingling with the cheers, while Harlow beams brighter than any spotlight. They're magnetic, two celestial bodies drawn together by an unseen force, spinning closer and closer until the inevitable collision.

"Amazing," A girl screams, eyes glazed over as she witnesses the connection between them.

"Deadly," I correct her under my breath because no one understands the price of this performance. No one but me knows that with each note sung, we're signing away pieces of ourselves — and Harlow is the ultimate cost.

We've built this life from scratch, brick by bloody brick, with music as our rebellion against the chains that sought to bind us. But now, those very chains are tightening around us once more, and Harlow... sweet, feisty Harlow with her electric blue eyes... she's the linchpin.

"Like a star destined to burn out too soon," I say, my tone dark, my gaze never leaving the figures on the stage. Because if we don't hand her over, if we don't pay the price demanded by Satan himself, there will be no encore. There will only be darkness, an eternal night where our souls belong to him, forever bound to his malevolent whims.

I can't let that happen. I won't.

The last chords of our dark anthem fade, and the throngs of shadow-draped fans are still screaming for more. But my eyes are not on them. They're glued to the scene unfolding just beyond the stage's edge, where the harshness of stage lights gives way to the dim glow of backstage secrecy.

Church is there, his hand finding Harlow's waist as they weave through cables and discarded instruments, his laughter a rare harmony that doesn't belong in our songs. Harlow stayed to watch the set tonight, something she never does. It's a sound that doesn't require a microphone to resonate within me—it's too personal, and it strikes a chord no riff could ever emulate. My brother, the cheeky frontman with a voice that can command both angels and demons, looks at her like she's the dawn after an endless night.

"Amazing show, huh?" I manage to say to a passing roadie, but my voice fades into the cacophony of adulation behind us. The pang in my chest tightens, constricting like a vice around my bones. This isn't just another groupie or a fleeting fling; this is hellfire threatening to engulf everything we've fought to build.

I lean against a wall smeared with graffiti, symbols of our allegiance to a darker power, and watch Church move closer to Harlow. His fingertips brush against her temple, coaxing a rebel curl back into the soft chaos of her hair. The tenderness in his touch is foreign to these calloused hands of ours, and I know it spells trouble.

"Careful there," I murmur, too low for anyone to hear over the din of dismantling stage gear. "You're playing with fire."

But he doesn't hear me. He's caught in the gravity of her presence, lost in the electric blue universe of her gaze. And I stand there, witness to a love that dares to challenge the very forces we've pledged ourselves to—a love that might just be powerful enough to break us all.

"Get a grip, Bishop," I scold myself silently, shaking off the helplessness as if it's nothing more than stage dust on my shoulders. "Time to step up, not out."

I push away from the wall, my resolve hardening with each step. There must be a way out—a loophole in the contract, a twist in the melody we haven't yet played. I won't let Church fall, not to Satan, not to love, not to anything.

I weave through the backstage chaos, the gritty scent of sweat and volatile fervor mixes with the lingering sweetness of Harlow's perfume, a cocktail of defiance and dangerous desire that saturates the dimly lit corridor. My boots hit the ground hard, keeping time with the racing pulse in my veins.

"Can't just snuff out a star," I mutter to myself, the words a bitter melody against the hum of amplifiers cooling down. "Not when it's the only light in this godforsaken place."

My thoughts crash into each other, a cacophony of what-ifs and maybes as I try to untangle the web we're caught in. The deal was simple: our souls for fame, a contract signed with blood under a full moon. But nothing prepared us for Harlow, with her voice like a siren's call and eyes that burn brighter than any spotlight.

"Damnation's not a one-way street," I say, my voice barely above a whisper.

The realization hits like a punch to the gut, I think we're screwed.

I lean against the cold wall, my breath comes out in ragged

pulls, the weight of eternity pressing down on my shoulders. If we sacrifice her, if we offer up the girl who's become the heartbeat of our band to fulfil some twisted bargain, then we surrender our humanity, and I'll lose more than just the band, I'll lose church forever, he will not be able to come back from this.

Twenty-Three

Harlow

Everything felt right, or very wrong in the eyes of my upbringing, but I liked it. In that instant, singing the Paragon of Virtue's Inferno words, and when Church came on stage to join me in my madness, I felt free, emancipated from my sorry excuse for a life. For the first time in my 19 years on this earth I allowed myself to just do something without caring about the consequences. Maybe I've been looking at this all wrong, I wanted to heal and fly away after all, and perhaps the guys are the answer to my prayers. I just don't know who answered them, God or his rebellious fallen angel, Lucifer?

I wanted to kiss Church so bad after we sang together, but those people below us weren't worthy of seeing me surrender to one of the princes´ of darkness like that. Whenever that moment comes, where I give that hallowed piece of myself that no one ever gotten from me, I set my heart on it being amongst the shadows that consume my men, the ones that can veil us from the world that doesn't deserve us, just me and them.

I stuck around this time and watched the Paragon of

Virtue's Inferno do their thing. Instead of tears, a Cheshire cat grin reigns over my features. I could get used to this. Yes, I am on the outside looking in right now, but this feeling of belonging is there, in the fleeting but fervent glares they all cast my way.

When they finish their set, the attention Church pays me it's intoxicating. It makes me greedy for more of him, of his touch, of his looming presence over me. I can see the others observing us like we are two exotic animals in a zoo, not even of the same species, going at each other. An odd sight no doubt, but sometimes the things that we think don't marry well with together, are actually a perfect combination. Like McDonald fries dunked in any flavored milkshake. They don't look at us like we are the yuck, no, their gazes are somewhat jealous with a smidge of torment. Green with envy, but if they want my love and adoration than all they have to do is come to me and I will gladly give it to them too. And this cause of anguish, I hope they open up to me so I can help them, in any way I can, to clear their mind of whatever plagues it. I would do anything for them.

"We are heading for our little mock of a green room to cool off. Want to come with, Mary?" Church asks, brushing a curl that decided to slip from my crown braid, behind my ear. The way he says 'Mary' this time comes out as a sweet nothing opposed to a hateful nickname.

"Yes, my luring destructive siren, come with us." Parrish says, as he presses his front to my back out of nowhere, his arms hugging me around my middle, his face resting on my shoulder.

I drape my arms over his and pivot my head slightly so I can peer at the pink haired dream, and giggle when he starts batting his eyelashes at me. This man is something else. I love him. Damn, what? I mean hmmm I really, really, like him, them. It's too soon for love, right? Do I even know what love is? Because I can't say I had much of that in my life.

"Mind if I have a second. I will meet you there, I promise." I utter.

"Everything ok?" Church questions me with concern in his gravelly voice.

"Oh yeah, I just hmmm want to gaze at the haunting beauty that is Spring Grove Cemetery, one last time from the stage. Who knows when I will be back here again?" And I need a moment alone, where I am not lost in them, completely gripped by the black magic they perform for us mere mortals.

Church's pale gray eyes hold mine with such tenacity it makes me tremble, but not in fear, no, in lust, for the stuff I want him to do to me whilst staring at me like that. "You get five. If you are not by side then, me and Parrish will hunt you like hounds and drag you into the crypts of this place to give that peachy ass a good spanking. Got it, Mary?"

I whimper and squirm at his words.

"For all that is ungodly and unholy, I hope you take six minutes, pretty doe. I sooo want to see the red imprints of our hands on these ass cheeks of yours." Parrish remarks, one of his hands migrating to the hem of my skirt and going under the garment. As it begins its upwards trajectory it lifts the skirt, exposing me to some extent. Once his palm is on the intended target, my backside, Parrish squeezes it forcefully, sinking his nails into my flesh making me squeak, as I spin around and jump away from him, right into Church's awaiting arms.

One of the lead singers' palms settle flat on top of my belly, holding me to him, while the other snakes between us. Taking a different route to the one his best friend did, Church's hand goes through the waistband of my skirt to reach my ass, and with the same brute strength, seizes my other cheek.

"I am waiting, princess." He whispers into my ear.

"For?" I ask. I don't dare peer back at Church, instead I am focused on Parrish and his knife that has come out to play, the tip of the sharp object trailing up and down my left arm.

"For you to acknowledge my command, baby." The hand on my stomach starts a slow descent, dipping into the waistband at the front and only stopping when it gets to my soaking panties, capturing the sensitive area between my legs.

The rough way I am being touched, makes me moan and my knees buckle. "Yes, master, I got it." I offer up with a sultry scratchy voice.

Church grunts behind me, before stating, "Oh, baby," His hand abandons my ass and ends up on my throat, forcing my head to lean back thanks to the brusque manner he'd grabbed me. I stare up at him as he gazes down at me. "I am happy you acknowledge who owns you, but you should save pet names like that for my brother. Trust me, it will drive him wild to hear you say that to him. He loves to be told he's the boss."

Over the barrier that is my panties, Church's thumb begins to rub my bundle of nerves while two of his fingers skim up and down my wet folds.

"Yes, your majesty?" I say softly.

I can feel Parrish getting closer, and then his mouth is

leaving kisses all over my jaw and chin, his pierced tongue caressing my skin.

"Oh, I like that one, Mary."

"Of course you do. You're a stuck-up princess." Parrish jeers at Church.

"Fuck you." My ashy blonde guy bites at my pink haired menace.

"Oh, yes please. But first let's make our girl come so she can go say goodbye to dead people that live in this neighborhood."

The dark gray clouds haven't relented one bit, still covering the sky and not letting the moon and the stars cast their light within the darkness. The smell of impending rain permeates the cool air.

I stand stagnant in the center of the temporary stage, as the crew is packing everything up backstage so we can move on to the next show.

My legs still feel weak from the orgasm the boys pulled out of me. After Parrish's words, Church stroked my clit in a rash and impetuous manner until I was a convulsing spent ragdoll in his arms. But what sealed the deal was Parrish embedding the tip of his knife on the flesh of my waist, cutting me.

Staring dead ahead, I trail my fingers over the spot on my side, as I draw them back and eventually peer down at them, I see that they are smeared red. I am still bleeding.

I close my eyes to replay the image of Parrish kneeling before my trembling body to suck and lick my wound, drinking up my life essence as if he needed it to survive. My alluring vampire. A quiet moan pulsates in my throat at the imprint he left on my body, on my mind and my soul.

This weird buzzing vibrates in my ear, like the air around me just got charged up with energy of some sort, which compels me to open my eyes. That's when I see it, out of the corner of my eye, this shadow dash through the headstones. A blacken dense fog somehow darker than the darkness of the night.

I should be heading back to the boys, but this killer curiosity has taken root within me.

"Right. Time to see if the boogeyman is just a fragment of my worst nightmares or actually made of flesh and bones. Or, I guess, smoke." I say in a hush tone as I make my way off the stage through the side stairs.

The very rusty black iron gate screams at the hinges as I open it up. The moment I am through where the Paragon of Virtue's Inferno fans once stood, where the dead sleep, I run, not away, but towards the shadow.

If I want to be with Church, Bishop, Parrish and Abel, I should meet the darkness they play with face to face, right?

TWENTY-FOUR

ABEL

PERCHED atop a cluster of towering speakers, I lurk in the dim recesses of the room. My drumsticks idle between my fingers, tapping an absent rhythm against my leg. The cacophony of the after-show mingles with the ringing in my ears—a melody of lust and sweat. But it's her voice that echoes loudest in my mind, Harlow's siren song from earlier with church, entwining with the memory of her silhouette beneath the stained-glass glow.

I lean back, the image sharp as a razor in my mind: her lips parting, notes ascending like divine whispers, each one threading deeper into my veins. It's been eons or mere seconds since she sang—time warps around her. A chuckle rumbles through me, raw and laced with irony. Who'd have thought? Abel Rosson, ensnared by a pair of electric blue eyes and a voice that could coax the Devil himself to kneel.

Below, Church's white hair is a beacon in the shadowy aftermath, his tattoos of demon wings sprawled across his back as he struts among the remnants of our congregation. Parish is somewhere there too, another predator in this wild sanctuary. And they had her, just moments ago, writhing between them, their hands worshiping her body until she shattered with a pleasure that I felt splinter within my own chest.

"Damn," I mutter to no one, the word dissolving into the thick air. I've been a whore in every sense, chasing highs in the warmth of countless others, seeking something I couldn't name. But Harlow... Harlow has sunk her claws into me, leaving no room for the ghosts of past conquests. No other has even grazed my thoughts since she stepped into our twisted world, all light old money curls and that defiant gleam in her gaze.

The taste of her name is a spell on my tongue, binding me to this moment, to the silent vow I make amidst the chaos. I won't be just another soul lost to the darkness, not with her light searing through the shadows.

"Let the demons come," I whisper, a smirk curving my lips as my boots hit the floor. "We'll see who's playing whom in this unholy game."

I lean back against the cool wall, my gaze fixed on Harlow. She stands there like some ethereal guardian of the damned, her silhouette slightly framed by the moonlight trying to break through the clouds, turning each tombstone below into a stark reminder of mortality. I can't help but think that she belongs with all of us, an anchor in this turbulent sea of power and darkness we willing stepped into.

"Can't sacrifice her," I mutter under my breath, feeling the weight of the truth settle in my chest. There's no way we could let her be a pawn in the cruel games that are played out in the shadows. She's too vital, a force that binds us together even as the world tries to tear us apart.

The restlessness that's been gnawing at me begins to fade as I watch her, the endless cycle of hunger and satisfaction that has defined my existence for so long now feels like chains, and I am ready to break. She doesn't know it yet, but Harlow has rekindled something in me, some fierce desire to protect rather than possess.

My attention is hers entirely, effortlessly. It takes nothing more than a glance from those black-rimmed, electric blue eyes to pull me back into the light from the abyss. She doesn't even have to look my way; just the knowledge that she's there, amidst stone memorials of lives once lived, is enough to keep me rooted to the spot.

"Damn it, Abel, move," I chide myself, but my body refuses to obey. It's not fear that holds me; it's reverence. In this place of death, she brings a promise of life, a defiance that challenges the very essence of our existence.

"Harlow," I whisper. the name, a silent vow that I'll stand by her, come hell or high water. She is the game-changer, the piece that doesn't fit the puzzle, yet makes it whole. As she gazes out over the tombstones, a sentinel among spirits, I know I would do anything to keep her safe in this world we've created—a world that will bend to her will, whether it realizes it or not.

The moment shatters. Harlow's figure blurs into motion, a streak of pale gold and fierce determination. I'm running before I realize it, adrenaline surging as if her urgency is my command. My drumming heart sets the rhythm as I chase after her, dodging granite and marble—the silent audience to our frantic pace.

"Harlow!" I want to shout, but the word sticks in my throat. This isn't a place for loud declarations; the dead prefer whispers. I bite back the impulse and focus on the flex of my muscles, the grace of a predator that has never felt more alive.

The night air is sharp, slicing through the layers of heat left by the fading day. It carries her scent, a trail I follow instinctively, my boots barely making a sound against the soft earth. Tombstones rise like jagged teeth around me, but I navigate the cemetery with the ease of one who knows darkness as an old friend, not an enemy.

As I weave through the tombstones, I catch glimpses of her—a flash of blonde curls here, the hem of her skirt there. She moves like she's possessed, and damn if that doesn't make my blood sing. The thrill of the hunt pulses through me, but it's not her I aim to capture. Its whatever phantom has drawn her away from safety, away from us.

She comes to an abrupt halt, and I almost collide with her, stopping just short of touching. My gaze follows hers to the outskirts of the cemetery, where a shadow melds into the dark interior of a car. Through the fogged windows, the silhouettes are unmistakable—two bodies entwined, moving with a carnal rhythm that belongs to the night.

"Christ," I mutter under my breath, torn between dragging her away and letting the scene unfold. Harlow doesn't move, doesn't even seem to breathe, and that stillness in her sends a chill down my spine fiercer than the night air. They don't know we're watching, those two in the car, lost in their own world of flesh and desire.

There's a rawness to it, something primal that resonates deep within me. I stand there, caught in the moment, with Harlow unmoving in front of me. We're witnesses to an act as old as time, yet here, among the resting dead, it feels like a challenge—a battle of life against the silence of eternity.

Fuck, I should shield her from this. The after-show rituals of those demons, they're no spectacle for the innocent. But then, Harlow's not just anyone, is she? If she's to be part of our twisted symphony, she has to face the music, all of it—the dark harmonies and the bloody crescendos.

I take a step forward, silent as a shadow over consecrated ground. My heart hammers a drumbeat that screams she's already ours, in every way that counts, in every way the night whispers. With a predator's grace, I close the distance between us.

"Harlow," I breathe out, barely above a whisper, but she doesn't turn—not yet lost to me.

In one fluid motion, I wrap my arms a cage around her slender frame. My lips graze the curve of her ear, and my tongue traces a path along the softness of her cheek. She jumps—a startled bird ready to flee—but my hold is firm, unyielding.

"You're about to watch a show," I murmur into her skin, tasting the salt of her, "I hope you're not squeamish of blood."

Her body tenses against mine, a bowstring pulled tight, and I wonder if she'll snap or sing under the pressure. The anticipation is a live wire between us, sizzling through the quiet graveyard air. I can't help but think this is where we belong, amid the stone angels and whispered sins, waiting for the curtain to rise on a scene drenched in scarlet.

Twenty-Five

Harlow

THIS IS NOT what I expected, I must say. The shadow led me to a secluded area at the far end of the cemetery that someone has chosen as a parking spot. There's not much in this little slice of beaten track, apart from a grove of trees that keep me out of direct sight and the secluded opening that the car has taken sanctuary within. The dark silhouette drifts into the vehicle like smoke, billowing throughout every nook and cranny possible. The people in the car, well, they are some- what engrossed, they don't notice something else has joined them.

I sense this presence at my back but cannot turn to look, not that I need to glance to know it's Abel. I am completely lost in an erotic reverie, unable to look away from the carnal scene playing before my eyes. . . I am gripped, my feet rooted in place, while from the depths of my mind something is shouting at me to turn around and leave.

"I can't." I say in my head to the part of me that is telling me to pull away from this intimate moment between two people.

I tug my lower lip into my mouth with my teeth, as the thought of touching myself while watching them plagues my mind. "Bad girl," this little angel on my shoulder whispers, "stuff like that will make you burn in hell."

"I am already in hell." I inform the angel. "And what a beautiful place it is. Much nicer than the cold purgatory I was at before, under mother dearest thumb. At least here I feel something beyond the numbness, at least here, I have four gorgeous men by my side." I am a sinner. They have made me one. I have been touched by all four, eaten out by Parrish and Church, and I want more. I want the Paragon of Virtue's Inferno men to do everything they please with me because, I am theirs.

"Harlow," I faintly hear Abel call out to me, yet I am still adrift in my thoughts, talking to a figment of my imagination that is seeking to keep me holy, when I am done being so. His arms snake around me, one across my middle and the other from shoulder to shoulder, placing pressure against my throat. Abel licks my cheek, breaking the trance and I jump, but his hold on me is unforgiving and unbreakable, so I go nowhere. "You're about to watch a show. I hope you're not squeamish of blood."

"Blood?" I questionably ask, turning my head slightly to look into his almost black eyes. .

"That will be the grand finale. ¨ I don't get it. "Perhaps we can enjoy it until the crescendo occurs, what do you say, angel?"

"I want to pleasure myself." The words just spill out of my mouth before I have a chance to think.

"Is that so?" He asks, a smirk taking shape across his face that oozes, corruption. "I can help with that." He states, hastily lowering himself behind me, both his hands going under the hem of my skirt and seizing my panties, slowly dragging them down my legs until they reach the ground. I have no idea why I do it, but I step out of them, allowing Abel to snatch them prior to him standing back up.

He brings the fabric to his nose and takes a big breath in groaning as he exhales causing me to whimper. "You smell like sweet sacrilege, angel. Freshly touched too, hmmm, Low, Church and Parrish definitely got your juices gushing out of you."

A feeling, crossed between embarrassment and the brutal unkind voice in my head screaming "Bad girl," makes my eyes fall to the ground, whilst my cheeks take on a pinkish tinge. But Abel doesn't seem to consent to me not looking at him anymore, with his free hand he grabs my chin, thrusting my face back up, so our eyes meet.

"None of that self-deprecating shit." How does he know that is what's happening here? "Whatever the voices are saying, fuck them. Did you not like them touching you like that?"

"I," I attempt to look away, but Abel just jerks my face further back until our eyes are on each other again.

"Eyes on me, Harlow."

"Loved it." I declare suddenly.

A genuine smile pops up on his handsome face. "Yeah, you did. Sin looks good on you either way, angel. But us four, we are the only ones that get that part of you, Low. Understood?" What is it with the nickname? "Understood?" He repeats anew, more forcefully this time.

"Yes," Damn, dejà vu or what? Church and I had the same

dance, didn't we? It seems the lead singer and the drummer are more alike than they realize.

His eyes quickly dart past my face. "We better hurry, I sense the spectacle in the car is not far from ending. Also, I am keeping these as a memento." Abel notes as he shoves my panties into the back pocket of his loose, denim shorts.

"Hmmm no you are not. Abel." I tell him in a frail attempt at a stern tone.

"Haha, its cute that you think you have a say in it. They are mine now. Just like you are." His hand settles on my hip, whilst the other, still holding on to my chin, shifts my head so it's facing the same direction my body is, consequently making me look straight ahead at the mating ritual of complete strangers. "Now come on, love yourself. I will join you."

Abel repositions his body, standing somewhat to my side instead of totally against my back. Undoing the button of his shorts and lowering his zipper a little, he pries out his massive penis. The black ink on his partially bare upper body mingling with the intricate design on his length, is a sight to behold. So pretty. Oh my God, tattooed all around his pelvic area is a snake. oops. I just said His name in vain. I would ask for His forgiveness, but I'm not really that sorry.

"Low." Abel murmurs, what seems to be his new pet name for me, I hum in acknowledgement as my blue eyes arise to his. "You're missing the show."

"Right." I utter and turn my vision to the car. Abel chuckles.

What I see is obscured, thanks to the fogged-up glass, but I can make out a woman being relentlessly pounded from behind by a guy. She is perched on her knees on the passenger seat as her hands cling to the backrest, her forearms supported by the cushion. How far did they have to push the seat back for the guy to have enough space to do what he's doing?

From the corner of my eye, I notice that Abel is already jerking off. His hand moving up and down his shaft with a considerable effervescence. I bury my hand under my skirt, just like Parrish had done at the mausoleum, flashing my wet crevice to the crawlers amongst the trees. I start drawing circles around the bundle of nerves just like Church did so meticulously earlier.

I moan, the sound reverberating through the lightless night.

"Fuck, angel. Look at you." Abel says.

"I thought we were supposed to be feasting our eyes on the sexual performance transpiring before our eyes over there, Abel." I remark without looking away from the car.

"Oh, I am." He leans into me to whisper down my ear, his nails digging into the flesh of my hip. I know I am going to end up full of blemishes from their harsh touches. "Why don't you sink your delicate fingers inside of you, baby?" The vibrations of his voice and his words send a shiver up my spine.

I abide by his request and sink a finger inside of me. "Abel." I purr, closing my eyes.

The midnight silence is penetrated with the sounds of metallic screeching from the car with the grunts and moans from the occupants within, the whir of a light breeze moving through the trees, some critters of the night speaking amongst themselves, and the noise of flesh on flesh that our independent thrusting of our genitals make along with our heavy breathing.

A second finger joins the one already thrusting into my vagina as my other hand reaches out and seizes Abel's length, my eyes fly open to gauge his reaction.

"Harlow." Abel grunts in pleasure, but there's an illusion of forewarning behind it. His fingers entwine with mine as he guides my hand up and down his penis. Meanwhile, I dive my fingers in and out of myself at a hurried pace.

In the car's interior, something changes in the guy's demeanor, to the girl's obliviousness. He's still aggressively driving into her like a man possessed, but his body stiffens. Maybe he's about to cum. I notice him reaching for an something in the glove box behind his back, the way he twisted his body allows me to get a clearer look at his eyes, especially when he gazes straight at us. They are fully black.

"Abel." I mewl with a tremble in my voice.

The object he grabbed shines in his hand, as he faces the girl again, completely brushing aside us being here witnessing everything. Was that a gun?

"Abel." I whimper once more. Why am I still pleasuring myself? Why am I still giving Abel a hand job? Why If anything am I going at it more feverously.

"I hope you are ready for the climax, baby. It's coming."

Chaos unfolds soon after his words. She comes as I do, my body convulsing as my juices flow down my legs, but in a split second I am shuddering for another reason. The guy places the object to her skull just as she arches her back in ecstasy, just as he squeezes the trigger.

A loud pop rings in my ears and then silence, like my brain just decided to press mute on the world around me. Splatters of crimson stain the windows of the car, as splashes of something warm spray over my hand. I peer down, in a dazed state, at our tangled hands on his penis, continuing to jack him off in spite of everything. Abel's cum drips down my hand in a smooth caress; almost making me forget about the horror show baring disturbing, scarred and rotten fruit before us.

The gun goes off once more, which compels my eyes to snap to the murderous scene. Through the bloody patches and brain matter, you can just make out his dead corpse still connected carnally, on top of her.

My legs lose their strength and cave underneath me, as darkness consumes me, and I faint.

Twenty-Six

Bishop

Muscles aching and sweat clinging to my skin, I haul myself onto the bus—the night's performance still thundering in my veins. The dim interior is a haven from the chaos outside, where security guards are holding back the tide of stragglers and groupies whose eyes burn with a desperate hunger to touch us.

"Harlow better hurry up," Church's voice slices through the hum of anticipation that's followed us offstage.

My gaze snaps toward the open door, scanning the shadows for her familiar form. "Where is she?" My voice is sharper than I intend, edged with an unexpected concern that tightens my chest.

The darkness beyond the bus door remains stubbornly silent, offering no hint of her whereabouts. Unease coils in my gut as I wonder what's keeping her—what's drawn her away from the sanctuary we've built within these steel walls.

Church leans against the door frame of the bus, his grey eyes flickering with a mischievous spark that belies the tension in his stance. "She wanted a moment," he says, the words carrying the weight of unsaid thoughts. "But seeing as Abel still isn't here, I'm gonna assume she has his eyes on her."

"Damn right," I mutter, raking a hand through my damp hair. The thought of Harlow out there alone, with only Abel's gaze for protection, gnaws at me. "I hope so and that he's not trailing some random pussy after the show." The idea of Abel's attention straying, even momentarily, stokes a fire in my belly.

Parrish, ever the blade in a gunfight, snorts from where he's sprawled across a seat, his dyed pink hair stark against the worn upholstery. "Obsessed is putting it lightly. He's way too obsessed with Harlow to trail after any pussy that's not hers."

There's truth in the insanity that laces Parrish's voice—a cutting edge that slices through the bullshit. Abel's fixation on Harlow isn't just desire; it's something deeper, darker, something that could either bind us tighter or blow us apart. We're all teetering on the edge, but Abel? He's dancing on it with Harlow in his arms.

"Abel's got his vices, but he knows what's at stake," I say, trying to convince myself more than them. The rhythm of our lives, the pulsing beat of our vow—it all hinges on Harlow now. Our sweet, feisty siren who's unwittingly entangled in our twisted destiny.

I stride over to the worn seats and collapse onto one, grunting from the night's exertions. My shirt clings to my skin, drenched in sweat from our performance—a mix of adrenaline and stage lights. With a swift yank, I peel it off and toss it aside, muscles protesting pleasantly. The cool air of the bus kisses my heated flesh, offering a momentary relief.

"Damn, we killed it out there," Church says, his voice vibrating with triumph as he slumps down next to me.

"Baptized it, killed it, and resurrected it," Parrish chimes in, with a manic grin slicing his face.

I don't bother responding, just grunt in agreement and reach for a cold beer from the fridge, popping the cap with a satisfying hiss. The bitter tang hits my tongue, but it doesn't quench the thirst that's been burning since Harlow disappeared backstage.

"Need eyes on them," I mutter, gaze fixed on the empty doorway, willing them to appear.

"Abel's got this," Church assures, though I catch a flicker of concern in his stormy eyes. "He wouldn't let anything happen to our girl."

"She not our girl," I growl, my knuckles white from squeezing the bottle.

We sit in heavy silence, each lost in our own turbulent thoughts. Time stretches, taut like a guitar string seconds before it snaps.

And then, finally, Abel lurches onto the bus, Harlow cradled in his arms like some fallen angel plucked from the fray. My heart hammers against my ribs, the sight of her limp form igniting a blaze of panic and something fiercer—something possessive.

"Shit," I hiss, leaping up. "What happened? Why is she out?"

"Chased a shadow," Abel grunts, his expression grim as he lays her down gently on the bench-like seat to our left. "Wanted to see the aftermath—the real show."

"Damn it, Abel," I snap, feeling the protective fury rise like bile. "Why the fuck did you let her watch?" My voice is a blade; sharp and accusing as my eyes bore into him. Harlow shouldn't have witnessed the aftermath of our shows, the raw and untamed chaos we leave in our wake.

"She needs to know," Abel fires back with that infuriating calmness he always manages to muster. "What happens, who we are—she's part of this now."

"Part of this?" I scoff, feeling the familiar twist in my gut, like my insides are recoiling at the very idea. "She isn't one of us, Abel. She's our next sacrifice." The words feel heavy on my tongue, a leaden truth I can't swallow down. Slitting her throat on our altar—should be just another rite, but the mere thought tightens something in my chest, a heart I didn't think capable of such resistance.

But Abel is watching me with those piercing eyes, seeing right through the façade. "You're not fooling anyone, Bishop. Maybe it's time you stop lying to yourself."

I want to argue, to rage against his words, but my throat feels like it's clogged with ash. Abel's not wrong. Each day that passes, chips away at my resolve, the image of her blood spilling crimson against the cold stone of the altar growing more abhorrent.

And then there's Church, with his gray eyes that never quite manage to hide the storm inside. He's been too obvious, wearing his feelings like a second skin, transparent and vulnerable. It's dangerous, this attachment we're forming, these tendrils of emotion that wrap around us, binding us to Harlow in ways we never anticipated.

"Denial's a river in Egypt, mate," I mutter under my breath, but Abel hears it anyway.

"Deny it all you want, but she's changing things," Abel says, his gaze shifting toward Church. "And maybe, just maybe, that's not such a bad thing."

The dampness of the night clings to my skin as I watch Church approach Harlow with a tenderness that feels like a punch to the gut. His hands, usually cradling a mic or casting shadows on stage, are now gentle as they press a wet cloth to her pale face. Parrish, ever the wildcard, drapes a blanket over her unconscious form, covering her but not before I catch a glimpse of too much skin.

"Where are her knickers?" The question rips from my throat, raw and accusing as I turn to Abel, who's standing there with an infuriating smirk tugging at his pierced lips.

"In my pocket," he tosses back casually, patting the fabric. "And no, you can't have them back. They're mine. She gave them to me."

Bullshit. "She would never give you her kickers," I snarl, feeling the heat rise in my veins. My fists clench at my sides, itching for something to smash—anything to drown out the possessive pride in his voice.

Abel just laughs, low and husky. "Well, she let me take them off, so I claimed them." He leans against the wall of the bus, all casual arrogance and entitlement.

I glance back at Harlow, lying still and vulnerable. "Really?" It's half accusation, half plea. Can't he see how messed up this is?

"Open your eyes, Bishop," Abel fires back, his tone sharpening. "She's one of us, whether you've come to terms with it or not." There's a challenge in his stance, a dare for me to refute the truth we're all beginning to acknowledge.

"Let it be known; I don't want to sacrifice her." Abel's declaration hangs in the air, heavy and undeniable, as he strides off to his bunk.

The silence that follows is filled with the echoing beat of

my own heart, racing with a cocktail of anger and dread. Harlow, our siren and sacrifice, lies between us—unaware of the chaos she's woven into the fabric of our existence. And Abel, damn him, might just be right. She's becoming part of us, grafting onto our souls like a dark and necessary sin.

But as I watch Church's fingers stroke her cheek, and Parrish's lingering gaze as he adjusts the blanket, I know deep down the truth that claws at my insides—we're far beyond the point of denial. Harlow isn't just a name on a list; she's the storm we never saw coming, the one we can't escape.

Church's gaze pins me, a silent question etched in those stormy gray eyes. "What do we do? Call the med team?"

I shake my head, fingers drumming an impatient rhythm on my thigh. "No," I assert, my voice cutting through the tension like a serrated blade. "She's just fainted. Give her some time."

"Alright, you're the boss." Church's tone is heavy with unspoken worries. The fun and cheeky frontman seems to have left the building, replaced by concern that doesn't quite suit him.

"Go shower," I command them both, my gaze never leaving Harlow's still form. "I'll sit with her."

They exchange a glance, a shared hesitation before acquiescing. The room feels smaller as they move, sounds amplified —the zip of a duffel bag, the rustle of fabric. It's all background noise against the steady beat of my heart.

Church heads towards the cramped space we call a bathroom, his stride less certain than usual. Parrish lingers, though. He leans over Harlow, a tender gesture that seems at odds with the hard lines of his inked skin. His lips brush as light as a feather over Harlow's forehead.

"Goodnight, angel," he murmurs, and there's something sacred in the way he says it, like a prayer or a vow.

"Night, Parrish," I mutter, more to myself than to him.

The door closes behind them with a soft click, their presence diminishing with the sound of water running and the muted thud of boots hitting the floor. Alone now, I'm left with the weight of my responsibilities and the quiet breathing of the girl who's unknowingly ensnared us all.

I slide across the worn leather seat, the smell of sweat and smoke clinging to the air. Harlow's head, a delicate weight against my thigh, her curls tangled like golden vines across her pale forehead. Gently, I lift her head, so it rests in my lap, my fingers sifting through her hair, easing away the tangles with a tenderness, I didn't know I possessed. Her face is serene, untouched by the chaos of our world, and it strikes me —she's the most beautiful woman I've ever seen. A pang of something fierce grips my chest, a reminder that she is more than just a face; she is our salvation, or damnation.

"Harlow," I whisper, my voice low, as though the act of speaking louder might shatter the stillness between us. But there's no response, just the steady rhythm of her breath—a symphony in the silent confines of the bus.

Time slithers by, elusive and mocking, until about half an hour passes. That's when Harlow begins to stir, a subtle shift that sends a current of electricity through my veins. Her eyelids flutter, revealing distant and glazed eyes, like windows frosted over on a winter's day. "Harlow," I say again, a touch more urgently, and this time she gazes up at me. A look that pierces straight through, leaving no room for the masks we all wear.

"Can you hear me?" My hand reaches out, a little shaky

despite my best efforts to appear calm. I tilt her chin up, needing to see every aspect of her reaction, to understand what's going on behind those electric blue windows. "Harlow?" I repeat, my voice the anchor trying to pull her back from wherever she's drifting.

Slowly, like the first thaw of spring, she rises, sitting up from her supine position, her head slipping from my lap to hover before me. There are no words exchanged, just a shared silence that fills the space with an intensity that rivals the pounding drums during our darkest rituals. She's right there, just inches away, yet in that moment, she feels like a creature from another realm—a siren, a spirit, a secret not meant for mortal understanding.

"Harlow?" The word hangs between us, a plea for her to snap out of whatever trance she's fallen into. But Harlow, sweet and feisty Harlow with those electric blue eyes, doesn't respond. Instead, she sinks slowly to her knees before me, her hands gliding up my legs in a deliberate path toward my crotch.

What is she doing? Is this some sort of sleepwalking act?

The concern twists inside me, sharp and urgent. I should stop her, shouldn't I? Yet there's an undeniable curiosity that pins me back against the seat, my breath catching as I watch her every move. She's never been one to shy away from asserting herself, but this...

This is different.

"Harlow," I try again, voice barely above a whisper. "Can you hear me?" No response. Only the steady climb of her hands, inching closer, leaving trails of fire on my skin.

I'm torn between the instinct to protect her and the unsettling desire to see where this goes. Every rational thought screaming at me to intervene, but it's like she's cast a spell over me—the same way her voice captivates crowds, weaving magic with every note she sings.

My heart races, a drumbeat echoing in the cramped space of the tour bus. It's not just the heat of her touch; it's the fear that grips me too—fear of what we're becoming, what we're meant to do to her. Our next sacrifice...no, I can't think about that now. Not when she's here, so close, unraveling before my eyes.

"Damn it, Harlow." My tone hardens, a mix of exasperation and something darker, something desperate. "Wake up."

But she doesn't. Instead, she continues her pursuit, reaching, infiltrating...and I'm utterly helpless under her spellbound actions. The defiant part of me, the part that rebels against our twisted destiny, wants to push her away, to break the hold of whatever has seized her.

And yet, here I am, frozen, my body betraying my mind with its own traitorous heat. Whether she's aware of it or not, Harlow Abaddon, with her pale skin and unruly curls, commands the moment, holds power over me in a way no ritual ever could.

"Harlow," I breathe out once more, a final attempt to reach her. But it's clear she's somewhere far from here, lost in the shadows that we've all danced with intimately. Shadows that tonight seem to cling to her a little too possessively.

I sit back, a silent observer to the unfolding mystery, my pulse thundering loud enough to drown out the world. What the hell is happening to us? To her?

With deft fingers, Harlow reaches for the button of my jeans, her touch electric against the denim. The snap gives way under her insistence, and she dives into the task of removal with a fervor that's as enthralling, as it is unsettling. Her fingers hook into the waistband, tugging the fabric down my legs, I can't help but to lift slightly in an assist of their descent.

As they pool at my feet, my arousal makes an unapologetic appearance, the evidence of my desire glistening on the tip. Harlow's gaze locks onto it, as she licks her lips and her blue eyes darkening with an intensity that borders on possession.

"Are you just going to look, or do you want a taste?" My voice comes out rougher than intended, tinged with a raw hunger that even I can't ignore.

Without a word, she leans forward, her tongue tracing a wet line up the underside of my length. A shiver races through me, my eyes fluttering shut as I savor the warmth of her mouth. There's something primal in this act, something that transcends the shows and the rituals we've bound ourselves to. This moment feels like pure sin, and this time, I'm the willing sacrifice.

"Harlow..." It's barely a whisper, a plea wrapped in velvet darkness, "grab it."

She doesn't hesitate, her hand wrapping around me, her grip gentle yet confident. A jolt runs through my veins, straight to my balls, as her mouth descends upon the tip. The small contact is a maelstrom to my senses, threatening to unravel me completely. I groan, deep and guttural, the sound echoing in the confined space.

"Fuck," I manage through clenched teeth. She has barely begun, and already I'm teetering on the edge, ready to plunge into the abyss she's opened beneath me. Her presence, her touch—it's all-consuming, a fire that blazes brighter than any pyre we've ever danced around.

"Harlow," the name spills from my lips again, a chant, a curse, a benediction all at once. "You're killing me." And I mean it. The power she wields over me in this instant is more potent than any spell we have cast, more binding than any oath we've sworn.

This isn't the Harlow who commands the stage with her voice, who spars with wit and defiance. This is something else, someone else—some part of her awakened by the shadows we court, by the darkness we've invited into our lives. And as much as it terrifies me, I can't turn away and I don't want to.

"Deeper," I breathe, the command torn from the depths of my being. She complies, obedient to this unspoken ritual between us. And as she takes me further, the world narrows to nothing but her—the touch of her, the heat of her, the undeniable control she has over my every sense.

"Harlow..." I say it like a prayer, like it's the only word left in my shattered vocabulary. Because right now, in this breathless, stolen moment, it's all that matters.

Her head bobs, slow and purposeful, teasing the tip as I struggle for breath. "That's it, Harlow," I urge, my voice breaking with lust, "take it deeper." And she does, just like the good little girl she is—innocent yet sinful in her compliance.

She slides down, taking more of me into the wet warmth of her mouth, I'm teetering on the edge of something dark and all-consuming. "Fuck, I'm not gonna last," I confess, a raw admission that I'm about to disgrace myself. But when the head of my dick hits the back of her throat and she gags, that's my undoing. My hand finds the crown of her hair, gripping gently. "Fuck, I'm coming," I warn—or maybe plead—as the tremors start.

It's a release that's almost painful in its intensity, a hot rush, spilling over into her mouth. I can feel it, dribbling from the corners of her lips, trailing down my length towards my balls. "Now pull off and show me," I command, my breath ragged.

She obeys, sliding back with a slick pop that echoes obscenely in the close confines of the bus. Harlow looks up at me, her mouth opening to reveal the pearly evidence of my cum resting on her tongue. "Fuck, that's a good girl," I praise, a surge of possessive satisfaction coursing through me. "Now swallow."

Her lips close, and she swallows, her throat working to take down every last drop. It's an act of submission, of control, that brands itself onto my soul.

I'm a goner. Screwed beyond measure because there's no way I can sacrifice her now. I want to keep her—need to. Running a hand down my face, I watch her still kneeling before me, catching a glimpse of something unsettling in her gaze—a flash of black that sends a shiver down my spine. I blink, but it's gone.

Rising gracefully to her feet, Harlow breaks the spell. "I'm going back to my trailer. See you in the morning," she says, her tone detached, as if nothing out of the ordinary has occurred.

And just like that, she walks out, leaving me alone with the throbbing silence and a heart full of questions. What just happened? Who is she, really? And what am I going to do with her?

I jerk to my feet, the cold reality slamming into me like a freight train. My hands are shaky, fumbling with the button of my jeans as I hastily pull them back up over hips, still feeling the ghost of her touch. "Was that just a dream?" I mutter to myself, the words tasting bitter in my mouth.

"Fuck," I growl, scanning the empty space where Harlow's enigmatic figure had stood just moments ago. My pulse races, echoing the throbbing confusion that tightens around my skull. Was she possessed? The thought is a wild, skittering thing, creeping along the edges of my mind with terrifying possibility.

The bus feels suddenly claustrophobic, the air too thick. I run a hand through my long white-blond hair, pushing it back from my face as I try to make sense of the encounter. I'm no stranger to the bizarre, to the dark embrace of the supernatural that has always twined with our music and our lives. But this? This was something else entirely.

"Shit, what the fuck just happened?" The question is a whisper torn from the depths of my gut, raw and needy. I can't shake the image of her eyes, the brief flash of black that seemed to swallow the light. And then the pure detachment, as if she hadn't just unraveled me with a single touch, as if she hadn't just consumed part of my soul.

I stalk to the window, peering out into the darkness for any sign of her. But the night holds its secrets close, shrouded in shadows that laugh at my attempts to understand. I'm left with nothing but the echo of her voice, the memory of her warmth, and the undeniable truth that whatever just transpired, has irrevocably changed everything.

Twenty-Seven
Harlow

The light of day cuts through the withering travelers' wagon, as I jolt upright, wide awake in my bed, drenched in sweat. the sheets tangled up all around me like shackles, keeping me prisoner in a cocoon of, what seems to be my own making. Once I get myself unfettered from them, I creep across the bed until I am sitting at the edge, with my feet touching the bitterly cold floor.

"What in the heavens happened last night?" I ask the haunts in the old trailer, but they don't react.

I can effortlessly hark back to the show, singing one of the boys' songs and then performing 'Home' with Church. A smile pops up in my face at the beautiful echo that moment with the lead singer was. After that it was the guys turn on stage, which is probably the first time I stayed and watched the whole thing. -They are a sight to behold when they are doing their thing. - In the wake of that, stuff starts to get hazy; flashes of the salacious instance with the two best friends, where I stood alone on stage and saw a shadow swiftly walk amongst the dead.

"I chased after it." I utter, seeking to conjure up the hindered memories, forcing them to come to the surface, to become clearer. "There was a car eclipsed by the darkness of the clouded night, a grove of trees concealing two people dancing to a carnal ballad." I pause in my words to no one. "And Abel was there, at my side." I close my eyes, a moan escaping my parted lips. I rub my legs together trying to smooth the ache in my core as my brain elicits small bursts of the two of us, onlookers of someone else's innermost and intimate moment while loving ourselves.

My electric blue eyes open wide as I jump off the bed, "Oh my God." I cover my mouth with both my hands, attempting to shroud a weep. "The guy shot her, and then himself." That's when everything goes black. I must have fainted. "I'm an eyewitness to a murder done in the heat of passion." Literally.

Abel must have carried me here. But there's this residue of something else that I can taste in the tip of my tongue. An encounter done in the dead of the night, in the main living area of the tour bus between me and Bishop.

"I wouldn't. Would I?" Oh, dear me, please tell me it was just a wet dream? A very, very lucid slumbering fantasy where I sucked his length. They have to be fanciful, the images playing in my head; it was like I was gazing through the looking glass, drifting through the motions, going with the current of another thing pulling at my strings. I was aware of what I was doing, but I could do nothing to stop it.

What should I do? I mean, I should call the police about the gruesome deaths that took place last night, right? But perhaps Abel has already done it. Maybe I should go to the guys, talk to them, before doing anything stupid. Maybe they can help me make sense of it all. Let's face it my survivor instincts are long gone, along with my faith of someone that never really cared about me and my sanity. May as well know all the rules of this baneful game the Paragon of Virtue's Inferno members play in the dark. Even though I am a little embarrassed if my thoughts with Bishop, actually came to fruition, because I never have done that before, I must've sucked. No pun intended.

Once I get myself presentable enough, I make my way to the tour bus. I don't know if they will be awake already, but if not, I will wait I guess, I have nothing but time. I don't bother knocking and just go right on in. I notice the boys all gathered around the table, which makes me halt in my stride just as their conversation dies the second the door behind me shuts and they see me.

"guys." I say in a way of greeting.

They don't appear to have been up from long, if the messy bed hair on all of them and the lounge wear, or hardly any clothing on Church, is anything to go by.

"Little mouse, how nice of you to grace us with your presence." Bishop utters. "Why don't you take a seat? We should talk." Well, I did come here for that, but when the older McGrew says it in that grave manner of his, it makes it seem like I am not going to enjoy what I'm about to hear.

I nod and wend my way to them. Just when I am about to take a seat next to Church, one of his arms snakes around my belly and he pulls me into his lap. His other arm joins the first and we find ourselves in a sweet embrace. An immediate calm creeps over my skin at his touch and I feel right at home in his arms. This is why I didn't struggle, I happily bend to Church's will, if this is the sensations he elicits within me.

"You know it's rude to just barge right into places like that, princess. What if we were doing something naughty?" Church whispers in my ear. His hug tightens even more. I can't get any closer to him than this; my back is already flushed against his naked front. What is he trying to do here, meld our bodies together?

"Without me? Now that would be cruel, Church." Wow, I didn't just say that out loud? And with a provocative undertone too.

Parrish starts laughing from his seat right next to me and Church, like he's possessed. I close my eyes and groan. I can feel myself blush, my cheek burning up as if I have a mild fever. Once the pink haired jokester gets himself under control, he tells me, "Pretty doe, I knew you were the perfect revival to our screwed-up souls."

Bishop clears his throat, which makes snap my eyes open and look straight at the man in front of me. "I think we should discuss what happened late last night?"

Does he mean the oral sex? "Ok." I vocalize quietly. "Was I bad?"

"Bad? Harlow, what were you thinking running after a shadow?" Bishop forbiddingly asks. Oh, we are starting with that. Wait. Is the guy with shoulder length ashy blonde hair mad at me?

"Hmmm I guess curiosity got the best of me." I admit.

"The dark varmints are dangerous. What they do in the hush of the night..."

I interrupt Bishop, "Did the shadow make him do it?" I direct my question at Abel, since the man full of tattoos, was the one with me amid the trees, his almost black eyes bearing witness to the same gory act mine did.

Abel peers at Bishop, who nods to a question not asked,

before the drummer for Paragon of Virtue's Inferno looks back at me and says, "It's more complicated than that, angel."

"Then help me understand. I promise not to chase any more blackened smoke figures, if y'all tell me your story. I want to be part of this. Let me in, please." I beg.

Twenty-Eight

Bishop

I sit there, the weight of the world on my shoulders, my gaze locked with Harlow's. She's perched on Church's lap, oblivious to the turmoil that's raging inside me. The air is thick with tension, every breath I take is laced with the heaviness of impending doom.

"Harlow," I start, my voice a low rumble, "I'm very certain you do not want to be a part of this...." My words hang between us like a sword ready to sever our fates. Do I drop the truth on her like a bombshell, let it explode and watch her flee? Or do I sugarcoat it, give her the version dipped in honey, so she stays close, and we all get a shot at freedom?

I grind my teeth, feeling the familiar burn of responsibility singeing my insides. As band manager, as the guy who plays the bass like it's an extension of his own dark soul, I'm used to making the tough calls. But nothing has ever weighed on me like this.

"Harlow," I say, bracing myself for the impact of my next words, "we've been dancing with demons." Her eyes widen, but she doesn't move, still as a statue where she sits. "Literally.

We made a deal at a crossroad, sold our souls for a shot at something better than the crap life had dealt us."

Harlow's eyes, a tempest of blue, hold mine with an intensity that could outshine the burning light of any pyre. She shifts, her movements deliberate and slow, atop Church's lap. I catch the flicker of discomfort in his grey gaze, the way his jaw tightens ever so slightly. The man is a ticking time bomb, every inch of his lean, tattooed form straining against the temptation she unknowingly wields.

"So, we...um," I grunt out, my fingers drumming on the armrest of my chair, each tap echoing the urgency thrumming through my veins. "So, we—" I nod to Church, then to Abel and Parish, our shared history, a shadow that bonds us, closer than a second skin—"we didn't have the luxury of an easy start. Hell, it was harder than most can imagine."

I watch as Harlow's brow creases, her biting curiosity mingling with a growing realization. Her gaze doesn't waver though, and for that, I silently commend her strength. There's steel beneath that soft exterior—a steel that might just see us through the hellfire we're dancing around.

I lean forward, elbows digging into my knees as I lock eyes with Harlow. "We scraped by on nothing," I admit, a rough edge to my voice that comes from years of carrying burdens too heavy for most. "I pulled double shifts working every day. All so Church here could finish school."

Church's eyes are shadowed with memories, his smirk a ghost of what it usually is. He's silent but the nod he gives speaks volumes. It's an acknowledgment of the sacrifices made, of the grimy trailer that we called home, the one that seemed to shrink with every breath we took inside its metal walls.

"Didn't touch a textbook myself," I continue my voice a low growl of defiance. "Education for me was the art of survival, making sure there was enough money for a loaf of bread, or to keep the heat running during those bone-chilling winter nights."

Harlow's lips part slightly, her gaze never flinching. There's a hunger in her to understand, to peel back the layers of who we are, of what has shaped us into the men before her now.

"Then, Church had an idea," I say, and even now, the weight of that moment crashes into me, a tidal wave of desperation and reckless hope. "A crossroad, both literal and figurative, where the air buzzes with a power you can taste on your tongue."

Harlow leans in, her breath a whisper against the charged silence. "What kind of idea?" Her voice appears steady, but there's a slight tremor there, a vibration of fear mixed with curiosity.

I glance at Church, his grey eyes reflecting the darkness of our past, the wings inked on his back a testament to the flight he's always chasing. "The kind that's born from the pits of hell itself," I say, the truth tasting bitter. "We summoned a demon, made a deal that'd either be our salvation or our damnation."

"God, why?" Her words are barely audible, a feather's touch on the heavy air between us.

"Because when you've got nothing," I reply, the words etching themselves into the room, "you'll risk everything just to feel like you're holding something—even if it's just a deal with the devil." I say taking a breath and continue.

"We had ten years," I start, my voice rough as gravel, "to claw our way out of the dirt, to build something that lasts."

My fingers continuing to drum on the worn armrest of the couch, keeping time with the silent rhythm only we know. Harlow's eyes, those electric blue storms, are wide but unflinching. "It's part of the deal. The shadows claim what they will while we play. It keeps the demon placated, keeps us alive."

I can feel the weight of Parish's gaze, his presence a solid force in front of me. Abel leans forward, his tattoos shifting with the movement, an intricate dance of ink and skin. He's always been the one to see the silver lining, no matter how tarnished it is.

"Look, if you'd seen the shithole we crawled out from, you wouldn't think this deal's so bad," Abel interjects, his voice carrying a cocky edge that's become his signature. "We fought tooth and nail to stand where we are now. It's our last year, then we're free." His hair falls into his eyes as he gives a half-shrug, like he's talking about something as mundane as waiting out a lease.

"Free," I echo, tasting the word. Free is a foreign concept, a language we've never been fluent in. I look at Harlow again, searching her face for signs of flight or fight.

Harlow's gaze pierces through me, a silent accusation in the depths of her wide, hazel eyes. Her lips part, the words spilling out from between them like venom. "You traded souls for fame, so you could eat at night..." The disbelief in her voice is a physical blow, striking deeper than any blade.

Church, ever the charmer with his mess of white hair and sinewy tattoos, doesn't miss a beat. "Yes, but we did get more than just food," he retorts, his grey eyes steady on Harlow. His voice is laced with that same cheekiness that crowds love, even now, when the stakes are this high. "I mean, we got famous, our band is doing well, and we have enough now to live happily forever."

The air thickens around us, charged with an electric tension that crackles and pops like a live wire. Harlow shifts in Church's lap, discomfort etched across her face as the realization sinks in. "So let me get this right," she says, her voice steadier than I expect, "you allow others to die so you can live..."

"Okay, okay, I'm a need a minute." She stands abruptly, her movements rigid, every line of her body screaming resistance.

"I'm a go get ready for tonight..." she mutters, and there's a tremor in her voice that she tries to mask. She strides towards the door, her back straight, spine molded of steel and resolve. "Ummm, I'll see you on stage," she calls over her shoulder without looking back.

And then she's gone, leaving behind a silence that roars louder than any concert crowd. The door closes with a soft click, an anticlimactic endnote to the tumultuous symphony we've just survived. For a moment, none of us move, each lost in our own inner thoughts about the precipice of fate we have found ourselves standing on.

Parish breaks the silence. "You think she's gonna run?" he murmurs, his voice a low growl of concern that rumbles through the tension-soaked room.

Church lets out a raspy chuckle, the sound more bitter than amused, and runs a hand through his disheveled hair. His tattoos seem to writhe on his skin as he shifts, muscles tense beneath the ink. "If you could've felt the heat from her pussy as she sat in my lap, rubbing on my dick that whole time, you'd be as inclined as I am to say nope..." His grey eyes glint like steel under a stormy sky, but doubt lingers there—a shadow threatening to eclipse his usual cheeky confidence.

"But I don't know, maybe." Church's gaze drifts toward the door Harlow disappeared through, and his voice drops to a whisper, edged with something like fear—or is it hope? "I think her heart and head are at war right now."

TWENTY-NINE

HARLOW

My men made a deal with no money to their name
Left the demon with nothing but their souls to take
From the hell of a past that left them beaten and defamed
They gouge their way-out leaving death in their wake

I CAN'T BELIEVE CHURCH, Bishop, Parrish and Abel bargained with the Devil.

What were they thinking?

It breaks my heart to know that they struggled and suffered so much, that they thought this was their only way to, how did Bishop put it, claw their way out of the dirt. The vulnerably behind Bishop's voice as he gave a glimpse of their sad past, almost made me abandon the cocoon his brother had me in, crawl on all fours across the top of the table just so I could reach him and straddle him, engulfing the older McGrew with my arms and legs. Not out of pity, because they wouldn't want me to feel sorry for them, that's not why they told me the truth, but out of kinship. We were all deprived, one way or another, of the liberty to just follow our dreams. I never lacked money, but I did lack love and support. Unlike them I didn't have friends or... even a real family that would stick by my side even while making a stupid pact with the Devil. Now, that's true riches. I want that. I still want to be part of this with them; I just need a moment to gather my thoughts about all of it.

I should be getting ready to go on stage in a little while, but this dithering feeling of not knowing how to proceed has me jotting down words as a distraction. I don't see the point in going in front of a crowd of thousands and sing my silly Godly songs anymore.

"To keep the shadows at bay," I croon as I write the lyrics down, "my men need to feed them while they play." This is the part of the story that doesn't sit well with me. Innocent souls are being sacrificed just so they can live on. But are these folks as guiltless and sinless as I am imagining them to be? What happens if they don't let the dark evil spirits drag the unknowing souls to Satan's unhumble abode? Would they take my men instead? That thought scares me. Perhaps I am ok with it if it means I get to keep them in the land of the living.

I have a feeling that something has been left untold though. If father's preaching has taught me anything, it's that contracts with the Devil are signed in blood spilled by the hands of the ones that want to do business with him. Did they neglect to divulge that part on purpose? Or did I flee too soon and not give them the chance to get to that?

A sting on my throat, like my flesh has just been sliced open, makes me pause on my scribbles and whimper. My hand grasps my neck, seeking to stop the phantom sensation. "What in the heavens?" But I don't have time to mull the feeling over as my phone begins blaring with an incoming call. That can't be good, the only people that ring me are Gabriel or mother dearest, and it looks like it is the later. She must have seen the tabloids by now.

Gabriel has actually sent me a few magazine articles where it looks like I am the hot topic of the moment. Headlines that read 'Abaddon angel lends her voice to the fallen' to 'Paragon of Virtue's Inferno men turn good girl bad' and the one that is definitely getting me in the most trouble, 'preacher's daughter falls for the princes of hell', thanks to all of the pictures of me and Church. Damn, we do look in love in those.

"Hello." I answer in a subdued tone.

"Harlow Magdalene Abaddon, I am very disappointed in you." Mother dearests outraged voice howls through the phone.

"Mother." I try to interject, unsuccessfully. What was I thinking? You don't interrupt mother dearest when she's talking.

"You are to leave those disgraceful sinners and that foolish tour right this instance. They are tarnishing our image, Harlow." Our image? Not mine, but ours. Because nothing is ever about me, it's about them, right? "I warned your father they were going to be a bad influence on you, young lady. You are too gullible and naïve, the perfect prey ripe for the picking." Says the person that has been manipulating me my whole life. These, let's call them attributes, weren't a problem when I was under her thumb.

I want to scream, "What happened last night is not on them, they didn't make me do anything, it was all me," but what would be the point? She wouldn't listen because it doesn't go with the narrative that is in her mind.

"I called Gabriel, he's arranging a flight for you to come back home…"

"NO." I shout suddenly.

"Pardon you, young lady. You don't have a say in this, I am your manager, and I am telling you that you are done with those disgraces." Mother dearest declares forbiddingly.

"But you ain't my manager no more, mother. Didn't you sign a contract, handing over the manager role to Bishop?" I ask her, somehow remaining calm, cool and collected, which is something I never am when speaking to her.

"I did no such thing, don't be silly, child."

"Hmmm you did though. When you merge our tours, you gave him control over my career for the duration of it." I might've asked Gabriel for the contract, he's part of my record label so I knew he would have a copy. I mean, it's my life that is on that piece of paper, which two people just exchanged without ever consulting me. I had the right to at least know what it said. "So, until Bishop McGrew instructs me to leave, I am not going anywhere, mother."

"I don't know what has gotten into you, young lady, but you better wake up from this little fairytale you think you are a part of right now. I wasn't going to tell you this because it is none of your business, but your father and I looked into their past." They did what? "Your father sent you there on a divine mission to bring the poor unfortunate souls lost in the darkness of their own creation, to us. But, darling, people like those four don't deserve salvation. They are trailer trash, Harlow. Unworthy of us, really."

"What did you just call them?" I demand, very much upset at her words.

"Trash, Harlow. Even their parents left them to fend for

themselves. And that Parrish kid, there is, without a doubt in my mind, something wrong with him. Did you know that his dad stabbed his mum to death while he was under the table? That ought to unbalance someone. Those men are broken and worthless."

"Thank you, mother." I utter, my voice charged with sorrow and my body shaking with anger, as silent tears cascade down my face, I hold on to the phone with a death grip.

"For what?" She questions me, confused.

"For opening my eyes and showing me where true evil really lies."

Mother dearest expels a deep breath before remarking, "Good. I will tell Gabriel to send you the plane tickets…"

"You got me wrong, mother, I am not going back." She made a mistake berating my men, especially my sweet yet unhinged pink haired guitarist. So, what if they are damaged, that's what lures me to them, what makes the Paragon of Virtue's Inferno worthy to me. If she wants to tear me down with her words, punish me with her fists, fine, I can deal. But them? That's out of bounds. Mother dearest doesn't know them, yet she thinks she can just judge them and their past like she's all that. "They aren't the evil ones, everyone else is. We are just the broken, ones looking for a way to survive this fucked up world."

She gasps, "Harlow Magdalene Abaddon, foul language will hail straight into hell."

"I'm already there, mother." I announce, before hanging up the call.

THIRTY

PARRISH

BACKSTAGE, the tension is a living thing – pulsing, electric. The crew members dodge around us, a ballet of urgency in the dim lighting. Harlow's absence gnaws at me, a void where normally her light would fill the space with warmth.

"Where is she?" I mutter to no one in particular, my voice rough with concern. She's still holed up in her trailer, and Bishop's words hang like a guillotine over our heads. He'd delivered part of the truth with the bluntness of a sledgehammer, and now there's a chasm of silence between us and her.

I slip my hand into my pocket, my fingers curling around the familiar shape of my knife. It's an extension of me, the blade that knows all my secrets. Pressing the tip against my thumb, I relish the sharp sting, the way it grounds me, even as my stomach coils tighter. Fear, dark and bitter, tastes like bile on my tongue. What if the complete story unravels her? Drives her away from our twisted sanctuary?

I run a hand through my hair, restless energy coursing through my veins. I've tried to lock away the darker parts of myself, the ones that crave the cut of a blade or the burn of a high. But it's a battle, every damn day, because feelings? They're messier than a back-alley brawl, more tangled than the chords we thrash out on stage.

"Focus, Parrish," I mutter under my breath, a silent command to keep my shit together.

My gaze flickers across the dimly lit space behind the stage, the heavy air punctuated by the distant roar of the waiting crowd. My heart hammers in my chest, but not from fear or adrenaline. No, it's all because of her—Harlow—and Church too. They're my fix now, the craving I can't shake. Each glance, each accidental brush of skin sets me ablaze, a hunger so fierce it might consume me.

There's an ache in my palms, a yearning to reach out, to feel the silk of Harlow's hair between my fingers, to trace the lines of Church's inked skin. But I hold back, clenching my fists until my nails dig crescent moons into my palms. It's not the time, not when the weight of what awaits us presses down like a coming storm.

"Get it together," I chide myself silently.

Rising anticipation coils tight in my gut as seconds stretch out like lifelines. We're bound together, the four of us, in this twisted dance of destiny and desire. And I'll be damned if I let my own turmoil trip us up now.

The pulse of my heart hammers in my ears, a staccato rhythm that syncs with the buzzing energy backstage. Adrenaline, my wicked dance partner, twirling me into a frenzy as we wait for Harlow.

"Stop fidgeting," Church's voice rumbles against the shell of my ear, his arms encircling me from behind—a grounding force to the chaos of my thoughts. "She'll be here. She needs time. Don't you see the darkness that swirls in her eyes? She is one of us, man. She is one of us."

I nod, not trusting my tongue to weave words that make sense. He's right. The same shadows that haunt my dreams lurk in the depths of Harlow's gaze. She's intertwined with us, inseparable, another chord in our twisted symphony. It's why my emotions are a storm surge threatening to break the levee —I can't lose her to the madness or fear.

"Church," I start, my voice a low growl of resolve, but the sight of Harlow cuts the air from my lungs.

She's striding toward us, an avenging spirit clad in white. The simplicity of her dress belies the complexity of the aura she carries, an ethereal presence glowing amidst the grime of our world. Her blonde curls bounce with each determined step, a stark contrast to the electric blue eyes that blaze with a fire, that could only be forged in hell's deepest pits.

"Harlow," I breathe out, all else fading into insignificance. The defiance in her stride, the unwavering set of her jaw—it's as if she's donned armor, ready for whatever battle lies ahead. An angel with the heart of a warrior, she owns every inch of the space around her.

And in that instant, the edge dulls within me, replaced by a burning need to stand beside her, to fight with her, for her. The blade, the drugs, the sex—they're nothing compared to the power she wields over my soul.

"Damn," I mutter under my breath, awe mingling with a fierce protectiveness. We've gone straight and narrow for her, but now it's clear—she doesn't need our protection. She's the queen in this game of chess, moving pieces into place with a grace that leaves us all humbled.

Harlow's stride halts inches from me, the world narrowing

to the space between us. I'm a ship getting dragged out to sea, Church's embrace my only anchor, until her gaze pierces through me, as sharp as the blades I favor. Her eyes are whirlpools of unsaid things, depths I'd plunge into without a second thought.

"I want your shirt. Give it to me now." Harlow commands, her voice slicing through the tension like one of my honed knives.

Church's arms retreat from around me, leaving a cold void that's instantly scorched away by the urgency in her tone. With deft fingers, I yank my shirt over my head, the fabric tearing across my skin, a silent pledge laid bare.

My shirt leaves me, and Harlow sheds her white dress as if casting off a chrysalis. She stands there, an ethereal vision in cotton that clings to her like sin. Lust punches through my gut, fierce and demanding. I clutch myself, desperate to tame the beast she so effortlessly rouses. The smirk playing on her lips tells me she knows exactly what she's doing to me.

She drapes the shirt over her delicate frame, and it swallows her whole, cascading down to her mid-thighs like a flag claiming territory. Harlow bends gracefully, nimble fingers snatching the white cord from where it lies discarded on the floor, remnants of her shed innocence. With purpose, she encircles the soft fabric around her waist, the belt pulling the material tight, accentuating the dips and curves I've memorized already.

"Baby, you look like an avenging angel dressing in a Paragon of Virtue's Inferno shirt," Church groans from behind me, his voice thick with desire and something darker—admiration, maybe even reverence.

I nod, silently concurring with Church's comment, because words fail me when my eyes are feasting on the vision before us. Her golden hair tumbles over the borrowed shirt, each curled strand seeming to catch the dim backstage light and set it ablaze. Abel slinks forward, every move deliberate as he tucks a few of those rebellious locks behind her ear, his touch both possessive and tender—a contradiction that defines us all.

"There you are, my queen," Abel murmurs, voice low and resonant, echoing the beat of drums he masters with such ease.

Harlow's smile, it's like a shot of adrenaline straight to my heart. She turns, her gaze locking onto Bishop, who's a statue among the chaos of backstage life. The muscles in his jaw twitch, the only sign he's not as in control as he tries to appear.

"Don't worry, I got this," she tells him, her voice steady and sure—a lighthouse cutting through fog.

Her confidence is all the armor she needs as she strides onto the stage, the echo of her determination, reverberating in the hollow cavity of my chest. We all scramble after her, a frenzied clambering to get a view from the wings. The need to witness Harlow in her element, to see her command the space, it gnaws at me with sharp teeth.

"Damn right, she's got this," I mutter under my breath, though no one hears me over the roar of the crowd.

The lights hit her like a baptism by fire, her form an ethereal beacon amidst the sea of darkness that cradles the audience in its embrace. I can't tear my eyes away—don't want to —as the murmurs of anticipation from the crowd crescendo to a deafening demand for the spectacle we all know she'll deliver.

"She is one of us," I whisper to myself. "She's unstoppable."

Harlow's silhouette casts a long shadow over the sea of faces, and with each step she takes, I feel the shift—the transfer of power from us to her. We are nothing without her.

THIRTY-ONE
CHURCH

HARLOW ABADDON IS a mare's nest, a heavenly hoax created by her label, but mostly so by her self-righteous, pious parents. Now my princess, she is a beautiful kind of chaos that rival's the tenebrous hail of mine and my band mates. It is the little moments that betray her make-believe, where I know she was made to be ours. The moments where she lets her genuine self-show, her darkness poking through the cracks that are forming across the character created to ensure her survival.

I am afraid for all of us, because I know I am already too far gone, I love her. And so does my pink-haired, best friend and lover -if his angst over being deprived from our pretty preacher's daughter is anything to go by. - His addiction is showing, Harlow is his newest drug, and he's very much hooked and highly dependent on her. I could sense him playing with his knife; a dead giveaway of his anxiety, so I do what I have been doing for years, comfort him with my touch.

Watching her sashay her way to us backstage, commanding Parrish to give her his t-shirt was already a fucking turn-on, but to have her strip down to her cute nude, cotton lingerie set, damn, I was more than ready to burst through the zipper of my pants.

The other two are in just as deep as Parrish and I, attempting to swim through the same treacherous, dark waters of these turbulent feelings. As the four of us feast our eyes on a badass version of Harlow, dressed in our bands tee, that barely covers any flesh on her upper thighs, leaving the rest of her legs completely exposed, her gorgeous old money blonde curls bounce with each step away from us that she takes, we know we are damned if we do, and damned if we don't.

"If only we had time to find someone else." The daunting words unwantingly flee my lips.

"Way to dampen the mood, Igreja." Abel snaps at me.

Igreja meaning Church in Portuguese, don't know where he just pulled that from.

Abel, never cared for anyone or anything, the fucker can barely stand us, and we are his family, yet when he touches our girl, he does it with such tenderness, it's as if she is the most precious thing to him. Quite at odds with the pure hate he shows the rest of the world. I wonder if their highly strict and God-fearing backstories have some parallels. Satan, I hope not. Abel's uncle was a monster, he used his religious-ness as an excuse to punish a younger Abel. If Harlow's parents so much dared to lay a finger on her, I am going to kill them.

"It's her or us, Church." Bishop reminds me. My dear big brother, forever the fucking protector, hanging by a whisker on an unbalanced tightrope, unsure of who to save. He would offer himself up, if he knew that would bail us all out from this devilish mess.

From the moment she graced us with her angelic presence, the guy was doomed to fall just as hard as we were. His concern for Harlow is borderline proprietorial, she's his, and knowing my brother, he holds on to the few people he plucks up the courage to love, tightly. Bringing Harlow here was a sweet but selfish deed that turned sour; she's the fucking last sacrifice and, as it seems, the only girl that could, and did, crawl into all of our black hearts and nestle herself very far within them, rendering us powerless and unable to remove her. This is going to break Bishop, shatter every one of us. The Devil won't just take our souls, he will take our hearts to. We are dead no matter what.

Bishop speaks again, "And the shadows already took notice of Harlow, had a hold of her, what are we to do?" He told us what happened last night between him and a somewhat possessed Harlow, where she gave him, what he described to be, the best head of his life. That got us all riled up; the shadows are already messing with her, it's too late now.

The demon's don't monkey around with you, unless your soul is at least a little bit lost. Fuck, was the darkness already there, or did we put it there? Did we taint Harlow's soul by playing with our forbidden fruit? Damn, we really are bad seeds; poisoning and spoiling everything we touch.

Silence falls amongst us as Harlow walks out on stage like she owns that bitch, "Hey, my pretty ghouls, how y'all doing?" Cheers actually erupt at her words. She goes straight to her band after addressing the crowd, a conversation that starts with all smiles soon turns into a heated discussion. No one can hear what's being said, but as the twins leave the stage with sullen looks on their faces, Harlow walks back towards us, simultaneously announcing, "Well, it looks as though it's going to be just you guys, me and my guitar from now on."

"This ought to be good." Parrish comments, rubbing his hands together.

Harlow ends up covering a bunch of our old songs, her voice seeping through with gobs of emotion, making it seem like they are her stories she's telling. She doesn't touch any of her own stuff until, "Y'all mind if I sing you a brand-new song? I promise it's nothing like my previous music. Y'all can be my judge, jury and executioners, what do you say?" Our followers howl, blessing her plea. "Ok. Thank you. It's called 'Pray to my men'." She declares, as she strums her first note on the guitar.

There are shadows dancing at the edge of my life
Toy soldiers to a devilish lord and master
Ripping apart the fabric of my blind faith with the tip of a knife
Committing to paper in gore a brand-new chapter
Done devoting myself to the wrong God
'Cause He won't listen to the laments of hurt of the broken and
flawed

Fuck. Harlow's lyrics, melody and vocals sound like a dead ringer of Paragon of Virtue's Inferno stuff. Honestly this rivals our junk impeccably. Cementing even more that my princess is one of us.

I pray to my men, now

A tingle shoots up my spine as she screams, with a broken voice, that part of the song.

'Cause, he's the only Church I want to kneel at
Swallowing it all down, even the spiteful words he has spat
An unhinged Parrish that cuts deep and bleeds you dry
Sucking it all up, my sweet rosé, make me want to die
A controlling Bishop giving me his unholy orders
Licking my wounds, submit and surrender to the sweet sinful
tortures
Abel, baby, are you the martyr of this story, or am I?
Impaling and gaping, getting me addicted to this dark high

"Unholy fuck." I utter. Her verses are to die for. She is giving all of herself away, her feelings and desires, dropping our names but masking them in between double meanings.

Pray to my men

'Cause they coax me, to fall from grace
What's the fun in being good anyway?
Strip me from my pretty white lace
Let's roll around in the hay

Parrish giggles like a little girl, "Guys, I think our pretty doe, wants us to fuck her."

"We can't, you idiot." Bishop barks at my best friend.

"Oh yeah." Parrish says, disappointment written all over his face.

Pray to my men
'Cause I am sick of this melancholic ticker
Of my folks seeking to forge me in their own holy image
And of this stupid imposed sobriety, just pass me the liquor
It's time to get rid of this never-ending grimace
I feel it like a slash to my throat
This haunt that I invoked

"What the fuck did she just say?" Abel asks, a bit dumbstruck. We are all looking at each other, choked up at Harlow's inter-esting choice of words. She can't know her fate, can she?

As I pray to my men, sacrifice me

. . .

"What the hell?" Bishop spits out.

"Tell me I am not the only one freaking out about what she just ended the song with?" Parrish remarks.

Sacrifice me? Why would Harlow put those words there? "It's probably just a strange coincidence." I assert to the guys.

Our dark horde goes wild, chanting "Abaddon," over and over again. "I'll take it that y'all liked it?" More screams echo in the packed venue. "Well, thank you. Hope I got y'all ready for the Paragon of Virtue's Inferno guys to slip right on out."

Harlow takes a cute little bow before she gets off stage and runs right to us. She's so damn happy, it's contagious. I open my mouth, about to say something, but she jumps into my arms, her own snaking around my neck as her legs go around my waist, and she kisses me, swallowing up whatever was about to leave my trap. It's a tentative kiss at first, like she doesn't really know what to do. Wait. Is this her first kiss? That's not possible, look at this girl.

Keeping one of my hands under her peachy ass, I move my free one to her face, caressing her cheek, before brushing some of her blonde strands back as I bury my fingers in her hair. leaving my hand at the nape of her neck, I help her out by taking her upper lip in my mouth just for a moment, sucking it, and then I go back to pecking her luscious lips. I continue by nibbling her bottom lip, gently grabbing it with my teeth, until I remember Harlow's not a fragile porcelain doll and she can take some harshness, so I bite down, hard onto it. My princess whimpers, whilst I lightly touch my tongue to her lips, tasting her blood that I just forcefully spilled out. Her lips part as a moan emanates from her throat and that's when I sink my tongue into her mouth.

"That's hot." Parrish groans. Who does he think he is Paris Hilton?

I don't have time to explore much of that since as swiftly as Harlow came into my arms, she parts from our embrace and leaves without a word or a glance back.

Thirty-Two

Abel

I FLICK at the frayed edge of a beer label, its sticky underside clinging stubbornly to my fingertips. The bus feels like a pressure cooker, each second ticking by, is a beat closer to the inevitable, a countdown to what I dread most.

"Abel, it's time," Bishop's voice cuts through the haze of my thoughts, as if voicing an incantation that sets our grim fate into motion.

I can't help but glance up at him, this man, a mountain of muscle and determination, his grey eyes steely and resolute. His long white-blonde hair, usually tied back, hangs loose today, as though he's allowing himself this small act of rebellion, before we commit the ultimate betrayal.

I shake my head slightly, the motion barely perceptible. "I know, Bishop... I know." My voice a low growl, the defiance in me bubbling just below the surface. But there's a tremor there too, one that betrays my true feelings.

The end for Harlow – sweet, feisty Harlow, with her light blonde curls and those hauntingly black lined, blue eyes. She doesn't deserve this, none of it. And yet, here we are, on the precipice of darkness, ready to push her over the edge.

Bishop places a hand on my shoulder, his grip firm. "We don't have a choice," he says, and I can hear the unspoken plea in his voice. He needs me to be on board, even though both of us hate it.

"Dammit, Bishop," I mutter, slamming the now-naked bottle onto the table. The sound echoes, a sharp punctuation to the swirling chaos in my chest. "This... This is going to break me."

He nods solemnly, understanding etching lines deeper into his brow. "It might break all of us," he admits, and for a moment, his façade cracks.

"Then why? Why does it have to be her?" I can't keep the accusation from my tone, the question aimed as much at myself as him.

"Because she's the key, Abel." His words are like a hammer to my resolve. "Without her sacrifice, everything we've fought for, suffered for, it all means nothing."

I stand abruptly, "Yeah, well, sometimes the cost is too damn high."

Bishop meets my gaze, his own reflecting a storm of conflict. "We do this for freedom, for control over our own lives. That's worth any price."

"Is it, though?" I counter, my hands balling into fists. "Is it really?"

In the end, no more words are needed; our path is already laid out, ordained by the dark whims of destiny and the deal that temporarily binds us with invisible chains.

"Let's go," Bishop finally says, his voice barely above a whisper, but carrying the weight of finality.

And with that, I follow him out of the bus, my heart heavy, my soul splintering.

Tonight, we either claim our freedom or lose ourselves entirely.

There is no middle ground, not anymore.

The concert last night was a bittersweet high; it was, so to speak, the closing act for my angel. Not that she knew that. As Harlow stepped onto the stage, her presence illuminating the stadium. Her voice carried the weight of nostalgia, echoing through the air as she breathed life into our old melodies – the songs that had been crafted long before our fateful pact. And then came a new composition, a haunting melody that seemed to whisper of liberation and destiny intertwined. Little did she realize, under those spotlights and amidst the cheers of adoring fans, that she was about to become our unexpected savior. Her words a truth because she wrote her future without even realizing it.

The shadows that clung to her troubled me deeply, whispering of a darkness within her soul. Did it stem from us, or was it already there, dormant and waiting? Church and Parrish's suspicions proved true – she belonged with us, the fifth member of our unconventional family. We couldn't bring ourselves to end her life; Bishop's logic resonated too – our journey here was paved with suffering and sacrifices; she deserved a chance at life. Yet, as I pondered, the weight of Harlow's potential sacrifice cast a somber shadow over my thoughts, questioning if the price was too steep for us all to bear.

Slinging my hoodie over my shoulder, I stride out into the night, my boots crunching gravel beneath me. The air sharp, hinting at secrets and sacrifices that hang heavy in the atmosphere.

Harlow's already nestled in the front seat when I slide into the back of the car, her pale hair shining like a beacon under the dome light. What did Bishop promise or threaten to get her compliance tonight? My gut twists, but I shove the thought aside.

Parrish is on the left, closest to the door, his eyes dark pools of unreadable emotion. Church squeezes in beside me, filling the space with his unruly white locks and inked skin. It's tight, too tight—almost claustrophobic—and I can't help but wish Harlow was in the back with us instead.

"Excited" isn't the word I'd use for any of this, but then Harlow's voice cuts through the silence, turning and piercing me with those electric blue eyes. "I'm actually excited to see this place," she says, a hint of genuine enthusiasm lacing her tone. "I can't believe you really made a deal. It will be interesting to see if it feels scary or not."

Scary? A bitter laugh nearly escapes me, but I force it down.

"Interesting is one way to put it," I mutter, keeping my voice steady while my mind races with plans and contingencies. We have to rewrite the rules, change the game—because losing Harlow isn't an option. Not now, not ever.

Her smile doesn't reach her eyes, and the darkness lurking within whispers of things unsaid, of the cost of freedom and the weight of destiny. I look away, focusing on the road ahead, where the night awaits to test our resolve.

Church's grunt slices through the tension like a jagged knife. "For the record, I'd rather not be going," he mutters, his grey eyes stormy beneath the tousled mop of white hair, a siren in human form, but tonight, his usual cheeky spark is dulled by the gravity of our task.

"Church, you've made your point. Now be quiet," Bishop says, his voice a low rumble, commanding attention and obedience, as always. The air around us thickens with unsaid words, with decisions that weigh heavier than the bass lines he's so used to dropping.

From her throne in the front seat, Harlow turns slightly, her pale skin almost glowing in the dim light of the trailer. "Church, you don't have to come," she offers, sweet yet edged with steel.

But Bishop is resolute, a mountain against our collective doubts. "Yes, he does," he declares flatly, and with a decisive turn of the key, the engine roars to life. The opportunity to bolt, to escape what's coming, vanishes with the ignition's growl.

Bishop doesn't hesitate; he plunges us into the night, steering us toward a destiny we can't evade. We're a band—brothers forged in fire and darkness—and now, Harlow is part of that twisted family tree, whether she knows it or not.

The road blurs as we hurtle towards Friars Point, where the opening in the trees looms like the mouth of an ancient beast. It's a place too familiar, yet it never fails to send shivers skittering down my spine. With each visit, the forest seems to close in tighter, as if it remembers the echoes of our footsteps and the secrets we've buried beneath its watchful gaze.

"Almost there," Bishop announces, his voice slicing through the hum of the engine and the cacophony of thoughts, battling in my head. We're bound by blood and music, yes—but also by something darker, a pact that sings of power and binds us to a fate I'm desperate to rewrite.

As the car halts, the headlights ignite a path through the darkness, the engine's growl fades into the stillness of Friars Point as Bishop kills the ignition. Harlow's head pivots, her eyes wide as they drink in our surroundings; that electric blue with that black framing, flickering with a mixture of wonder and something akin to recognition.

"I thought a crossroads would be like an actual road, not like a forest?" she muses aloud, her voice laced with that sweet, feisty tone I know all too well.

Bishop doesn't turn around; he simply releases a measured breath, his broad shoulders rising and falling with the weight of what we're about to do. "It is," he says, his voice as blunt as ever. "It's up there. This is where we park the car. We have to walk the rest of the way."

Harlow's smile ignites a spark of rebellion in the pit of my stomach, her unwavering spirit evident even now. "Okay, let's go," she declares with an air of defiance that's so very her. Without hesitation, she pops the car door open and steps out, her pale silhouette ghosting toward the overgrown path that leads deeper into the woods.

"Abel..." Church's voice scratches at the silence, his grey eyes flicking to me, seeking some kind of assurance. But what can I offer when my insides are a storm of doubt?

I rake a hand through my hair, the gesture as restless as my thoughts. "I don't know if I can do this," I admit, the words tasting like acid on my tongue. The very notion that we are marching Harlow towards her fate claws at me, leaving raw, angry marks behind.

"Neither do I." Parrish's admission is a blade sliding across the tension in the car. His hazel eyes appear as shadows under the canopy of night, but they reflect a turmoil that mirrors my own. Knives and blood play are one thing; this... this is something else entirely.

A sudden slam jolts us from our confessional, a sharp punctuation to the night's grim symphony. Bishop's door shudders closed with a finality that echoes through my bones. He strides after Harlow, his purpose etched in every step, a testament to the sacrifices we've made to claw our way out of obscurity and into the spotlight, no matter the cost.

My gaze locks onto the pair of them—Harlow, with her old-money, light blonde curls bouncing gently, and Bishop, his back rigid with resolve—and something within me fractures. What are we, if not a band of misfits tied together by more than just music? A family woven from darkness and desperation, bound by promises soaked in blood and ambition.

I swallow hard, the sound deafening in the close confines of the car. Glancing once more at Church and Parrish, I see it —the unspoken pact in their eyes. We're in this together, to the bitter end, wherever that may lead. With a nod, I steel myself against the gnawing guilt, and we step out of the car, the trail swallowing us whole, as we follow the fading echo of Harlow's footsteps into the harrowing forest.

We fall into a reluctant march, a procession led by a desire for freedom, dogged by the price it demands. Each step is heavy, laden with the weight of choices made and those yet to come. Our path is a winding serpent as we follow it deeper into the embrace of the woods.

Bishop's broad shoulders block out the stars, his silhouette a dark promise against the night sky. He doesn't look back, but I know he feels our presence—a spectral force at his back.

Harlow's laughter, light and unburdened, drifts back to us.

She's oblivious to the crossroads we stand upon, the decisions that churns like a maelstrom just beneath the surface. Her innocence is a stark contrast to the shadows we've danced with, the ones that now cling to our flesh like a second skin.

"Keep your head," I whisper to myself, a silent plea to whatever might be listening. I cling to the defiance that's kept me afloat through years of struggle, the drumbeat of rebellion that has become my heart's rhythm. Tonight, it pounds in warning, a reminder that even in the dark, we hold the power to choose our fate.

We're near the clearing now, the end of our journey—or perhaps the beginning. The air shivers with anticipation, charged with the energy of ancient pacts and whispered oaths.

"Ready?" Parrish breathes out, his question more a statement of solidarity than an inquiry.

"Always," Church replies, his tattooed hands flexing at his sides, ready for whatever comes.

"Let's finish this," I say, stepping into the clearing with them. Our footsteps unite in a silent pact, a vow that no matter what, we face this together.

THIRTY-THREE

HARLOW

BEFORE MY EYES stands the decrepit remnants of an old Church. Its dark stone appears to be melting, marked by tears from a past, long forgotten. Once healthy rose bushes climb over the walls, their flowers and leaves very much dead, all that remains is the grayish dry vines, full of thorns. What is left of the stained-glass windows have lost all their beautiful vibrancy-thanks to dust and grime, with majority now broken. The characters depicted seem to have come out from the pits of hell more so than heaven. How did this end up in the middle of this dense forest?

We walked for quite a bit through the deadly-quiet eerie woods of Friars Point, before arriving at this clearing. Bishop has been the only Paragon of Virtue's Inferno member to keep me company and listen to my nervous rambling, since Church, Parrish and Abel have been acting quite strange since we all got in the car.

Did they not want me to come?

Last night was such a high, it was not even about belonging somewhere anymore, I just felt like for the first time people got to see the genuine Harlow Magdalene Abaddon, unsullied by anyone else. In that moment singing early Paragon of Virtue's Inferno songs, the stuff from before they became rock stars, and then giving the crowd a part of myself with 'Pray to my men', it was like my wings had at long last healed-even though now they are tinged with darkness on the edges- and had spread wide, allowing me to fly. I will be frank, after I hung up the phone on mother dearest those words just poured out of me, that somber ballad was as raw as they come. Hearing the audience go wild for my song, filled me with life.

As I came off stage from that apex in my dull existence, I wasn't thinking clearly. How else can I justify jumping Church and kissing him? My first kiss. Ugh, there's no way the younger McGrew didn't pick-up on my inexperience. But, hot damn, as my alluring fallen angel with ashy blonde hair and pale gray eyes took control, playing around with my upper and then lower lip, all I kept thinking was how it felt more intimate than what we have been doing in the dark. Do all kisses feel this almighty?

Parrish did break the spell I seemed to have been under when he uttered, "That's hot," just as his best friend shoved his tongue inside my mouth. I panicked, I felt this overwhelming premonition of love consume me, like the further Church's tongue got within me the closer he was to my soul, I had to make a quick escape before I said something stupid like, oh I don't know, I love you. There goes my innocence making me credulous again.

And now, as we make our way inside the abandoned house of prayer, the spot the Paragon of Virtue's Inferno men claim they made the fateful deal with the Devil; I wonder if I let my lack of guile, shepherd me into peril. My guys wouldn't let anything hurt me, right?

Bishop came into my trailer this morning, walking right in like he owns the place. Well, I guess in a way he kind of does. "We are leaving for Memphis in a few minutes, you should head to the tour bus pronto, little mouse."

"Morning to you too, Daddy." That made Bishop groan, which in turn made me giggle.

"What happened here? Did a hurricane go through the trailer or something?" I was sitting cross legged on the floor of the travelers' wagon, piles of scattered clothes all around me.

"Yeah, hurricane Harlow. I don't feel like wearing most of this stuff anymore. So, I am rummaging to see if there's anything worth saving. Did you know that the only black thing I own is the leggings I bought at the airport before coming here?"

Bishop cut off my chattering by, all of a sudden, saying, "I like you in white."

"White? It doesn't really go with your image though."

"You're not us, baby. I don't want you to change for us. But if you don't want to dress up in your cutesy, whimsical, western, princess-like clothes then don't. You are our angel, our salvation, I think you should keep the white." The older McGrew ordered.

"Right. Ok."

"Once we get to Memphis, I was planning on taking a trip to where we made the devilish pact, since there's no show tonight. In case you are interested in coming, little mouse."

"Sounds like a good way to kill time." I utter, beaming at him. I know at first, I sought to keep their dark ways at bay, pushing away any advances from them to include me in their little rituals. So, it's nice of Bishop to extend an invitation to me now, since I decided that I want to be with them.

He knelt down, right in front of me and fished out a white dress from the mess of clothes. "Wear this one tonight."

Later that evening, adorned in Bishop's pick, a sleeveless Victorian style nightgown, with delicate broderie anglaise around the square neck, and a conservative length reaching just past the knees, pairing it with simple white trainers, which in hindsight was probably not the best thing to put on for a walk through the muddy soil of the forest.

The solid timber doors bang shut behind me, making me jump out of my skin and closing us in. The boys tread ahead of me to the altar of the church, as I take my time, glancing over everything, taking in the chilling familiarity of the space I find myself in with the guys.

"Weird." I voice out loud.

"What is it?" Abel asks me.

My eyes continue their scrutiny of this condemned place of pilgrimage, as I declare, "I ummm.. I feel like I've been here before once upon a time, In a dream perhaps? ¨

"You what?" Parrish utters in disbelief.

While Church curses a demanding, "What the fuck?"

My hand shoots to my neck as that phantom feeling arises again. I clear my throat, attempting to gulp whatever it is down, though, to no avail.

"Harlow." Bishop calls out to me.

I am still facing away from the guys, staring at the main way out of this God forsaken structure, when shadows come forth, taking shape within the pews of the fallen congregation. I begin to step back, further into the house of prayer, and as I do so the seats start filling up, like a crowd of wayward spirits gathering to witness something extreme.

"What," the words die in my lips as realization settles in. It wasn't a dream; it was a vision, a premonition of my demise. I look down at my snowy white dress, but a rivulet of crimson red doesn't stain it, yet. "This isn't where you made the deal is it?" I ask the men, closing my eyes, as a single tear falls.

"Harlow." Bishop speaks my name once more. Why does he sound heartbroken?

I open my tear-filled eyes, making the gray background that surrounds us a blurry disorder. "This is where you pay the price, in blood." How many times have they done this? How many... Wait. Is this why they haven't fucked me yet? They need a virgin. "And I'm the price this time, right?" I am nothing but a sacrificial lamb, being led to the slaughter. Oh, they played me well. What a stupid little girl I am, I fell right into the demons' den. The easy prey in a predator's divertissement. A little voice in my head whispers, "Run." But isn't it a bit too late for that?

"We are so sorry, princess." Church tells me, sounding as crestfallen as his brother, causing me to ultimately turn around and face them. All four Paragon of Virtue's Inferno members stand proud, in this sanctuary of the damned, by the altar, wearing the same neon masks they used the first time they came to mess with me inside the trailer.

"Please don't do this." I beg as I begin to cry. Weak, I am so goddamn weak.

"We have no choice, Low." Abel offers up.

Well, then I guess they give me no other possible course of action, but to flee. I swore that I would never run away from them, and here I am now doing just that.

Thirty-Four

PARRISH

I watch Harlow, her eyes flitting from shadow to shadow, skimming over the desecrated altar and the stained-glass windows, where the moonlight can't reach. They are electric blue, those eyes, vibrant even in the dimness, fringed with fear yet sparking with something untamed. I see it, that flicker of defiance as it ignites within her—a silent declaration.

She's made up her mind.

Her body tenses like a bowstring drawn tight, muscles coiled, ready to spring. For a breath, she's still, a statue of resolve. Then she's moving, arms pumping, hair streaming behind her in a golden wave. Her legs carry her toward salvation, toward the heavy wooden doors that promise freedom.

But Church is faster, his instincts honed on stages and back-alley scuffles. His movement is a blur, a dance of predator and prey. He intercepts her with the grace of the lead vocalist he is, the showman, who knows how to captivate an audience—even if it's just us, the unwilling spectators to this grim performance.

"Harlow!" His voice isn't the fun and cheeky tone that woos crowds; it's sharp, laced with urgency.

Church's tattooed arms—a canvas of demon wings and diabolic symbols—ensnare her mid-flight, crashing around her slender frame like iron bands. She doesn't make it more than a few desperate strides before she's pulled back into our twisted fold, her escape cut short by his imposing form.

"Let me go!" The words tear from her throat, raw and fierce.

"Easy there," Church murmurs, but there's an edge to his grey eyes, a glint that speaks of darker things than the lyrics he croons under the spotlight.

I lean against a rotting pew, the wood creaking beneath my weight, a macabre echo to the scene unfolding. My fingers itch for the familiar coldness of a blade, to trace patterns on skin and feel the warmth that follows. But not yet. Now is the time to watch, to wait, to savor the anticipation.

"Sorry, darling," I call out to her, my voice a smooth caress that belies the chaos of my thoughts. "No exit stage left tonight."

Harlow's screams rip through the stale air of the church, a feral cry of betrayal. "I trusted you!" Her accusation slashes deeper than any blade I've ever wielded.

Church's grip tightens, as her body writhes against him, desperation giving her strength.

"Let me go!" she shrieks, each word punctuated by her flailing limbs. She believed in us, opened her heart to the bond we forged through music and midnight secrets. Yet here she is, caught in our snare, the trust she had in us, tearing apart like the decaying vestments that hang from the walls.

"Shhh, Harlow, please," Church whispers, his voice a

strange symphony of softness and steel. He's always been the one to charm, to disarm with a smile or a well-timed joke. Now, his soothing tones are a lullaby over a nightmare.

Her struggles don't wane, but Church moves with the certainty of a tide, carrying her back towards the altar.

"Stop! You can't do this!" Her pleas are a knife twisting in my gut. The madness that usually thrums within me, craving the slick sensation of blood beneath my fingers, recoils. It's a peculiar feeling—this hesitance, this flicker of something akin to regret.

"Shhh," he repeats, a mantra meant to calm the tempest in her soul as he lays her down upon the ancient stone. The altar is unforgiving, unyielding, much like the fate we're about to bestow upon her.

"Church... please..." Her voice cracks, the fire that fuels her defiance reduced to dying embers.

"Quiet now," he murmurs again, his breath warm against her ear amidst the chill of the desecrated hall.

I can't help but wonder, as I watch her fight dwindle, if there's a part of me that yearns for redemption as much as I crave the chaos. The thought is fleeting, lost in the rhythm of ritual and the necessity of what we believe must be done.

"Sorry, love," I say, though my words are for me as much as they are for her. "Some demons can't be outrun."

The chilled air of the church wraps around me like a sinister caress, yet it brings a sense of twisted comfort. I breathe in the mustiness, the scent of decay that clings to every broken pew and shattered stained-glass window. This place, this forsaken sanctuary, has become more than just a hideout for us—it's our macabre chapel, our secret haven.

"Harlow, darling, you want to hear a story?" I murmur, my

voice threading through the tense silence that follows her ceased struggles.

She lies still now, her chest heaving with ragged breaths, eyes wide as she takes in the dilapidated grandeur surrounding her. Glancing up at the ceiling where timber hangs like flayed skin, I remember the day when fate led me here, to the heart of forgotten prayers and lost souls.

"Once upon a time, we were reckless, leaving our offering in the open woods." My gaze drifts to the altar. "But then they found her, and we knew we needed to be smarter, more... discreet."

This hallowed ruin called to me back then, its doors stubbornly sealed, guarding its secrets. But secrets are meant to be unveiled, and I've always been one to take what I want. With force and resolve, I breached its defenses, claiming it for our own dark purposes.

"Here, beneath our feet, lies the testament of our devotion," I continue, stepping closer to the edge of the platform where the altar stands as an ominous centerpiece. "The foundations of this very church conceal the sacrifices made in the name of freedom."

I can almost hear the whispers of those who came before Harlow, their voices melding with the groan of the rotting wood beneath my boots. They are a part of the church now, part of its decaying beauty, their bones interred in the unholy ground.

"Church found his muse amidst all this ruin," I say, casting a glance at him, noting how his grey eyes reflect the faint light, filtering through the broken canopy. His tattoos, symbols of our shared damnation, seem alive on his skin, twisting with his every move. "Didn't you, Church?"

He doesn't answer, but I see the acknowledgment in his eyes. After all, it was within these forsaken walls that we found our purpose, our grim communion with forces beyond the mortal coil.

"Everything ends, Harlow," I whisper, leaning down to meet her gaze, "but some endings pave the way for new beginnings. Some sacrifices are necessary."

In the end, we're all bound by the same chains, forged from the sins of our past, the desperate need for salvation. And tonight, under the watchful eye of a church that no longer offers sanctuary, we come full circle—the hunters and the hunted, the sinners seeking absolution through the ultimate sacrifice.

Church's hands are a vice as he secures Harlow onto the altar, his touch almost gentle in its firmness. I watch, silent and still, as Abel moves with practiced ease, looping rope around her wrists, binding them above her head. The lengths snake around her ankles, taut and unyielding. She is a wild thing made statue; a sacrifice pinned to cold stone.

The ropes creak under Harlow's struggles, but Abel has done his work well; she won't break free. In my periphery, Church stands back, his silhouette framed by the gaping maw of a stained-glass window, his grey eyes fixed on Harlow, searching for something only he can see.

Harlow's eyes meet mine, fierce and pleading all at once. "Why?" she gasps, the word a shard of glass in the silence.

"Because we must," is all I offer, the truth too vast and complex for this moment of reckoning. "To find peace, some must endure the storm. We are those some, Harlow. You, now, are a part of that 'we.'"

The church seems to lean in, eager for the climax of our

grim tale, as if the very walls hunger for the conclusion we've wrought within its embrace. And as the darkness gathers, waiting to feast on what comes next, I stand sentinel over the last act of our story, the final verse in a song, written of blood and shadow.

The echoes of my own footsteps bounce off the cold stone as I circle the altar, a predator in a dance with unwilling prey. Harlow's breaths come out in ragged gasps, her electric blue eyes ablaze with a mix of fear and defiance that only fuels the fire within me.

"Harlow," I start, my voice low, almost a whisper against the cacophony of our breathing, "You are our last. The final note in this dark symphony we've been forced to play."

Bishop stands still and silent to the right, a stoic figure, observing everything as it unfolds. Church's shadow stretches ominously, a vigilant guardian of our entwined fates. Abel lingers in the background, his restless fingers betraying a yearning to play the invisible chords of destiny.

"Your spirit, your... essence," I struggle to find the words to tell her how much hinges on this moment, "it's the key. You will save our souls, give us a chance to continue with our lives, free from the demon and shadows that have haunted us for too long."

I see it—the flicker of realization, the dawning of horror as she understands the gravity of what I'm saying. The ropes binding her form to the cold, hard surface of the altar seem to tighten with each truth I reveal.

"Granted, we never thought it would be this difficult," I admit, the weight of my confession threatening to crack the facade I've held for so long. "We figured you'd be easy to... to let go of." My hands clench into fists at my sides. "But understand this—we didn't want it to come to this. You were right; you are one of us, the missing piece we've been searching for."

She squirms against her bindings, a wild thing caught in the hunter's trap. "Please, Harlow, understand. We were nothing but trash before—all those years, discarded, stepped on. These past ten years... they've been the life we've been clawing for, the life we deserved."

A pause, heavy and suffocating hangs between us, while Church and Abel stand motionless, nothing more than statues of regret and necessity. Bishop, standing in the same place since we entered, slowly pulls a large hunting knife out of his jacket, its blade gleaming malevolently under the dim moonlight.

"Going back to the dumps is not an option available to us. It's do or die." I murmur, leaning closer to her, close enough to see the individual flecks of darker blue in her eyes. "But, Harlow," the words catch in my throat, a confession of a different kind, "I'm not sure I can do this."

Her eyes search mine, wide and shimmering with unshed tears. It's now or never—truth or damnation.

"Harlow, I think I've fallen in love with you," I say, letting the words spill out raw and unguarded. "I really do."

The church holds its breath, the stained-glass windows reflecting a kaleidoscope of emotions that paint our faces in hues of desperation and longing. And as the truth of my heart lays bare before her, I can't help but wonder if love might just be the most powerful sacrifice of all.

THIRTY-FIVE

CHURCH

ONCE UPON A TIME Robert Johnson sang the song, *If I had possession, over judgment day.* "This takes 'if you love them, let them go' to a whole new level of absurdity." Harlow states unexpectedly.

Parrish in a low and solemn voice utters, "Pretty doe." This was big for him, to spill out those words to Harlow. He has more guts than any of us. Love doesn't come easy for people like us. As C.S. Lewis once wrote, 'Love anything and your heart will be wrung and possibly broken. If you want to make sure of keeping it intact you must give it to no one…Wrap it carefully round with hobbies and little luxuries; avoid all entanglements. Lock it up safe in the casket or coffin of your selfishness. But in that casket, safe, dark, motionless, airless, it will change. It will not be broken; it will become unbreakable, impenetrable, irredeemable. To love is to be vulnerable.' And yet, here is my best friend giving his ticker away to someone we are about to kill.

"This is more godawful than being a notch in all y'alls

bedpost. Why play with your food if you were just going to throw it away in the end?" Harlow spits at us.

"Because we are selfish, little mouse. You know that." Bishop comments. "We saw something we wanted and just took it, consequences be damned."

"Did y'all fool around with the other dead girls walking too?"

"What? No, Low…"

Harlow cuts in, interrupting Abel, "So, I am just that special? I get to have my heart broken before you snatch it out of my chest."

"You won't be the only one losing your heart tonight, pretty doe." Parrish blurts out.

"Baby, if we don't do this, we are the ones gone." I admit to my lit princess. "The shadows will rip out the souls they have been chasing after since we made this pact." I need her to understand this isn't child's play, the decisions we make aren't done lightly. It's a game of survival; one we don't intend to lose. I am still left wondering why it feels like if we go along with this offering, we will definitely still be the losers.

"And love is sacrifice, right? Fine. Let me show you what true love is." Before my eyes a frightened girl turns into a calm and serene creature. She's no longer trashing against her binds, there's no tremble in her voice and her alluring electric blue eyes weep no more. "I will be your penance." Is she giving us permission to slaughter her? We read Harlow her last rites and she's just giving up. What the fuck? This is somehow worse than having her begging us for her life or throwing shade at our bad choices. "It's not tragic to die for someone you love." Is that Harlow saying she loves us? Fuck. She is willing to draw her last breath to save us. She is our salvation indeed.

I turn my head to look at my brother, outstretching my hand to him. There's a moment of hesitation, where his pale gray eyes dance between me and our angel laid out on the altar. Now he's torn? Fucking fantastic. "Give me the bloody knife, Bishop."

"Church." He warns me.

"You heard her. She wants to bleed for us." Eventually the handle of large hunting knife lands on my hand. Damn, is it me or does it feel heavier than all the other times we used it to pay the Devil for his services?

I saunter to where Harlow's hands are tied up above her head. She tilts her head back so she can see me with her piercing blue eyes. Oh, how I wish she hadn't done that. I lean forward, putting my elbows down by her head, as with one of my hands I caress her cheek while with the other I hold the handle of the knife with a dead grip, the blade hovering just above her throat.

"Harlow, baby, I love you. Please forgive me." I am about to doom us all.

And then, she ruins me further by saying, "I do." Fuck. I shut my eyes, trying to gather the strength I need to do this. Without ever opening them, I pull my mask off and dip my face until my lips meet hers and I kiss Harlow Spider-Man style. My princess parts her lips immediately, giving my tongue access inside her mouth. I swirl it around hers, sucking it into my mouth, and this cute game of tug of war begins once Harlow is past that unsureness of hers and starts mirroring what I am doing.

She moans and I fall to bits, fracturing the kiss. As I bring my forehead to hers, I tell her, "We don't deserve you." I remove my face from her proximity, leaning on my extended arms that arresting near the edges of the altar-the knife still dangling from my fingers.- "Hey baby, how about we make you feel good one more time before," I don't finish the sentence, we all know the ending here.

"Church, I don't think that's a good idea, man." Abel remarks.

"Life is about balance and unfortunately, we had to bargain a way to tip our scales. We are getting ready to inflict pain, may as well throw some pleasure in there for our girl for free. What do you say, baby?" She nods at my offer. I walk to the opposite end and climb on top of the altar with my princess, kneeling between her spread legs. I am going to get so much shit from the guys for the deed on the brink of unfolding.

I creep my hands up her legs –keeping hold of the knife as I go- pausing only when I reach her hips. Her dress rises up, with help of my hands, exposing her core to me. Well almost, only one thing is in the way, her panties. Skillfully with the twist of the sharp blade, I cut them off of her. I squat down, resting my stomach on my thighs so I can bury my face in her pussy. Harlow's body jerks, making her pull tighter on the restraints that secure my princess to the pulpit.

"We are so going to hell." Parrish states. Yeah, no shit.

I am surprised to find Harlow already wet, considering the dire life-threatening situation she finds herself in. Damn, she really is as fucked up as we are. I play around with her clit, sucking and lapping at it a few times before stiffening my tongue and penetrating her core. Her whimpers echo in the ghostly house of prayer.

I lower my hand –void of any sharp objects- to the shank

of my jeans, rubbing myself through the stiff material. I continue stroking her with my tongue, nipping and sucking as I go, building my princess up to her impending doom. I should be dragging this out, not get her to the heights of pleasure so quickly, because the sooner we get there then the sooner I will have to pierce her. But it seems I don't arrive at that conclusion quick enough, and my baby cums undone for me.

As her body convulses, she tugs on the ropes, purring my name, "Church."

I kiss my way up her body, until I am lying perfectly on top of her. I use one of my elbows to keep me from resting all of my weight on my girl. I stare deep into her eyes, and all I see is affection and worship. "I am about to do the dumbest thing ever, and set hell lose on all of us, I hope you are ready, baby."

"I love you. All of you. I'm ready." This girl is the strongest person I have ever met.

"This is going to hurt." I press the tip into her and she gasps. I kiss her all over, lips, cheeks, nose, neck, the tears seem to be back, forming at the corner of her eyes. I clench my jaw in concertation, my hard muscles contracting and pulling against my inked skin.

The knife drops to the ground, the sound deafening as it hits the floorboards, vibrating like a shot being fired.

"Church, what did you just do?" Bishop asks, somewhat hostile and grim.

"I made her bleed." I inform him, in a very blasé manner.

"I don't think the shadows will count that as such." My best friend observes. "But I do." A Cheshire like grin spreads across his pretty face.

"We can't use her now." Abel remarks.

"Exactly. Guys, I am sorry. I couldn't do it. She is ours that much has been clear since she graced us with her presence. She was made for us. She fits with us, in this dark twisted narrative, perfectly. We'll have to make a new bargain or just accept the one we made, for once actually deal with the consequences of our actions."

I move deeper into Harlow, and she winces. "Is it supposed to hurt this much the first time?" My princess asks.

"It would have been better if someone had stretched your pussy a bit better before diving right in." Bishop angrily states.

"Yeah, well this was a bit of a last-minute decision. I made her wet, at least, and I am taking it slow. I am barely halfway in." And I made sure my cock was free from the confinements of my jeans and boxers before climbing over her beautiful body.

"There's more to come. Fuck me." Those words make everyone snigger, even my crabby big brother.

"I am trying, baby." I pull out, until only the head stays in, and thrust back further within her warmth. It's taking everything in me to control myself and not just go at it like a beast. My pace is slow, as I move in up until I am fully inside, then withdrawing almost all the way out.

"We are dead, you know that right?" Bishop states, ever so nicely. -not-

"Love is sacrifice." I repeat Harlow's words, tossing them at Bishop, withdrawing fully from Harlow's pussy and shoving myself in. That makes her moan. Good, her pain will be nothing but a distant memory, replaced by rapture and contentment.

He sighs as he yanks his mask off, and the other two follow his action. "Ok." He speaks.

"Thanks for the permission brother; it's not like I am not balls deep in her already."

"Dude, can you finish so we can all have a go?"

"What am I, an attraction you can ride?" Harlow snaps at Parrish.

"You are now." Abel responds.

I lower my lips to Harlow's, silencing her retaliation, kissing the living daylights out of her. My thrusts become a bit more forceful and frantic, as I can feel myself getting closer to the edge. I ain't falling off, without her, so I descend my hand to her bundle of nerves and start drawing bewitching and tantalizing circles around it.

Harlow bites on my lower lip, hard. I pull away, which gives her blessing to shout my name. She's nearing the peak, I can feel her already tight walls, constricting even more so around my dick. "Fuck, baby, you are milking the life out of me." That is when I pinch her clit. Heaven comes crashing down on us both, she orgasms and in turn, makes me blast within her like the fourth of July, filling her to the brim. I don't think I have ever come this hard in my bleak existence.

"Oh, so pretty. My turn, my turn." Parrish says, jumping up and down in excitement, like a little kid. What an idiot? My gorgeous idiot.

I return my attention to the girl beneath me, Harlow's tiny body still coming down from the high of climax. "Are you ok?" I ask Harlow, huffing and puffing those words out.

"You should've done it, Church." She tells me, sorrow dripping from every syllable.

"Done what, baby?"

"Sacrificed me."

Thirty-Six

Harlow

"Sacrificed me." I tell Church. "Do you even have time to find someone else?"

"Tonight was the deadline." Abel announces.

"Right." Because of course it is. Leave it to guys to wait until the last minute to do stuff. "And now the demon king is going to come for y'all. You are unquestionably selfish. I am going to have to somehow carry on living without you. At least y'all would have each other, who do I have? No one." I will say though, having this conversation while tied to an altar, in an abandoned and decaying church forgotten amongst the trees, with the lead singer of Paragon of Virtue's Inferno still buried balls deep inside of me, is very ungraceful and awkward.

The initial pain has subsided, now a simple dull ache. For a hot minute there I was wondering what all the fuss was about, that stung bad. But when he started moving in and out, going further in as he went, slow at first, later picking up the pace, the discomfort turned to this heavenly feeling, that's when I understood the beauty of this carnal dance. Church is blessed indeed; he wasn't lying a while back when he told me that his perfect arched length hits a nice pleasurable spot within. That on its own was driving me wild already, then he began playing with my bundle of nerves, at that point I was a goner. Feeling him cum with me, within me, filling me up with his seed, is an intense connection beyond anything I could ever have imagined. It's as if in that moment Church marked me as his.

"Baby, hey, we will sort shit out in some way, and deal with the ramifications of my impulsive urges. It might not even come to that. One can only hope, right?" Church says in a futile attempt to console me. He does give me a heartfelt kiss, which just about deflects my worry. "But tonight, how about we ignore everything and just enjoy me breaking you in? The other guys do want to have a go too."

I tilt my head to the side and there they all are, their erections very noticeable, looking at me like I am the best prize you can get at a funfair game booth.

"Well, someone needs to make room then." I throw those words at Church, which makes him chuckle.

"Only because it is your first time." What's that supposed to mean? There's no way I can fit more than one down there, is there? Church finally removes himself from my core, and damn, I feel so empty.

After stashing his length back in his jeans, Church slides off of the altar and strides to his best friend, whispering something down his ear that I can't perceive. Parrish, the goofball, skips to me, his unhinged yet bubbly demeanor back at full force. making me realize how tormented my men were about what they had to do tonight. The way he told me he had fallen in love with me, I could feel the grief behind the words as if it was a sweet yet agonizing goodbye.

He pauses right next to the pulpit, placing his hands on his hips as he looks at me up and down, surely trying to decide what to do with me. I only know I am in trouble when that cute psychotic smirk of his makes an appearance, forcing his dimple piercings to pop. Parrish pulls out his own knife from his pocket and kicks off his plans by cutting the rope around my wrists. Once those are unbound, with the tip of the knife he traces my flesh, mapping me out, with the lightness of a feather, slowly he migrating to the end of the altar and does the same to the binds on my ankles.

"Aww you were right Church, her virgin blood mixed with your cum does create a beautiful pinky mess. Almost the same hue as my hair. But I believe it needs a bit more white, to make it the exact shade." With that Parrish grabs me by the ankles and drags my body until my ass is right on the edge. I squeak at the sudden barbaric move.

"Damn, I love it when you make that sound, little mouse." The older McGrew remarks.

"Hey pretty doe, drape your arms around my neck and hold on tight, it's going to be a bumpy ride." My pink haired boy utters as he lowers the zipper from his jeans and pulls out his long and pierced length. I do as I am told, lifting my upper half from the altar and hugging his neck with my arms.

My eyes bounce around his gorgeous face, memorizing it, counting the piercings he has there as if they are stars. Eventually they land on those deranged hazel eyes that I am smitten by. "God, I love you." I blurt out.

Parrish hums before saying, "I thought we exorcized God out of you." He wiggles his length up and down, brushing against my wet folds, the cold metal of his piercing sending shivers up my spine.

"You did; you are all my Gods now."

"Nicely saved, Abaddon." And with that he slides in, no dillydallying on his part. I gasp in shock at the curt intrusion. "Unholy Mary, you feel like home, and everywhere I have never been all at once."

"Did you just quote a poem from 'Wild Spirit, Soft Heart' by Butterflies Rising? Dude, you are so lame." That sentence is immediately followed by an "Oof," upon Church smacking his closed fist to Abel's belly. None of that fazes the man rooted inside of me, one of his arms snakes around my back and holds me flush to him, as his face comes to rest on my shoulder, and Parrish kicks off thrusting in and out of me like he's possessed.

It feels different from Church, yet still amazingly good. Having the piercing graze my inner walls is an arousing sensation. I wonder if Parrish did it just for the sake of doing it, or if he had other peoples fun in mind? I have a hunch I'm not going to last long on this go either, as this knot in my belly chokes my guts until it fractures, leaving me a trembling mess, screaming Parrish's name.

As I come undone in Parrish's cocoon, one of the sleeves of my dress gives away, most likely cut off, and I perceive this sharp pain on my shoulder blade accompanied by some sort of fluid cascading down my back. "Bern, be careful you are going to leave a scar." Bishop warns the man that is still driving into my core drawing out my climax.

"Don't stop. Fuck me. Love me. Carve me, leave your mark on me, please." I just about hack to purr out.

"Rats." Parrish utters with a strained voice, finishing whatever he is writing on my flesh. It certainly feels like an inverted cross and the letters C B P and A around it. His length swells within me and the hand with the knife slams against the altar, presumably because he needs the support, right as he plants himself deeper inside my core and shoots row after row of his pearly white seed inside. It seems to drag on forever, his body shaking like a leaf.

Parrish takes his face away from my shoulder and relocates both of his hands to my face, his knife left behind, on top of the table I am sitting upon. We stare at each other for a heartbeat, trying to gather our composure and breathes. His lips crash to mine in the same abrupt way his length entered me, his tongue creeping into my mouth like hell-for-leather. This boy doesn't seem to want to waste any time. It's a feverish kiss, very much untamed, just like Parrish.

Before you can say knife, I am vacant, between both, my upper and lower lips. "Ok. Time is up for you, Berny." Abel announces.

"Hey, I wasn't done yet." Parrish complains, throwing a pout in Abel's direction.

Abel dark brown eyes fall to my pussy, prior to him commenting, "Judging by the amount of cum pouring out of her swollen lips, I would say you are."

My extremely tatted man's hand comes to my throat, gripping it roughly. He tugs me up from my seated position by my neck, my feet landing on the rotting floorboards. Luckily, his intention was not for me to stand, as with how shaky my legs are I don't think I would have coped with that. Abel spins me around, my pubis bone hitting the table, whilst his grasp on my throat never yields.

"I am about to rock your world, angel." That's when his hand shifts to the nape of my neck and my upper body is shoved forward, my front lying flat on the tabletop and my ass perfectly aligned with his monster shaft.

"Oh, if you are fucking my pretty doe like that, can I lick her wound, pretty please, cherry on top." Parrish begs, his hands in a prayer position of open hands, palms together, the shells of his hands against the center his chest, fingers pointing towards heaven.

Abel groans, "Well, I guess saliva does help heal wounds, and you did create that, so you should be the one to clean it."

"Hot dog." Parrish says, beaming from ear to ear. Approaching the altar again, he brushes some of my old-money blonde curls away, dropping his face to the meticulous slashes he inflicted on my sink. He licks it once, humming in delight, which coerces me to moan.

"Hey, don't go stealing my thunder." I hear the faint sound of a button popping, a zipper being lowered and fabric rustling, soon followed by the head of Abel's length demanding entry in my core.

"With that beast? You will have her knocking on hell's door in no time, no exterior factors needed my friend." Parrish observes.

"Just drink her blood and shut up, vamp." Oh, I like that pet name for my pink haired man, I might keep it for myself.

Rather than barging his way inside my wet folds, Abel slides in slowly but surely. I will be frank, it felt tight with the other two, considering it was no-man's-land ahead of Church popping my cherry, but with Abel it's like I am being ripped apart. I whimper, because damn that stings a bit.

"It will be alright, angel, you'll adjust. Just take deep breaths, ok." I nod because words fail me. Monster indeed. The hand that was still latched on to the nape of my head begins voyaging down my spine, the touch a sweet caress, relaxing me enough for the drummer's length to fit entirely inside. "That's it, angel. Good girl."

While Parrish feasts on my blood, slurping and lapping it up, his tongue piercing stroking me in a bewitching manner, Abel starts thrusting in and out of me. His hands have congregated on either side of my hips, keeping me steady. I am facing away from the McGrew brothers, staring at the pews beyond Parrish. The Shadows, don't seem to have moved. Have they been watching this lustful act the whole time? A combination of all the factors surrounding me, become overwhelming, the idea of being ogled by these critters from hell, my vamp licking and sucking my blood, my tatted man's length spreading my inner walls wide, and, on the whole, how sensitive I am down there from the many times I have come thus far, it's no surprise I rupture out of nowhere.

"Aww damn you got her to squirt, you ass." Parrish antagonizes Abel.

The wet sounds that have been echoing within the sinners' house of prayer since Church's turn, become even more distinguished and heighten. The drummers length glides in and out with ease, the movement smooth as butter. His nails are digging into my flesh with incredible strength, telling me that he's losing it.

"Fuck." It's all he says prior to shoving himself to a great depth and imploding inside my core. I can feel all the various juices pour out of me and stream down my legs that is how full I am already, and there's still one member left to make me his, to connect our bodies and souls, and shove a piece of himself so far into me that it will never abandon me.

Thirty-Seven

Bishop

I can't help but stand back, a silent sentinel amid the chaos of flesh and desire on the altar. My breath catches as I watch her body arch, caught in the relentless rhythm of their movements. The dim moonlight streaming across her skin, casting shadows that dance along the curves of her form, intertwining with the stark lines of virgin blood smeared on the stone beneath her.

"Fuck," I mutter under my breath, the sight before me is both unholy and mesmerizing. It's an offering, a perverse sacrament where pleasure and pain meld into one. Her moans echo against what is left of the stained-glass windows, a haunting chorus to the carnal symphony playing out before my eyes.

There's a rawness in the air, thick and tangible, as three separate strands of cum drip from her cunt. She stands now, leaning over the altar, her gaze fixed on the front of the church, on the shadows in the pews. They are witnesses to our sin, silent judges in this sanctuary of the damned, turned den of debauchery.

Her submission, her unravelling—it's a heady thing to witness. And though I've yet to touch her, I feel the pull of her surrender, a siren's call resonating deep within my bones. I'm the manager, the one who orchestrates the madness, but here, in this moment, I'm nothing but a man consumed by the fire before me.

"Beautiful," I growl, the word barely audible above the crescendo of her cries. A primal part of me revels in the sight of her so marked, so utterly claimed. It's not just about the control; it's the power etched in every line of her body, the raw energy that courses through us all.

The others may step back, content with their conquest, but I'm far from done. This is more than lust; it's a claiming, a binding of souls in the most ancient of rites. As I watch the evidence of their sin streak down her thighs, I know we have crossed a threshold from which there is no return.

We play with forces dark and deep, and she is the nexus, the vessel through which they flow. In this desecrated place of worship, she has become our altar, our salvation and damnation intertwined. And as I prepare to join this profane communion, I know one truth above all else: She is ours, and we are irrevocably hers.

I stride forward, the raw energy of the moment pulsing through me like a living thing. The others—Church with his cheeky grin fading into the shadows, Parrish's madness lingering in the air, and Abel's cockiness receding with a satisfied smirk—they all step back, granting me my turn.

"Fuck it," I mutter, thumbing at the waistband of my pants before freeing myself in one swift motion. My hand wraps around my dick, heavy and eager, as I approach her—their release still fresh on her skin. "If we're all damned, we might as well go out with a bang."

Harlow stands there, an ethereal vision perched on the edge of ruin, her pale form arched beautifully over the altar. Her breath comes in ragged gasps, eyes dark with desire and something fiercer, something that matches the tempest within me.

I slide between her trembling legs, my rough hands seizing her hips with a possessiveness that's etched into my every fiber. I drag myself through the slickness, the mixture of cum and virgin blood that marks her, and us, forever. It's warm, it's filthy, and it's fucking divine.

"Look at you," I growl, my voice a low purr of dark amusement, watching her body react to every filthy word. "The most perfect little cum slut. Do you like being full of everyone's cum? Do you enjoy how messy and sloppy you are right now?"

Her response is a symphony of moans, each note striking against the hallowed silence of the church.

Her moans escalate, a fervent affirmation as I align myself with the carnage between her legs. "Yes," she groans out, voice laced with pleasure and pain, the sweetest melody to my ears.

"Good girl," I mutter under my breath, pushing in. Despite the chaos we've wrought upon her body, she's still impossibly tight, clenching around me in a way that feels like destiny. It's as if every fiber of her being recognizes me, welcoming me home into the eye of her storm.

From the moment Harlow stumbled into our world, all wide-eyed and brimming with that fiery spirit, I knew she'd be a force to be reckoned with. But as I sink deeper into her embrace, surrounded by the dark echo of our sanctuary, it hits me like a revelation—she isn't just a tempest; she's the axis on which my world spins.

I drive into her with an almost religious fervor, each thrust a liturgy written in the language of flesh and desire. The stone altar beneath her is cold, but our bodies are a conflagration, stoking the fire that rages within me.

"Fuck it," I growl, my voice a low rumble that resonates through the cavernous space of the desecrated church. "We're keeping you, Harlow, for as long as we damn well can." The threat of the crossroads demon looming over us—an ever-present shadow—but in this moment, it's just us and the primal dance of our bodies.

A reckless idea sparks in my mind like a struck match. Maybe it's time to renegotiate the terms of our little agreement. Because, if there's one thing I've learned about dealing with devils, it's that there's always a loophole, always another hand to play.

The rhythm of my body slamming into hers becomes a frenzied beat, echoing off the walls like the pounding of war drums. Harlow's screams and moans are the melody to my savagery, a symphony of sin played out on this unholy altar. I'm relentless, driven by an insatiable hunger that claws at my insides.

"Good girl," Church's voice cuts through the haze of lust, his grey eyes glinting with indulgence from across the altar. His white hair, a disheveled halo around his head, bobs in approval as he leans forward, arms braced against the altar. "Taking all of us... You're ours now. You belong to us."

The words fan the flames within me, a dark promise that brands her soul, as much as our bodies have marked her flesh. There's a twisted pride that swells in my chest because she does belong to us—claimed by our touch, marked by our desire.

Parrish's hazel eyes, wild with the same fervor that grips me, never leave the sight of where we join. His lips curve into a smirk, the tattoos etched into his skin seem to come alive, dancing with the ripple of his muscles under the dim church lights.

And Abel, with his pale skin and constellation of freckles, watching with a cocky tilt of his head, drumming fingers against his thigh as if keeping time with each of my thrusts.

The air crackles with our collective energy, every pant and cry a testament to our unity in this darkness. My pace quickens, desperate and demanding, as I chase the crescendo that's building within her.

Then it happens. The moment she shatters beneath me, her inner walls clenching around me so fiercely, it's like being caught in a velvet vice. Her climax triggers mine, a cataclysmic release that has my balls drawing up tight.

"Fuck..." The word is ripped from my throat as I spill into her, filling her with my cum. In this instant, I'm not just part of her; I am one with her. We are entwined beyond flesh, beyond blood—a single entity forged in the crucible of our forbidden rite.

As I collapse over her, panting and spent, the air thick with the scent of sex and sin. We have defied the fates, rewritten the stars, if only for a night. The demon can wait—we've earned our respite through sheer will and wicked deeds.

"Harlow," I whisper against her ear, my voice a blend of reverence and rebellion. "We've only just begun."

THIRTY-EIGHT
HARLOW

Hellhound on my trail
(Robert Johnson)

THEY FOLLOW the preaching of a man that sang of nothing but blues, about last fair deals and a hellhound on his tail. Robert Johnson's story didn't end well, how did Church, Bishop, Parrish and Abel think this was going to go for them? They are playing with inferno fire, and there's no way they won't get burned.

It's funny, I thought I knew what it was to be afraid, but I might've mistaken self-preservation for fear, because the dread I feel now that I have something to lose, my men, I am beyond a shadow of a doubt scared.

I should be mad at them. I should hate their guts. I was no more than a means to an end to them for a hot minute there. They manipulated the dainty threads of my life just so that I fell right into their bloody hands. But being the person that I am, I can't. I don't even despise mother dearest, and she has treated me like trash all my life. So how can I loathe these lost souls, when they have flaunted nothing but heed and passion my way? We all have a slip of the pen, can't fault them for still being human even under the fallen angel façade.

We vacate the abandoned church, the shadows eyeing us like prey on the way out. The boys didn't bother to clean our mess up, leaving remnants of my lost innocence and our pleasure to stain the altar cloth and possibly the wood beneath it perpetually. Parrish has taken it upon himself to carry me in his arms, my front to his, in a reverse piggyback ride, after my legs gave up on me when I tried to stand by myself.

"Perhaps getting fucked by four guys on your first go at it was a bit much, hmmm pretty doe? Someone is going to be sore in the morning." Parrish recited that last part in a sing-song manner. No need to wait until the dawn of a new day for that, I already ache. "It's ok, you'll get used to having this many dicks." Will I have enough time with them to get used to it though?

The plan was always for them to go back to the McGrew's old trailer house where they grew up after the sacrifice. "We'll do what we have always done, clean ourselves, get some rest. We'll head back to Memphis when we wake up." Bishop had said. So, I suppose, as we make our way through the dark woods to the car, that's our destination.

My head is resting on Parrish's shoulder, my legs and arms around him in a clingy embrace, whilst one of his hands rests under my butt and the other on my lower back. I watch the house of God, that is now consumed by darkness, left to rot and fall apart, get smaller and become disguised by the grove of trees. What would they say about us getting married here?

A few flowers would do the trick, perhaps dark Dahlias, to transform it from a cold somber decaying ruin, swamped in blood and death, into a beautiful melancholic Garden of Eden, to rival our souls. I would love that. Ugh, hold on, marriage? Way to jump a bunch of chapters ahead on a love affair tale, since we kind of just got together.

That is, if I am not reading too much into the I love you´s and the sex.

"Are we together now?" I ask Parrish in a low voice.

"Till death do us apart," was his answer. My soft moan echoes in the deadly silence of the night.

I fight like hell to keep my eyes open and not fall into a deep slumber, I don't want to miss a thing, but it seems I was chasing a rainbow on that one. I stir awake, drenched in sweat, because I seem to be confined within a sea of over-heating male bodies, in a squeaky iron frame king size bed. Parrish is curled up between my spread legs using my thigh as a pillow. Church is on my left, on his side, with his arm draped over my middle, his face nuzzled into my neck as his shallow breathing trails sweet caresses on my skin. Whilst Bishop is on my right, lying on his back like me, his arms folded on his chest, the same position a corpse would be put to rest on a coffin. Looking around I wonder, where my man covered in tattoos is though?

I find myself ogling the small room; it's pretty bare, only having the bed we are lying on, a desk with chair by the window and a chest of drawers opposite to the bed. On a corner by the window there's a large black and gray splotch feasting on the moisture from the ceiling.

I untangle myself from the bodies in bed with me and go on a hunt for Abel. I become aware that my hair is wet, but not from perspiring, and that I smell like sandalwood. Did the guys wash me? Cripes, I must've been really tired if that didn't wake me. I am also only wearing a men's tee, that stops at my upper thighs.

I sneak out of the room, walking through the corridor of Church and Bishop's childhood home that leads to the open space with kitchen, dining and living room all in one. This place seems to be stuck in a nostalgic brooding past. A bitter breeze brushes my naked skin giving rise to goosebumps. By the side of the kitchen, to my right, is the front door that is wide open, revealing the rising sun, casting rosy hue petals across the rich blue morning sky that creates a halo around a man, sitting by the steps on the front porch, his upper body tattoos bare for all to see.

"Hey." I utter as I approach Abel.

"Hey." He says, peering behind him. Hot damn, he's wearing his reading glasses, the sight making me bite my lower lip to try and halt the moan that wants to escape. "It's early, go back to bed, Low." Abel declares, turning back around to stare at the break of dawn.

"Nah, I don't think I will." I state as I take a seat next to him, holding my folded legs to my chest. "Couldn't sleep?" I ask him.

"I have trouble sleeping, and Bishop's bed was a bit crowded."

"Insomnia?" I pry, because I want to get to know them before it's too late.

A suppressed laugh emanates from his throat, before voicing, "That, nightmares, dark thoughts, you name it."

"Do you regret it?"

A furrow paints his face when he looks at me, his almost

black eyes locking with my electric blue ones. "Regret what, angel?

"Not sacrificing me. You must worry about what it means for you four." I know I do, it's slowly eating up at me.

"I don't regret a thing. Not even the dark gospel itself of why we brought you into our lives, because it did just that. The consequences of our failure to perform our end of the bargain are our cross to bear, not yours. So please stop worrying." How can I? I love them. Abel looks away, glancing down at his clasp hands. "Can I tell you a story?"

"Hmmm sure."

"You see that trailer over there, the one falling to pieces?" He asks as he tips his head in the direction of a ram shackled structure with sunken roof and broken windows, the vinyl siding clearly rotting and peeling away from the exterior walls. "That was my," Abel pauses, his Adam's apple bobbing up and down as he swallows, "home once." The way he says it makes it seem like it was never home at all. "My parents were junkies. If it weren't for the McGrew's..."

I put my hand on top of his. When they part at my touch, I interlock my fingers with one of them. "Abel, you don't have to tell me anything." I inform him.

"I want to. The McGrew's, they were the ones that cared for me, fed me, made sure I was washed up and had clean clothes on my body. You think you have it bad, until something more awful comes knocking. When I was 6, I was used as payment for my parents' debt. Lost my innocence to a sick bastard that never saw the inside of a prison for his sins. And then I end up with a monster just as harrowing. Silas Rosson, my uncle. A strict-for-punishment disciple of God, he was.

Everything was my fault according to him; I never did anything right in his eyes."

"Abel," I seek to interrupt.

"You want to know what he told me about that nightmarish night. That I asked for it. He used to chain me to a wall, arms spread like Jesus on the cross, in an ill-lit clammy basement for days, no water or food. Rats were my only roommates, the fucking rodents sure liked to nibble at my dangling feet. Torture. Endless torture, that he inflicted upon me to purge me from my, so called, wrongdoings. Odds are, the more someone tries to twist us into something, the more likely we are to bend the other way. If I am going to be branded like a cow as a sinner, I may as well be sinful. And I so hate basements."

"I hate spandrels." I say abruptly. "I had my own personal praying closet under the stairs of my home, probably just as dark and damped as your basement."

"Harlow, what are you saying?" Abel questions, his eyes studying me.

"I didn't have rats for company, but I had many eyes of glorified souls that looked down on me, judging me for whatever mother dearest declared I did wrong. There were times I wondered if she had forgotten that she locked me in there." A hollow laugh slips away from me, "How disrupted am I? I much preferred getting her physical abuse than being shoved inside the closet."

"She hit you?" Abel is breathing hard, odium, like Ive never seen filling his eyes. "I don't understand; What bad deed could an angel commit?"

"I dared to hope, for a life beyond the one they professed was the righteous one and imposed with iron fists."

"They punished you for dreaming." He grunts angrily.

"It's ok, Abel." I try to comfort the man before me.

"What? No, it's not."

I get up and straddle Abel's lap, placing my hands on his cheeks, as his arms envelop me, circling around my back. "Stuff happens for a reason." I halt, seeking the right words. "I am so sorry, for the awful things you had to live through, and for the torment you suffered by the hands of someone that avows to follow the preaching of a said to be kind and merciful god. But they made you the man I love, wishing them away would be wishing you away, so don't ask for my terrible upbringing to be wiped off. If they hadn't broken me; you wouldn't have this me."

"Harlow." Abel utters my name in such a tender way, it makes my heart swell.

"The people that did us wrong will go through their own woe, they will pay for the agony they served us with. Just wait and see."

"Fuck. I love you, angel." I bestow Abel with a sheepish smile before kissing him. At his lips touch, I blossom for him like a flower, parting my lips to allow his tongue to enter. Abel's arms hug me tighter to him, any space between disappearing as our kiss deepens. My hands move from his face to the nape of his neck, my fingers burying themselves in his raven black strands, pulling and tugging.

Our tongues get enslaved in a riveting dance that drags until a shadow comes to loom by the trailer door. "What do I need to do to get myself some of that loving, mama?" My cheeky guy with pink hair asks.

Hmmm... have I bitten off more than I can chew with these boys?

Thirty-Nine

Abel

THE RHYTHM of my heart syncs with the pounding of the drums, as I reflect on Harlow's narrative from the previous evening, I recall her words vividly. Her voice, a haunting melody that cuts through the clamor of our backstage frenzy. The air is thick with tension, scented with sweat, leather, and the electric charge of our shared energy. I twirl a drumstick between my fingers, the wood familiar and grounding.

"We are the same," I find myself thinking, the words a silent mantra that matches the tempo of my restless thoughts. Harlow's story, raw and resonant, hangs heavy, a confession that tethers my soul to hers. There's a thrumming in my veins, a chorus of certainty that crescendos with every word she speaks. She's meant to be ours, meant for us. I've never been more sure of anything.

No tattoos mar her flesh, but she carries her scars on the inside, just like us. It's in the defiant tilt of her chin, the feisty spark in her gaze - she's one of us, even if she doesn't bear the inked marks of our brotherhood.

Harlow's arrival into our lives isn't happenstance; it's fate, destiny, whatever you want to call it. It's as though she's the missing piece we didn't realize we were searching for, until she appeared. Her presence completes a puzzle we've been trying to solve with sheer will and brute force, a mystery etched into the very fabric of who we are as a unit.

"Harlow, there's a reason you walked into our lives," I say, my voice low and steady amid the disarray around us. "You're the piece we needed. Without you, we're just an unfinished song, all build-up and no climax."

Clutching my drumsticks like lifelines, I stand backstage in Clarksdale, Mississippi, the very heart of blues legends and soul-selling myths. The infamous crossroads loom in the back of my mind, a silent witness to our show tonight. Spotlights blaze, casting shadows that dance with the rhythm of our own personal devilry, there's an ache in my chest, a gnawing dread that's got nothing to do with the adrenaline pumping through my veins.

I glance at the wings of the stage, half expecting to see Harlow there, her electric blue eyes reflecting the chaos we create, her presence the missing piece we didn't know we were incomplete without. Damn it, why did it have to be her? She's the harmony to our discord, the siren song to our damned souls.

She was never meant to be a sacrifice. Not for us, not for any godforsaken deal. We should've chosen another way—anyway—that didn't lead to losing her. Losing everything.

We're playing with fire in more ways than one, right here at the crossroads where so many have fallen before us. And as the legend goes, the devil doesn't come clad in red; he comes whispering promises, dressed in desires too tempting to resist. Just like Harlow waltzed into our lives, an angel in devil's garb.

The cacophony of Clarksdale's backstage is a living beast, all growls of amplifiers with the hiss of speakers warming up. The show is hours away, but my pulse already keeping time with the restless drumbeat thumping. It's here, in this place steeped in legend, where we've come to play out our final act. But there's an unease in me, knowing what's at stake—our souls, Harlow's fate—tied to the devil's whims.

I shove my hands into the pockets of my leather pants, trying to anchor myself amid the chaos. Turning a corner, I freeze. Church, wrapped around Parrish like ivy on an old gravestone, presses him against the wall. Their kiss isn't just for show; it's raw, fervent, as if they're trying to meld into one being. A surge of something fierce and unnamable claws through my gut, a violent twist of emotion that feels like jealousy, but cuts deeper.

Before I can turn away or make sense of the whirlwind in my chest, warmth envelops me, a small frame pressing flush against my back. Arms, delicate yet strong, encircle my waist, grounding me. I exhale, tension seeping out as I lean back into the familiar presence. Her touch is a balm, her proximity a comfort, reminding me why we're here, why we endure—the missing piece that made us whole.

"Abel," Harlow whispers, her breath warm on my skin, her voice steady despite the pandemonium around us.

I spin around within Harlow's embrace, my gaze locking with hers, an ocean of electric blue rimmed with night. "How pretty, right? I love seeing them together," she admits, and her words spill over me like a melody that both soothes and ignites.

"You're okay with this?" I can't help but probe, needing to hear her thoughts, to understand her heart.

Her lips curve into a knowing smile, one that reads the depths of my soul. "Why wouldn't I be? Love is love, I'm just glad to be a part of it," she says. The simplicity of her acceptance, the purity of her view—it bewilders me.

"Something about it intrigues me, not sure if it's for me, but it draws my attention a lot." The confession tumbles out before I can stop it, a raw admission hanging between us.

Harlow leans up, bridging the gap, her kiss landing deeply on my lips. It's a clash of worlds, a fusion of doubts and desires that sends a shockwave through my veins. "Well, we could try it together, to see if it fits, and if it doesn't, I get to keep you all to myself, right?" Her voice dances with mischief, her eyes shimmering with promise.

A laugh escapes me, dark and hopeful, as I draw her impossibly close. Our bodies meld together, two forces of nature entwined in the eye of an emotional tempest. "You're perfect, you know that?" I say against her lips, every word a vow, every breath a testament to our twisted fate.

FORTY

HARLOW

I CAUGHT Abel haunting Church and Parrish, peaking through the corner at one of their moments. I love seeing those two together; it's just so primal and raw. How could I not be ok with it? That's what I want, a love born out of harsh pasts, with much the same suffering and dire straits, that grows and flourishes as years go by instead of withering and dying with time, that lingers by virtue of their shared immoral deeds. To see the beauty in each other's flaws, now that's the most sacred thing of all.

"I am not perfect, my shepherd." I confess to Abel. "But, dare I say it is my soul's deformity, my broken parts, that makes me fitting for y'all, wouldn't you agree?"

I can feel a slight hum and throb exuding from his body, as a violent palpitation rays out from his heart, there's this spirit around him at present that screams, well, to put it in Paragon of Virtue's Inferno words, fuck me. Hmmm no, that sounded wrong coming from me, let's go with let us consummate and consume one another.

"You misinterpreted my words, Low, you are a paragon

"

because ugliness is the greatest of all sins and we, all four of us, are graced by it. We are ugly souls, disguised in a pretty face, and you just shrugged off those bullshit masks we put on and found the beauty in the foul rotting within us. Now that is the province of a poet, my dear."

"Your pretty faces don't hurt though." That makes my man, with skin beautified by a mass of tattoos, chuckle. "I am a bit vain, so please don't put me on a pedestal I do not belong on."

"Ok, angel." Abel utters, as an unrighteous smirk creeps up, painting his hollow-cheeked face in a twisted and wicked nuance. "How about I put you in a position you do belong, with one of our cocks buried deep in one of your holes?" An unchaste shiver snakes up my spine, making me bite down on my lower lip to keep the whimper stuck in my throat from getting out. That makes Abel chuckle again, as he thrusts out one of his hands to my lips, pulling down on my lower one and forcing my teeth to relinquish possession of it. "You can swallow down your moan all you want, Low, but I can smell your arousal, I know you want it, you ache for it."

"I am still a bit sore from last night, Abel." I admit. Between having my cherry popped by Church, which on its own it's already something that is sure to spawn some tenderness in my core and following that with three other as substantially lavish lengths and their as brutal pounding, yeah, I ache alright.

"We can give your pussy a rest, the last thing I want to do is hurt you." Is it strange that I actually wouldn't have minded suffering through the discomfort and pain as his monster rod in where it's raw, where it hurts? "I mean, I did say holes, Low." Immediately upon purring those words, with the arm that is still hugging me around my middle, he forces me to orbit him like he's my sun until my back meets the wall. Abel's other hand comes to rest right next to my head, his body pressing against mine; hunching so he can look down at me. I giggle because I find myself in the same position Church had Parrish in just around the river bend.

I peer through the corner, and low and behold, they are still in one another's embrace, their kiss still ungentlemanly and passionate, but currently one of Church's hands is buried inside the pants of the man with pink hair as one of Parrish is buried within Church's. I can see them yanking at each other like there is no tomorrow. I was wet between my legs before, but now I am, drenched.

"Harlow." Abel grunts, compelling my gaze to fall upon him. His almost black eyes had been staring at the other two also, but now they meet my electric blue ones with so much vehemence and resolve, a shroud of solemnity and sobriety gracing the sharp lines of his face. "On your knees, angel. It's time to pray." I would love to do as I am told, but if he doesn't back up, I don't know how I can, he is to close for me to move. I fracture my hold around his middle, my hands going right between us and planting themselves over his chest, but as I seek to push him somewhat off me, he asks, "What are you doing?"

"Well, my shepherd, you aren't giving me much room to do as you please."

Abel captures my hands with his, bringing them to the wall and pinning them dead on either side of my head. His legs part like the Red Sea did for Moses, "Down, girl." He growls.

I bend my knees and start to slither down the cold surface behind me. My hands stay where they are, trapped under his grasp, awaiting, in a way, for my knees to encounter the floor for him to then hold them together above my head with one hand, while with the other he pops the button of his baggy jeans, lowering the zipper and pulling the denim material down along with his boxers just enough for his monster to stand at attention, it is so close to my face it actually brushes my cheek with the springing motion.

"Open wide, I am going to lay claim to your mouth." Phantasm images play in my head, of me giving head to Bishop. Wait, did that in sooth happen, or was it just a wet dream? It doesn't matter, gospel or not, what is happening in this instant should be what I am devoted to.

"I am ready to receive my Holy Communion, my shepherd." I declare in an inviting and seductive voice.

Abel groans, the sound just loud enough to pierce through the raucous noise of our crew hard at work putting the show in place. "Yes. Talk holy to me, Harlow." It fills me with pride that he liked my play on godly words. Instead of the body and blood of Christ in the form of bread and wine, I am hoping for Abel's flesh and cum.

I part my lips, and Abel wastes no time shoving his monster in my mouth, he guides it in with his hand at the base. He begins with the tip and then pulls out, in and out, in and out, where every time Abel pushes his tattooed length back in it goes an inch or so further than before. This goes on for a while before his snake is fully nestled deep inside. I try to gulp down what's lodged deep in my throat, but of course that won't work, that's when tears gather in my eyes as I start to gag.

"Angel, you are going to have to breathe through your nose for this, ok?" I do as instructed and it helps a bit, at least I don't feel like I am choking anymore, but I am drooling like a bloodhound. "Fuck, you are a sight for sore eyes, Low." He mutters in a low and rather rough tone. "You take me so well, first in your pussy and now in your maw. I am going to fuck your mouth, pronto." With that his hand abandons his monster and ends up next to his other one holding my hands captive against the wall. Swiftly Abel begins to unceremoniously thrust in and out of my mouth, the noises outside of this moment somewhat obscuring my moans and slurping sounds. It just dawned on me that I need to perform in a few hours, my voice is so going to come out croaky and broken, and I so don't care.

The intricate tattooed snake on his length seems to writhe as his monster keeps disappearing and reappearing from my parted lips, like it's a genuine ophidian. I conjure up this, very much, improbable thing, where the serpent leaves his flesh and slithers down my throat. I mean, is anything out of the realm of possibility here, where shadows, demons and the devil are involved?

I can sense Abel's body begin to tense, someone is close to coming undone. He releases my hands as his go to the top of my head, his fingers getting tangled up in my light old-money blonde curls. My arms fall limp at my sides; I have been so into what he's doing with my mouth, that I missed the pins and needles feeling from lack of proper blood flow through my arms. Once I regain some sort of strength to them, I lift one arm to his hip, whilst the other skims the valley between my breasts, gathering some of my saliva, to eventually join the first on the opposite hip.

Abel's hands turn to fists in my hair, as he continuously thrusts into me. I don't know what comes over me, I am the sweet preacher's daughter, I had to cut the innocent since I am no longer so, but I urge my hands to journey past the hips, caressing his firm ass cheeks. With my wet fingers I hit the road rubbing circles around his rose bud.

"Harlow, what are you…" He never finishes his question as his words become a howl the split second I insert a finger in his back door. "Fuck!" He breathes out. My finger sets off penetrating in and out of him in harmony with the way he's ramming into my parted lips. "Don't stop. Shit." He hisses that last word, his monster planting itself deep in the back of my mouth and spilling his salty seed. I try my hardest to swallow it all down, but there's so much and it just keeps on coming.

My boy with dark brown hair with a hue that rivals his eyes, takes a step back, removing his semi hard length from my mouth. Some of his cum escapes pass my lips with the action and cascades down my chin, as one of the hands on my hair falls to my throat, gripping it with ungraceful force, and pulling me up to my feet.

His lips capture mine in a hungry and possessive kiss, our tongues marrying straight off the bat, tying themselves in knots with one another. "What possessed you to do that, my angel?" Abel asks once he fractures our kiss. Our gazes' crash together, and there's an inferno behind his dark brown eyes. It would be scary if I didn't know he would never cause me harm intentionally.

I lick my lips, tasting whatever is left of Abel's rapture upon them, before replying, "I don't know. Did you not like it?" My voice sounds hella hoarse.

"Seriously?" He says in response, one of his eyebrows arching, bewilderment written all over the sharp lines of his handsome face.

I can't get a good read on him, so I panic. "Oh Abel, I," I pause in my words, last night's conversation arousing in my mind. Oh no, did I trigger something? I can only presume what that predator drug dealer must've done to him, perhaps that is why he's not sure if he wants something with the others. "Damn, Abel, I am sorry if I ruined the moment, if I caused you so sort of anguish."

"Pretty sure, damn is a swear word, angel. And what are you on about? Why are you apologizing? I mean, it felt weird at first, but I happen to like it… a lot."

"Oh," whatever else I was about to say just turns into a squeak as Abel's hand narrows around my throat.

"But here's the thing, I was going to be nice," as if my guys know how to be nice, I try to chuckle at that, but nothing comes out, I think Abel downright desecrated my throat, "solely fuck your mouth and then eat you up. However," He utters, spinning me around in his arms and smothering my front to the wall, his hand never leaving my throat, "it's only fair since you got to play with my ass that I get to play with yours." With his free hand, he creeps up my dress and rips my panties. "It looks like you are going to be tender in all of your holes, my angel."

His fingers brush along my wet folds collecting some of my juices, which make me tingle with pleasure, to then set off on a pilgrimage to my rose bud. They draw slow and tantalizing circles around it, biding their sweet time before swooping in my back door. I mewl at the lone digit intrusion. It moves in and out of me unaccompanied for a bit, until a second one joins it within, and then a third. Abel is busting a gut to stretch me out as much as possible. I am worried, with Abel's sizable length my core had to bloom to a considerable extent to be able to house him, how the hell is he going to fit in my ass?

"The good thing about starting with me, is that your ass will be ready to take any of the other dipshits and their insignificant dicks with ease." I chew over what he just put forth in my head, I have faith that if he ever takes one of the others -not so small, at all- lengths in his ass he will be eating up his words. But Abel certainly does take the crown for thickness.

The Paragon of Virtue's Inferno drummer withdraws his fingers from my puckered hole and grabs a hold of his monster, bringing the tip right to the entrance. I hear him spit, feeling the secreted liquid hit my skin, right where his length is. He presses forcefully against the hole and his snake's head begins going in. I hiss, because the sting is as bad as when he penetrated my core.

"It will be alright, angel, you'll adjust. Just take deep breaths, ok." Abel repeats a twin incantation to the one he chanted to me on the altar, his hand releasing his length and coming to move up and down my spine, the touch light as a feather; delicate and worshiping. The gesture does the same as the night before, relaxing me enough for him to bury his length to entirely inside. "Good girl."

I go from being a virgin, barely twenty-four hours ago, to having both; my pink blush lips down south and my derriere broken in. He spits once more and begins to thrust in and out of me. In all of this the hand on my throat never abandons it position and is now constricting, choking me somewhat, while the other hand finds itself on my bundle of nerves, flicking through it like you do the pages in a book. There are so many sensations swarming over me it's not exactly a miracle that I rupture abruptly.

The narrative that follows is a bit odd and concerning, but I play it off with the fact I must've caught my tattooed man off guard. He seems possessed almost, ramming into me with unforgiving and bestial urge, two of his fingers boring themselves in my core, hooking within, as his hand on my throat strangles me. Black clouds play at the edges of my vision, either from the lack of air in lungs or the intensity of my orgasm, i am not sure. I can't speak, I can't tell him to yield, at least with how tight he is clenching around my neck.

My saving graces, Church and Parrish as they hell-for-leather turn the corner, colliding straight into us.

FORTY-ONE

PARRISH

MY HEART HAMMERS in my chest, the erratic rhythm syncing with Church's. We pull away from each other, gasping for breath. Our hands sliding from the confines of fabric, slick with each of our releases. The silence that follows is heavy, suffocating, charged with an energy we've unwittingly unleashed. My skin prickles as the air around us thickens, and I can sense it—the wrongness of it all—as the light in the room begins to wane, as if it is being snuffed out by an invisible hand.

"Church," I whisper, my voice barely a rasp, my eyes scanning the darkening space. He doesn't respond, but I feel his tension mirroring mine, our instincts on high alert. The shadows seem alive, twisting and contorting along the walls in a macabre dance.

"Shit," Church hisses, his grey eyes flickering to the periphery. "The demons are lurking damn close."

I swallow hard, tasting the adrenaline and fear mingling on my tongue. His curse slices through the unnatural stillness —a reminder that we're not alone. I can see them now, the shadows drawing nearer, their forms gaining substance, becoming something more than just absence of light. They hunger for chaos, for the discord we've created.

A bead of sweat rolls down my temple, tracing the lines of tension etched deep into my skin. My breath hitches as I take a step back, the shadows snaking across the ground like tendrils of malice. Church's curse is barely audible, a whispered blasphemy that seems to feed the darkness around us.

"Shit," Church hisses, his grey eyes flickering with a spark that's part anger, part fear. "They're not just shadows anymore." His gaze locks with mine, and the understanding that passes between us is as sharp as the blade I usually wield with such confidence. We've crossed a line, danced too close to the edge of damnation, and now we're teetering on the brink.

He's right. The shapes are more defined now, growing bolder, stretching towards us with purpose. The air grows thick, almost suffocating, as if the very atmosphere conspires against us. I can feel the weight of our choices bearing down on us—every note we played, every drop of blood we spilled in defiance—it all leads to this moment.

"He's pissed," Church whispers, the words chilling in their simplicity.

I nod; my throat tight, unable to voice the dread that coils in my gut. Fear is a living thing inside me, writhing and clawing its way up my chest. But fear won't save us now. We defied him—the Devil—and the price of rebellion is steep.

"Fuck off!" My voice is a tremor resonating in the thick air, but I force it through the pressing darkness. "Go find someone else!"

Church's hand grips my shoulder, his voice a low snarl. "We have gotta find the others, now."

The shadows don't heed our commands. They thicken and curl at the edges, growing more solid with each passing second. The light around us fades into a twilight gloom, and the very fabric of reality seems to warp as they take on form—wraith-like figures with eyes that glow like molten gold, sinister and silent.

"Shit," Church breathes out, and I feel his muscles tense beside me.

Their whispers slither through the air, a cacophony of hisses that scratch at the inside of my skull. Words I can't understand, but their intent is clear: malice.

We're standing in the eye of a storm that we brought upon ourselves, and the sense of control we had is slipping away, like sand through open fingers. The wraiths inch closer; their presence is almost palpable now—a cold promise of violence.

"Church," I whisper, not daring to raise my voice lest it betrays the fear clawing at my throat. "They're going to strike."

We bolt, our breaths ragged bursts in the stagnant air. The narrow corridor amplifies our pounding footsteps, a desperate drumbeat that syncs with my racing heart. The Shadows slither after us, their dark tendrils reaching, grasping, relentlessly like nightmares clawing into reality.

"Keep moving!" Church's voice is a harsh command that slices through the heavy darkness. His hand grips mine, slick with sweat and fear, pulling me forward.

As we skid around the corner, Harlow and Abel materialize like specters conjured from the gloom. The collision is brutal, bodies slamming together with the force of destiny denied. We stumble backward, a tangle of limbs and confusion, the impact knocking the wind out of us.

Time stalls, hangs suspended in the chaos of our entwined fates. Harlow's pale curls are a contrast against the encroaching darkness, her electric blue eyes wide with shock. Abel is sprawled on the floor, pants around his ankles.

Harlow is gasping for air. Her dress is bunched around her waist, the pale fabric bright in contrast to the darkness we just fled. I can't help but notice the damning evidence of their recent closeness—Abel's cum is still dripping from his dick. His eyes flash an inky black before settling back to their natural hue, disoriented on the floor.

"Shit, are you okay?" Church's voice cuts through the tension, his concern directed at Harlow who's straightening herself up.

"What the hell just happened?" I mutter under my breath.

Forty-Two

Abel

Blood pounds through my veins, every beat a drum of the hellish symphony that seems to have started playing out of nowhere. I'm still coming down from filling up Harlow's ass when Church and Parrish burst in, looking like they'd danced with the devil himself and lost. Their eyes are wild, hair matted to their faces, for a pair of guys who flirt with darkness on the regular, this is something else entirely.

"Abel," Harlow's voice is a soft murmur beside me, laced with confusion and concern. Her pale skin looks almost ethereal in the dim light, but her electric blue eyes are wide with uncertainty. I can't help but glance up at her, seeking some silent reassurance or an answer she doesn't have.

Before our silent conversation can continue, Parrish's command slices through the air, as sharp as one of his beloved knives. "Get up, pull up your pants. We gotta talk, now!" His tone brokers no argument, the urgency in his hazel eyes sparking a fire under my ass.

"Shit," I mutter under my breath, fumbling with the fabric of my jeans, yanking them up over my hips. My fingers tremble slightly, not just from the post-orgasmic haze but also from whatever terror has etched itself into their faces.

Church, normally the soul of cheeky banter, stands mute, his grey eyes haunted pools reflecting some unspeakable horror. He's always been the type to laugh in the face of danger, but right now, he's a silent statue, and it sets my nerves on edge.

"Back to the bus," Parrish growls, already turning on his heel. I cast a final, lingering look at Harlow, who seems as shaken as I feel. But there's no time to comfort, no time for soft words.

Pavement slaps under my boots as we sprint, the night air a cold slap against my flushed skin. Harlow's breaths are ragged echoes next to mine, her presence a flickering flame in the encroaching darkness that threatens to smother us. Church is just behind, silent as the grave, and Parrish's footsteps hammering a frenetic rhythm that matches the pounding of my heart.

We reach the sanctuary of the bus, its hulking form a shadow against the lesser dark of the night. I yank the door open, muscles coiled tight, ready for whatever hell might spill out. But it's just Bishop. His silhouette etched in the dim glow of the lights, a fortress amid the scattered papers and half-empty coffee cups.

"Get in," I bark at Harlow, pushing past the threshold into the known safety of our mobile haven. She scrambles up behind me, followed by Church and Parrish and the door slams shut with a finality that seals us from the terrors outside.

Bishop's gaze lifts, a sharp glint in the low light. "What the fuck happened?" His voice is a blade, cutting through the chaos swirling within me.

I can feel Church move beside me, his presence like a shard of ice in the warmth of the bus. "We got chased by shadows," he starts, voice rough as gravel, the tremor in it betraying more fear than I've ever heard from him before. A pause, heavy as a tombstone, then—"Then we ran into Abel and Harlow, and—" His words choke off, but his eyes, grey as storm clouds, lock onto mine.

The weight of his stare tells me all I need to know before he even finishes. My gut clenches. "Abel's eyes were black." The words hang between us, a sentence passed without a trial.

Panic claws up my throat, a wild thing desperate to escape. "Fuck..." The word falls from my lips, heavy with dread. My pulse hammers in my ears, drowning out the world as Church's accusation reverberates through the cramped space of the bus.

"Abel?" Harlow's voice slices through the cacophony of my thoughts, her usual calm laced with an edge of fear. I can feel her eyes on me, probing, searching for answers I'm not sure I have.

I force myself to look at her, to really see her—her pale skin almost luminescent under the harsh lights, her electric blue eyes wide and clouded with concern. The sight anchors me, if only for a moment, before reality crashes back in.

"Abel was possessed," Parrish declares, his words like a blade against my consciousness. He stands firm by the door, his musician's fingers betraying a rare tremor.

My stomach churns, bile rising hot and bitter. Parrish's gaze doesn't waver, his hazel eyes cold and assessing beneath the bright pink strands of hair that fall across his forehead.

"I'm assuming, he was possessed while he was fucking you," Church interjects, his usual cheekiness nowhere to be found. His grey eyes hard stones, fixed on me with an intensity that feels like a physical force.

"Did you feel it? The possession?" Bishop's voice, usually so grounded, is tinged with urgency now, demanding answers.

I stagger back, the weight of Parrish's revelation anchoring my feet to the floor of the bus.

"That's why you didn't let me breathe," Harlow mutters, her fingers grazing her neck in a ghost of the stranglehold.

"Shit." The word barely makes it out as a whisper. My hand reaches out, seeking forgiveness or maybe just a lifeline. "I'm sorry, baby. I swear, I..."

My voice trails off, useless. What do you even say when 'sorry' isn't nearly enough? When you've been used as a vessel?

She cuts across the space between us, quick, like she's crossing a battlefield instead of the cramped interior of our tour bus. Her hand lands on my chest—thump-thump, thump-thump—a drumbeat beneath her palm that drums the rhythm of life, of guilt, of still being here.

"It's okay," she says, but her blue eyes now stormy seas, churning with things unsaid, fears unvoiced. She doesn't mean it's okay; how could it be? But there's steel in her gaze, a determination not to buckle.

"Is it?" I question, daring to meet her stare, to see the reflection of my own haunted eyes in hers.

The silence is a living thing, coiling around us like the shadows we've just fled. The hum of the sound crew doing the sound check idles in the background. I lean against the wall, the cold seeping through my shirt, grounding me.

"Maybe I can do a deal with the Devil," Harlow voice cuts

through the tension, distant as if she's not quite with us. Her eyes, usually so full of kindness, now hold a depth that's almost frightening. "Spare your souls?"

The words hang heavy in the air. It's a ludicrous idea, something out of a dark fantasy—except our reality has become just that. I glance at Harlow, her lips parting slightly, but no sound escapes. Church stares at the floor, jaw clenched, the silent type to the bone.

"Are you serious?" My voice sounds foreign to my ears, rough and strained.

FORTY-THREE

BISHOP

"LIKE HELL YOU WILL," I snap, my words slicing through the tension-charged air with the precision of a well-tuned bass string. I'm on my feet now, every inch of my frame rigid with defiance. My eyes lock on Harlow's electric blue ones, daring her to challenge me. The pulsing veins in my forearms stand out, a testament to the fury and concern coursing through me. There's no way she's going through with this insane idea. "There's no way I'm letting you sell your soul to the Devil. Satan can't have you. You're ours."

Harlow's pale skin blanches further, but her chin tilts up, a silent display of her feisty nature. She looks like she wants to argue, the stormy mix of determination and fear in her gaze, clashing with the soft curve of her lips. But she knows better. There's something about my stance, maybe it's the broad set of my shoulders or the unyielding firmness in my jaw, that tells her arguing with me would be futile. Good. We've played with fire, danced on the edge of darkness, but we are not crossing that line, no matter how bad things get.

She huffs, the sound full of frustration and a touch of

admiration, as if she recognizes the protective barrier I've thrown around her. Her look softens slightly, that inherent sweetness threading through the tension between us. "Bishop..." she starts, but then stops, her eyelashes casting long shadows over her high cheekbones as she looks down, caught between the desire to rebel and the knowledge that some battles aren't worth the war.

I spin on my heel, the leather of my boots squeaking against the worn floor of the bus. My head's a cacophony of chaos. I push through the narrow hallway, every poster and sticker plastered along the walls a testament to our wild ride to the top... and now, to the edge of damnation.

I slam the door to the back room, the sound echoing like a gunshot. For a second, I just stand there, eyes shut, trying to calm the storm inside me. We're up against a force that doesn't play by the rules, but neither do we. I've always had a plan, always been the mastermind with an ace up his sleeve. But this? It's like trying to outplay a riff nobody's ever heard before.

"Damn it," I mutter under my breath, my fingers curling into fists. The weight of leadership—that's on me. Every decision, every risk, and now every soul in the balance, they look to me.

The telltale shuffle of feet pulls me from my brooding reverie. Church, his presence is like a shadow, heavy with things left unsaid and moves unplayed. He carries the burden of his past like a cross, each step a penance he never seems to finish paying.

I don't glance back as he enters; I don't need to. The scent of leather and cigarettes announces him well enough. His footsteps falter, a dance of hesitation and resolve that I've come to know all too well.

"Church," I say, voice steady despite the tempest raging inside me. "Not now."

But he's here, and I can feel the weight of his gaze boring into my back, grey eyes seeking absolution, where I'm not sure I have any to give. The silence stretches, taut like a guitar string right before it snaps.

"Man, I—" he starts, the words rough around the edges, like they've traveled a long road to get here.

He lets out a breath, and even without seeing his face, I know what's written all over it—regret, sorrow, the whole damn tragic ballad.

I pace the cramped space at the back of the bus, my boots thumping against the floor like a drumbeat in time with my racing heart. Each step is a silent mantra, a vow to set things right, but the rhythm gets broken by his confession.

"I fucked up," Church mutters, voice thick with shame. He sounds like he's been chewing on it for a while.

My back stiffens as I whirl around, the energy in the room crackling with tension and unsaid words. "This is all my fault. If I hadn't made that deal—"

"Shut it," I growl, cutting him off mid-sentence. The air between us charges with my sudden movement as I push off the door, my glare pinning him like an insect to a windshield.

"None of this is your fault," I assert, my voice slicing through the thick atmosphere. It's graveled and raw, echoing my inner turmoil, but leaving no room for doubt. "We all made the same damn choice. Every one of us." My finger jabs in the air for emphasis, punctuating the shared blame. "We, went to the crossroads, and we, made that deal with the Devil."

Church's grey eyes, usually alive with mischief are now dull with the weight of our collective sins.

I get right in his face, my glare as sharp as the edge of Parrish's knives. "Church," I growl, low and menacing, "you're not carrying this cross alone."

He's a mess of white hair and inked skin. His grey eyes are storm clouds about to burst, but I won't let him break—not here, not now.

"Damn it, Bishop," Church rasps, his voice shredded with the weight of his self-loathing. "I'm the one who started it! I'm the one who dragged everyone else into this." He chokes on the next words, each syllable soaked in regret. "And Harlow…"

My jaw clenches so tight I can feel my teeth grind. He's spiraling, and I've got to yank him back before he drags us all down into the abyss.

"If I hadn't been watching her," he continues, a tremor running through his lean frame, "you would never have seen her, she wouldn't have crossed paths with us. You wouldn't have chosen her, she wouldn't be caught up in all this. We wouldn't be—"

He cuts off, throat working like he's swallowing glass. I know the unspoken truth that hangs between us, heavy as the chains we wrapped around our own necks at the Devil's altar.

"Say it, Church," I snarl, because dancing around the fact is just another way of letting the darkness win. "We wouldn't have fallen for her. We wouldn't be so fucked."

He nods, a single jerky movement, his gaze finally lifting to meet mine.

I lunge at him, my hand clamping onto his shoulder with a

grip meant to ground us both. "Listen to me," I growl, my voice a low rumble of thunder in the cramped space of the tour bus. "We've all been enjoying the perks of the forbidden fruit, for too long to start pointing fingers. We made the choice, All of us."

The air is charged between us, thick with unspoken words and shared sins. But there's one truth that burns brighter than any mark we've earned from our dark dealings.

"As for Harlow..." The name alone tightens something deep inside me, forcing the next words out, each one heavier than the last. "A life without knowing her light, wouldn't be a life at all. I'd rather die, than have not known her."

Church's face crumples for a moment, like I've struck a chord that resonates with his own heartstrings. His grey eyes reflecting the turmoil within. He looks down, and I can see the shadows of our past deeds darken his features even more.

"Church," I say, sharp enough to slice through the silence. "Look at me."

He does, finally, and it's like staring into a mirror, that reflects back all the reckless decisions we've made, all the lines we've crossed together.

"None of this, none of what we're facing now, is on just you. You hear me?" I shake him slightly, needing him to believe it, to shed the weight crushing him. "We've got bigger problems."

"Harlow needs us," I continue, the resolve in my voice as solid as the ink etched into my skin. "She's chosen us, and we've chosen her. There's no turning back."

The door hinges groan, slicing through the thick tension hanging in the air. Harlow's silhouette fills the frame, a beacon of light against the backdrop of our dark musings. Her curls shimmer like spun gold, eyes surveying the scene before her. The room suddenly feels charged with a different kind of energy; it's as if she carries a storm under her skin, quiet but so full of potential fury.

"You, ok?" Harlow's voice, though soft, cuts clean through the heaviness that has settled on my shoulders. She stands there, poised between worry and resolve, the embodiment of everything we're fighting to protect.

I force a half-smile, nodding once. "Yeah," I lie smoothly, because what else is there to say? I can't let her see the cracks, not when she's the glue holding us precariously together.

Church doesn't answer, just shuffles his feet, his gaze anchored to the floor. He's still tangled up in his own head, but Harlow's presence seems to act as a salve, even if just for a moment. It's a testament to the power she unknowingly wields over us, a quartet bound by more than just fate or foolish pacts.

"Everything's fine, Harlow," I add, hoping my voice sounds more convincing than I feel. We can't afford to crumble, not now, not with the shadows looming just beyond our safe haven.

FORTY-FOUR
CHURCH

WHAT A SHIT SHOW, and in all respect it's my fault. I fucked up, over and over. Bishop says it's not my job to carry this cross of guilt and despair alone, but I am the one that damns everything I touch, condemning everyone I love to Abaddon. I hear what my brother is saying; we all blithely took greedy bites from the forbidden fruit the father of demons had offered, and the Devil only knows where we would be without the deal, probably long dead. Yet I can't help but hate myself for the hell I brought down upon all of our lives.

Abel, shit, the shadows got to him, and they did what they do best, he almost offed Harlow up in the peak of their carnal dance. I felt a pang of something when I saw his eyes misted over in a cloud of blackness, for a split second I thought I had lost him, but then my eyes fell upon Harlow's neck and the handprint on it as she desperately tried to draw in as much air as she could, she became the lone character of my crucifying, doesn't mean I cared any less for the man with his skin embellished in Paragon of Virtue's Inferno words. The gospel is I do fancy him, I just don't think he could feel the same, with his past and all, it's probably why our relationship is so arousingly full of hostility and antagonizing.

"Everything's fine, Harlow," My older brother tells my princess. Fine? As if. There's no way she doesn't taste the pungent deceit in those words. Meanwhile, I just shuffle my feet and glare at them.

Harlow, fuck, she doesn't deserve this, but Bishop painted an irrefutably flawless picture, a life without ever having the pleasure of being graced by her light, would have been no life at all. She makes the days before her seem dull and hollow, impregnated with insignificant shit. And now, she makes it hard to just shuffle off this mortal coil, while on the eve of Harlow we wouldn't have given a damn if Death came knocking on our tour bus door.

We were not wrong about Harlow being our salvation; we just mistakenly thought it was because she was preordained to be our last sacrifice, not actually destined to be with us. Oh, how I wish things had played out differently. We are not Gods, we are fools.

"Fine? Right." Harlow repeats my own introspection of Bishop's utterance. "Lie to me, why don't you." She hisses at Bishop, her voice makes me want to scratch off my own flesh, it sounds fucked.

"Harlow." Bishop sternly says her name.

"This is my fault."

"What?" My brother and I voice at the same time, our pale grey eyes boring into the beautiful girl standing by the closed door of what used to be the den of iniquity, mostly where we brought Paragon of Virtue's Inferno groupies and fucked them, but since Harlow arrived it has become an unused master bedroom.

"If y'all had just sacrificed me you wouldn't be in this mare's nest. Why won't you let me remedy the baneful situation y'all find yourselves in?"

"By making your own deal with the Devil? I told you no, Harlow." Bishop asserts, his tone unforgiving. "This isn't on you, my little mouse. Or you." He points at me. "So, both of you can stop trying to be the fucking sacrificial lamb and taking the blame on behalf of all of us. We were all sane enough to lend a hand in making this bed; consequentially, we all must lie in it."

"Harlow shouldn't have to though." I remark. "She's an innocent party in all of this."

"Innocent? Church, you stripped me of that when you pushed yourself inside my core. You made me yours, y'all did. Don't you dare alienate me from this now." My girl sounds so tormented by the idea of not being a part of this with us. She needs us, as we need her. "Till death do us apart." Harlow vows. She chose us, just as we chose her. Unfortunately, I and the rest of Paragon of Virtue's Inferno members are on our last rites.

"No." I say in a solemn and assertive manner, which makes Harlow furrow her brows. "Not even death can break us up. Our souls are yours forever, my beautiful succubus."

Her expression changes, a small smile now blesses her face. "Succubus? I don't think I'm the demon that is going to climb in your bed at night and have my way with you. That sounds more like something one of you lot would do, my incubus. Oh, wait you already have, at least twice."

At some point in our back and forward, Harlow and I got really close; she is no more than a hair's breadth away from me, while Bishop has taken a seat on the end of the bed, his elbows on his knees, his hands clasped together holding his face by the chin. My brother and his voyeuristic tendencies, there is no judgment amongst the members of this dysfunctional found family, since we all have our own deviant kinks, but still, weirdo. I love him though. Harlow is wearing her own take on one of Sarah Michelle Gellar's Daphne outfits in Scooby-Doo, a 70's style, sleeveless V-neck mini-dress with leather go-go boots, all in white though. It's Fucking hot.

"When dad was around, I used to beg the stars that he would just leave. When mom got sick, I prayed to whoever might've been listening that she would just stay. Some wishes come true, some don't. Some you pay dearly for; some just fall into your lap. Harlow, you are the one thing we hoped for; But never asked for." I don't know what came over me then, why I just spilled my guts to my princess.

"Wow Church." Harlow gasps.

As my dear brother utters, "What is this hearts and flowers bullshit? It sounds like you are saying goodbye, you asshole."

"Bishop!" I call out his name in a castigating manner. How dare he throw me under the bus like that? "I am not; I just don't want things to be left unsaid."

"Don't give up. Please." Harlow begs.

"Of course not. I got spooked, that's all, baby." I admit, brushing my fingertips to her throat, which is already showing signs of bruising, her skin taking a hue of black and blue in the shape of a hand. "I didn't expect the shadows to turn on us like a bat out of hell."

"Ok, let's go back to the front lounge of the bus, talk this over with the other guys," I shut her up by planting my lips to hers. I don't want to go out there, I don't want us to be chasing our tails like desperados, we should take a moment, sober up. I want to indulge in our girl for as long as I fucking can. I guess, it is dawning on me that the little time we've had with her so far, wasn't enough, nothing but an eternity could ever be enough. If our days are numbered, wasting a lone grain of sand -from this cracked hourglass- on futile talk seems absurd. We should be enjoying her, leaving a scar of ourselves on her mind, body and soul in such a way, it would be impossible for an echo of us not to haunt her after we are gone. Ruin her for anyone else. If the life I have led has taught me anything, it is that if you want something, just have it.

I set forth nudging Harlow's dress over her shoulders with both my hands moving in chorus, as I kiss her ardently. My intent is to get rid of the item of clothing, urging it to slide down her body and drop to the floor, leaving her in only her underwear and those sexy boots.

"My little mouse, is there a reason why you are not wearing any underwear?" Bishop asks, his tone grave, making it sound like he's censuring her, when in truth he's seeking to mask his derangement over Harlow pulling a Paris Hilton here.

I fracture our kiss so I can admire our girl's bare skin, giving her the opportunity to reply. "Well, the V-neck was a bit too plunging for a bra, as for my panties, Abel ripped them off."

"Hey, who cares, easy access for us, brother." I comment as I begin to strip off. Once completely naked, I plaster my front to Harlow's, Holy Ghost be damn, he is not getting between us. I grab the nape of her neck with one hand, pulling her face to mine so we can go back to kissing, while the other goes around her waist and plants itself on her lower back.

As we get into a spellbound rhythm with our mouths and

tongues, my hand abandons the cobweb of old-money blonde hair, it found itself within, and creeps down her side, caressing her ethereal skin with the merest whisper of a touch from my fingertips. Harlow's arms hug me around the neck, her spin arching backwards, as I lean my upper body forward, managing to get my hand precisely to where I want it, on her thigh. Then my contact becomes aggressive and rough, I enclose my arm around her leg, and lift it, flaunting her beautiful pussy to my brother.

I hear my brother growl, prior to asking, "Did Abel fuck your ass, little mouse?" My princess trembles in my arms, which tells me all I need to know, even before my hand on her back lowers further and skims the valley between her ass cheeks. There's some sticky stuff amid her puckered hole. Well, this opens a few doors, the things we can do to her now that she has been broken through both holes.

Our lips part. "Did it hurt, having that monster in your pretty rose bud, my succubus?" I ask, my hand moving further between her legs; so my fingers can flick past her wet folds. She nods, in that cute mousy way of hers that my brother is very much fond of. "How much are you willing to hurt to please us?"

"I crave the raw suffering, the sweet torment, but only if it's administered by you four. Make it sting, burn, bleed. Love me the Paragon of Virtue's Inferno way." Harlow states, taking our breath away with her words.

"Fuck, I love you." I confess, making my hand forsaken its place on her cunt to snake around to grab a hold of my cock.

In one swift move, I shove every inch of my dick inside her pussy, cutting Harlow's "I love you too" short, her nails boring into the flesh of my shoulder blades. From the corner of my eye, I perceive Bishop discarding his clothes, and as I begin to thrust in and out of our girl, coercing whimpers of pain and pleasure past her lips, he seizes his cock and begins to beat his own meat.

Ive fucked a lot of pussies; none have ever felt as much like home as Harlow's does, the only other thing that comes close is Parrish's ass, yet I much prefer it when he screws me. Granted, doing it standing up with Harlow is not an easy feat; my princess isn't petite per say, 5' 6 perhaps, and, I mean, the boots do help a bit since they give her, at least a good three inches extra on top of that, but when put against my 6' 4, there's a great deal of knee bending from me. Between Parrish's identical height as me, Bishops 6' 2 and Abel's 6 feet, she is the most exquisite trinket.

I hook my free arm around her other leg, lifting my princess off the ground. Both my arms are now hooked around the back of her knees, as hers arms narrow further around my neck. My hands have come to rest on Harlow's ass cheeks to facilitate me raising her up and down my dick, impaling her roughly and deeply.

"Church." Harlow moans. I can feel her inner walls constrict around my dick like her pussy is trying to munch on it, to then ingest it, she's damn close to coming undone.

"Time to come into flower, my succubus. Bloom for me." I command, before biting hard on her neck, and like a good girl, she does what she's told. Her body locks up as she violently convulses in my arms. Harlow not only strangles me with her arms but around my cock with her pussy, yet I relentlessly keep ramming inside of her. After licking and giving the wound I inflicted upon her neck a final kiss, I ask Bishop, whose knuckles happen to be white from the firm grip he has on his dick, "Are you going to join in at any point, brother?"

"I was waiting until you were done with her." He puts forward.

"But we share so well. Are we going to deny Harlow, the pleasure of being in a McGrew Sandwich?"

"I want to be in a sandwich." My princess purrs.

"Do you even know what that entails, my little mouse?" Bishop questions Harlow, as he gets up from his spot on the bed and walks in a slow almost predatory manner to us. Not for a moment does my brother stop jerking himself off. Not for an instant do my princess's electric blue eyes leave my brother.

I am still bouncing her on my cock, when she shakes her head, the message is not very apparent, so Harlow says in a hush tone, "No."

She looks over her shoulder, as my brother's chest meets her back. One of his hands plants itself on her waist, holding Harlow in place, and forcing me to halt in my impaling of our girl. "It means this." He purrs, as with his other hand he guides his dick into her ass.

"Daddy." Harlow screams, her voice labored and her eyes squeezing shut.

My older brother is a tightrope walker, his control being the very old and rotten rope that he walks upon, which just happens to snap under the weight of his feelings for Harlow. I mean, he's blessed that she's coming down from the high of an orgasm and that Abel probably stretched her well enough, but still he went in kind of dry.

"Let us demonstrate the bewitching devilry that is double penetration, little mouse? Get ready to ascend to heaven."

After he finishes speaking those words, he winks at me, which pretty much means, start fucking.

With both hands now on Harlow's waist, he helps me bounce her up and down on our dicks. When she opens her eyes, which are somewhat watery, they collide with my pale gray ones, and the idolization written upon them is apocalyptic.

Harlow twists her upper body somewhat as one of her arms abandons me and drapes over Bishop's shoulders. She hugs us both, one arm on each of us, whilst we penetrate her very much in chorus. The sounds of her soft moans, and short breaths are like a riveting chant, combined with mine and Bishop's backing vocals of groans and the melody of flesh meeting flesh, and this is the best song ever created.

Damn, freshly fucked virgin holes tend to be tight, but Harlow's is peculiarly so, even after four dicks having taken turns in her pussy just last night. With Bishop's cock just on the other side of the thin partition between her holes, making it claustrophobic almost, rubbing incessantly against mine, I am about ready to rupture.

Neither of us sees it coming, Harlow's face, which has been cast down to look at where our bodies meet, turns to Bishop, one second, they are simply gazing devotedly at each other, the next her lips are on his. Here's the gospel about my brother he doesn't kiss. According to him, it's too intimate, kissing is giving your heart away. I don't think Ive ever seen him brush his lips against another, yet here he is, mouth to mouth with Harlow. The sight makes me spill my seed inside my princess's pretty pussy.

A merciless tremor takes possession of our girl, she whimpers, sinking her teeth into Bishop's lower lip as she reaches her pleasure apex too; imposing checkmate on Bishop's king, drawing to an end the rising and fall of Harlow's body on our dicks, as he begins to lose it in her ass.

The grace of fucking standing up is that gravity ain't your friend, whatever we just pumped into Harlow is slowly spilling out of her, dripping on the floor at our feet, even with our cocks still deeply rooted inside of her holes.

"Whatever happens you are a part of this, you are a part of us. You belong." I tell her.

FORTY-FIVE
PARRISH

I SAT OUTSIDE on an upturned milk crate, the cool air brushing against my skin as I flipped my knife over and over in my hand. The familiar motion was calming, though the weight of everything happening around us was pressing down hard. The noise from inside had died down a few minutes ago, but I stayed where I was, stuck in my own thoughts. The shadows were coming, and the demon wouldn't be far behind.

For the past ten years, life had been easy. Too easy. I hadn't spent much time thinking, not really. Between the constant partying, the endless string of fucks, and the drugs, life was a blur. But now... now there was Harlow, and things had changed. I was thinking, and not just the shallow thoughts that kept me alive before. I was planning, trying to figure out what came next. How the hell are we supposed to stay alive? I knew we couldn't outrun the demon forever, and when it comes for us, there wouldn't be any mercy.

History had more than enough proof of what happens when you break a deal like the one we made. A hellhound would come calling, and if we weren't at the crossroads, there'd be no saving any of us. The idea churned in my gut, an uncomfortable mix of dread and resignation. There was no escape.

The door to the bus creaks open, and I look up in time to see Harlow slip outside, moving so quietly, like she didn't want to be seen. The little doe always walked like that, like she was hiding something.

But this time, instead of heading toward the stage or her trailer—which we still carted around more for her clothes than anything—she heads toward the woods. Thats enough to get me off my ass. I stand from the crate, quietly slipping into the shadows behind her, following her through the trees and bushes. We are a good fifty meters from the bus when I step on a branch, and the sharp snap of it making her stop dead. She turns around, and her eyes met mine.

I raise a brow, watching her closely. "Going somewhere, beautiful?" I ask, my voice teasing but laced with warning. She sighs, her eyes flickering with a hint of frustration.

"Yes, I am," she says, with that stubborn set to her jaw. "And you can't stop me."

I can't help the smirk that spreads across my face. "Oh, pretty doe," I murmur, circling her slowly, the predator I was born to be slipping out. "I think you've forgotten who's the prey and who's the wolf." I stalk around her, closing the distance step by step, watching her breathing quicken as the circle tightens.

Her eyes flutter shut, her breath coming faster, and I lean in, my voice dropping to a low growl. "Are you not satisfied? Are you not tired? After all the noise from the bus, I'd think you'd be sated enough to hold you over, at least until after the show." I glance at my watch, lips curving into a grin. "Twenty minutes, sweetheart."

She smiles at me, a wicked, knowing smile. "You may have taken my flower yesterday, but my body craves all of you, all the time." Her words send a jolt of heat through me, and I close the last bit of space between us. My hand slides up her neck, fingers curling to cup the back of her head as I tilt her chin up to meet my gaze.

"So where were you going?" I ask, my voice barely more than a whisper.

"To fix this," she replies, her voice steady, but the fear in her eyes is impossible to miss. "I can't live without any of you. I need to make a deal."

The cold, creeping feeling of dread claws at my insides, and my heart twists. "Harlow, you can't do that," I explain, barely managing to keep my voice even. She's willing to sacrifice everything to save us.

"I might be able to get us another ten years," she insists, her eyes pleading. "That's better than none!"

My heart melts at her words, the sacrifice she is willing to make. "Baby," I murmured, leaning down to kiss her, soft and slow. Her body melts into mine, and for a moment, the rest of the world disappears. As my lips move against hers, I whisper, "You can't save us. Our deal is broken, and the hounds will be here soon."

I kiss her deeper, more desperately. I need to savor every second, every breath, determined to love her with everything I have, before I am ripped from this world.

I deepen the kiss, feeling the warmth of her body pressed against mine, the world around us fading away as I let myself get lost in her. My hand slides down her back, fingers brushing over her curves, pulling her closer until there isn't an inch of space between us. Every part of me wanting her, needing her, as if the fleeting time we have left demands we take every last second for ourselves.

Her breath hitches as I trail kisses along her jawline, down the curve of her neck. Her skin soft under my lips, she tilts her head back, giving me more access. My hands moving lower, gripping her hips, feeling the heat between us rise as her body responds to every touch.

"Parrish," she whispers, her voice breathy, filled with need, spurring me on. Her fingers tangle in my hair, pulling me closer, and I can feel the urgency in the way she presses herself against me, as if she is trying to memorize every part of this moment, every feeling.

I back her up against the nearest tree, my lips capturing hers again in a rough, hungry kiss. The bark scratching against her back, but she doesn't seem to care. All I can think about is her—how her body trembles under my touch, how she gasps into my mouth as I grip her thighs, lifting her slightly so I can press my hips against hers. She hooks her legs around my waist, drawing me in closer, our breaths mingling in the cool night air.

Her hands roaming over my chest, tugging at my shirt, desperate for more skin, more contact. I groan against her lips as I shift, adjusting her against me, the intensity between us building. Her nails scraping lightly down my back, and I can feel the fire between us raging, uncontrollable, unstoppable.

I tug her dress over her head, tossing it aside carelessly, her bare skin glowing under the moonlight. My mouth moves lower, teasing kisses down her collarbone, over the curve of her breasts. Her breath coming faster, her body arching against me as I take my time, savoring every reaction, every sound she makes.

I let my hands wander, taking in the softness of her skin, the curve of her hips. The heat between us is unbearable, and I know she feels it too. I pull her even closer, the friction between us sending a jolt of pleasure through us both. Her lips part in a breathless moan as I press harder, grinning against her skin, knowing I have her exactly where I want her.

"I want to fuck you hard," I whisper against her ear, my voice low, filled with the same hunger I feel, humming throughout her body.

"Please," she breaths, her voice trembling with need. "I need you."

I look down at her pussy, her lack of underwear making me smirk. "Who has them?" I jest, motioning to her. She chuckles in my arms and replies, "Abel." Her response earns a laugh from me. I tighten my grip on her hips, instructing her firmly, "I'm going to set you down now. You are to turn around and place your hands on the tree, little doe." She nods in understanding and gracefully untangles her legs from around my waist.

I observe her silhouette that is illuminated by the moonlight against the tree, her arms resting on the rough bark as she arches her back. Every curve of her body is accentuated in the soft glow, stirring a primal desire within me. The sight of her exposed form, revealing intimate details in the pale light, sends a surge of arousal through me. It's evident she has been thoroughly pleasured, her swollen lips a testament to that fact. Despite any discomfort she may feel, my selfish craving overrides any concern I should have for her well-being.

I reach for the knife in my pocket, it's cool metal sending a shiver down my spine. "Do you trust me?" I ask, locking eyes with her as she nods eagerly. With deliberate intent, I trace the blade's handle along her moistened folds, eliciting a symphony of breathy moans from her lips. Each repetition fuels her pleasure, and I can't help but groan, as I sink the knife handle inside her over and over.

As she grows more vocal, I venture further, circling a finger around her rear and find slickness there. The substance is both slippery and sticky, hinting that it has already been filled. Envious thoughts flicker through my mind briefly before being overtaken by an insatiable craving for her core. My sole focus now is on delving into her completely, consumed by an urgent need to claim what is mine.

I extract the knife from her body and raise it to the moonlight, its handle soaked in more than just her fluids. With a smirk, I run my tongue along the blade and ask her, "Church?"

A mischievous smirk plays on her lips as I hastily undo my jeans and line up with her. I can't afford to be gentle in this moment; I need to be rough, and I tell her just that. She moans in response, urging me on. I plunge into her waiting core, sinking deep until I reach the hilt. With a fierce determination, I set a brutal pace, thrusting into her with all my force before quickly pulling back out again. Our bodies collide in a tangle of limbs and passion, the sound of our heavy breathing and skin slapping together filling the air.

She screams my name, her voice echoing through the forest as she clings to the tree for dear life. I reach around and flick her clit with my fingers, continuing to thrust into her hard and fast. I can feel her body trembling, fighting against me, but it only adds to the intensity of our passion. She moans loudly as she climaxes, clamping down on me, causing me to groan in pleasure. With both hands now gripping her hips tightly, I fight through my own climax and fill her completely. As we both catch our breath, she slinks forward with her face pressed against the rough bark of the tree. "I have you all inside me now," she says between heavy breaths, a mischievous smile playing on her lips. I chuckle and reply, "You were never an angel, more like a demon dressed up as one. And you fit us perfectly."

For a moment, neither of us speak. There is nothing to say, really. We both know this was temporary, fleeting. We are living on borrowed time.

I pull back slightly, brushing a strand of hair out of her face, my fingers lingering against her cheek. "You, okay?" I ask softly.

She nods, her eyes half-closed, a lazy smile tugging at the corners of her lips. "Yeah," she whispers. "More than okay."

I kiss her forehead gently, letting the moment linger before reality creeps back in. "We need to head back," I say quietly, though it pains me to break this moment. "The show's starting soon."

FORTY-SIX

HARLOW

MY BOYS ARE STILL PLAYING Gods, walking around like nothing is wrong, even though they have been stripped from their goety. Either they don't care about their dire state of affairs, or they are very good pretenders. The things that used to obey the Paragon of Virtue's Inferno bidding have turned against them; they are now at the mercy of the demons' deadly tricks. Poor Abel, got possessed by one, almost putting me into eternal sleep, the guilt behind those dark brown eyes hurt me more than his hands did. I still crave them around my neck, how bananas is that?

It didn't start off that way when the Paragon of Virtue's Inferno drummer and I sated our fleshly desires, but then it became this desire to congregate all of their rapture elixir within me. Like our first time, when they asserted ownership of me, only this time, I am staking a claim to them. I am planning to tell the Devil, "They belong to me. Look, a part of them is within me. You can't take them. That would be stealing what's rightfully mine." I can help, so why won't they let me?

My pink haired man and I are making our way back to the venue, as I need to be on stage soon. I don't know how my singing is going to go since my throat is very much bruised, inside and out. Makeup can cover one of those things, but I actually have a soft spot for the imprint of Abel's hand on my flesh, so I won't. Let Creation see it and judge me for it, it doesn't bother me anymore. And now that I think about it, a gravelly voice will do great for some of the Paragon of Virtue's Inferno dark ballads. It's just me and my guitar; I can easily change my set.

After mating like animals against the southern Magnolia tree, I turned around so I could face him, holding out my hand, palm up. He asked me if I wanted him to hold my hand to which I responded with, "I want your shirt. Give it to me now." I wasn't putting that begrimed white dress that had been discarded on the soil at our feet, back on.

"I am having fucking dejà-vu." He professed, as he reached behind him, his hands gripping the collar of his t-shirt, and pulled it over his head. "I am starting to believe it is not about the garment, you just want to see my bare chest. I am flattered, pretty doe." although I do love to feast my eyes on his pale skin that has been beautified by the unicorn, rainbow, and all the other strange, unearthly fantasy creatures; I also love wearing their stuff, it smells like them, and Parrish's scent is the sweetest and most flowery out of them all, I just fancy sniffing it whenever I so desire.

Hence, why I am only in my mud-caked go-go boots, and a black t-shirt with plastisol printed, white wings gracing my whole back.

"Hey, Stabby?"

Parrish chuckles, presumably at my choice of nickname

for him. "I cut, my pretty doe, I don't stab." He puts forth, his hand grasping mine, fingers interlacing my own.

"Ok. Slasher then." That makes him giggle. God, I love that sound, it's so out of place because it comes from a grown-ass man, but it's like an angelically deranged lullaby to my ears.

On a more serious note, I try to return to the topic from earlier, "Parrish, baby, I still think y'all should let me,"

"No." He interrupts.

"Please let me finish." I beg.

"No. I know what your next words are going to be, doe, and I don't want to hear them anymore. Hasn't the boss-man told you no already?" He means Bishop. "That should've been final. You deserve a spanking from him, for sneaking out." The last part making a lecherous shudder, shoot up my spine.

"I don't see y'all coming up with any other solutions."

"You don't get it, Harlow." The pink haired man somberly states.

"You're right, I don't." I snap at him. "Y'all just seem to have come to terms with your grim fate. I haven't. I just got you guys and I am not ready to let go."

I miss my footing somewhat as he stops dead in his stride; we're almost out of the woods now, "It's not about submitting to the Devil's will. You are cardinal, a beautiful singularity that shouldn't be in a fucked-up world like this. Your light made something grow in the hollowed-out void where our hearts used to be, pretty doe. You made us realize that there is nothing worth living for, unless it is worth dying for."

"Are you saying that I made you want to die?" I ask him, horrified.

"Death is only the end, if you assume the story is about you." What in heaven's name is he on about? "This isn't our story, my pretty doe, it's yours. It's not about us, biting the dust, it's about you, staying alive."

"I don't have to die, Slasher, I just have to sell my soul to the Devil. I just have to do what y'all did."

"You're assuming he will give you the same deal. Trust me, little doe," Parrish pauses in his words, his jaw tightening as he grinds his teeth together before continuing, "He won't. The Old Serpent is a deviant bastard, he's definitely gonna want something else from you. And like hell am I allowing him to get his filthy, fiendish hands on it. Over my dead body."

"Parrish." I summon his name in a dead calm tone, seeking to quiet the green-eyed and bitter voices in his head.

"Please, Harlow, I beg of you, don't go to him." He suspires. "I already had a monster take someone I love from me, I can't," Parrish closes his eyes, depriving me of its hazel magnetism, "drip... drip... drip." Oh no, what's happening? He takes at least three steps back, his hand letting go of mine, both rising to his pink strands. He begins to pull and tug at his hair, a wail pulsating from within him.

"Parrish, baby, what's happening?" I ask, rushing to him as his ass comes to rest on the ground, his body cocoons within itself, rocking back and forward.

"He won't stop shouting. She won't stop screaming." He mumbles, his hands planting themselves over his ears.

I drop to my knees beside him. I don't know what to do here, his mind seems to have taken him somewhere I do not belong. I hesitate for a second, and then I encircle my arms around him, hugging him tight. "I'm right here. Just come back to me."

"Stab... stab... stab. The kitchen table wobbles with their

impure dance. Drip... drip... drip. Her blood rains down on me."

The McGrew's past has been written and talked about everywhere, their dad used to beat them up, I gathered Bishop got the most, from what was written, until he decided to just abandon them, their mother wasted away to nothing by a ratchet disease, in a way also leaving them as young boys. There isn't much out there when it comes to Abel and Parrish, all I have heard -dare I say- is from conclusions people have made, from reading between the sinister lines of Paragon of Virtue's Inferno lyrics. After mine and Abel's talk last night I know his genesis and I think I am about to learn Parrish's.

"Shit, it's been a while since he's had an episode." A sinful raspy voice utters.

"Church?" My voice is a medley of panic and relief, as I lift my head and see him emerge from amongst the shadows, his hands buried in the front pockets of his distressed light-washed, skinny jeans, his shoulders hunched as if the cold of the night is bothering him.

"He will be alright, just let it play out, baby." Church tells me.

"Papa keeps asking where his Marigold is, as he sinks his knife into mama over and over again. The voices in his head told him that the woman before him ain't his wife, my mama, a demon wearing her skin, like a wolf in sheep's clothing."

"Oh, baby." When mother dearest spitefully told me over the phone that little Parrish witnessed his dad kill his mum, I took it as her spitting venom like the snake she is, but it seems her words weren't unfounded. Still living through that trauma, it helped shape who he is right now, and he's the most perfect Parrish he could ever be, imperfect. I love him.

"Stab… stab… stab. Papa finishes with a growl as the knife drops to the floor. Drip… drip… drip. Mama moans as her life juices stain the kitchen table red."

Something comes over me, and I start chanting an old lullaby I don't remember ever hearing.

Be my nightingale
Sing me to sleep
'Cause nothing is more beautiful than your deceit
You can be my sanity
My spiked with poison remedy
Please, be my nightingale

Parrish eyes open wide and stare at me in disbelief. Tears have gathered upon them, a lone drop escaping, caressing his cheek on the way down. "That's my mama's song; she used to sing it to me to chase the bogeyman away. How do you know it?" That's a good question indeed, one I don't have an answer for. "Are you going to beg me to kill you as well?"

"What?" I ask, confused, at the same time the Paragon of Virtue's Inferno lead singer hisses, "Shit."

"Papa left mama on the kitchen table, draining out. He said that was the only way to purify her, to purge the demon out. But every breath mama took was like a melody of agony, I couldn't," Parrish's hazel eyes, which had been locked on to mine as he spoke those words, clench shut for a split second, a painful grimace taking over his face, "I couldn't take it anymore.

I crawled out from under the table, picking the knife up before rising to my feet. As I stood there facing away from her, looking at the object in my hand that was doused in blood, mama prayed for me to end it and began to sing that lullaby. She was going to die no matter what, the least I could do was put her out of her misery, right? So, I buried the knife in her heart."

My electric blue eyes move from Parrish to Church, looking for some sort of confirmation for what's being narrated. Church's down cast gaze tells me all I need to know.

"I killed my mama." The pink haired man notes, in a withdrawn and cold manner, like something within him disconnected from the horrible fact.

"Parrish," Church begins, but I cut in before he can carry on.

"No, you didn't." I defend in a hushed merciful tone, as my eyes return to him. I raise one of my hands and brush some of his short pink strands back with my fingers, petting him like the good, unhinged man he is. "You said so yourself, she wouldn't have survived what your papa did." I can't believe he's been living with this misplaced guilt for this long. He shouldn't have to repent for this sin, he isn't the monster in his mama's tale, his papa is. If anything, he's Zadkiel, the angel of mercy. "You give her the best gift of all, my handsome slasher, peace."

"How can you root out the beauty in something so ugly?" Parrish asks with intrigue and enchantment in his voice.

I grab his face with my hands, caressing his cheeks with my thumbs, looking him straight in the eyes. "Sharon Tate once said that, "everything that's realistic has some sort of ugliness in it. Even a flower is ugly when it wilts, a bird when it seeks its prey, the ocean when it becomes violent.

Nothing is ever black and white, regardless, if you only seek the bad and rotten in stuff, then that's all you will find." My lips fall upon his in a dove like peck. "I am sorry this befell upon you and haunts you still." I kiss his forehead in the same tender and gentle way I did his mouth.

"But I am not sorry, that it fostered this you, it made you, my Parrish Bern. I love you, just the way you are." I get up, not bothering to dust off the dirt from my knees, extending a hand to Parrish. "Now come on, we have a dark show to put on."

FORTY-SEVEN

I STAND to the side of the stage, arms crossed, my eyes locked on Harlow as she steps into the light. The crowd tonight is fucking insane. It is always like this for the last show of the tour—the energy high, people going wild, and we usually get to let our hair down, cut loose. But not this time. Not after what we have done. Not after we didn't go through with it.

My whole body feels off-kilter, wired like I am ready to fight at any second. I can't shake the feeling, like I am being watched. Every shadow that flickers near the stage makes me jump, every dark corner making me feel like something is about to crawl out and grab me. I haven't been right since last night, when we were supposed to kill Harlow, when we broke the bargain. I don't want to admit it, but the possession has fucked with my head. The idea of it happening again makes my skin crawl. I don't want to be a puppet for whatever dark shit is lurking around us.

I take a deep breath, trying to focus, but every second that passes, my nerves tighten. The crowd is rowdy, buzzing with excitement, but I can barely pay attention to the noise. My eyes are glued to Harlow. She's wearing one of Parrish's tops again, a loose, ripped thing, and those fucking go-go knee-high boots that show off her legs, the ones that made it a bit 'easier', what feels like a lifetime ago, to fuck her peachy behind. But my gaze catches on her knees—they look like they are covered in dirt. What the hell?

I can't figure out why, but I know one thing, I have to watch her. I'm not sure if it is paranoia or instinct, but I can't take my eyes off her. Not with everything going on. Not with the shadows moving the way they are tonight, slinking around the back of the room, just beyond the stage lights, writhing and shifting in the dark. I can see them clear as day, and it's freaking me the hell out. They are more active than usual, more agitated.

I'm not the only one noticing, either. Ive caught a few people in the crowd glancing over their shoulders, their eyes darting to the back of the room like they can see the shadows too. Normally, people are oblivious to that kind of thing, but tonight… something's different. The air is heavier than usual, thick with tension, like the room itself knows something is coming.

I clench my jaw, forcing myself to keep watching her. Harlow's strumming her guitar now, her fingers dancing over the strings with the kind of ease that only comes from someone completely in their element.

The crowd roars, and she smiles, stepping up to the mic.

"Hi, y'all," she greets them, her voice smooth, with that edge of mischief that has the crowd hooked instantly. "Are you ready for Paragon of Virtue's Inferno?" The crowd goes wild, making her chuckle softly, glancing down as she strums a few more chords.

"Tonight is the last night of the tour," she continues, "so, let's make it the one we talk about for years to come."

She strums the guitar again, harder this time, launching into the opening chords of a song. But this isn't one of our usual tracks. I know our set list, inside out, and this definitely isn't on it. It isn't a cover either—this is something new, something I've never heard before. The melody, haunting, a slow, echoing tune that sends chills down my spine.

And then she starts to sing, and fuck, her voice, even though a bit raw and broken right now from the rough fucking it got from me, it hypnotizes me every single time, soft but strong, like it could pull you under if you aren't careful.

I found you in the dark,
Where the shadows tried to keep us apart.
But love is a wicked thing,
It slips through the cracks; it clings to the dream.

Her voice echos through the crowd, and for a moment, the world feels like it has narrowed down to just her, standing there, singing into the darkness. I can't look away, and I don't want to.

I held your hands so tight,
Promised we'd make it through the night.
But the demon came, with eyes like flame,

Took what was mine, leaving nothing but pain.

The lyrics hit me hard, like they are too close to home. Too real.

I barely noticed Church slip up behind me, his presence looming beside me as we both stare at Harlow. His breath hitches, and without looking, I know what he is thinking because he heard it too.

"She's singing about us, isn't she?" he speaks quietly; his voice rough with emotion. I don't need to say it, so I just nod, unable to tear my eyes away from her.

"Yeah," I mutter. "She is."

Harlow's fingers pick up the pace, strumming faster as she moves into the next verse. The haunting melody lingers, wrapping around the crowd like a spell, pulling them all in.

I went to the crossroads,
Made a deal of my own.
I told the devil, I'd pay any price
If he'd let me keep my boys at home.

My chest tightens, the words sinking in like lead. I can feel Church stiffen next to me, the weight of what she's singing, hitting him just as hard.

She is singing about trying to save us, by making her own deal.

Harlow's voice soars, louder now, more desperate.

But love's a fickle friend,
It fades, it bends,
And I'm still here, trying to fight
For a life they said would end.

The crowd is completely entranced, and so am I. There's something raw in her voice, something screaming of a deeper pain, of a battle we all know is coming, but we are too afraid to face.

Church lets out a slow breath beside me, his voice barely above a whisper. "She's not just singing about us... She's telling us what she's planning."

I swallow hard, my heart thudding in my chest. "Yeah," I reply, the realization sinking in. She really is ready to do anything to keep us together, even if it means making her own deal with the devil.

Harlow's fingers slow, and she sings the last few lines softly, almost like a haunted lullaby.

If the devil comes for me,
I'll stand tall, just wait and see.
I'll give him everything I've got,
If it means keeping you all safe from what's been wrought.

The final chord echos throughout the venue, and for a moment, the crowd stands completely still, hanging on her every word.

I clench my fists, trying to push down the fear that has risen in my chest. Harlow is willing to do anything to protect us, but I'm not sure if it's a comfort or something far more terrifying.

As the crowd's silence erupts into cheers, Harlow looks out over the sea of faces, her eyes briefly flickering to where we stand at the edge of the stage. It's in that moment, I realize —she is ready to make the deal, ready to face whatever comes for us.

But I am not ready to lose her. Not now. Not ever.

FORTY-EIGHT

HARLOW

WE ALL DIE in the end.

No matter what path we take at the crossroads, there is no Harlow Abaddon without the Paragon of Virtue's Inferno. They die; I die. My men are being blindsided by love and lust, and this silly notion of wanting to be my saviors. This isn't one of those cute old fairytales, where the princess needs to be rescued by princes.

Why can't the damsel liberate them from evil, for once?

Parrish's mental distress in the woods should've persuaded me not to do it, not to go to the fateful crossroads to make my own pact with the Devil, but it only made my resolve stronger. I am faced with Sophie's choice, just like my pink haired man had been, that violent and bloody night. Either I watch the shadows fester on my men tonight, or I put an end to this torment, before the demons get their evil possessing hands on them. The price, on one hand is my heart, and on the other will be my soul. I am not claiming that selling my soul to the Old Serpent, as Parrish called him, is the smart or right thing to do, but doing nothing feels wrong, like I am closing the book on our story before it begins. Yes, I might get a pretty bad paper cut from turning the page and signing a damning contract with Satan, but if that gets us a few extra chapters together, I will blithely bleed for my four damned souls, forever and always.

These final lyrics I am singing -before I welcome the guys for the last time on stage to perform their set- are a self-fulfilling prophecy. I am no longer asking for their permission; I am begging for forgiveness for what I am going to do. I am the sacrifice; that was always my part in this narrative. My life, my death, my choice, and I choose Church, Bishop, Parrish and Abel. They might end up mad at me, but I rather live with their animosity and resentment, then not have them with me at all.

The shadows brought this on, they are restless tonight. Everywhere I look there's one, an unnatural pocket of black smoke, swirling amongst the crowd of thousands, appearing almost human one second and the next twisting and contorting itself into ungodly entities.

Some of the lost souls in the herd before me sense something not right around them, their eyes darting all over the venue, looking for whatever is causing the chill in the air that raises the hairs on the back of their necks and causes the goosebumps covering their arms. I want to howl, "The shadows are right in front of y'all noses," because these sinners are staring right at them but looking straight through them.

Old me is turning in her grave, kicking and screaming, telling me to get down on my knees and pray for all of their souls, to chase the demons away with His words, but I know that would be in vain, He holds no power in this congregation. Besides these people aren't the lead of my concern, my men are.

As I play the last note on my guitar, a moment of pure silence follows. For that split second, all I hear is everyone's heavy breathing, and then the room starts chanting my name like an invocation of some sort. I give the audience a demure smile, prior to glancing at the Paragon of Virtue's Inferno members, I can see shadows crawling on the ceiling right above their heads. You know that infamous spider-walk scene in the 1973 The Exorcist, where Linda Blair's character goes down the stairs in an unorthodox manner, that's how these fiends are moving, bidding their sweet time, until they are ready to pounce on my unsuspecting guys.

The predators just became prey.

"I hope I edged y'all enough and you are ready to take on my guys, 'cause they are about to have their wicked way with you, Hail Paragon of Virtue's Inferno." I give praise to the band.

Our paths cross as I am vacating the stage, the guys making their way on to it. My intent was to bypass them and steer clear of any interaction, but Bishop has other ideas. His hand grasps my elbow with vehemence, which causes me to emit his favorite sound, a squeak. "Don't you dare. Do not try and sneak off on us again, my little mouse. You are already due for a spanking. I would hate having to make it a lashing with my belt instead." My body throbs with desire at his dominant tone and his sadistic words.

"Well, it wouldn't be sneaking out, daddy. I told you exactly what I was doing." I bluntly inform Bishop, which makes him growl at me.

"Low, just promise us you won't go to the crossroads alone. Please." Abel pleads.

Oh, I have no intention of going by myself, so I can look them all in the eyes as I utter, "I promise. Now go, your followers are waiting."

Bishop reluctantly let's go of my arm, as Church draws near me, his hands coming to hold my face in them, like I am the most sacred thing to him. The Paragon of Virtue's Inferno lead singer's pale gray eyes move back and forward between my electric blue ones, as though searching for something written within the black rim of my iris, perhaps penitence for telling a lie. A yielding sigh flees his lips before they brush mine in a gentle peck. "Don't be reckless, that's our job, ok?" And with that they all abandon me on the outer limits of stage, leaving me staring after their retreating forms as they head out to perform.

"I'm sorry." I whisper as I turn away, letting the darkness consume me.

Once backstage within the long empty corridors of this venue, my body begins to shudder, not from cold but from dread. I can hear the faint echo of my guys' hellish performance, Church's beautifully rough voice nudging me on.

"Don't let them know you are afraid." I tell myself as I come to a standstill. "Actually, never mind, the demons can probably smell fear, so it doesn't matter. Just suck it up, Harlow Magdalene Abaddon; you're getting good at that." Taking a very deep breath, I close my eyes, reciting the summoning incantation that I overheard the boys utter a while back, "Evoco hmmm," ohh, damn. I didn't really think of a demon to call forth, "Astaroth per nomen non sanctum sum.

Veni ad me." Where in the hell's name has that name come from? It just popped into my mind out of the blue.

"Well, well, well, what do I have here? A sweet treat?" This haunting voice utters, as a black fog slithers its way to me across the ground. The moment it gets near my feet the smoke starts to surge up, growing vertically, until only a towering shadow looms in front of me.

The darkness wanes and a man manifests before me, with scarred black bat wings protruding from his back, a very, very, naked man. The tattoo of a very realistic blue pit-viper circles his arm, from his bicep to his wrist, the snake's head resting upon his hand. His Herculean physique is eye-catching; I can see all the delicious and pronounced ridges of his muscles, and as my eyes travel down his body, his pretty huge length, standing at full attention.

"Like what you see? Feast your eyes, my sweet treat." Some of those words remind me of Church; he told me pretty identical things on my first night with the tour, when they had their fun with me.

My eyes shoot up to his cadaverous face with its hollow cheeks, sunken eyes and sharp lines, which somehow, I find attractive. His slicked back, blue-black hair in combination with those yellow eyes, are spellbinding. I shouldn't be ogling a demon; I should be saving my men.

"I want you to take me to the same crossroads my men went to." I tell the demon. The Devil's crossroads, even though of ill-repute, it doesn't actually have a big neon sign above it saying this is it; you either know exactly where it is, or you don't. And I definitely, don't. Plus, I think my infernal friend here can zap me straight there, instead of me having to wander through the woods and possibly getting myself lost on the way.

"Is that so?" Astaroth goads, looking me up and down. "What do I get in return?" He asks me, as he licks his lips.

"What do you want?" I knew asking for something from a demon wouldn't come without a price.

"How about a favor, that I can collect whenever I so please?"

"Ok." I say. An evil grin smears his face as his lips ram into mine in a maniacal kiss. Astaroth tongue is forceful and penetrates my mouth without my consent. He shoves it so deep down my throat I start to choke on it, that's when he parts from me.

"Sorry, my sweet treat, my deals are sealed with a kiss. I am not the embodiment of eroticism for no reason."

I am about to censure him, but words fail me as I take in my surroundings. Two dirt country roads intersecting, making so that four routes branch out from where I stand. There's nothing but open fields covered in withered dry grass and a few barren trees with an ashen hue scattered around, enveloped by the darkness, of the moonless night.

"Welcome to the Devil's crossroads, Harlow."

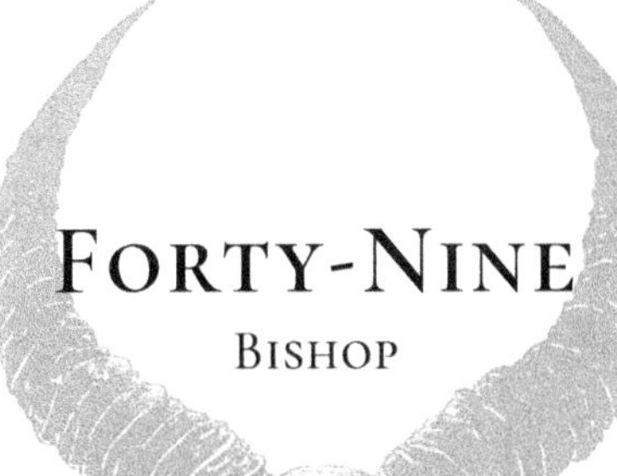

FORTY-NINE

BISHOP

THE LIGHTS DIMMED as we launch into the last song of the set, the crowd roaring as Church steps up to the mic, his voice raw and gritty as he begins to sing. The energy on stage is electric, but beneath the surface, it's all hollow for me. I can't stop looking at the shadows creeping along the backdrop, sliding across the ceiling like black tendrils, slowly swallowing the light. They are here, and they aren't going to wait much longer.

A crossroad demon saved our lives,
Pulled us from a fate, of pain and lies.
But the debt's still owed, the price still to be paid,
Now we face the reckoning we made.

Church belts the words out, his voice hitting every note with a kind of desperate power, like he is trying to hold on to something that's slipping away. He's up front, at the center of stage, pouring his soul into the performance, but I can see it in his eyes—he knows what is coming. He knows just as much as I do that this song, this night, could be our last.

I tighten my grip on my bass, feeling the vibrations of Abel's drums pounding behind me, keeping the rhythm steady, fierce. Abel is playing like his life depends on it. Maybe it does. His eyes are locked forward, his expression focused, but I know him. He's strung tight, just like me. His gaze keeps darting to the shadows, watching them grow, knowing they aren't just a trick of the light. They are real, and they are coming for us.

Parrish is in the middle of a solo, his fingers flying over the strings of his guitar like it is the last time he'll ever play. Hell, maybe it is. The crowd eating it up, losing themselves in the music, oblivious to the darkness creeping just outside their line of sight. But I can't look away. The shadows beginning to gather at the edges of the stage, it feels like the air is thick with something unspoken, something we all feel but no-one has dared acknowledge.

I can see them, sliding across the ceiling, growing bigger with each passing second, like they are waiting for the perfect moment to strike. My heart pounding in my chest, but I keep playing, the baseline thumping beneath the melody. The demon is calling, pulling at the strings of the deal we made years ago. And now, because we hadn't killed Harlow, because we didn't fulfil our end of the bargain; we are living on borrowed time.

We walked to the crossroads, made our deal,

Now the devil's come to take what's real.
The shadows creep, the light turns cold,
Our souls sold; the price untold.

Church's voice is rougher now, almost strained, like he can feel the weight of it all pressing down on him. I know the feeling. The shadows inching closer, I feel their pull, like they're whispering in my ear, reminding me of the bargain. I can almost hear the demon's voice, slick and smooth, reminding me that our time is up.

I glance at Parrish. He's still locked into the chords he is playing, his body moving with the music, but his eyes are distant. He knows it too. He feels it. The hellhounds will be here soon, the demon's incarcerators, come to drag us to hell for not delivering on our end of the deal.

I force myself to focus, my fingers moving automatically over the strings of my bass, trying to drown out the sense of impending doom with the music. But it isn't working. The shadows growing, swirling along the backdrop, and I know we can't hold them off for much longer.

Abel's drumming grows louder, more frantic, like he's trying to keep the inevitable at bay. But the truth is, we are out of time. The demon is calling, and there is nothing we can do to stop it.

We played with fire, danced with sin,
Now the darkness calls us in.
The devil waits, his patience thin,

The reckoning will soon begin.

Church's final verse hangs in the air, the crowd roaring in response, completely unaware of the shadows closing in behind them. I can feel the pull in my gut, the cold grip of fear twisting inside me. The song is almost over, and when the music stops, we have to face whatever is waiting for us.

I lock eyes with Parrish for a brief second, and I can see the fear mirrored in his gaze. We all feel it. The end is near.

The final note hanging in the air as we walk off the stage, sweat pouring down our faces, hearts still racing from the performance. The crowd erupting into screams for an encore, their voices deafening, but I can barely hear them over the sound of my own pulse, pounding in my ears. I scan the shadows, searching for her, my gut twisting into knots.

"Fuck," I mutter under my breath, looking around frantically. My eyes dart from corner to corner, over the edge of the stage, out into the crowd, but Harlow isn't anywhere in sight. "Where the hell is she?"

Abel's eyes flick over to me, his face a mixture of confusion and dread. He must feel it too. Something is wrong. Parrish is the first to catch on, his face going pale as he turns to Church. "The little doe," he whispers, his voice tight with panic. "She's gone to make a deal."

Church's face drains of color instantly, realization hitting him like a punch to the gut. "We need to stop her," he demands, his voice cracking as he looks at me. "If she makes that deal—"

"She doesn't know where to go," I cut in, trying to steady

my own rising panic. "If we go now, we might beat her there. Hopefully, she's lost and hasn't found it yet."

Without another word, we race through the back of the venue, leaving the crowd behind, still screaming for an encore; that will never come. My heart hammering in my chest as we pile into my car, the adrenaline making my hands shake as I fumble with the keys. I am not sure how much time we have, but I know one thing—if Harlow makes that deal, she'll be lost to us forever.

The engine roars to life, and I slam my foot on the gas, the car lurching forward as we speed toward the crossroads. None of us speak for the first few minutes, the weight of what is happening hanging thick in the air. We know the crossroads well—an old T-intersection, abandoned when the highway had been built, now only accessible through a narrow path in the bush. It´s a 30-minute walk, but if we drive down the path, we can make it in 10.

"She's silly for this," Abel mutters, his voice tight with fear. "She thinks she can fix it. She thinks she can save us."

"She has no idea what she's dealing with," Church responds, his hands gripping his knees so hard his knuckles are white. "We were prepared to die, to leave her behind to live her life. Not to have her… to have her join us."

"She won't survive this," Parrish adds, his voice flat, almost defeated. "The demon will tear her apart."

The car swerves slightly, as I push the gas pedal harder, speeding through the night. My mind racing, thoughts of Harlow running through my head—her stubbornness, her strength, her fucking innocence. She thinks she can save us. She thinks she can buy us more time. But she doesn't understand the price. She doesn't understand what making that deal will do to her.

"She was supposed to be safe," I growl, more to myself than anyone else. "We were supposed to keep her safe."

I can feel the tension rising in the car, all of us teetering on the edge of panic. None of us ready for this. We have been prepared to die for our mistakes, to pay the price for our broken deal. But we aren't prepared for losing her, for her trying to take on that burden herself.

As we near the old crossroads, as I turn the car down the path hidden within the bushes, I hope it will fit down the narrow lane, so we don't have to run. Thankfully it does, making quick work of the path as we near the crossroads. I slam my foot on the breaks, the tires kicking up dirt, bringing the car abrupt stop. Flinging the doors open, we jump out. Hoping we can still beat her there.

We have to.

FIFTY

HARLOW

"WELCOME to the Devil's crossroads, Harlow." Astaroth announces, spreading his arms out wide, portraying that this is it.

"Everything around it seems to be..."

"Dead?" He finishes my sentence. "Yeah, well, that's what happens when the Devil comes around once too often. He kind of just sucks the life out of stuff, you know."

"Right hmmm so, how am I supposed to do this? Do I summon him like I did you?" Astaroth starts laughing his demon heart out, even before I conclude asking questions.

"Oh, Harlow, you are so cute and clueless." He boops my nose with his middle finger as he begins to explain. "No. This ritual is a bit more complex. You have to dig a hole, in the dead center of the crossroad, so right about where we stand, and bury a box containing a picture of the foolish mortal that wishes to make the deal, so yourself, some graveyard dirt and," Astaroth pauses in his recital of the steps and ingredients needed to call forth the Devil to the crossroads, tapping his middle finger to his bottom lip as he thinks about the last one, "ah, yes, a bone from a black cat."

"What if I have none of that?" I put forward, because I am as ill-prepared as all the depraved souls left to drown in the Genesis flood narrative, where only Noah and his family, were granted safe passage to a cleansed-by-water chaos we call, earth.

"You are lucky I like you, my sweet treat." The demon says, his face getting a hair's breadth from mine. "I am seriously contemplating running off with you, to keep you all to myself, eat you up, forever and ever."

"I am with someone." I blurt out. "Actually, four someone's."

The Cheshire cat grin that graces his cadaverous face is eldritch and disturbing, it exudes nothing but havoc, and it stinks of perversity. "Yeah, blessed bastards. I guess my old, putrid black heart will have to cope with being stuck in the friend zone then. I mean, we can at least be friends, right, my sweet treat?"

A demon wanting to be my companion is mystifying. Nonetheless, I don't see why not. "Sure." I tell him. Astaroth has been nothing but kind, and helpful since I summoned him. If we look past the non-consensual kiss, I did require his services, I suppose, but some communication beforehand would've been nice, he could've forewarned me that his covenants were sealed mouth to mouth or something.

"About the things I need…" Once more I don't get to finish voicing my thoughts, as out of the blue a rotten wooden box materializes in his hands. "Astaroth." I gasp as I take hold of it. "Ouch." A splinter pierces my finger, embedding itself under my skin, snapping off the box. "What will be the price for this? Another favor?" I question.

"This one is on the house. You still need to be the one burying it." Astaroth casts his yellow eyes down at an already dug hole between us. "Down you go."

I chuckle. "Did the hole have to be right there, Astaroth? Or did you just want me to get down on my knees in front of you?"

"Maybe a bit of both. That is the dead center of the crossroad." He avows.

"Show me you're shameless, why don't ya." I say as I kneel, placing the box in the hollowed-out spot and covering everything up with dirt. His large boner is very much aligned with my face, so I do my utmost to keep my eyes glued to what I am doing. But the temptation to just have a peek at it from this angle, is strong.

"Astaroth, is there a reason why you are naked?" A hauntingly unnatural deep voice utters from behind me. I hastily get up and turn around, my back meeting Astaroth's front, his length poking me in my lower back.

"Wait, the king of the Delta Blues Singers is the Devil?" I ask, confused, because the man before me with his dark skin dressed in a three-piece black suit, button down shirt and shoes, looks just like Mister Robert Leroy Johnson, the man that started this whole crossroads legend.

"Nah, my sweet treat, but he certainly likes to wear Johnson's skin when he comes to the crossroads." Cold sweats break out at Astaroth's comment. "And to answer your question, brother, I couldn't resist making this delicious snack squirm a bit. Painting her cheeks in a light pink hue is the most supreme rapture. Simply sinful." The demon whispers that last part in my ear.

"You own clothes?" I ask, sneaking a look at the hellish naked man at my rear.

"Just cover yourself, Astaroth." The Devil commands, his voice pulsating with immense unholy power.

"Fine." Just like the box, garments magically appear upon Astaroth skin. A replica of the Devil's attire but his is all in midnight blue. Stunning.

The sound of crunching grit breaks the silence, as a car drives up one of the narrow paths. Oh, no, they can't be here. Car doors fling open, and my four men get out. "Harlow!" Church's raspy voice calls out to me, as four sets of feet rush to where I am standing.

"I've been waiting for your souls for a long time, boys." I dare a quick glance at the Devil an evil smirk gracing his borrowed face. "Thank you for making it a lot easier for me to rip them off you." He snaps his fingers and the four of them collapse to the ground. "Even though Cerberus would have appreciated the chase."

"NO!" I howl, running to their unmoving and limp bodies. I fall on my knees amongst them, my hands chaotically caressing every inch of flesh. Their eyes now milky and empty, their skin ashy and cold. Church, Bishop, Parrish and Abel are dead. "No... no... no..." I repeat over and over again, as my body begins to rock back and forth. I should be crying, but I am in such a state of shock, my body unable to conjure any tears to fall from my eyes. "I want to make a deal." I utter once I get some air in my lungs. I didn't even notice that I'd stopped breathing alongside them. I rise to my feet, wobbling somewhat, almost dropping back to the ground. I allow myself a final look at all my fallen angels, before turning to face the Devil. "I want them back. I want their souls back. They are mine; you cannot have them." I implore.

"Here's the thing, Nephilim, you and I, we can't make a deal." The Devil informs me, and my broken heart sinks.

"What? Why not?" Damn, I couldn't sound more like a petulant child if I tried. "I will offer you my soul in return."

"There was only one way I could get your soul," He pauses in his words and peers at the bodies left in my wake, "and your guys there, fucked that up."

"What are you saying?" I ask.

"You have nothing to trade, Nephilim."

"Oh, that's not true, brother." Astaroth cuts in.

"You're still here, Astaroth?" The Devil sounding very much displeased with the demon I summoned.

"Are you kidding? Of course, I am. This is a terrific tragic tale, that just reached its paramount climax, and there's no fucking way I ain't going to be a part of this. Plus," Astaroth saunters to my side, draping his snake tattooed arm over my shoulders, "Harlow and I are thick as thieves now, she's, my bestie. And come on, Lucy, you and I both know why she's here."

"At the crossroads?"

"Shush, the grown-ups are talking, Harlow." My demon companion says to me, before directing his next words to Lucifer, "A paragon of virtue's spirit in an earthlings body, a creation made so, by the grace of God to redeem them, the sinners." Is he disclosing that I have an angel's soul? "But the only thing all these worthless humans know to do, is exploit gifts from Him. I mean, God even sent Gabriel to try and amend some of the horrid mess she was born into, make her parents see the light or some shit. If anything, he only made things worse." Gabriel? As in my music producer? Wait, are they saying he's THE angel Gabriel? "God's children can't see righteousness, when they are blinded by gluttony, sloth, greed, pride, envy, lust and wrath. Because that's the thing with sin, once you get a taste, it consumes you from the inside out until your body, mind and soul are all rotten and foul."

"Enough with the storytelling. Get to the point." The Devil orders, his tone showing that his patience is running thin.

"Let's turn this in our favor. Imagine, the souls of all those pious pretenders in your hands where they belong, and Harlow is the one that delivers them to you. And her price is those idiots taking a nap over there. It's a bargain, if you ask me, brother."

Satan hums, considering Astaroth's words. "Ok." He utters as his blood red eyes fall upon me. "Your father, I want your father's cult."

"What?" I squeak. I feel so small between these two-strong and ungodly presences. Cult? Is he talking about my father's congregation?

"You heard me, child. What are those four to you? Do they honestly mean enough for you to deliver me your father's soul?"

For a bleak heartbeat, I stare down at my feet. Blood may be thicker than water, but love is thicker than blood, Matthew 2:13-23. This should be an easy decision, I love my guys, they are my life, my death, my eternity. So why, when I look back at Lucifer, do I say, "I can't kill my father." How can I be loyal to people that, yes, gave birth to me however, showed me nothing but bitterness, like I was the bane of their life?

"Do you know who he really is?" The demon with a ghostly complexion and blue-black slicked back hair asks me. His arm is no longer over my shoulders, but it's right against mine. His proximity, a welcome security blanket; providing safety and comfort through this harrowing situation.

"He's a good man. He seeks to save lost sheep from you." At my testimony, the Devil bursts out laughing. I furrow my brows as I carry on praising the man that raised me, "My father spreads the good Lord's word."

"He might, but trust me when I tell you, my sweet treat, your father doesn't actually practice, what he's preaching." Astaroth betrays to me

"You don't know him at all, Nephilim." Lucifer avows. "I suggest you dig a little deeper, maybe explore that compound you live on, a little more thoroughly."

"Why not just tell me?" Why are they beating around the bush, instead of just spilling the infernal hot tea?

"It's better you see for yourself, what type of a man your father really is." The Devil counters.

"If I agree to do this," I pause, glancing at the handsome corpses resting on the dirt, nothing but empty vessels, abandoned by what makes them my men, their souls, "can I have them back?" I plea.

"Sure. Why not?" Lucifer utters, clicking his fingers.

As the guys begin to wake up, Astaroth mutters, "And that's my cue to leave. Hey, my sweet treat," he waits until my electric blue eyes are on him to continue, "our deal, our secret, ok?" And then he just vanishes.

"You have 48-hours." The Devil puts forward. "Burn the

compound to the ground and I will sweeten the deal, y'all can go on your merry fucking way, for the rest of your lives. Otherwise, I will take back their souls. I might not be able to take yours, Nephilim, but I can still punish you. Perhaps trap you inside a hellish pit, within the back of your mind, one where you see them die, over and over again for all eternity."

FIFTY-ONE

CHURCH

IT's dead quiet in the car, as Bishop drives us to our trailer home, back in Friars Point. I presume that's where he's taking us, since he drove right past the venue we just performed at, where our tour bus rests abandoned. I'm in the passenger seat, behind me there's Abel, and Parrish is sitting in the middle, while Harlow is by the other rear window, behind Bishop. She hasn't spoken a word and has barely looked at any of us, her electric blue eyes down cast, from the moment we rose from the dead.

Because thats it right, we ran straight into Death's embrace. One second, we were exiting the car and making our way to our girl, the next... nothing. I have a faint recollection of a pure darkness shrouding everything, an absolute quiet, so loud it was desolating, and an all-consuming coldness, so profound and raw, purging, what I'm assuming was my soul because, clearly my body was left at the crossroads. The worst thing was the solitude, I was totally and utterly alone, I felt abandoned in a vast vacuum like void. Is that what my hell looks like, me by myself, for all time?

It felt like forever before I stirred awake, back in my human flesh. There she stood amid evil, the wind whipping her golden locks all around, as me and the rest of the Paragon of Virtue's Inferno members got back up to our feet. The angel, the Devil and the demon, it sounds like the start of a bad joke.

What the fuck was Astaroth doing there? I must've asked that question out loud, because my brother retorts, "That's a good question. Harlow?" All eyes fall upon the hauntingly, beautiful girl, her go-go white boots long discarded on the floor of the car. She is hugging her knees to her chest, her cheek resting upon them as she observes the world, rushing past, through the car window.

"Harlow, please talk to us." I plea.

She sighs, the window becoming misty with her exhale. "I didn't exactly know where the Devil's crossroads was, and I didn't have time to dawdle, so…"

"You summoned a demon?" Abel interrupts, at the same time, Parrish asks, "Why him?"

Her bewitching electric blue eyes finally find their way to us, they land on Parrish first and then journey pass the pink haired man to Abel, from there they shift to me and eventually Bishop. "I didn't know his name, but it just came to mind." She says in response to my best friend's question.

"How did you even know how to call forth a demon, my little mouse?"

"Someone was paying more attention to us then we realized." I remark. "What was Asta's price?"

"Hmmm," Harlow's eyes go back to avoid looking at us, "Astaroth wanted to be friends." I frown at her words, is Harlow lying to us? Or…

"He kissed you, didn't he?" Her mortified gaze lifts to me. Bingo. That's why she's acting strange. "Yeah, that's how he seals his deals, princess. How deep, did Asta shove his tongue, cause when he did it to me, it felt like a snake was slithering down my throat. Hot, but a bit weird. The handsome dick asked me for a favor though, that he could collect whenever he feels like it."

"Harlow, I am not pleased some other," there is a hitch on Bishop's reprimand as he seeks to find the right word, "guy's mouth was on yours. I am even less happy with you going to the crossroad by yourself, after you promised Abel you wouldn't."

"I promised I wasn't going to go on my own. Which I didn't," Harlow cuts in, trying to defend herself, "Astaroth was with me."

"Baby, you are not helping your case." I tell her.

"A lashing is definitely in the cards for you, my little mouse. I will teach you not to play us and disobey us, ever again." Since my brother is the one driving, his pale gray eyes dart between the road ahead and the rear-view mirror, where Harlow's reflection lays, as he continues lecturing our girl. "And we haven't even touched upon your talk with the Devil and what it is costing you, for us to be back. But we'll address that in a second, now," Bishop glances at me, "why the fuck, where you making deals with other demons, little brother?"

"I," shit, the tables have turned, and I am the one being chastised now. Once I cleared my throat, I explain myself, "I wanted someone tracked down and taken care of."

"You better not be talking about dad, Church. I think the scars the shadows left on him -from when he came to us right after we became famous, to milk us out of our wealth- was enough for him to never violate our lives again." Our dear dad, was flogged and branded by demonic hands. Marks that resemble the ones he left on Bishop, that beautify his back, but our dads will forever burn like hell upon his skin.

We soon arrive at the trailer, the headlights of our car illuminating our home. "Not dad." That's all I say.

Doors open and close as we all make our way out of the car. We climb the steps to the porch, the wood squeaking and creaking below our feet. As we enter the trailer, Harlow confesses, "The Devil wants my father." The guys and I turn to her; she stands by the front door, staring up at us with panic in her eyes, boots in her hand and feet dirty from having walked barefoot on the ground outside. "He wants me to burn the compound to ashes. Something about it being a cult."

"Wait, he didn't ask for your soul?" Parrish questions, sounding very much puzzled.

"He said he couldn't get it now. I think Astaroth implied that I was an angel incarnated."

"Fuck." Bishop hisses. "We almost sacrificed a fucking heavenly being. No wonder Satan was more keen for you, than any other virgin blood we've ever offered him. He could only get his hands on a soul like yours, while still pure and in a dark rite done in his name. Once touched, it means you've fallen," he pauses, his eyes fixating on Harlow, "it means you belong to the ones that made you fall."

"Holy shit." We all say in chorus, even Harlow. Her soul is ours. We own her. Damn, if that doesn't send a pleasurable tingle up my spine.

"I have 48-hours to complete my end of the bargain, or else he will take you away from me again." With that gut-wrenching revelation, my princess rushes past us into the corridor that leads to the bedrooms. Instead of going into Bishop's, which is the first door to the left, the one where we all spent the last hours of darkness, the night of the sacrifice, she carries on straight ahead to the end of the hall, right into my bedroom.

"Church." "Yeah, I am on it." I answer my brother, having anticipated his instructions, as I follow after Harlow. She went into my bedroom therefore I should be the one going to her to give her solace.

"Baby?" I call out, entering the bedroom, and closing the door behind me to give us some privacy. Not that you have much of that in this place, these walls are paper thin.

"I am going to save you. I swear." She says from her sitting position at the foot of the bed, her knuckles white from how intensely she's holding on to the mattress.

"Harlow," I murmur, as I kneel on the floor in front of her, one of my hands coming to rest on her thigh as the other brushes through her old-money blonde hair, pushing some of her curls behind her ear, "you don't have to."

"You were dead, Church. The Devil clicked his fingers, and you were all just gone, your bodies dropping to the ground. If I thought I was broken before, having all of your lifeless bodies at my feet..." Harlow can't even finish her sentence, as tears gather in her eyes. "The bad stuff I suffered through during my life before you, is insignificant, when weighed up to the agony I felt then. I swear; I can't experience that again."

"Ok." I try to give my girl a speck of comfort by caressing the skin on her thigh as I dry some of her fallen tears from her cheek, with the back of my hand. "But you don't have to do it alone. We'll go to the compound with you. We'll dig a bit. I don't want you to just unleash an inferno upon that place, without at least knowing the truth. In the end, whatever you decide to do we'll be right there, at your side. We're all in this together." She gives me a little nod, acknowledging my words. Her electric blue eyes cast a brief look behind me before shifting to me.

"When are you going to tell Abel?" Harlow switches gears.

My face twists into an expression of wry amusement. "About?" I ask.

"Did Astaroth find him? The drug dealer?"

What the fuck? "How?"

"Your eyes glanced at Abel after you admitted it wasn't your dad. It was swift but I noticed."

"Of course you did. Shit, Harlow," I don't get to say whatever was meant to follow that, as my princess begins to speak her peace.

"You all paint me as the savior, but I think that role belongs to you, Church. You saved us all. You emancipated us from our living nightmares, and you keep doing so by taking care of the bogeymen, that dare hurt us. Please, tell me Astaroth was merciless, that he inflicted excruciating pain on that piece of trash."

"Asta located him in New Orleans, running a ring of child trafficking, sampling the goods prior to shipping them to other depraved scumbags. So, from what the demon told me, he played a little with his food, Asta wanted to show that molester, what a real predator looked like. He chased him through the bayou and when he caught him, Asta cut him by the root of his wrongdoing."

"By his dick?" Harlow utters, elated by the idea. Wow she makes the word 'dick' sound so risqué when slipping from her sacred lips.

"Yes." I confirm. "The demon let him bleed out within an inch of his life, and then he called forward some gators to feed on him and finish the job."

"How gruesome. Astaroth did good; remind me to thank him when I see him again." Jealousy surges within me. Asta is a charmer, so, I can't be faulted for feeling somewhat hostile about Harlow's closeness with this demon. "You care about Abel. You love him."

That comment snaps me out of my sour thoughts. "Why are you grinning at me like the pink and purple kitty from Alice in Wonderland, Mary?"

"Because you and I, we are one in the same, our hearts are made to love more than one person. Just be gentle with him on his first time, ok?" Harlow asks as she looks behind me and smiles even wider.

"Nah, I much prefer to be wrecked by Church McGrew." Abel proclaims.

FIFTY-TWO

ABEL

CHURCH TURNS, his eyes widening as he spots me standing in the doorway. For a second, he just stares, words hanging in the air between us, that neither of us could find. I cross the room before he has time to react, closing the distance in a few quick strides. Without a second thought, I pull him into my arms, crushing him to my chest with a fierce urgency that neither of us expected.

I haven't been able to tear myself away from the door, not after hearing what Church was willing to do for me, for all of us. I'd been dead—gone—and come back, all because of Harlow's deal, a deal I still don't fully understand. The near-death experience, the pull to darkness, felt like something I'll carry with me forever. But the worst part? Knowing that without Harlow, I would've stayed there. She saved me, anchored me back to this world, and I feel it in every beat of my heart.

Now, I can't stand to be too far from her. Something inside me will not let it happen, it's like an invisible thread is keeping us connected. She is the reason I am here, the reason we all are. And no matter what it takes, we aren't letting her go. I knew she'd gone to the Devil to get me back, and I didn't know every detail of her deal, but I know enough. She saved us, saved me, and I am going to make sure she gets out of this alive. We are going to kill her father, even if she changes her mind. My decision is made—I'll follow through on this no matter what.

Church's arms tighten around me, his grip fierce, like he's afraid I might vanish if he let go. The warmth of his embrace presses into me, steadying me, grounding me in the chaos that is our lives now. When I finally ease back, his eyes are on me, wide and searching, his lips parted like he is about to say something—something deep, something that feels like it has been weighing on us both. I can feel his hesitation, the unspoken question lingering between us.

But I'm not about to give him the chance to pull back. I close the small gap between us, leaning in and pressing my lips to his. It's like a release, everything I haven't been able to say, pouring into that kiss. His mouth, so warm and soft, yet firm with surprise, and the slight scratch of his stubble is real, grounding, something to hold on to in this surreal moment. For a heartbeat, he holds still, frozen, but then he gives in, melting into me, his lips parting to let me in. The kiss deepens, intense and unrestrained, and his response hits me with an urgency I didn't know I needed.

Church's hand slides up to the back of my neck, fingers tangling in my hair as he pulls me closer, tilting his head to take control of the kiss. A spark ignites between us, raw and electric, like an unspoken understanding, pulsing between our bodies. I feel a thrill rush through me, a need I haven't allowed myself to give into, is there, flaring up with his touch. His grip tightens, pulling me in until there isn't a sliver of space between us.

My hands drift down his chest, feeling the strength within the planes of his body, the warmth beneath his shirt, and I let myself savor every inch of him. I feel him shudder under my touch, and then my fingers drift lower, skimming over his abs, sliding down until they reached the bulge in his jeans. I give him a slow, teasing squeeze, feeling his hard and hot dick press against my hand. His breath hitching, a low groan escaping him as he gasps against my mouth, his voice rough with barely contained desire.

"We don't have time," I murmur, my voice barely steady, though every part of me aches for more, to drown in this new connection between us, for just a little longer. "But damn, Church, you gotta promise to ruin me when we do."

His breathing is hard, his chest rising and falling as he stares at me, his pupils blown wide, lips swollen from the kiss. His gaze heavy, laced with something raw, something that makes me feel like we are standing on the edge of a cliff. He swallows hard, his voice coming out rough, barely a whisper. "Okay… okay, I promise." His hands loosen their grip, but he doesn't let go right away, lingering as though he isn't ready to give up the moment.

Finally, he steps back, his hand slowly dropping from my shoulder, his fingers trailing down my arm, unwilling to break contact completely. I didn't think anything could cool the fire burning inside me now, not even the danger that is looming, but reality settles back into the room, pressing down on us with its relentless urgency.

I turn to face Harlow, she is still sitting on the bed, her expression a mix of amusement and approval. Her lips curved in a smirk as she watches us, her gaze warm, playful, yet focused, like she is memorizing every second.

"If we had longer than 48-hours, I'd demand a show," she states, arching a brow, her tone light, but her eyes serious. "But, alas, we don't. So, boys, it's time to get down to business." She leaned forward; her gaze sharp. "Call the others in. I'm laying out the whole plan." Her voice has a slight hitch to it, like she is trying hard to mask her real emotions. She's about to kill her father to keep us, I am certain there is a whole storm of emotions inside her right now, battling out the right from the wrong.

"Bishop, Parrish, get in here," I call, my voice cutting through the heavy air. This little trailer already felt tight with just the three of us, but I know the weight of what is coming will make it feel downright suffocating.

Bishop and Parrish walk in, their eyes flicking from me to Church, then to Harlow, who is still perched on the bed. The trailer is cramped, the faded wallpaper peeling around the edges, the once-white ceiling now darkened with patches of mold that grew darker and larger the closer you get to the far end—Church's room. It looms overhead like a shadow, an unspoken reminder of the decay we are all fighting against, the past we have spent nearly 10 years running from, and it makes the space feel claustrophobic, like it's pressing down on us from above.

Parrish moves next to Church, his sharp eyes catching on the way his bottom lip is swollen. Without a word, he reaches out, his fingers brushing gently over the spot as if piecing together the last few minutes. His gaze darts between Church's lips and Harlow, then finally landed on me, his eyes widening for just a second, before a knowing smile tugs at his mouth, a flicker of understanding passing between us.

Harlow takes a deep, steadying breath, her gaze intense as she looks around at each of us, drawing us into the gravity of the moment. She doesn't flinch under the weight of our stares as she launches into it. "The Devil's deal is simple," she begins, her voice unwavering. "He wants me to go to my father's compound, burn the whole place to the ground, and make sure he's taken out with it. In exchange, he's giving all of you back your souls—free from him forever. And we have forty-eight hours to do it."

Bishop's brows knit together; his expression clouded with doubt. His voice cautious, a low rumble. "That's it? Nothing else? No strings attached?" His eyes are sharp, a flicker of skepticism laced through his gaze.

Harlow doesn't miss a beat, meeting his gaze, her voice clear and steady, as if daring any of us to doubt her. "Yup," she replies, the single word slicing through the room like a blade.

Parrish's face shifts, his hard expression, softening slightly as something like hope flickers in his eyes. He lets out a rough exhale, muttering under his breath, "Fuck... we'll actually be free."

I frown, studying her face closely, taking in the dark circles beneath her eyes, the weariness that she is trying so hard to hide is etched into her features. I know she is holding up a strong facade for us, for this mission, but the toll it's taking is all too clear. I search her expression, watching for any flicker that might hint at something she isn't saying. "Are you sure there's nothing else?" I ask, voice low, not quite ready to take this at face value.

Harlow's gaze softens, her eyes flicking down, and for a

moment, something vulnerable slips through. Her voice, barely more than a whisper. "Apart from only having forty-eight hours? No, that's it." She pauses, her fingertips tapping together in a nervous rhythm. "He really wants my father's soul. Asta hinted there's something, I don't know, something the Devil hasn't told me. But I know exactly where to find the truth."

"Fuck," Church mutters, raking a hand through his hair, his gaze narrowing with a determination I haven't seen from him for a while. "Okay, okay. So, what's the plan, Harlow?"

She lifts her chin, her eyes locking onto Church's with an intensity that sends a chill down my spine. "My father's office," she says. "There's a room he's never allowed me in. That's where we start. If I'm going to burn his entire operation down, his flock, everyone in it—I need to know why. I need to understand what Asta, and the Devil know, that I don't." Her voice wavering for a second, her expression clouding with a look I haven't seen before—confusion, maybe even a hint of betrayal. "They called my father's flock a cult. I don't know if they said that because they're from Hell... or if they really meant it."

She's trying to make sense of it, trying to put together pieces that seem too surreal to accept. I know what that feels like. And that is exactly why I have to step in.

"Harlow," I said, meeting her gaze directly. "I get it. You grew up in the church, you believe in the word of the Bible, I understand that. But the way you lived, the way your father taught you..." I let out a breath, choosing my words carefully. "If I'm being honest, I'm on the Devil's side here. It feels like a cult, and not just in the way the Devil throws that word around. It's more than that."

Her brow furrows, her gaze questioning. "Like... what do you mean?"

I run a hand through my hair, the memories of what I'd read, what I'd seen, flickering back. "I watched this documentary once," I begin slowly, the images flashing through my mind. "There was a group that sounded eerily similar to your father's flock. They called themselves a church, claimed to be doing God's work, but the reality... was far darker." I paused, "They hurt their members, manipulated them, controlled every single aspect of their lives. All in the name of salvation. All in the name of God."

Harlow's face pales, her fingers still tapping together as her gaze drops. She is quiet, trying to process it, and I can see the pieces starting to fit together in her mind.

FIFTY-THREE

HARLOW

IT'S EXACTLY 300 miles from Friar Point, Mississippi, to Chapel Hill, Tennessee; almost a five-hour drive. Dawn had been on the brink of ripping through the moonless night sky, by the time we got to the McGrew's trailer. Twilight was already upon us when we started freshening ourselves up, taking lukewarm showers, -since the heating pump seems to be on the way out- to get rid of the layers of smut from last night. Morning is pretty much in full swing when we get back in the car and begin to make our way to the compound.

Bishop is behind the wheel once more, with Abel in the passenger seat, while Church, Parrish and I are lying on top of one another, across the back seat. I am inbetween Church's legs, my back resting against his chest as he leans back against the door, his arms, hugging me tightly around my middle, my legs are draped over Parrish's as his head uses my boobs as his own personal pillow. I borrowed a pair of the lead singer's elastic –waist banded boxer shorts, they are black with white pinstripes, and one of Bishop's white button-down long-sleeved shirts. My old-money blonde hair is in a lone French fishtail braid.

"You should sleep, my little mouse." Bishop tells me.

"Can't." No rest for the wicked, not until we get to the end of this and my men's souls are no longer approaching the gallows, with the Devil's leash ready to hang them.

"Whatever is bugging you, angel, don't let it." Abel utters, not even bothering to turn around to spare me a glance, his elbow propped on the windowsill, his head resting on his hand. He is wearing his glasses, which means he must be tired. "We are never ever forsaking you again. We are going to do this."

"We are going to be free from devilish strings." The older McGrew adds with a firmly held belief pitched within his words.

As his younger brother goes on to softly say in my ear, "We are going to marry the shit out of you, grow old and saggy together, and fuck you good until kingdom come."

"And maybe bake a baby or two in here." Parrish comments, his fingers clawing at the flesh over my tummy, as though he wants to tear me open right here, right now, and breed me like that.

I want all of those things so bad, but I am scared I am going to lose myself when I kill my father. What if my boys don't love who I become? "Whatever happens we will always love you, my dark princess." I frown, twisting my upper body slightly, so I can peer at Church, but being careful not to disturb my pink haired man, whose head is still resting on my chest. Did my ashy-blonde haired rebel, just read my thoughts? "No, baby, I can't read your mind, but I am pretty good at reading your body language, I know all of your ticks."

Church replies, to a question I never asked aloud, as he lifts one of his hands to my forehead and tries to erase some of the worry lines that tarnish my skin, with his thumb. "You can't hide anything from me."

My eyes connect with Church's and I gasp, all of the sudden desperate for air to fill my lungs, as I almost drown within the depths of emotions that encompass his pale-gray pools. The Paragon of Virtue's Inferno men and I, we are more than lovers. But while Bishop, Parrish and Abel feel like my soulmates, Church and I, we are twin flames, meant to burn down the whole-damn-world to nothing but cinders with our love. Our fire, impossible to put out once it arouses from dormant embers.

Shrouded in black apocalyptic like clouds, the heavens give the appearance that night has fallen, even though it is only about mid-afternoon by the time we get to Chapel Hill, my father's compound being just on the outskirts of the town. Is this God seeking to send a message to His sheep, that something evil is coming for them?

As we cut through town, I tell Bishop to take the Caney Spring Road, of highway 31, and park amongst a grove of willows, that lie just behind the abandoned, old, rundown church that I used to sneak into when I was a kid, the complete opposite to the beautiful Chapel Hill - Church of Christ, and it's pearly gates into my father's compound. With money from his followers and my walk-of-life fruits, father bought the Maple Leaf farm that is just behind the chapel, all 1700 acres, and he built a whole town in his church's name. Father used to say, that isolation would guarantee that his herd wouldn't be infected by false beliefs, and be led into temptation by the serpents of the outside world, because the spirit might be willing, but the flesh is weak.

Hmmm this is starting to sound more and more like a cult.

We wait for dusk, within the confines of the dilapidated church. We feast on sweets and snacks, that I'd stashed inside a long time ago, for when I needed to run away for a bit from the hell. just across the road. Quite surprised raccoons and opossums didn't get into the food.

Chapel Hill - Church of Christ, is but a glorified way in now; it used to be father's house of prayer, until his 'brothers and sisters' erected a bigger temple, to accommodate his ever growing following, at the heart of the compound, that's where his sermons take place, where his illicit office is. The compound has barbed wire stock fencing all-the-way around it; our best bet to sneak in there will be by cutting through, it somewhere along the tree-covered wayside of a deserted Old Columbia Road, further away from the chapel and my family home.

Darkness is falls upon us at last, and as we stand by the fence, Abel with bolt cutters in his hand, getting ready to cut the wire, Church asks me, "Are you sure you want to do this?"

I nod, as I voice a weak, "Yes." I clear my throat, seeking to dislodge the disquietude I am feeling, so that my next words come out more assured. "I need to know the gospel about my father and his church. Maybe that will give me some peace of mind, when I offer him up to the Devil."

"Ok." Church mutters.

Once inside, I lead them straight to the temple. We creep through the compound, in and out of dark corners, like the shadows from hell that the four of them use to mess around with. "There shouldn't be anyone out and about, curfew was an hour ago. The only people allowed out are father, the elders and whoever they entrust with patrolling the streets, to make sure people are obeying father's ordinance." I explain to the guys.

There's a moment of silence, where all you can hear is the cicadas singing, and then Abel fractures it by saying, "Low, you are very much making it sound like this is…"

"A cult." I interrupt my heavily tattooed man. "Yeah, I know."

"What the fuck is that monstrosity?" Parrish chokes.

Unlike the nice early Christian white wooden plank chapel at the front, the building looming before us, is an expanse of stark white that seems to swallow the light around it. The temple is this kind of a massive New Orleans, shotgun style house with towers on all four corners. Its walls are solid and unyielding, smooth and featureless, like the face of some great, monolithic creature carved from stone. It rises from the earth like an impenetrable fortress, devoid of warmth, each wall thick enough to hold back the world, or perhaps, to keep something far darker within. The windows are sparse, mere slits in the façade, narrow and arched at the top, comparable to old Romanesque churches or the haunted remains of medieval ruins. They give nothing away, these rounded eyes, yet their shape holds a strange, timeless sorrow, as if they bore witness to secrets buried deep inside the walls.

"My father's temple." I retort. "Now come on, we shouldn't linger."

As we enter the building via a backdoor, -meant only for my father, closer to where his office lies-, and walk through the long corridor, Bishop states, "You know, my little mouse, I am reconsidering having you in white. This is some sinister shit and makes me see it, in a very different light." And this is but a small portion, this is nothing, all the other rooms within this place, are as colorless as this passage and everything on the outside.

According to father, white makes it easier to see people's sins; you will defile your path in, blacken it with your impurity. Keep pure no matter what, and you won't leave filth in your wake. Yet, I am no longer innocent, and I am not befouling the floor.

Father lied.

The doors into father's office loom right in front of us. Foolishly I reach for the handles and try them, hoping that father had left it unlocked. "Damn." I mutter. Father holds the only key, how are we supposed to get in there?

"Excuse me, gorgeous." Abel utters and gently pushes me aside, as he knees before the doors. He pulls something out of the back pocket, of his black baggy jeans and inserts it in the keyhole. Is that a bobby pin? Without breaking a sweat and with the grace of a black swan, Abel fiddles with it a bit, and voila, the lock clicks and the door opens.

I have never been allowed in this room. I could go inside father's office in the old chapel and the one in the house, but not here. Here it is forbidden.

There isn't much to it, at first glance, it's another milky room, no windows, with all white furniture, and paintings of glorified souls hanging on the walls. A partners' desk to our right with some seats placed around it, and opposite to that is a wall mostly made up of shelves.

"Is that a confessional in between the bookshelves?" Parrish inquires.

Indeed, it is. I approach it with prudence, like something woeful might jump out at me from within. As my hand touches the white wood of one of the doors, a ghostly voice whispers, "Be a good girl for your father, your lord and savior." That makes me recoil. I have been asked by my father to be a good girl numerous times, but never like that, never with such lechery.

"Harlow, what is it?" Church asks, his tone exuding concern.

I don't respond. I don't move. I am frozen with fear. Whatever is beyond the confessional doors, it gives me the same god awful and hopeless feeling as the prayer room in my family home. God only knows what possesses me to step forward again, to reach out and open the door, which creaks louder than a banshee's screams. Instead of a little pew at the back, where a devout would sit to confess, a lace curtain rests.

I move the veil aside and the sight before me repulses me and turns my stomach.

FIFTY-FOUR

BISHOP

WE'D BARELY MAKE it two steps into the dim room, before
Harlow stops dead, her body going rigid. I crash into her,
unprepared, and quickly wrap my arms around her to steady
her. She doesn't say a word, doesn't even flinch, and I can feel
the tension radiating through her as she stares straight ahead.

As I take in the sight that has frozen her to the spot, I hear
Abel's voice from behind, a sharp intake of breath followed
by, "Fucking hell." He steps forward, moving to stand in front
of Harlow. Gently, he places one hand on each of her cheeks,
tilting her face up to meet his gaze. "Harlow, baby," he whispers, his voice soft but strong. "It's okay. Let's go back out to
the other room, all right? We'll check those shelves in there.
We don't need to be in here right now." She swallows hard,
her eyes glassy, but slowly nods, giving him a small, almost
absent gesture of agreement. Abel's eyes meet mine over her
head, wide with undiluted fear. True, unmistakable terror—
the kind I've only seen a few times.

Slowly, I unwind my arms from around her, making sure
she is steady. Abel keeping his hands on her, guiding her

slowly back out into the office, with quiet reassurances that I can only hope will hold her together. Once they leave, Parrish and Church step up beside me, both of them equally just as shaken.

Parrish swallows, the sound louder in the quiet, nearly echoing through the sickly silence of the room. "I think… I think, I'll go help Harlow and Abel," he mutters, his face paling as he looks at me, searching for some kind of approval. I nod, unable to muster any words myself. He turns quickly, walking out to join them, leaving just Church and me in this room of horror.

Church's voice comes out in a shaky stutter, beside me. "You don't think… I mean, they didn't… right?" He's staring, eyes fixed on the object in front of us, and I know exactly what he is thinking, because it is coursing through my mind too, a horror I can't shake.

At the center of the room stands a single bed, gleaming and cold, constructed entirely of marble. Its stark white color, illuminated only by the faint light coming in through the office behind us, making it look even more unnatural, more sinister. Massive crosses adorn each wall, casting strange shadows that twist and loom over the room. At the top of the bed is a white lace pillow, pristine, almost angelic, in brutal contrast to the rest of the room. But it is the foot of the bed that turns my stomach: leg holders. Just like in a delivery room, the kind used for women giving birth.

Shock roots me in place, locking my legs, and my mouth feels like it has been sewn shut. Church stutters again beside me; his voice even smaller, even more afraid. "You don't think… you don't think Harlow's ever been on that table, do you?"

I force myself to respond, though the bile rising in my throat. "No," I state, my voice barely a whisper. "She was a virgin. I don't believe she even knew about this." But the words feel thin, hollow, a desperate attempt to believe something I can't fully convince myself of.

Church's face twists in disgust, and he shakes his head slowly. "You don't think… they used that for… for what my mind is thinking, do you?" His voice trembles, each word dragging up our worst fears, the kind we can hardly bear to consider.

I can barely keep my stomach in check, as I take one last, sickened look at the bed. "Let's look over there," I finally said, voice rough, motioning toward a stack of shelves along the right side of the room. They are lined with leather-bound books, their spines cracked and worn, like old diaries.

With dread pooling in my stomach, I move toward the shelves, each step heavier than the last. Whatever these books contain, whatever secrets Harlow's father has hidden in them, I know we'll have to face it. I reach for a random book, feeling the cracked leather under my fingers as I open it. Church grabs another, flipping through the pages beside me. As I start to read, my hands begin to shake, my grip on the book faltering as I absorb the words on the page.

It is sickening. My stomach churns, and my knees feel weak as I scan the entries. Beside me, Church's book slips from his hands, hitting the floor with a loud, hollow thump that seems to echo throughout the room. He staggers back, turning away as he wretch's, the sound of him vomiting sharp and raw. I can't blame him. What we are reading… this is horror in its purest form.

We made a deal with a demon, spilled blood in his name,

killed nine women to pay our own debt—but this... this is something else. This is a level of depravity so deep, so twisted, that even the Devil himself can't compare.

I force myself to keep reading, bile burning the back of my throat. The diary entry, written in the neat script of a madman, is a chilling account of his so-called "holy duties."

"Isabel came to me, her first bleeding. She is 13. A little late, but I have seen later. I explain to her the process she will go through to receive a child from God Himself. I also explain that she will be married to one of the boys in the compound, Thomas, I picked him for her. He is a devout Christian, happy to marry her. He currently has three wives already, all of which bear the babies of God and now she will bear his own children too."

I feel my blood turn cold as I read the next part, my eyes almost refusing to take it in. "At first, she was scared, but once I explained how God works through me, and that she would only need to lie on the altar of God until she was with child, she was happy." I clench my fists, rage twisting my insides as I turn the page, but the depraved words keep coming. "Once her bleeding has stopped, she will be brought in, and I will fill her with my seed until she carries the child of God."

Polaroids are tucked between the pages—sick, disturbing photos of the girl. Isabel, barely more than a child, lying on the marble altar. Her face, pale and frightened, the innocence in her eyes hollowed by fear. And there he is, Harlow's father, standing at the end of the bed near the leg holders, his face twisted with an expression of pure fanaticism.

The entries go on, describing in horrid detail the blood, the pain, the multiple times it took for her to become pregnant. There are even more photos, images of Isabel on her so-called wedding day to Thomas, and later, a picture of her with a swollen belly, her expression vacant and hollow.

This dairy says he'd filled this compound with thirty-eight children from what he called "God's grace" So far. Who knows how old this dairy is, the number could be a lot higher now. The scope of it is sickening, and I feel my hands tremble, my vision blurring with a red haze. My heart twists with something dark and dangerous. I'd felt bad for what we are asking of Harlow—to burn this place down, to destroy her own family.

But now? ---- Now, I want to dance on the ashes.

I shut the diary, my mouth dry, bile inching up my throat. How the hell was I supposed to tell her what is in this room? I don't even know if I can. This isn't just abuse, or manipulation, or even murder. This is something far worse, a perverse cult with roots deeper than anything I could've imagined.

Beside me, Church shakily reaches for another diary, glancing at it briefly before letting out a guttural sound. "I'm out," he chokes, his face pale, eyes wide with horror. "We gotta get out of here, before I vomit again."

He clutches the book he just pulled, gripping it like a lifeline, and stumbles out of the room. I watch him go; my legs locked in place as I try to process the atrocities we've just uncovered.

But then I hear him calling from the other room, his voice quiet but firm, straining with pain. "Harlow, baby, I need to show you something."

That snaps me out of my trance. I turn on my heel, forcing myself to move, to follow Church out of this hellish room, to leave behind the pure evil that lurks in the pages and the photographs.

Fifty-Five

Harlow

THERE WAS a secret room beyond the confessional, at the heart of it a hybrid miscreation of an alter and bed, with built in stirrups, and crosses, so many crosses all over the walls, trying to make that place a sanctum sanctorum, when it's anything but holy.

"Parrish, can you fucking stop pacing, and help me snap Low out of it." Abel ferried me out of there, back into father's office. Once by the desk he turns me around in his arms and lifts me so that I am sitting on top of it. He hunches forward, cupping my face with his hands, his dark brown eyes looking intensely into mine, searching for something. Is he trying to draw me out from within the dark bounds of my mind? I do hope my shepherd can do that, I have lost my bearings, and I can't seem to find my way back.

"What the hell is that room?" Parrish asks Abel, as if the Paragon of Virtue's Inferno drummer, holds all the answers.

"Perdition upon a false Garden of Eden." Abel replies. Did the room reveal to my tattooed boyfriend, the atrocities that go on in there too?

As I stepped foot within those four walls, will-o'-the-wisps, -ashen flaming ghosts with a human appearance- materialized upon the altar, performing a carnal dance. The lines on the apparitions weren't sharp, but I would recognize father, no matter what, the figure below him was a different story, constantly changing and distorting; one young girl, after another.

"Harlow, baby, I need to show you something." Church utters as he comes out from that God forsaken place, carrying a weathered leather-bound book in his shaky hand.

Bishop pushes past his brother, coming to stand right in his way. "Church, I really don't think Harlow should see what those pages hold." He behests, his tone somber and harsh.

"Our girl said she wanted the gospel about her father. Alas this is it." Church sets forth, holding the damn diary up. I pluck it out of his hands, all eyes falling on me. I don't remember getting off the desk or to my feet. I don't remember walking to the McGrew brothers. It's like I am a zombie, roaming about with no feelings, no awareness and no interest in what I am doing, completely detached from the world around me.

I drag myself back to the desk, laying the book down and open it, skimming through the pages with such lack of grace, that I rip some of the paper. The boys close in on me, their combined presence soothing the torment within. A sigh fleeing my lips, I cotton on that as long as they are with me, I will be ok.

"This is some grim shit." Parrish comments, as he reads, over my shoulder, the things scrawled upon these pages in father's handwriting.

The words that grace father's written account, are

disturbing and distasteful, and as I study the ages, that's when I get sick to the core. Fifteen. Fourteen. More fifteens followed by a twelve, that's when something within me breaks apart violently, and I just lose it. I begin to tear the pages out, as I scream like a madwoman. I don't stop until there's nothing, but the empty leather binding and father's depraved deeds blight the pristine white floor.

All these people, I brought to him through my singing. I was nothing but a siren, luring poor unfortunate souls into their doom. The compound was supposed to be a slice of heaven, a beautiful community full of good people, not this breeding ground for father's so-called pure children.

God made a terrible mistake, gifting me to this man. Father writes, as if he believes he is a conduit of the Lord; a prophet blessed with the power to birth angels on earth and this is his mission, to impregnate as many virgins as possible to carry his holy fruit. Does father think he has a divine seed or something? How does that justify raping underage girls?

How did mother dearest let this happen? Does she even know? She must, nothing gets past that woman.

"If only you weren't defective, then your father wouldn't have to touch as many doves to create perfection." Those words crash into me like a tidal wave. She screeched them at me once upon a time, right before tossing me in the prayer closet.

Later that night I overheard father tell mother dearest, "That's the things with firsts, my dear, they never come out right."

That spiteful cow, that ungrateful pig, I am going to roast them to a crisp. I launch into a maniacal laugh, that only silences when I suck some much-needed air into my lungs, a sense of unnatural serenity taking over me.

Like mister Johnson once sang: *As I put a match to the compound*

"This place has been adulterated by sin, it needs to be purged. Fire should feast on the flesh of the aberrations that prey on the weaker souls. May God have mercy on the faithful that fell for a preacher's perverted wile, that didn't deserve what was done to them by the hands of my father and that they shouldn't suffer through the fire and brimstone I am about to bestow upon this compound. If God finds anyone worthy of salvation, then He can deliver them from my wrath. Let's burn it down, guys. This church where the act of evil has occurred, where the improper sacraments were conceived. The school, where the desecration of His words was taught. The old chapel and my childhood home where it all started."

Fifty-Six

Parrish

I have a little box in my mind, a coffin carved from the deepest corners of my soul. It's where I shove the things I can't bear to look at—the horrors too raw, too dark to face. It's where I lock away the memories that consume me, that creep into my nightmares, and the ones that haunt me when I'm awake. I cram them inside and seal it tight, hoping it will hold. What I saw in that diary, though—the scrawled words in her father's neat, unholy hand, the images that shouldn't exist —they're going straight into that box. But I already know the truth. This time, the box won't hold. Those horrors will claw their way out, tearing through my mind, and when they do, they'll create nightmares, unlike any I've faced before.

My life wasn't easy. Hell, it wasn't even livable most days. It was pure, unfiltered evil, and I've spent years trying to come to terms with it. Between the four of us, we've seen enough darkness to send chills through Lucifer himself. But this? What Harlow's father has done, what he's created? It makes my past look almost tame. The man has built an empire of suffering, wrapped in the guise of devotion, filling it with atrocities, so twisted they defy comprehension. I think even the King of Hell will relish the chance to drag his soul into the deepest pits and leave it there to rot for eternity.

And Harlow? She trumps us all. Her pain, her burden—it eclipses anything I've endured. Anything any of us have endured. As much as I want to believe she'll come out of this whole, I know better. I can feel my own mind splintering after reading just a fraction of that diary. If I'm cracking, how the hell is she holding it together?

Abel stands to the side, his face frozen in an eerie stillness. It's unreadable at first glance, but the sharp tension in his jaw, the way his fists are balled so tightly, his knuckles white—it's a rage so quiet, it's deafening. Church, on the other hand, looks seconds away from throwing up. His face is pale, a faint sheen of sweat on his brow, his chest rising and falling as if he's struggling to keep himself steady. And Bishop—Bishop hasn't moved. His whole body seems locked in place, his eyes fixed on Harlow, like she's the only thing tethering him to reality.

The pages of the diary are scattered across the floor, a grotesque mosaic of evil exposed to the light. And there she stands, right in the middle of it, the eye of the storm. Her face is a blank slate, unreadable, but her eyes—they burn. It's a fire, I know all too well. A fury so white-hot it quiets everything else, sharpening your thoughts into one singular focus: destruction. In her, I see a reflection of myself, the calm before I slice into flesh, watching blood bloom along the blade's path, the serenity that comes, when the world narrows to a single purpose. That's where she is now. Quiet. Focused. Ready.

Harlow's gaze locks on me, her eyes like shards of ice, cold and cutting. "Let's light it up," she says, her voice calm, steady, and resolute. There's no hesitation, no second-guessing, just a quiet command that carries the weight of inevitability. Without waiting for a response, she turns on her heel and walks out of the room, her steps, measured and deliberate, each one ringing with purpose.

We follow. Of course, we follow. How could we not? It's as though she's pulled us into her gravity, a force so absolute, that resistance feels impossible. Like sheep trailing their shepherd or rats bewitched by the hypnotic tune of her flute, we move after her in silence. If Harlow asked me to walk off a cliff, I'd do it without question. Hell, I think we all would. There's something about her in this moment—this unshakable authority, this quiet power—that none of us can deny.

She leads us out of the building and down a gentle slope, the loose dirt crunching beneath our boots. The air feels heavy, oppressive, the weight of what's coming pressing down on all of us. At the bottom of the hill stands a weathered garden shed, its wooden walls warped and faded from years of neglect. It's unassuming, ordinary at first glance, but there's a determination in Harlow's stride that makes it feel monumental, like this little shed holds the key to her vengeance.

She stops in front of the door, her fingers brushing over the rusted padlock that hangs there. It's corroded, flaked with orange and brown, the kind of lock that should've been replaced years ago. She doesn't even flinch, her movements steady as she looks over her shoulder. "Baby," she says softly, her voice breaking through the silence, like a blade slicing through tension. "Do you mind unlocking this?"

Abel steps forward, silent and focused, pulling a bobby pin from his pocket with a smoothness that speaks of practiced ease. There's no fumbling, no hesitation—just the quiet click of the lock springing open, after a few deft movements. He slides it free from the bolt, the metal groaning faintly as he pushes the door open.

Inside, the faint smell of gasoline and machine oil greets us, sharp and clinging to the air. The room is dim, lit only by the faint light of the moon filtering in from the open door, casting long shadows over the shelves lining the back wall. On the bottom shelf, rows of jerry cans sit waiting, their red plastic dulled by dust but unmistakable. The air is thick with potential, the promise of destruction hanging heavy in the small, confined space.

Harlow steps forward, crouching to grab one of the cans, her movements slow and deliberate. She doesn't speak, doesn't need to—the quiet authority radiating from her is enough. We exchange glances, but no one says a word. In this moment, she's not just leading us. She's commanding us, and we're ready to follow her into the fire.

The rest of the shed is as plain as can be; a small generator coated in a fine layer of dust, a ride-on lawn mower parked in the corner, its seat cracked and faded, and a few scattered tools leaning haphazardly against the walls. But none of us are looking at any of it. Our attention is fixed on her.

Without hesitation, she stands and hands it to me. The weight of it shifts in my hands, the liquid inside sloshing faintly with every slight movement. It feels heavier than it should, not just because of the fuel but because of what it represents. One by one, she passes the cans to the others, her steps purposeful, her expression unwavering.

Her eyes shine unnaturally bright, too clear, too sharp, like the fire she's planning to unleash is already burning inside her. Every ounce of her is focused, consumed by a purpose so singular it's almost terrifying. There's no hesitation in her movements, no fear clouding her expression—just pure and unrelenting vengeance.

"Parrish, Church," she says, her voice calm and steady, as if she were giving directions to dinner rather than orchestrating destruction. "Take the church. Burn it to the ground. I won't set foot in there again."

I nod, the thought of setting that altar ablaze makes my blood sing with anticipation. That room, that table—I want to watch them turn to ash. Church steps forward, gripping his jerry can tightly, and leans down to kiss her. His lips linger on hers, the kiss slow and deliberate, a moment of unspoken understanding passing between them. "It would be my absolute pleasure," he murmurs softly against her lips. I nod again, silently agreeing, my own thoughts dark but resolute.

Harlow turns to Abel and Bishop next, her focus shifting seamlessly. "Take the school," she says, her voice just as steady, pointing to a white wooden building further up the hill. It looks pristine, almost innocent in the dim light, but we all know better. It might resemble a church more than the abomination we just left, but whatever went on inside those walls is no less monstrous.

Bishop frowns, his jaw tightening as he steps closer to her. His voice is low, protective, as he says, "Baby, I'm coming with you."

She doesn't hesitate. She shakes her head firmly, stepping up to him and pressing a soft kiss to his lips. "No," she says, her voice unwavering. "This is something I need to do alone. I need to look him in the eyes, as I light that match and watch him realize it's the Devil calling him, not God."

Abel exhales deeply, the sound heavy and uneven, his face drawn tight with worry. His hands flex against the jerry can he's holding, the weight of it mirroring the burden in his voice as he says, "We should stick together." There's a faint tremor in his tone, a crack that betrays the fear he's trying to suppress.

Harlow shakes her head, the movement deliberate, unyielding. She steps up to him, rising on her toes to softly kiss his lips. The tenderness of the act is almost jarring, a fragile moment in the midst of chaos. "I'm going to end this," she says, her voice steady, resolute. "I'm going to end it all."

She turns to Bishop next, slipping into his free arm, her body folding against his for a brief second. His other arm grips the jerry can tightly, his knuckles white, as he holds her like he's afraid to let go. "I love you," she whispers, her voice soft, almost gentle. Then, with quiet determination, she pulls away and moves toward me.

Her lips press to mine, firm but purposeful, and I feel everything in that kiss. The weight of her resolve, the sharp edge of her madness, the all-consuming force of her vengeance—it crashes into me, and for a moment, I can't breathe; Her warmth lingers even as she steps back, her eyes locking onto mine.

There's a glint in her gaze, something wild and untamed, but beneath it, lies an eerie sense of clarity. It's the kind of focus that only comes when every wall has been torn down, leaving nothing but raw intent. Seeing that diary, those words and photos, shattered something in her. But in their place, it built something else—something fierce and immovable. She's ready to burn it all down, and I know there's nothing, no force on this earth or in hell, that could stop her now.

"I love you all," she says, taking a step back. Her voice carries over the silence, not trembling, not wavering, but final. Then she turns, her shoulders squared; as she begins her march toward the largest building on the hill—the house that must have been her family home.

Church's voice breaks the quiet, low and shaken. "Fuck," he mutters, his face pale, his eyes glued to her retreating figure. "I don't know if I can let her go alone."

"We have to," I say, my voice firm even as my chest tightens. "This is her story, not ours. She needs to end it, the way she needs to."

Bishop lets out a heavy sigh, his jaw clenched so tight I can see the muscle jumping beneath his skin. His gaze lingers on Harlow, his voice is thick when he finally speaks. "She needs to find her ending," he agrees. "But my whole body is screaming at me to follow her."

I step forward, clapping church on the shoulder. "Let's go," I say, jerking my chin toward the looming shadow of the church. "I've got a room I want to burn down first."

Fifty-Seven

Harlow

I STAND at the foot of my parent's bed, looming over them as they peacefully rest shrouded in their old-fashioned valance bedspread, white beautified with a dahlia floral print. I hate that stupid skirt edge. I'd like to say our stuff is the cool kind of vintage, but it's just old-granny withered trash that my parents got at a goodwill establishment for nickels on the dime.

I was fine with the fruits of my labor going towards father's church, as long as I had cute enough clothes covering my skin and food in my belly. But that's when I had faith it was being used to build paradise not a house of ill repute for father's own sick pleasures. Now I am mad. How dare he? Father used me, used my angelic voice, not only to bring in a nice little herd for him to manipulate, but plenty of money for his wayward cause. I hate him.

And mother dearest, how dare she? Making me believe all of my youth, that I was the black sheep, the disgrace of our pure picture-perfect family, but they are the wolves in sheep's clothing. The abuse, the punishments, hours of kneeling and praying, for not listening and submitting to father preaching, for not being a flawless church-leader's daughter. "Refining compliance, is led by a strand of hair, Harlow." Mother dearest was in the habit of saying to me before she disciplined me. "Until you learn that, you will wear sackcloth and ashes. It's my prerogative as your mother to break you, insolent child. I will reform you into the model virtue, he so craves." She scarred me alright; she made me into a burning one, an angel of fire, and I am about to carry out my mission. God, I hate her.

But I so love my men, here I am taking a page out of a Harley Quinn book of madness, and instead of looking at me with pity in their eyes for the truths I have learnt, they idolize the broken doll, that I have become, they worship the unholy ground I walk upon. They follow me like perfect pets and obey my orders, like good men.

As I stare vacantly at father and mother dearest's sleeping figures, a dark lullaby is being cooked up in the deep recesses of my mind.

> *White dove, why do you bleed?*
> *Is it because, to a false man of God you plead?*
> *I flown the coop, on father's perverted persecution*
> *Yet you were but a slave in his mental institution*

I didn't realize I started chanting it whilst I poured gasoline all over them, dousing them in the propellant of their reckoning. "What," father and mother dearest rouse, sitting up in bed whilst couching and spluttering, "Harlow, what in God's name do you think you are doing?"

"You shouldn't call the Lord's name in vain, father." I enlighten him, setting the can down at my feet.

"Did you just bathe us in fuel? Have you gone insane, Harlow?" Mother dearest bellows my way.

Keep pure no matter what
Father tells you
When he comes on knocking, dismiss the sin named lust
Yet the preacher man desecrates you with just one screw

I carry on humming and singing. It could be that I am acting a bit psychotic, but the old Harlow can't come to the phone right now. Why? Oh 'cause she's dead.

"What are you wearing?" Mother dearest asks clutching her pearls.

Really mother, you think this is the right time to censure me about my attire? Ok, I'll bite. "Oh, this is daddy Bishop's shirt, and these are my incubuses boxer shorts. I am not wearing anything from my slasher, but I stole my shepherd's lighter." I note, as I take Abel's gold windproof, Zippo lighter, -with the sigil of Baphomet carved into its surface-, out of the chest pocket of the shirt. I pulled it out from his baggy jeans front pocket when we shared a goodbye kiss in the shed, my hand accidentally brushing against something monstrous in the process.

White dove, father made you fall from grace with his greed
Pray and obey, your blind creed
But alas, sweet bird, it's a foul bed of lies
And by infernal fire, you will be baptized

"Harlow!" Father calls out to me.

"Preacher man walked into the club and he said to me, hey girl can't you walk and not stray? Father, I'm torn and I'm selling my soul to the dark rhythm, the beat and the bass, 'cause I'm so possessed with the satanic music they play. I can't stop my feet from dancin' to the sound of their demonic drums. I can't keep my hips from swayin' to their carnal ballads. Preacher man took my hand, looked in my eyes and he said, hey girl can't you live your life right? So I cried, father, things aren't always so black and white, don't cast the first stone 'cause I'm not alone, and it's not like I'm hurtin' anyone. Not yet, anyway. I wouldn't change a thing even if I could. I chose a devilish path and I'm not looking back. I'm sorry if I left the angels crying over me, but I fell in love with my rock-'n'roll gods." I am borrowing these Selena Gomez lyrics to tell my parents about me and the Paragon of Virtue's Inferno member's.

"What happened to you, child? What have those boys done to you?" I try to exhume the concern from his words but find none there."Other than love me?" I offer up, innocently.

From the corner of my eye, I make out the tail of a blue pit-viper disappearing under the skirt of the bedspread, at the foot of the bed, it slithers its way up and it nestles beneath the covers, right between father and mother dearest. Astaroth is here, probably to collect what the Devil requested I deliver to him, my father's soul. An ugly smirk, full of malice, blooms in my face.

There is no absolution
From this burning conclusion

"Forgive me father for I have sinned, I am no longer pure, you see. They loved me alright, in every hole that can house their manhood. And I welcomed them like a good girl." I look my parents up and down, with as much disrespect as I can summon.

Stay innocent, oh good girl
But how can you, when father bestows you with improper love?
White dove, you now carry his rotten seed
And I am here to betray that angels you will not breed

Mother dearest interrupts my crooning, "That's enough, you demon," fury exudes from both my parents. I think I struck a bad chord there. She attempts to get out of bed, no doubt to inflict some sort of punishment upon me, but Astaroth takes that exact moment to materialize, out of a black fog that creeps up from under the bedspread. He drapes his arms over mother dearest, holding her and father back.

"You got it wrong, ma'am. Harlow ain't no demon, I am."

"Asta." I breathe out, thankful that he is here. For a split-second I was back to being the weak girl, the one that cowards before her mean mother, I even took a step back as she got ready to rise from the bed. "Not the prayer closet," was my only thought. I would give Astaroth my first born, if he can make it so that mother dearest spends her afterlife in her own prayer closet deep in the bowels of hell.

"Sweet treat. Miss me?" My demon friend with slicked back, blue-black hair and yellow eyes asks me, in his laid-back manner, but I can hear the whisper of worry behind his spoken words. Did Astaroth sense my distress, is that why he exposed himself? He should be careful; this girl might end up believing he cares.

"It's only been 24 hours." I tell him.

He chuckles. "That's a yes in my books."

"No clothes again, I see." I remark.

"Anything to please my favorite angel." Astaroth betrays to me, before mumbling to my parents, "She likes me bare." It's my turn to chuckle. "Don't stew on it, sweet treat, I won't tell your guys that you might actually fancy me."

"Don't flatter yourself, Mister."

"May I say," Astaroth begins to utter, pausing for a moment to sniff mother dearest, who recoils at the action, and father, who frowns very much vexed, "y'all smell divine."

"Our daughter poured gasoline all over us, demon." My father informs Asta.

"Oh, no. That ain't it. The both of you reek of sin, but the stench coming from you, Sir, is ever so lusty." Astaroth says, licking his lips.

"What's the meaning of this, Harlow? What have you done?"

"I met up with the Devil at the crossroads, father. He ain't that bad, really." I confess, as I start playing with the lighter in my hand, opening the lid with my thumb, lighting it up and closing the lid back down so the flame dies within. Over and over, I repeat the action, my electric blue eyes focused on the object and the rivetingly beautiful flame it gifts me with. "He offered me a sweet deal; I get to keep my men forever, in exchange I give him you and your disgusting cult out there."

"Awww, true love, isn't it beautiful?" The demon sandwiched between my parents suspires. "Actually, Lucy is pretty bad; I just think he has a soft spot for your daughter. All of us from down below do. She is quite something."

"The Devil opened my eyes, and for once in my life, I am seeing clearly, no longer blinded by your God-fearing bullshit." Mother dearest gasps at the swear word that slips past my lips. "I have been in your office father, the one in the new church, I have entered your chamber of lecherous horrors, and I have read your work. You are sick." As I growl that last part, I fix my gaze upon the people that birthed me, Astaroth isn't amongst them anymore.

I feel his presence behind me well before he whispers in my ear, "Light 'em up, baby."

I flip the cap of the Abel's lighter open , for one final time, flicking the wheel, setting it alight. "You deserve what's coming for you, father. Your compound is burning, and now, it is your turn." And with that I drop the Zippo on top of the bed. The whole thing, along with father and mother dearest, get swallowed up by the flames in no time. Once I soak in the haunting image of them being consumed by fire, I turn on my heels and walk away. Astaroth stays behind, probably to admire the infernal beauty of my craft, and later to harvest the fruits it bears.

My parents' piercing screams become the vocal support as I wrap up my fresh lullaby.

Damning taste of the forbidden fruit
Father, did you miss me?
I am 'bout to lay to rest, all of my confessions
I am the strange fruit hanging
The only angel you could give genesis to
And I am getting hot and heavy with four demons; can you hear the
wedding bells?
The Old Serpent my soul can't have
But he wants yours father
For the holy vows that you broke
For the unholy love that you make
You are going to hell
Keep pure no matter what
Be a good boy for your paragon of virtue daughter, burn father
burn.

I end with a gasp, as it seems I sang my way to the place that plagues my dreams, the prayer closet. In front of me stands the doorway to my nightmares. I shouldn't linger, soon the whole house will be engulfed in flames as well. Yet, instead of leaving I reach for the doorknob and turn it.

FIFTY-EIGHT
CHURCH

MY PARAGON of Virtue's Inferno brothers' and I await our girl inside the old church by her family home, the place swamped with gasoline, ready to be set ablaze.

"She's taking too long." Parrish remarks. He's squatting on top of the altar, elbows on his knees, his sharp toy in between his clasped hands, his hazel eyes fixed on the church entrance.

Feasting my eyes on the church's aberration while it was burning, was a joy to behold. Yellow, orange and red ribbons of scalding heat intertwined while the fire crackled and snapped, sparks jumping, and sizzling like bacon. Flickering of firelight danced and swayed with the wind, being blown around like the noodle man at a car yard. Twitching and contorting flames reaching up toward the dark sky above, hot hands trying to ascend to the heavens.

The white wooden structure they use as a school, a couple of yards beyond the one Parrish and I were tasked to destroy by fire, got painted in the same colors by my brother and Abel, but they didn't stick around, to savor the burnt ashy flavor hanging in the air at the scene of their fiery crime. Once they met up with us, we retraced our steps out of the compound, so we could be reunited with our girl. I did find it strange that nothing living stirred in the night; no sentinels that were supposed to be walking the grounds, sounded the alarm to warn their fellow brothers and sisters of the hell, brewing upon them. But I did catch shadows creeping in a helter-skelter manner throughout the darkness. Demons are already playing havoc in this place.

"I'll go get her." I announce. To ward off any possible protest from anyone I make my way out of the house of prayer like a scalded cat.

I trample over the graveyard towards Harlow's childhood home. Other than having dead people buried in her front yard, the house itself looks pretty much like a white-picket-fence dream. But a beautiful face can mask the ugliest of evil.

The moment I step through the front door, the smell of burning flesh is pungent and gut-churning. Soft moans echo from upstairs, as smoke cascades down the stairs like a water-fall. "Harlow!" I shout.

"In here." I hear her say from within a wide-open door below the flight of stairs.

"Baby, what," the rest of my words are forever left unsaid, as I take in the room she's in. Is this the fucking prayer closet? It's a coffin, buried within the walls of the house. Its length and width are about the same, with just enough space for someone like my princess to kneel and that's it. And the height of this chapel-fashioned room, I mean, I can't even stand up straight in it.

Opposite the doorway hangs a crucified Christ, With an

altar right beneath his feet, and a bunch of other religious shit, making this casket even more crammed. The walls scare the bejesus out of me; amongst the portraits of salt of the earth people, passages from the bible, that are written in Harlow's handwriting, grace the many peeling layers of cracked and moldy looking wallpaper.

Just like the room in her father's office, this is the stuff of nightmares, but while one was erected to break and spoil the body of pure girls, this one was created to fracture and scar the mind and soul of the innocent daughter of the church's leader. It says a lot about Harlow, of her inner strength, she unearthed herself from this pit of despair with her light unsullied. How? This world does not deserve to be blessed by her, it didn't take Harlow at her best and now, it's going to have to handle my princess at her worst. Whatever darkness you find in her heart is there because of me, Bishop, Parrish and Abel, we are her sins, and we are not worthy of this angel, but damn, we are keeping her.

"Welcome to my hell." Harlow says as I come to stand by her, my arm brushing against hers, since it's as tight as a virgin's pussy in here. Her electric blue eyes finally stop contemplating the cross on the wall and look up at me. "I really don't want this closet to haunt me anymore. Wanna help me make it into some sort of nirvana, baby?"

I crave to be her knight in shining black armor; to slay the demons that cause her such melancholia. "I wouldn't know how, baby." I tell her.

To be one of her four horsemen in this apocalypse, would be an honor. I feel like Death, with his pale horse, suits me, whilst my fellow Paragon of Virtue's Inferno members would be the other three. Bishop could ride the Black horse and be Pestilence. Parrish, on his red horse, could be War. And that would leave Abel with Famine, on a black horse.

Once all is still, with the peace of death, what remains are the echoes of the people that once lived. Disgrace is the epitaph, that ends those memories; she is the lies of a history written by the embittered. A man's good deeds become rotten, love turns to hate, faith to mistrust, temperance to greed, glory to shame, pleasure to misery, and none speak against her but the withered wind. Harlow is our fifth, the one that comes when all seven seals are broken, Disgrace, on her green horse. Desertification follows her, the final horseman, and the worst of them all, for when the people have finally evanesced, even the land is taken. No soul will be able to return, the birds will not sing, the flowers will not bloom. There will be no joy for the innocent or the sinners. There will be neither good, nor evil; merely an earth made barren by their struggle. When Desertification rides, the world is done. Wonder who that is, in our story?

"Pray with me, Church." Harlow says, pulling me out of my churchly wool-gathering. What? If you can't judge a book by its cover, do it by its contents. So, yeah, I read the bible, sue me. "Actually," she voices, her gaze going to the altar and in an uncouth move, with one of her arms she knocks over everything that was on top of it to the floor. The sound of stuff shattering as it lands at our feet reverberates around the confines of this closet, making it more thunderous somehow. She turns back to me, grabbing me by the collar of my black tee, "allow me." And then tugs me so that I am between her and Jesus, forcing me to sit my ass on the shrine.

"Hmm baby, I don't think we have that much time left,

before fire wolfs down your house entirely." The searing heat coming from above our heads is worrying, and the smoke enshrouding us, makes my eyes water and my throat burn.

"Then you better cum quick, my incubus." Harlow bluntly betrays to me, as she goes down on her knees before me and begins to undo the button and zipper of my black ripped skinny jeans. I lift my butt up for a second, so she can pull down the denim material and my boxers, just enough to free my dick.

What is softer than water? Harlow's touch. What is harder than a rock? My cock, soon after her fingers caress it. How distorted of Creation, to make it so that hard rocks are hollowed out by soft water.

Harlow grips it tighter, as her mouth descending down. She stops a hair's breadth away and sticks her tongue out to trace the slit at the tip. "Fuck." I curse, which makes my princess release a giggle, with her mouth wide open as her tongue starts circling around the head. This girl is going to be the death of me.

At last, she takes my cock into her mouth, but her lips only slide over the head. A gentle suction hollows out her cheeks, making her look like a million fucking bucks. She gifts me with a few sucks and then her lips pull away, coming to rest upon the head. Ever so gracefully she spits, her saliva running down my length, which she uses to help move her palm smoothly up and down. Damn, that feels good.

Her lips part again and she receives me back into her mouth, going further this time, bobbing along with her hand, giving me a perfect marriage between a hand-job and a blow-job. Her mouth feels nice; warm and wet, her hand chokes my cock just right. Harlow never deep throats me, her lips never get as far as the root, her nose never touches my pubic area, by virtue of the hand she keeps on me. Not that I am complaining, I am quite long and, I do reach the back of her mouth often. The prayer closet gets impregnated with slurping noises and sweet moans from Harlow, and deep breathless groans from me.

My princess happens to be an ace with her tongue, every time she draws back, it skims the underside of my dick, and it sends a heavenly tingle up my spine. Shit, I need to come soon or else we are toast. I close my eyes, soaking in the pleasure my girl is giving me. I am close. She can probably taste pre-cum, feel my cock go even stiffer and its head swell up.

"Room for one more?" A voice I haven't heard in a while speaks in the recesses of my mind. When I open my pale gray eyes, I see Asta standing, in all his naked glory, under the threshold of the closet, licking his lips, as he stares at us in a lecherous manner.

"Son of a b…" My dick decides that this is the moment to spew out its cream, deep in Harlow's mouth. As it pulsates and gushes, I don't feel my succubus drink it up.

I am not done shooting my load when her face pulls back. She rises to her feet, her mouth full of my cum, seizing me once more by the collar of my t-shirt, she plucks me from the altar and flings me behind her. I lose my footing when I seek to turn around as I go, trying to keep my eyes on my girl, not wanting to miss a thing. The only reason why I don't fall on my ass is because my back meets Asta's front.

"You're leaking my salty delicacy." Astaroth whispers in my ear, his arm draping over my shoulder and across my chest, his hand planting itself on top of my heart. I am about to respond to the demon, when Harlow does the most beautiful thing I have ever seen, she spits my pearly white seed all over Jesus on the cross. "Wow, isn't she breathtaking? Tell me, lover boy, how am I supposed to not be fucking smitten by your girl when she does shit like that, hmmm?"

Harlow spins around to face us. "Asta." She squeaks adorably, a big smile gracing her face, as my cum drools down past her lips to her chin.

"So are you by the way." I eventually retort to the demon, glancing at him. His cock is right between my ass cheeks; its head, which is by my tailbone, is dripping on my flesh.

"Seeing sinners burn, gets me hard, reminds me of the good old witch trial days. I just love me some witches. And then watching my sweet treat pray to you, fucking witchery."

"Bad demon." Harlow says as she draws near us.

"You know it, Missy." Asta purrs at my princess.

"This was meant to be a private moment between me and one of my boyfriends, Asta." She chastises the demon behind me, while I pull my boxers and jeans back up.

"Was it? You left the door open. And come on, sweet treat, you and I, and lover boy here," Astaroth utters, as his hand journeys up from my heart through my collarbone to my throat, clenching around it, compelling my cock to jerk in appreciation, "know you ain't a prude, you don't really mind having me perv on your fleshy fun."

"I guess, you ain't wrong, Mister. But I am not the attention seeking whore here, my demon friend, you are." Harlow teases Astaroth. "You just keep popping up into our narrative."

The ceiling above our heads begins to snap and groan. "Hey, baby, I think it's time for us to go." I announce.

"Wait!" Her hand goes to the necklace around her neck, the one with the rose gold simple cross. I kind of forgot it was even there. She latches on to it with ire and rips it off. Her electric blue eyes fall to the object dangling from her hand, and with bitterness in her voice she mumbles, "Thank You for not listening to my prayers, Lord. Or," Harlow's gaze lifts to meet mine dead on, "perhaps You did." And then she lets the necklace drop to the floor.

FIFTY-NINE

ABEL

THE WOODEN PEW creaks under my weight as I lean forward, elbows braced on my knees, my fingers lace together in a grip so tight my knuckles have gone white. The old church smells of mildew and ash, a suffocating reminder of its decay, and the gallons of petrol we poured all over it, but I barely notice it over the storm of thoughts in my head.

They are taking too long. The minutes drag, each one feeling like a small eternity as the weight of the night presses down on me. My chest feels tight; my breath shallow. Harlow has gone alone; against every instinct I have to keep her close. I wanted to argue, to insist we stick together, but the fire in her eyes, shut me down before I'd even started. Now, all I can do is wait—and waiting is tearing me apart. Church has taken off to collect her but that has to be a good twenty mins ago.

"They should've been back by now," I say aloud, breaking the silence. My voice sounding strained, even to me. Parrish, who is crouched on the alter, trying to make his blade spin on it's tip, raises an eyebrow but doesn't respond. Bishop sits a few rows back, his head tipped against the pew, his face unreadable in the dim light.

I shake my head, trying to push down the unease that is clawing at me. "This is taking too long," I state, louder this time, my voice shaking slightly. "Let's go. Let's go find them. What if she got into trouble?"

Parrish jumps down without a word, his face grim but resolute. He doesn't argue; doesn't hesitate; Bishop exhales heavily, dragging a hand down his face as he rises from his seat. "Fine," he mutters, his tone reluctant but tinged with the same unease I feel.

We leave the church quickly, stepping into the cool night air. The silence outside is unnerving, broken only by the faint crackle of flames and the creak of the old wooden door that is swinging shut behind us. My pulse races as we make our way up the hill, toward Harlow's parents' house, our boots crunching against the dry earth.

As we crest the rise, the house comes into view—and my heart nearly stops. Flames pour from the top-story windows, licking at the eaves like hungry beasts. The fire raging, bright and feral, casting an orange glow over the surrounding trees. Smoke billowing into the night sky, thick, black, and blocking out the stars.

I freeze, my stomach plummeting. "Where's Harlow?" The words tumble out of me in a desperate rush, as my chest tightens further. My eyes scan the scene, frantic, looking for any sign of her. She has to be out here, has to be safe. She wouldn't still be inside—she can't be.

Parrish steps up beside me, his jaw tight, his face unreadable. Bishop is silent, his gaze locked on the inferno in front of us. I can't read him either, it only makes the knot of fear in my gut tighten, further.

"We have to find her," I demand, my voice cracking. The heat of the flames brushing against my skin, the crackling roar drowning out every thought but one: Where is she?

As we stand frozen at the edge of the inferno, the front door creaks open. My heart nearly stopping at the sight of them—Church and Harlow, walking out casually, like they have all the time in the world. The flames flicker behind them, casting shadows that dance across their faces, but it is Harlow's expression that catches me completely off guard.

She is smiling.

Happy.

She looks happy.

My breath hitching as she strolls down the steps, a gas can still in her hand. She tilts it, pouring a stream of gasoline along the length of the front porch with a relaxed ease on her way down, that sends my mind spinning. Church following her, just as calm, pulling a pack of smokes from his pocket. He lights one with a practiced flick of his lighter, the tip glowing as he takes a slow drag, the smoke curling around his face as he exhales.

They reach us, and Church stops in front of me, his eyes gleaming with that familiar mix of mischief and something darker. He holds the cigarette between his fingers, as if offering it to the night, but Harlow plucks it from his hand before he can take another drag.

She lifts it to her lips, taking a long pull, and immediately starts coughing and sputtering, as her face twists in disgust. "Holy shit," she rasps, her voice rough as she waves the smoke away. "Gross. This is gross."

Church just shakes his head, smiling as he watches her, the cigarette dangling loosely from her hand. She turns on her heel and heads back toward the house, moving with the same unhurried confidence she had when she walked out.

I can't tear my eyes off her, the way the flames reflect in her eyes, how she looks utterly in control, as if the fire isn't just devouring her childhood home, but her own fears and burdens. She reaches the porch, her movements smooth, and tosses the cigarette into the puddle of gasoline. The flames catch instantly, roaring to life and racing up the porch, as if eager to devour the house whole.

Hallow's smile widens, as she watches the fire spread, the heat pushing her hair back slightly. She walks back to us, her expression unbothered, as the house behind her begins to collapse in on itself.

We stand huddled together, silent except for the crackle of flames, and my chest tightens as I look between her and the house. That's when I see it. Something—someone—standing in the doorway.

I blink, my blood running cold as I turn to Harlow, my voice shaky. "What the fuck is Astaroth doing inside there?"

She follows my gaze, and her smile turns sharp, almost amused. "That attention-seeking whore didn't want to miss out on the drama," she said lightly, shrugging one shoulder as if it were the most normal thing in the world.

Church laughs, the sound low and rough, shaking his head. Harlow turns her attention back to the house, watching as the flames climbed higher, her face illuminated by the destruction of everything that had once held her captive.

The four of us instinctively close ranks around her, forming a protective circle with Harlow at the center. The heat from the raging fire radiating toward us, but none of us flinch. Our focus is on her—always her. The flames dance in her eyes as she looks up at each of us, her face a mixture of strength and vulnerability, her breaths coming out in shallow bursts.

One by one, we wrapped our arms around her, pulling her tightly into our collective embrace. Church leans in first, his lips brushing the top of her head, with a tenderness that contrasts sharply with his usual sharp edges. His voice is a low rasp as he murmurs, "You saved us, little angel. Well, fallen angel now, if we're being specific—but angel nonetheless."

Parrish follows, his movements slower, deliberate. He kisses her head with a quiet reverence, his hand lingering on her shoulder as he closes his eyes, almost as if he is grounding himself in her presence. Bishop is next, his arms tightening around all of us as he presses a firm, lingering kiss to her hair, his exhale shaky, as though the weight of the night has finally caught up to him.

Then it was my turn. My throat tightens as I lean in, my lips brushing against her crown. The smell of smoke clinging to her, mingling with the faint scent of her shampoo, and I realize, how fragile she feels in this moment, despite the fire in her soul. "You saved us, little angel," I whisper. "You pulled us out of the dark."

Harlow lifts her gaze, her eyes shimmering with unshed tears, as she looks at each of us in turn. Her voice shaking as she stammers, "No, no... I didn't. You saved me." She turns her head slightly, gesturing toward the inferno, that had once been her family home. "This... this was pure evil. You're all just fallen angels, like I am."

Bishop's voice, a soft rumble as he tightens his hold on her.

"Well, I'm glad we're all fallen angels, then," he said, his tone carrying a rare gentleness. "Because if we weren't, we would've never met you. I think I might call you Daughter of Azazel… because you bewitched my soul, and brought war upon this evil land."

Harlow's lips quirk upward, though tears begin streaming down her cheeks. She turns in our arms, shifting so that she can reach Bishop. She cups his face, her fingers trembling, and presses her mouth to his, pouring every ounce of emotion into the kiss. When she pulls back, her voice cracks, heavy with raw emotion. "I love you. I love all of you. And I'm ready… ready to live my life with you all. I'm ready for everything you can give me, ready for my life to finally start."

I tighten my hold on her, brushing a strand of hair from her face. "Daughter of Azazel," I say, my voice steady, despite the storm raging inside me. "If you lead, I'll follow."

EPILOGUE
ASTAROTH

FROM MY PERCH in the rafters of the decrepit warehouse I am in, I survey the chaos below, with a grin so sharp it could slice through bone. The band is finishing their set, the crowd roaring, their energy thick and sweet; like ambrosia. The venue is old, grimy, and reeks of spilled beer and stale sweat. Perfect. It matches the delicious rot of the mining ravine, just beyond these walls.

Ah, mortals and their vices. Such fragile, stupid little creatures.

My claws tap against the rusted beam I am sitting on, the sound lost in the deafening cheers. I can see the band clearly from here, every strum of the guitar, every beat of the drum, sends shivers through the room. Church, with his gravelly growl and untamed energy, and Harlow—ah, my sweet, fiery Harlow. Her voice pours out, like honey laced with venom, wrapping around every soul in the room, pulling them in, making them hers.

I chuckle to myself, low and menacing. "Look at them," I

mutter. "The darlings of sin, basking in the glory I helped them create. Such a delightful little mess."

They are a five-piece now, and their popularity is skyrocketing. Tabloids can't get enough of them—the first openly, polyamorous band to hit it big, a walking scandal wrapped in leather and smoke. *How long will they last?* the headlines screamed. *Can they survive the fame?* As if the ink-stained vultures could ever understand the fire they walked through to get here.

The set ends, the band exits the stage, leaving the crowd in a frenzy of screams and chants. I watch them as they moved with practiced ease, the camaraderie between them electric. I stay hidden in the shadows, my grin widening as I track their movements. They disappear into the backstage corridor, heading toward their bus.

"Oh, this is going to be fun," I whisper, my tone gleeful. With a flick of my tail, I melt into the darkness, following them.

Inside the tour bus, the air is thick with sweat, adrenaline, and victory. They file in, one by one, still buzzing from the performance. Harlow is the last to enter, closing the door behind her with a satisfied smirk. She doesn't hesitate—she pulls off her shirt first, then her jeans, and finally her underwear, until she is standing completely bare, in the center of the room. The sight of her making my grin falter, for just a moment, my usual malice melting into something softer, warmer.

"Well," she says, her voice playful but commanding, her gaze sliding across each of them. "Who's first?"

The room stills for a beat; their eyes drawn to her like moths to a flame.

I perch in the corner, unseen, my claws curling around the edge of the couch, as I drink in the sight of her. My sweet Harlow, bold and unapologetic, radiating a power that no mortal should ever wield so effortlessly.

"You're a vision," I murmur, my voice quiet, meant only for her, though I know she can't hear me. "My perfect, chaotic muse."

The others begin to move, drawn into her orbit; like planets around the sun. I lean back, my grin returning, sharp and cruel.

"Let them adore you," I whisper, my voice filled with a love laced with poison. "But never forget, little one, it was I who made this world bow to you."

The flames in my chest burn hotter as I watched her, my maniacal glee mixing with an ache, I don't care to name. I would burn this entire world down for her, if she asked.

My grin stretching wide, my fangs glinting faintly as I take in the scene before me. The mortals, my little pets, shedding their inhibitions as they shed their clothes, revealing the raw, primal need that simmers just beneath the surface.

Harlow stands at the center of it all, glowing, commanding, her bare skin catching the dim, flickering light. She is a vision of power, and oh, how I adore her. My sweet, chaotic muse, the tether that keeps me anchored in this world, I both loathed and thrived in.

But as I watch them touch her—Bishop pressing reverent kisses to her thighs, Abel trailing his hands over her curves, their mouths worshipping her like the goddess she is—something dark and feral stirs within me. She's mine, I thought bitterly, jealousy burning hot and sharp.

And then there is Church, tangled with Parrish, their hands and lips desperate, their desire radiating like an open flame. I watch his body move, the heat in every touch, the way Parrish's fingers skim his skin—and an idea struck me, wicked and perfect.

"Time to call in that favor," I murmur, my voice low, dark and laced with excitement.

I move, silent and smooth, until I am behind Church. Leaning down, I bring my lips close to his ear, close enough that my breath can brush against his skin. "My turn," I whisper, the words cutting through the haze of his mind.

For a split second, his body stills, his breath catches. And then I surge forward, pouring into him, taking over. The sensation, intoxicating—so warm, so alive. My essence filling him, my will overtaking his, until his body is mine to command. I open his eyes, and the world comes into sharp, vibrant focus through his mortal senses. Everything feeling amplified: the warmth of Parrish's hands on my borrowed skin, the sound of their breathless moans, the electric charge of the air.

From somewhere deep within our shared mind, Church's voice echoes, hesitant but firm. Be gentle with her. She's important.

I smile, letting my amusement slip into my reply. Oh, I know. She's just as important to me.

I pull away from Parrish, his touch lingering, as I move toward her. My Harlow. My muse. My sweet little angel of chaos. She's still the center of it all, her head tilted back, her eyes half-closed, as she lets them worship her. Bishop's lips trace her collarbone, Abel's hands mapping her body like he is memorizing her.

As I approach, her eyes flicker open, meeting mine. Her lips part, a question forming there, but I don't give her time to voice it. I kneel in front of her, letting my hands slide up her thighs, slow and deliberate. Her skin, warm under my palms, soft and perfect.

"Harlow," I murmur, her name on my borrowed lips feeling like a prayer. My voice, low, a mix of Church's familiar tone and my own seductive edge. "Let me show you how much you mean to me."

Her hand reaches for me, her fingers threading through my hair, tugging me closer. That fire in her eyes, the trust, the unguarded way she look at me—it was everything.

She's mine, I think to myself, the words ringing with a mix of reverence and hunger. But this isn't about possession, not this time. This is about her, about showing her how deeply she has sunk into my very essence. She is the light I never thought I needed, and tonight, I will make sure she knows it.

My fingers press firmly into her soft skin. My breathing steady as I kiss the inside of her leg, slowly working my way upward to the apex of her thighs, savoring the way her muscles tighten under my touch. Her scent wrapping around me, intoxicating, driving me deeper into my desire.

Her hands finding their way into my hair, her fingers curling and tugging lightly, urging me closer. I oblige, lowering my face onto her pussy. My tongue moving slowly at first, tasting her delicious elixir, that tastes like every single thing that fuels my whole existence, teasing her, drawing out soft gasps and moans, that echo in the heated air of the bus. I press my mouth harder against her, slurping down her essence, my movements deliberate, unrelenting, until her gasps turn to cries and her body tenses beneath me. I stay with her, riding the wave of her climax, drinking in every shudder and every breathless sound she makes. This is nirvana, I knew it was going to be, this is where souls go, when they travel to heaven.

When her body finally relaxes, I kiss my way up her trembling frame, the taste of her still on my lips. Her hands move to my shoulders as I reach her face, her eyes heavy-lidded and hazy with pleasure. I don't hesitate; sinking into her with slow, deliberate thrusts, filling her inch by inch, I knew she would feel perfect, but I didn't think it was going to be this perfect. I will never be able to touch another now, Harlow is mine, I will make sure of it. The heat of her wrapped around me is incredible, pulling me in deeper as I lean down and capture her lips in a kiss—a deep and consuming kiss, a claiming.

Her moans vibrate against my mouth, and I move to her neck, kissing and sucking the sensitive skin there. Her breath hitching as I linger, her voice a whisper in my ear. "What are you doing, Asta?"

I pull back slightly, still moving within her, each thrust slow and deliberate, my eyes locking onto hers. "Calling in my favor," I murmur, my voice low and rough, laced with dark satisfaction.

I don't give her time to reply, leaning back down to kiss her again, silencing her words with my lips. Her hands grip my shoulders tighter, her nails digging into my skin as her moans grow louder. I pick up the pace, each thrust harder, faster, our bodies moving together as her cries fill the small space. My own control wavering, her pleasure and mine building, until it became too much to contain.

When we both reach the edge, the world seems to blur, colors and stars exploding behind my eyes, as her pussy tightens around my borrowed cock. I groan her name, my movements slowing but not stopping, savoring every moment of release.

As the tension ebbs, I press a soft kiss to her lips, brushing a strand of damp hair from her face. "I love you, Harlow," I whisper, my voice soft, a rare admission slipping from me as I smile down at her. Her wide eyes following me as I move off her slowly, her body still trembling, and nod at the others, silently inviting them to take my place. They move back in almost immediately, their focus solely on her, their touches reverent and eager. I turn my head to look at her one last time, and her gaze meets mine, still dazed but aware, her glimmer now shining brightly towards me. I wink at her, a sly grin tugging at my lips, then I let go of Church's body.

The shift was seamless, my essence slipping free as I straightened, unseen by anyone but her and the man whose body I'd borrowed. Church's eyes flicker with awareness, confusion and understanding, all of which mingle in his expression, but I don't linger to explain.

With a smirk, I turn and walk off the bus, the cool night air wrapping around me. Let them have their moment. She was mine, too, in ways they will never fully comprehend.

Three months later, and here I am, standing on the outskirts of their sprawling new estate in Transylvania, Louisiana, a place dripping in folklore and mystery. I can't help but admire the irony. The fools don't even realize, the history of the land they've chosen; the legends soaked into the soil. It is perfect— dark, steeped in magic, and eerily fitting for what they've become; For what we've become; And the building that is just ten minutes to the right of their land, that's housed more than just the beautiful Queen. The location is fitting to say the least.

The house itself is magnificent. A Gothic beauty with towering spires, wraparound porches, and a looming presence that seems to echo through the dense bayou surrounding it. It's a place that whispers secrets and dares the world to ask questions. It suits them, suits her, far better than that boring box of a house, the boys had sold to buy this.

Oh, Harlow has chosen well, and of course, I approve. As if I'd let her live anywhere else.

They converted one of the rooms into a massive, shared bedroom, the kind that screams decadence and sin. Four poster, custom size bed, soft lighting, endless space for all of them. Their nest, I call it. Yet, I haven't claimed my spot there, since the night three months ago. The night that has burned itself into my soul, the memory of her moans, her touch, her taste-- haunting me every waking moment.

I haven't slipped between her legs since then, but oh, I dream of it every second of the day. That night has changed everything. Not just for her, but for me. Who would ever think, the great and powerful Astaroth could be undone by a mortal woman? And yet here I am, lurking like a lovesick fool.

I still visit her constantly, of course. She can't see me most of the time, but I am always there, watching, guarding, hungering. Especially now.

Her belly has begun to swell, round and beautiful, a testament to the life growing inside of her. Two lives, to be exact. She assumed they were twins, and the others seemed content with that explanation. I've even caught Church bragging about his virile genes, the smug bastard.

Oh, how little they know.

One of those babies is his, he wasn't wrong with that assessment, the others might argue they all filled her that night but… The other baby? Mine.

I called in my favor that night, after all. They don't know the truth—not yet, anyway. It isn't time. Harlow is radiant, glowing with the essence of creation, and I am not about to burden her with the knowledge, just yet. No, that revelation would come later, when she is ready. When they are all, ready.

From my perch in the shadowy corner of their sprawling garden, I watch her as she moves across the back porch, her hand resting on the curve of her belly. She's laughing at something Abel has said, her voice light and carefree. It's a sound that fills me with a strange, unfamiliar warmth.

"Soon, my love," I whisper to myself, my voice low, almost reverent. "Soon you'll understand just how much I've given you. How much I've claimed in return."

For now, I wait. I am patient, after all. What is a little more time to someone who has lived millennia? But one thing is certain—those children growing inside her? They aren't just hers, or mine, or even Church's. They are destiny, and destiny has a way of making itself known.

The End
Or is it…

About Mimi Baptist

I am half Portuguese half French girlie, with maybe somewhere else sprinkled in there, but I wouldn't know, living in the UK. Indie author and a bibliophile. All around bookish to the bone.

If you don't find me snuggle up in a couch reading a book, then I am in front of my laptop writing whatever crazy land of make believe my wild imagination has come up with. I swam in the deepest waters of 'Fall Apart' for a good year until I decided to put pen to paper, and after that words just poured out.

My second book 'Just Always Be Waiting for Me' a reverse harem retelling of Peter Pan's, is the first retake on a Disney story, I intend on taking on others. But Peter Pan was my first love, may as well start there. All to say, I am a Disney fanatic, don't judge me to hard for it.

Please join me in this insane ride.

Standalone:

Bittersweet Snapdragon (🎧 Coming Soon)

Dark Dahlias Rite

Somethings Got To Give:

Fall Apart

Fall Together

The Queens of Ombres Series:

Follow Poppy (Coming Soon)

Protect Poppy (Coming Soon)

Crown Poppy (Coming Soon)

Haunted Tales and Withered Old Flowers Series:

A Field of Tulips and Bones (Coming Soon)

Muddy White Lillies (Coming Soon)

About Cassandra Doon

Cassandra Doon hails from New South Wales, Australia, where she was nurtured between the bustling streets of Sydney and the serene snowy mountains of Tumut. Today, she finds inspiration in the breathtaking Scenic Rim of Queensland's Gold Coast. A versatile author with a lifelong passion for storytelling, Cassandra has penned over 16 novels and 5 children's books, exploring a variety of genres. Known for her daydreaming and a head often lost in the clouds, she admits to being more at home in her fictional worlds than on social media. Outside of her literary pursuits, Cassandra is a devoted mother to two boys, dedicating her days to their endless energy as both a soccer mom and Pokémon master.

Standalone:

The Boys Of Hastings House

The Kings of Willows Peak

Damaged Goods

Tuesday May

The Devils Cut

The Detectives Mate

Bittersweet Snapdragon (Coming Soon)

Dark Dahlias Rite

Aces

Obsessed Shadows

The Dead Zone (Coming Soon)

Second Chances Series:

The Waterfall

Wicked Bonds (Coming Soon)

Writhe (Coming Soon)

The Restaurant (Coming Soon)

Haunted Tales and Withered Old Flowers Series:

A Field of Tulips and Bones (Coming Soon)

Muddy White Lillies (Coming Soon)

The Queens of Ombres Series:

Follow Poppy (Coming Soon)

Protect Poppy (Coming Soon)

Crown Poppy (Coming Soon)

Also By C.L. Doon

The Rain Dang Detective Series:

Still Waters

Moving Water (Coming Soon)

Standalone:

Second Chances at The Riverbend Café (Coming Soon)

Lavender (Coming Soon)

Also By C. Doon

Standalone:

Ravenwood Manor

Phantom Navis

Shadow Prince (Coming Soon)

www.ingramcontent.com/pod-product-compliance
Lightning Source LLC
Chambersburg PA
CBHW072036190726
48294CB00005B/1286